SO VERY LUCKY

ALSO BY CAITLIN DEVLIN

The Real Deal

Born For This

SO VERY LUCKY

Caitlin Devlin

LAKE UNION
PUBLISHING

Published by Lake Union Publishing, Seattle

www.apub.com

EU product safety contact:
Amazon Media EU S.à r.l.
38, avenue John F. Kennedy, L-1855 Luxembourg
amazonpublishing-gpsr@amazon.com

ISBN-13: 9781662536168
eISBN: 9781662536151

Cover design by Will Speed
Cover image: © KOTOIMAGES © TanitaKo © tomertu
© KDdesign_photo_video / Shutterstock

Printed in the United States of America

For Mum and Dad, for everything

Chapter One

Ask yourself – where do rumours this ridiculous come from?

The obvious answer is, of course, that they come from the internet. Or before that, the tabloids. Or before that, the town gossip, who would inevitably be drowned for witchcraft. The vague, all-encompassing-and-helpful-to-no-one answer is that they come from people. That is to say, our innate need to speculate. Which brings us closer to the real answer, or at least the answer that I consider to be real. Rumours this ridiculous come from our need to be the one who knows. To be the man on the inside. To see something that no one else sees. To be included. To be special.

Because, you tell yourself, if you can see it but other people can't, it doesn't mean that you're wrong. It means that you know Calista better. That *you,* set apart from the average fan, have a relationship with her that allows you to see past whatever story is being told and get at the truth. That's what we all want, anyway: to feel like we know Calista better than other people. That's the spell she puts us under. That's how it was for me.

Except it was different in my case. Because I always was special to Callie.

The night that it happened, Rich was supposed to be out. I never liked Rich to be in the flat when I checked in on Callie, not because it made him jealous, but because it didn't – at all. He accepted the reality of our relationship like one accepts the reality that dinosaurs once walked the earth – fact, but *almost* fantasy, and certainly nothing to do with him. Early on, he asked lots of questions, like everyone did when they found out, but over time, after he had seen that these days I had about as much to do with Calista as he did, he stopped talking about her like I'd ever known her. One of our stupider arguments had begun with Rich turning to me in the middle of Calista's Grammys performance to ask, 'Is this song about Bruno Hoffman, do you think?'

I stared at him. 'Rich, this song is about *me.*' It was a song from her debut album, not a big hit at the time but it had become a cult favourite among her fans. It was smaller in scale than much of her later stuff, more tender and intimate. All of her stuff about me had been like this, although most of it was never released.

'You?' And he looked from the screen, Callie crooning into a standing mic in a long sapphire-blue dress, to me eating gyoza in my pyjamas. 'Really?' he'd asked.

I'd said to my friends for a while now that I likely wasn't going to stay with him. My friends had begun to point out that I'd said this several times and was still staying with him. I had begun to wonder if I needed new friends.

I'd planned my night perfectly. Rich would be out with his friends until late. I had sushi in the fridge – not particularly nice sushi, but not the awful supermarket stuff I often had for lunch, so it felt like a treat. I had a foot mask on, something I couldn't do around Rich because he'd wax lyrical about what a scam it was on the part of the beauty industry (always a vague, undefinable force) to make me feel like I had to deep condition my feet, and that I shouldn't soften them on his account. I'd explained enough times that I didn't feel like I *had* to. It wasn't anything to do with beauty, and it certainly wasn't anything to do with him. I liked the days afterwards of peeling all the old, dying skin off my feet and renewing, like a lizard. Rich said that was even weirder.

I was sat with my sushi on my lap, my feet in the strange white bag full of goop, when the door opened. The first thing I felt was intense annoyance. I thought, *God, I have to break up with him. I might even do it tonight.*

'Where's my girl?' he called from the hallway.

Definitely tonight, I thought.

He appeared in the doorway, grinning at the sight of me in candlelight with my bagged feet. 'What do we have here?'

'Self-care,' I said.

A roar from the TV as the twenty-year-old warm-up act bounced off down the enormous stage in her platforms. She looked like a doll. She didn't have Callie's otherworldly something. The broadcast cut to interview footage, music industry has-beens popping up to give soundbites on a 'decade-defining musical legacy'. For the crowd at Copacabana Beach, it must have been an agonising wait in the sun, all of them straining their necks for that first glimpse of her. The sky over the stage, before the livestream had cut away, had been threateningly bright. People would pass out if it got much hotter. Perhaps an ambulance would be called for someone. Perhaps Callie would get to do that thing where she raised a hand in the air to pause the music and say, with compassionate concern, 'Does someone need help? Can we get some help over there?' Only resuming once she was assured that everything was fine. 'I love you guys,' she would say. 'I want everyone to be okay.' They would clap like she was laying down a manifesto for world peace.

When I knew Callie, her shows weren't like this. When I first knew her, right at the beginning, she played half-empty pubs and cafés, perched on whatever wobbly chair or stool they could spare. People talked through her sets. It was a toss-up as to whether they would applaud her or not, or whether they would even notice she had left the stage. Men twice her age would come up afterwards to hit on her, their access to her unbarred. I had seen her open for terrible bands at dingy clubs, play in park bandstands where people yelled at her to shut up. There had been a show where the only people in the audience were the bar staff, wearing pitying smiles. And me, stood by the stage with a vodka coke. Cheering loudly enough to fill the empty room.

I'll never forget the night she played Brixton Academy. She asked if I wanted to stand at the side of the stage and watch, but I told her that I wanted to be in the crowd. 'You'll boil, Stevie,' she said. It was mid-August and oppressively hot. The venue was organising water handouts and anxiously prepping for a medical emergency or several. I didn't care. I wanted to be in the middle of it all. I wanted to feel them loving her.

'Silly Stevie,' she said, and she kissed me on the cheek. Her curls were stiff with product.

The TV was now showing a supercut of Callie's last ten years in music – producers she'd worked with and peers she'd outstripped popping up to comment on some of her key moments. 'When she appeared in that ballet skirt on the steps of the Met to announce *Pointelle* . . .' sighed an ex-member of a girl group. 'She just looked like something out of a fairytale.'

'That's her weakest,' said Rich, mouth full with one of my avocado rolls. '*Pointelle.*' Privately, I agreed. Callie's sixth album was a little too sweet and empty for my taste, computerised pop without any of her usual bite. She'd taken on an airhead-blonde persona, an artist's impression of her most popular hate comment, but in the end that persona hadn't really had much to say. People loved it, though. By that point, they loved anything Callie did. 'Did you get wasabi?' asked Rich.

I threw the packet at him. His eyes widened but he didn't say anything. His face as he dabbed wasabi on to the side of his plate told me how impressively restrained he thought he was being.

My phone was buzzing.

@steviestone5 are you watching?

People were already posting clips of the warm-up act to social media and Callie's fans were tagging me. Not in huge numbers – most of them weren't that interested in me anymore – but there were still a loyal few that refused to let me fall out of her story. Rich always told me to turn off my notifications when Callie was in the news, but I liked hearing them ping in. It was nice that people remembered how much I used to matter to her.

'Did you see that tennis guy's cheating on her?' asked Rich. His feet were now up on the coffee table beside mine. I shuffled my white bag of goop away.

'What do you mean?'

'It was in the news.'

'*Which* news?'

'God, Stevie,' he said, 'I don't know. It's true, though.'

'Please. People are always claiming that.'

'They say there's videos.'

'Like you can't deepfake anything these days.'

'Your bag smells,' said Rich.

'It's the oils.'

'They reek. You shouldn't have it near food.' He reached forward and picked up a prawn cracker from beside my foot. 'Mixing cultures here,' he said.

On-screen, Callie in 2016, opening up the VMAs in a thin layer of silver.

'Because sushi's Japanese.'

Callie in 2018, in a long white dress against the red rocks of Arizona, guitar slung over her shoulders, honouring Dolly Parton.

'And these are Chinese.'

Callie accepting her Woman of the Year award, teary-eyed as she made her way through her speech.

'Good though,' said Rich, and crunched into my ear. 'You should have got more.'

'I didn't know you were going to be here.'

'Wasn't feeling it. Liam flaked – argument with his girlfriend – and Harry's a boring shite since he started teaching.' He rolled his eyes at my silence. 'I didn't mean it like that. Just that he's not who he used to be, you know? It's great for him; he loves it. Putting more good into the world than any of us.'

Callie in the director's chair on a music video shoot, clapping her hands excitedly at the playback.

'Still,' said Rich.

Callie performing at the Super Bowl half-time show, glittery pop star in a white blazer and tiny silver shorts. *Dry Ice* was her most commercial era. Lots of her fans still haven't forgiven her for it, and lots still haven't forgiven her for not staying in it. She always said that you couldn't please everyone and she never does. But, paradoxically, they love that about her.

'I think Liam and Jewel are going to break up, you know,' said Rich.

'What's it about this time?'

'Oh, nothing in particular. That's what's driving him crazy. Some shite about he never *anticipates* her needs, the romance is always *performative.* God, I'd hate if someone gave me that kind of weak crap in a break-up.'

'Hm,' I said, taking mental notes.

'But it's on him. Dating a girl called *Jewel.*' He gestured to the screen. 'Then again, who am I talking to? *Calista.*'

'That's not her real name. It's a nickname.' He knew this. He routinely forgot. (Callie crying into her third Grammy. Her tears running down the side of the trophy's gaping mouth.) 'Anyway, what was wrong with Jewel? I liked her.'

'*Jewel.* I always thought she was a bit . . . What is it people say? Crunchy?' What he wanted to call her was a 'hippy-dippy bisexual', which was a phrase I had heard him use, although never knowing that I could hear.

I would do it tonight, I thought. I was suddenly astonished at myself for letting it go on this long. For how long had I thought I would keep this man in my flat, scoffing at my skincare, eating my dark chocolate, not reading any of the books I gave him? Skulking around in my slippers and pretending to be a modern, liberal-leaning example of non-toxic masculinity, but I'd never heard him say out loud he was a feminist and he'd once admitted that he considered taking a finger up the bum to be 'a slippery slope'. I was exhausted. The very act of sitting there next to him had become exhausting. Didn't it tire him out, being so objectionable?

He scooted up the sofa and put his arm around me. 'Can I pick a bit of skin off your feet, when they start peeling?' he asked. 'Also, I got you a KitKat on my way home.'

'Thank you.' I laid my cheek against the cotton of his jumper. Maybe tomorrow.

On-screen, they had cut back to Copacabana Beach. The roar of the crowd was immense now, filtered through the TV but still powerful. We had a front-on view of the stage – the screen displayed a giant hourglass, the sands slowly collecting on the base. A minute to go, maybe less. A commentator spoke over the crowd to the TV audience only.

'Calista has always had a knack for surprising us, so we should prepare ourselves to expect the unexpected. This is the culmination of her last ten years in the music industry – eight albums under her belt – and she's dropped many heavy hints that after tonight, after this celebration, we can expect something completely different from her. For an artist who manages to become someone new with each release, this is a heavy promise. Let's see what she has in store for us.'

The last grains of sand ran through the timer. It shimmered, then disappeared from the screen. In its place was a shadow – the outline of a woman, her hand on a standing mic, which she held tilted away from her slightly, a thin line at an angle to the line of her body, straight and determined. The noise from the crowd was subdued over the live feed, but I could envision how it would feel to be among it, the way it would go right through your head sideways, make your ears feel full of water for hours afterwards. The shadow shifted, just a little. Not an animation, then – it was really her behind the screen. My breath caught.

She tipped the mic towards her.

'Shall we?'

The introduction to her latest album, *Dinner At Mine.* Another bellow from the crowd. The camera found a group of fans at the barrier, my age or a little younger, looking like they were about to pass out. Their eyes devoured her, hair matted on foreheads shiny with sweat, spit flying from between their teeth as they screamed.

A door opened in the screen. From it protruded a long leg in a strappy silver shoe. I put a prawn cracker in my mouth and sat back, as if this was just another thing on TV.

She was all in white, with two small silver wings protruding from her back, gossamer thin. Her hair was loosely curled. Her skirt, unevenly cut at the hem, dangled down her thigh as she ran forward, the mic in her hand an extension of her.

'She looks beautiful,' I said, before I caught myself. Rich, who for all his faults had never felt threatened by Callie, made a sound of acquiescence.

She raised a hand, jostling the wing on her shoulder, and waved it, the movement large and deliberate. Thousands of hands waved back at her. An overhead shot showed them jumping on the spot, clawing at the air. Callie raised the mic to her lips. Paused. Smiled, in recognition of their anticipation.

'Hello, Rio,' she said, in her soft voice.

They lost their minds. They cried in each other's arms like the world was ending. There was a crush at the barrier – they were pulled towards her involuntarily, all in one sweep. The camera found a mother clutching her young daughter to her chest, both weeping. A boy of about eighteen, his hand to his mouth, shook all over so violently that I thought he might collapse.

Rich snorted into the prawn crackers, then offered me the bowl.

Dinner At Mine's lead single, 'Eat Me', was one of my favourites of her newer songs, a commentary on her own consumption under the public gaze and her constant cannibalisation of herself and her own image. The central refrain of '*eat me, I like it*' wasn't, as I tried to explain to Rich over dinner, purely sexual – it was an acknowledgement that she benefited from being placed before the public as a delicacy, that if she pretended she wanted privacy, ordinary boundaries, a normal life, she would be a hypocrite. Rich pretended to listen. Afterwards he asked me if Callie was actually saying any of that in the song or if I was just reading into it.

'But that's the point,' I said. 'It's art. You're supposed to read into it.'

'Seems like Calista can write something silly and meaningless and then you all do the work for her, turning it into something deeper than it actually is.'

That was one of the times I hated him the most.

'I like this one,' he said now. I was still pressed against his chest.

'No, you don't. You called it silly and meaningless.'

'Catchy, though.' He hummed along.

Under the applause, the music transitioned into something slower and sadder. Callie kicked off her silver shoes – 'Some perv just came in his trousers,' grinned Rich, in a way that made me want to slap him – and she turned and walked towards the back of the stage, one bare foot in front of the other.

'I love you already, Rio,' she called over her shoulder. More screams. 'I promise you, we're about to have lots of fun tonight. But I wanted to start the show by bringing it way back to the beginning.'

She could have said anything and they would have screamed for her. She could have announced that she was going to perform a one-woman version of *The Sound of Music* that evening. She could have declared that she was running for president of the UN. She could have told them to run down the beach and light the ocean on fire and they might have tried.

'Ten years is a long time,' she said. 'We're going to go on a journey through those ten years tonight, Rio. We're going to talk about it all. But this is where I have to start.'

Rich tried to say something. I shushed him, flapping both hands.

'There's this person who was there for me, right at the start,' she said. A white bench had appeared at the back of the stage, descending on two wires. She walked over in her bare feet and sat herself down on it, crossing one leg over the other. The crowd filled every long pause between her sentences with endless, adoring noise. 'She's someone I've been thinking about a lot lately,' she said.

She. You'd think I was the only woman who had ever been in Callie's life to judge by the leap my heart made at that word. No change in Rich's face. It didn't even cross his mind as a possibility.

On her bench, she smiled, lips brushing the metal of her mic. She didn't speak softly, exactly, but she gave you that impression – she'd never had much of a stage voice. She turned it on now and then, but she also had this extraordinary ability to chat to the crowd like it was one individual and the two of them were engaged in easy conversation. The air around her was gold – the lights, or the evening, or just her aura – impossible to say from our limited view through the TV screen, but lovely all the same. She opened her mouth to continue talking, then pressed her lips together and smiled again as the crowd cut her off; benevolently, like a child was telling her a story. *Let her speak,* I thought wildly. She raised the mic to her lips again.

'Rio,' she said. 'One thing I do believe – one thing I've always believed – is that you should never forget where you came from.'

She wasn't looking at the camera. It was possible that she wasn't even aware where the cameras were positioned. Still, she stared out into the crowd, and her eyes were endless, and I saw what they searched for, impossibly.

'So, Stevie. This one's for you.'

Rich dropped his prawn cracker.

'Fuck,' he said. 'Wow, Stevie. A shoutout!' He nudged me. I couldn't speak. 'What a win for you, hey?'

My phone was blowing up. Hundreds of her fans in my mentions now.

'You okay?'

'Yeah,' I said, turning my phone over in my lap.

'Who's messaging you?'

'Just randoms.' People knew who I was, of course – as her star had risen, mine had blundered up a few rungs as well, just to the point that her most dedicated fans recognised me by name if not by face. But it had been five years at least since there had been even a passing mention of me, other than in the songs she sang. I'd never seen people flock to my profile like this before.

It didn't feel real. Callie, at Copacabana Beach. Saying my name. If Rich hadn't been sat next to me making his unromantic comments, I might have cried.

The bench started to rise, with her on it. The first few chords of 'Again, Again, Again' began to play – chords that were ingrained in me, that I would be able to pick out in a wall of sound. The camera pulled back and we saw that the bench hadn't descended from the top of the stage – it was attached to a crane-like structure, one that towered far above the stage, arm reaching out over the heads of the crowd.

'Shit,' said Rich. 'Is she going to fly over the entire beach on that thing?'

She had started to sing. I tried to tune Rich out and focus only on her and the words. But she wasn't singing them to me – she waved to the crowd as she rose, picked people out, smiled. It had only been a moment. I had vanished from her life again.

There had been a moment, though, where she had searched for me and remembered. I knew that moment would spin my world.

She was above the stage now, high in the air on her white garden bench. The crane had begun to carry her over the crowd, pulling her first to the left, where eager hands stretched upwards, tried to bridge impossible space to receive her. She smiled down at them. Her voice sailed over their heads. Her hair had grown, or maybe it was extensions. It fell almost to her waist now and it was blonder than ever, almost the same white as her dress. She looked entirely unreal. *Like an angel,* I thought, and immediately loathed myself for it. She leant down towards the eager fans like a religious figure, there to answer their prayers.

'Shouldn't she be on some kind of harness?' asked Rich.

The crane lifted again, presumably to carry Callie to the other side of the crowd. But the movement was sharp – a jolt. One of the wires jumped. I saw a flicker of uncertainty on Callie's face, a moment of fear. Then the wire fell away, snaking frantically down through the air. The bench tilted, plunging vertical, dangling. It happened so fast that Callie didn't have time to find a handhold – her fingers reached out, and clutched on to nothing.

She fell.

'Fuck!' cried Rich. He jumped up, knocking the bowl of prawn crackers to the floor. I was frozen, stuck to the sofa like there was a hand on my throat pressing me down.

The bench swung. Callie tumbled from it gracefully, almost as if it were intentional. There was a brief second of suspension, a point at which she hung in the air like a star, the trailing material of her dress rippling upwards as she, still surprised, fell down. Then she slipped off the screen.

The bench hung, empty, against a clear blue sky.

A wide shot of the stage showed confusion, a hint of white fabric, people in black running, fans moving in mass panic. Some screams, but mostly hushed bewilderment. The swirl of frightened bodies made my stomach churn. Then the feed cut. Suddenly we were watching a woman open up her dishwasher, delighted by the difference that her new tablets had made to the cleanliness of her wine glasses.

Rich looked at me. I felt the turn of his head, but I still couldn't meet his eyes. 'What the *fuck*?' he asked.

I was doing silent calculations, making maps of the stage in my mind. She'd swung to the right of it. Had she fallen into the crowd, or on to the stage? Which would be better?

My phone buzzed.

Rich and I stared at it. When I didn't pick it up, he reached forward and placed it in my hand.

@steviestone5

Someone had tagged me in a picture. Blurry and pixellated, zoomed in from far away. A crumpled figure in white, lying on the floor just in front of the stage, between the edge of it and the barriers that held back the crowd. Her head was turned away, so that all you could see was a tangle of blond. The shape was too blurry for anyone to tell the damage. But people in the comments had already drawn their own conclusions.

Dead.

what happened????? asked someone.

She hit the side of the stage and then the ground, replied someone else. *My friend is there and she's pretty sure she hit her head.*

omg I'm crying, replied a third person.

Rich watched me scroll through these comments. 'Jesus,' he said.

'Do you think she really is . . . ?'

'I don't know. I couldn't really judge the height of the thing. It didn't— I mean, it didn't look . . . survivable.'

'No. That's what I thought.' My voice was cold in a way I'd never heard it.

'Jesus,' he said again. He'd angled his body so that he was looking at me front on, hands holding on to the back of the sofa and the arm. 'I'm sure she's okay.' I knew he was resisting the urge to point out that he had *said* she should be wearing a harness. We waited, unsure what to do.

My phone buzzed again. I looked down.

@steviestone5

A video. Rich decided, for reasons known only to himself, that *this* was now too much for me and tried to take the phone. I held on to it and pressed play. The second the video started, he stopped trying to prise it out of my hand and watched, rapt.

It was a long fall. She slipped from the bench and fell the height of the whole stage and then some, hitting the edge of it with violence. It was her back that hit it, not her head. The bounce from the stage to the ground was not graceful. Her limbs flew, like she was a soft toy. She landed heavily. The video was silent, but I saw hands reaching for her, people pushing through the crowd to get to her.

'No blood,' I said to Rich, raspy, like my throat was full of sand.

'No,' he agreed.

The news alerts were starting to pop up, but they didn't know any more than we did.

BREAKING NEWS: Calista appears to be seriously injured mid-Copacabana Beach broadcast.

Eventually, the TV itself switched into a breaking-news announcement, with a bleary-eyed presenter informing us that the broadcast would not continue and that they would fill the scheduled time with a screening of Calista's 2023 documentary, *Grenadine*.

Rich's hand drew circles on my back.

'I bet it's a stunt,' I said finally.

His hand slowed. 'Do you really think so?'

'You never know with her.'

'I know she's theatrical, but this would be another level. Don't you think? I mean, this would be pretty fucked-up.'

Another buzz in my lap. *@steviestone5*

This video was taken from a distance, but what it showed was inarguable. A stretcher, carried away from the stage into an ambulance by paramedics. Police held back the crowd, their arms moving into shot. You could hear the mass panic. Most people had their phones out. On the stretcher was a figure all in white – but not the ethereal, half-finished white of Callie's dress. A white sheet. It covered the entire body, pulled over the face. None of her was visible.

Rich's breath caught. 'Oh,' he said. 'Stevie.' He pulled me to him.

I believed it then, and it hurt. Such a straightforward, uncomplicated pain.

I almost miss it.

Grenadine (2023)

Calista's seventh album is all colour. Oranges, greens, yellows and reds – shades so vibrant as to be obnoxious and garish on anyone else, but she surrounds herself with them and glows outwards, overpowering them, and it looks like the most natural thing in the world. This is the gift she has. Anything can read intentional.

Still, 'Who Loved You First' is not my favourite music video of hers. The song is a solid second single, vindictively bubbly. 'When she's got you at your worst, remember who loved you first,' she sings, bright and optimistic about her life versus that of her unnamed ex – likely model Beau Joali, but there's speculation. The music video is too dependent on the album visuals, tropical and fruity but without much of a concept.

'You still can't stop staring at it,' says Mel, and she's right.

Mel is drinking prosecco. This year she's decided that drinking prosecco on every night out will make every night out feel like a celebration, and thus remind her that every night out is to be celebrated purely for what it is. It's a pathology of hers, this need to romanticise her life, and one that is beginning to grate on me. Still, after almost two decades of largely wonderful friendship, I've had to let go of the things Mel does that grate on me. This, I've learnt, is what you do in long relationships – you let go of things, or you bury them very insistently and pretend not to be aware that they haven't gone away. Otherwise, you part. I learnt this with Leonora and with Jeremy, even with my dad, to an extent, but I don't remember ever feeling it with Callie. Maybe that's why I still watch her, like this, every time she comes on-screen. Sooner or later I'll have to spot something I hate or be reminded of something that turns our split, in my mind, from a dumping to a mutual parting of the ways. It never happens. I don't like this music video very much, and that's about as close as I get. Even that dislike is lukewarm. She's still Calista.

'Big fan?' says a voice behind me.

It's a man's voice. That's good – I'm ready to hook up with a man again. I've seen a couple of women casually since Leonora, and am a little tired of being seen for what I am. Men treat everything you do as a sexy mystery, up until they're a little bit tired of you, and then you start to become the kind of mystery it takes far too much effort to crack. Women can spend one evening with you and say, 'I don't want to assume, but it sounds like you have some generational trauma in your family. Have you ever been in therapy? Talking therapy? I can see how you might be the type to over-intellectualise CBT.' Then again, maybe that's just the kind of women I'm attracted to. None of Mel's girlfriends have ever tried to get her to go to therapy and I'd argue she needs it more than me.

The man standing behind me is good-looking in that safe kind of way that means I'd never feel inadequate standing next to him but I also wouldn't have to give caveats when showing his picture to my friends. Jeremy wasn't a bad-looking man but he photographed so terribly that when friends asked to see what he looked like I would give them a pre-prepared monologue before handing over my phone. 'He was quite tired here. This isn't his best light. He smiles very differently off-camera – you'll see when you meet him.'

This man smiles in a slightly superior manner that should turn me off completely, but I'm me, so it doesn't. 'I think she makes good music,' I say. He keeps smiling, but his eyebrows go up. 'You don't agree?'

'No, she must do. It just isn't really my thing.'

I'm ready to turn away. I'm not really in the mood to defend Calista to strangers – two years on from my break-up with Leonora, and I'm still not quite over the role Callie played in it.

'But her artistry is great,' he says, surprising me. 'Her sound isn't really my thing, but I like that she's always doing something interesting with her visuals. And she keeps people talking about her. That's worth a lot, right? I mean, you have to be smart to manage that for as long as she has.'

I look him up and down. I don't even care that it's obnoxious – I've learnt that men are hard to scare off. He's still smiling in that superior way, but maybe I'm reading into that. People can't always help the kind of face they have. Poor, lovely Jeremy, for example.

'What's your name?' he asks.

I look over his shoulder for Mel, but she's engaged in conversation with some blonde girl. 'Stevie,' I say.

'Like Stevie Nicks?'

Inevitable. 'Sure.'

'Rich,' he says, holding out his hand.

'Like Richie Rich?'

That gets a laugh. The first time you make a man laugh, he always looks at you afterwards like you've surprised him, like he came over to talk to you as a matter of manners, a social obligation, and has found himself unexpectedly charmed. 'I think you're very pretty, Stevie,' he says. 'Do you want to have a drink with me?'

I check that he's not here alone to pick up girls – always a red flag, in my experience – and no, his friends are a little way off, pretending not to watch, smacking each other's shoulders when they think we can't see, like Rich is about to lose his virginity. Oh god, maybe he is. How soon is too soon to ask if someone is a virgin? I've never taken a virginity before. Callie took mine and look what happened to me.

'Sorry about my friends,' he says. I realise he's followed my gaze.

I sip my drink through my straw. 'They seem to think you're getting lucky.'

He grins. 'They think all kinds of crazy things.'

◆ ◆ ◆

Mel leaves with her blonde, and Rich and I walk down Dalston High Street, towards my bus stop. Of course, we aren't really going to my bus stop at all, but to his flat, which is only ten minutes from here. Neither one of us has acknowledged it yet. 'Okay,' he says, after our conversation about university courses and number of siblings has petered out. 'What is it about Calista?'

'What about her?'

'I mean, you were staring at that video. Properly staring.'

'I hadn't seen the full thing yet.' A lie. 'She's good at what she does,' I said. 'You admitted as much.'

'Right, and I do think that. But I don't get her stuff, not really. I mean, I only know the big ones, and they're all quite factory pop to me. They all sound quite manufactured.'

'Well,' I say, 'what's wrong with that? Everything that's created is manufactured. That's what creating is. You just mean they aren't manufactured to your tastes.'

'Sure,' he concedes, 'maybe. I guess when I say manufactured, they sound built for radio. They sound built to sell records. They don't sound like they come from the heart.'

A plastic bag blows over our feet. Across the road from us, a drunk couple embraces, mid-argument, and yell lovingly into each other's faces. The girl wears a big fur coat, which she winds around her boyfriend, pulling him into her warmth.

'That's a common misconception,' I say. 'Everything she does comes from the heart.'

He smiles. 'You talk like you know her personally.'

'I do.'

He looks at me sideways, deliberately chill, unsure whether to take me seriously. 'Oh yeah?'

'We dated.'

He laughs – this is safely a joke. It must be. Everyone's reaction. 'Fuck off.'

'I'm not joking. You can google it.'

A pause. Still unsure if I'm kidding, he slides his phone out of his pocket and unlocks it with the resigned air of a man who is ready to be the butt of the joke. 'What's your last name?'

'Stone.'

'Stevie Stone,' he chuckles. 'You've got rock and roll built into you. Why aren't you a musician?'

'Tone deaf.' I watch him scroll headlines. He switches over to the images tab, and there we are, fresh-faced eighteen-year-olds smiling in selfies. We never got papped together much – she wasn't famous enough for that back then – but we did used to post each other online.

'Fuck off,' he says again, but the inflection is different. When he looks up at me, I know he sees me differently. I've watched that change happen to so many people over the years. I've watched them type my name and her name into search engines and then I've watched the raise of their heads, and I've looked into their eyes, and I've seen myself transformed. Un-ordinary. And I love it. Every single time.

'It was a while ago,' I say.

'Pop star's girlfriend,' he says. He slides his phone back into his pocket. 'You're sure you want to be hanging out with me?'

'Not yet. Guess we'll see.'

He laughs and takes my hand. I feel the metal of a ring and look down, concerned, but it isn't a wedding ring, just some cheap blackening silver on a different finger. He's one of those boys who probably used to paint his nails and doesn't now because he works in an office and his band broke up. But he's still skinny in band tees, wearing cheap silver jewellery, talking about artistry and scoring brownie points for not shitting all over commercial pop. I haven't been out with a man like this in a while. Maybe it's what I need. He seems like a good person.

We go back to his flat. He takes my coat and fixes me a Baileys on ice. His heating isn't running – maybe he's cheap, or maybe he's broke. We shiver in his bed together. His hands are cold when they touch me. When he goes down I close my eyes, tightly, and the colours blossom bright.

Chapter Two

We heard nothing for fourteen hours. I didn't sleep, refreshing her social media pages over and over underneath the duvet, jumping between tabs. Eventually Rich reached out and tried to pull me to him, mumbling something that was probably supposed to be consoling. Notifications knocked steadily, commiserations from fans and the few people in my life who knew of or remembered my connection to her. Friends from university sent short paragraphs to let me know they were thinking of me. I hadn't held on to many friends throughout my life – Mel and I had our group who we got drinks with every other month or so, but they were all more Mel's friends than mine. They were kind to me, but in a very deliberate way, so that I always knew they were being kind rather than feeling it. I had been too absorbed in Callie at university to make many other real connections. Sometimes I wished I could go back and change that, but I knew that really it could never have been any other way. The girls in our group who had never known Callie were confused by me – I wasn't what Calista's ex was supposed to be like. The ones who had been around when Callie and I were together brought her up now and then, but I could never stand the way they spoke about her, like they'd actually known her at all.

She was always a fighter, said one girl, over text. Callie had never been a fighter, more of a gentle, insistent presence with a quality that made everyone want to help her. Other people did the fighting for her. I deleted the message.

Mel tried to call me. When I didn't pick up, she texted, a long paragraph that jumped erratically between eulogy and list of medical miracles. I skimmed it, numb.

At seven, Rich woke up and started dressing for work. When I didn't follow him he stopped, one sock on, halfway into his shirt, and said, 'Aren't you going into the office?'

'Obviously not.'

He came and sat on the edge of the bed. 'Don't snap at me,' he said tenderly. 'It's not productive.' I threw both his shoes into the hallway and, when he left to retrieve them, closed the bedroom door. I could hear him hovering outside for a few seconds, trying to decide whether or not he was being mistreated. In the end he seemed to determine that even if he was, it was a good moment for him to practise being the bigger person, and he left.

I hunkered down in bed. At first I read speculation about what might have happened, but that made me feel worse. Then I engaged with other people's grief and that made me feel worse as well. Some fan posted about the 'lovely chat' she'd had with Calista in 2018 under a black and white selfie of the two of them. *You didn't know her,* I thought. Then I scolded myself. When was the last time I'd had a lovely chat with her? It might have been further back than that.

I'd known her, and I hadn't. I suppose that's why I couldn't really make up my mind whether or not to mourn. If I was mourning the girl I'd loved, hadn't I already done that by now? She'd been gone for years. If I was mourning Calista, then I would have to do it like a fan. And that made me feel sick.

Then, at 11 a.m., as I was just starting to nap, my phone started vibrating even more insistently.

She'd posted.

Hello my loves! she'd written. *I'm so sorry that it's taken me a while to let you all know that I'm safe. But I'm awake and doing well all things considered and I'm going to be absolutely fine. I'll be taking a small break from everything to let my mind and body heal from what happened but know that I would never leave you for long. Big things are coming! Kisses, C x*

A minute later, she posted a gif of a woman in a white dress rising slowly from a grave. It looked to be from some old movie, but nobody in the comments had identified the source yet. There was an outpouring of relief and love. Famous friends commented underneath it – *So glad you're okay. Been thinking of you non-stop.* The most mundane well wishes from any verified account gathered thousands of likes. I stared at the post, and then I started to sob. I cried violently for a few seconds before I stopped myself and went to do my laundry. I'd been putting it off for three days and even the act of separating it felt exhausting. I took a break halfway through to lie on top of the dirty clothes and stare at the ceiling.

Rich rang. 'God, what a relief,' he said. 'That would have been awful. You must be so relieved.'

'Big relief.'

'Why are you angry at me?'

I didn't answer, because I didn't really know.

'I'm sorry if I wasn't very sensitive about it,' he said. 'You know it's hard for me to understand the relationship you have with her. I mean, a lot of the time you talk about her like she's just another celebrity.'

'Do I?'

'You know, speculate about her relationships and her next move and all that, just like the girls at work.' I was quiet. 'Sorry,' he said, 'I keep saying the wrong thing, don't I?'

'I was in love with her.'

'I know,' he said. 'But I was in love with people at eighteen as well, you know? Or I thought I was.' *I'm not weird about it,* was what he wanted to say. He would never really get it. I asked him to pick up sushi for dinner, and when he said, 'Again?' I hung up.

For a while I sat on the sofa and thought. I was fine, objectively. Callie was fine, as much as she could be. Perhaps it was just the reminder that even someone as untouchable as Calista could be gone in an instant that had unsettled me. I logged on to my laptop and wrote three descriptions of almost identical nail colours, as if each one had its own distinct personality, and that calmed me down. Callie had always predicted that I would be a journalist when we left school, perhaps a profile writer, one of the sort who hangs out with a famous person for two days and then writes a cover feature for *Rolling Stone.* 'I could be your first one!' she'd said, lying on her back with her guitar on her chest. It had sounded so reasonable when she said it, me sitting in the front seat of some rock star's car, a notebook in my lap, asking them how they balanced work and family life. Callie had ended up exactly where she was supposed to, and maybe I had too, writing copy for an online beauty and wellness store. The dullness of it overwhelmed me sometimes, particularly when Calista was in an album cycle, but mostly I didn't mind my job. I could do it almost without thinking, and the brand tone of voice was quite pretentious, which meant I could be too.

> *Have you met Rosa? Trust us – you'd remember. She's the gentle kiss that leaves you wondering, the perfume that lingers in the room when she leaves. She isn't bold, but she's always noticed. She isn't loud, but she's always heard. Her subtlety steals focus. She's the rarest of blooms. Vegan friendly and cruelty-free. Made without formaldehyde.*

I checked the comments section on Callie's first post again. Most of it was still positive, but there were a few outliers.

wish you'd died

Something off about this . . .

girl you literally fell to your death??? make it make sense

This last had a few replies under it. Most were weak jokes, but one caught my eye.

We obviously have no way to verify if this is really her. A lot of people are out a lot of money if she doesn't 'recover' from dying . . .

Jesus. People were crazy.

My dad rang, which was unusual, because it had been less than two months since we'd last spoken on the phone.

'I was worried about you,' he said. I could hear that he was doing the washing-up. I was touched that he'd called – he'd barely acknowledged that Callie and I had been dating at the time, let alone referenced it since.

'I'm okay. I'm sure she's fine.'

'One of my old school friends died a couple of years ago. It really knocked me sideways.'

'She isn't dead. She already posted on social media.'

'I don't know,' he said. 'Looked pretty lethal. Ridiculous that she wasn't wearing a harness.'

'Yeah,' I said, already regretting picking up. He walked away from the phone to put something in his cupboard. I heard him huffing with every step he took. He'd always been overweight but since I'd left home he'd grown concerningly fat, the kind of fat that made people turn their heads in the street and gape. 'Are you feeling alright at the moment?'

'Oh, fine,' he said, 'fine.' That meant no, but he wasn't going to go to the doctor and do anything about it. When Callie and I had been together I'd worried about his health. Now I'd had to adjust to the knowledge that any day I might pick up a call and find out he'd had a heart attack. I'd prepared myself for it several times over. Rich swore that I'd still be knocked sideways when it happened, but I'd already lost one parent and he hadn't lost any, so I reckoned that made me the expert on parental deaths. I listened to Dad shuffle around the kitchen. He'd done his job by calling me, so now it would be on me to keep the conversation alive.

'What have you been up to?'

'Not much. Keeping busy.' It was at least a positive that he was doing his washing-up. In my first year of university I would go home almost every weekend just to tidy the kitchen for him. Eventually, Callie and Mel between them convinced me that I was enabling his behaviour. I spent many nights in the years that followed lying awake, torturing myself over the fact that I had doomed him to a dirty house and a bad diet. Over time, the feeling sort of slid away, and I stopped thinking of him as someone that I had any responsibility towards. He could keep his house clean when he really wanted to, it turned out. As for keeping himself alive, that would have to be his decision to make. 'Some bloke on Facebook was saying her death's been covered up,' he said.

'Well, you shouldn't believe anything you read on Facebook. I've told you that before.'

He muttered something to himself.

'What was that?'

'Mainstream media never has the whole story, Stevie. You should remember that.'

'Thanks, Dad,' I said. 'I'll remember.'

I hung up the call feeling considerably worse than I had before. His intentions had probably been good.

◆ ◆ ◆

Two days later, it was more than just one bloke on Facebook. I was back in the office in Shoreditch now, smelling fragrance samples and trying to think of synonyms for 'overpoweringly floral'. My boss, Kiera – who was only five years older than me but seemed to be in a completely different, far more adult phase of life – came over to my desk and said, 'Hey, Stevie,' in a voice that suggested I needed to be treated gently. I had always wondered if she knew about me and Callie. She tapped my desk lightly with her pen, gave me a smile, and said, 'We've got offers going up on all of the in-house perfumes, so we really need those done in the next three days or so.' She said this with a sort of knowing sympathy, as if she felt the best thing she could do for me was to let me throw myself into doing my best work for her. 'I'll be in my office, if you need a word about anything,' she said, and left me to the curious stares of everyone else. Kiera's office was really just a sectioned-off portion of the studio space, with a pastel-pink divider to separate her from us – I could see her popping her head over it every now and then, to look at me. She'd definitely watched the Copacabana Beach performance – she'd definitely heard Callie say my name. Maybe the whole office had heard it. There was something very satisfying in that, as much as I didn't want to be stared at.

I checked Calista's socials intermittently as I worked. I had always checked in on her like this – not daily, but regularly, whenever the workflow was slow and one of her songs came into my mind. Today, it was an obsession. Minute by minute, I needed to know what people thought. I searched her name on various platforms, and though most of the videos that popped up were generic adoration, some were more interesting.

> 'Here are all the clues that Calista's fall was actually a planned publicity stunt.'

> 'Why haven't we seen Calista's face in the last forty-eight hours? I get that she's recovering in hospital, but she could take one selfie from bed and put this all to rest.'

> 'Let's unpack all five theories around what might have happened at Copacabana Beach, and guys, the fifth one is where it gets really crazy.'

I scrolled ahead on that last one. Some American girl in pigtails and a trucker hat explained there was a theory going around that there were multiple clones of Calista – Callie had actually died years ago, apparently – and the most recent clone had been neatly disposed of after she failed to stay under the thumb of the record label. I thought 'neatly' was an interesting word choice. I also wondered where she'd found this theory – I'd been immersed in all things Calista for the past two days and I hadn't seen anything like this floating around. The more popular conspiracy was that this was all promo for her next album. The slightly more fringe one was that Callie was dead and her management were posing as her on all her socials while they figured out a game plan. This was the first time I'd seen it suggested that the girl onstage hadn't been her at all. Apparently there were corners of the internet that even I hadn't been able to follow Calista into.

'Oh, I *love* her,' said Rosie, next to me. She was twenty-four and the first person to really make me understand the phrase 'chronically online'. At first I thought she was talking about Calista, because I knew she loved Calista. It had created an ongoing strangeness between us in the year and a half I had worked there – we both knew that she must know who I was, but neither of us had acknowledged it. 'That girl,' she said, pointing at the pigtailed American. 'She always talks about the *best* conspiracies.'

'Oh god,' said Vera, who was fifty-four, also a Calista fan, but not of the internet variety, so blissfully unaware of my connection to Callie. She heaved herself around in her chair. 'What is it now? Lizards in 10 Downing Street?'

'No,' said Rosie, in a tone that meant, *god, no, nothing so dull.* 'You saw what happened on Sunday night, right?'

'Of course,' said Vera.

'Well,' said Rosie, putting an arm across the desk so that I could see the lipstick samples on the inside of her wrist, 'there's all sorts of speculation about what *really* happened.'

'I think everyone saw what happened.'

'Well, it was just so random. People think maybe someone sent her up there without a harness on purpose. Or it was all orchestrated. Or she jumped.'

'Don't be so insensitive,' said Vera, turning back to her monitor. I wondered for a moment if she did know. But she was just a good person, the sort who thought that being a good person meant not speculating online about other people's misery.

Rosie leant over the desk towards me. 'I'll send you a link,' she said, winking. She was a good person of a different sort.

◆ ◆ ◆

She sent me the link when Rich and I were halfway through our tikka masala. It wasn't to a video, like I'd thought it might be, but an entire Instagram page: *@whathappenedtocalista*

really interesting reading!!!!! she'd written.

'Shall I wait?' asked Rich, holding the remote. I always paused the TV when he went on his phone and he relished any opportunity to hold me to my own standards.

I didn't answer. The page was mostly full of old pictures of Callie, with long captions that ranted about everything that might have happened to cause the events at Copacabana Beach. A few posts put old pictures of her side by side with more recent ones, circling apparent differences between them.

Callie's song 'Jessica' talks about a girl who has to live as someone she isn't, says the caption of one. *Could she have been hinting at the name of her doppelganger even then?*

'Jessica' was a private joke that Callie had with herself, the name she gave to any straight girl who she assumed to be closeted. It made me want to laugh, to think how far off base they were. Still, there *were* differences between the pictures. In one, her nose was straighter, her jaw sharper. I couldn't quite remember which one looked more like my Callie.

Rich, still holding the remote petulantly aloft, peered over my shoulder. 'God,' he said, 'what rubbish. Who's sent you that?'

I swiped out of the app and closed my phone. 'You remember Rosie.'

'Yeah,' he said. 'Batshit. Your curry's getting cold.'

◆ ◆ ◆

After he fell asleep that night, rolling over to lay a hot arm on me no matter how many times I rolled him away, I watched that moment from Copacabana Beach on my phone. Not the fall, but the moments leading up to it. The gentle introduction to 'Again, Again, Again'.

'She's someone I've been thinking about a lot lately.'

Sat on her bench, fabric blowing gently against her legs. Everything around her a glorious gold, and Callie the white-hot heart of the star.

'So, Stevie. This one's for you.'

I stopped the video as the bench began to rise.

It had been so many years since she'd said my name. Not since our fateful meeting on Carnaby Street five years ago had she even acknowledged that I existed. She had breathed life back into me, reminded the world that I wasn't ordinary, that this dull, cyclical life I was living had never been meant for me. I should have been stood under that bench, in the boiling heart of the crowd – god knows I had never minded sweating in a crowd for her – watching it rise. If she'd fallen – and somehow I couldn't imagine that she would have done with me there, but if she had – I would have held my arms out, and her white clothes would have caught on the wind like a parachute, and she would have drifted safely down to be held by me.

Had she looked for me in that crowd as she fell?

The next day, Calista posted again.

Doing so much better! Thanks for all the well wishes!

I stared at it for a while.

'Good that she's doing better,' said Rich.

'It doesn't sound like her.'

'Pretty reasonable that someone might be posting for her, given her condition. Don't you think?'

It was reasonable. Still, the post only fuelled the online speculation. Videos putting forward their own theories got hundreds of thousands of likes. The page that Rosie had sent me jumped up massively in followers. The comment section was flooded with self-confessed reluctant believers.

> *I thought this was all crazy . . . but it's getting undeniable now. Why isn't she posting for herself if she's doing so well???*

She had an appearance scheduled at Yale. People thought she might do it over Zoom, but it was cancelled without much fanfare. She was meant to be performing at a memorial concert for some guitarist who had recently overdosed and her name quietly disappeared from the line-up there as well. Fans waited for a statement – she and the dead guitarist had been close, apparently – but nothing. The silence moved like smoke across my laptop screen. People gestured through it. *She's sicker than we thought. She's taking on a new persona.* Increasingly louder, these days: *She's dead. She's dead, and they haven't told us.*

I lay awake at night and tried to imagine the world without her in it. People who didn't know her family history would go to her parents' house in Brighton and lay flowers outside, like they had for Princess Diana. There would be countless television specials. Someone was likely already working on a documentary. Maybe she would have a memorial concert of her own. But she couldn't be dead – they would have said something. *Someone* would have said something. If Calista had dropped out of the world, we would have felt it. We were tied into the very bones of what she was. And even if the rest of them weren't, *I* was. Wasn't I? Surely I was.

Even a photo of her from her hospital bed didn't end the speculation. It was a selfie with a black and white filter on it. She lay with her head bandaged so that her face was partially obscured, a tube in her arm. She was giving a thumbs up. When I first saw it, I wanted to kiss the phone. There she was. She was fine. Right away I felt embarrassed at the rush of affection. I'd become so much better at creating emotional distance.

I opened the comments.

why is she hiding her face???

She literally has a head injury, someone had replied. Lots of commenters claimed the picture was AI. *Her thumb is wobbly.* It was, very slightly, but that sort of thing wasn't new. Callie often edited her pictures. When one fan pointed this out, someone else replied, *She's face-tuning a picture of her in hospital with a bandaged head? You guys will believe anything honestly.* I couldn't even tell what side they were on.

'Do you feel better?' Rich asked.

'Yes,' I said, doubtfully.

Rich cooked every night for a week, which had never happened. He did it without even drawing too much attention to it, delivering plates of food to me on the sofa with no smart-arse comments or passive-aggressive smiles. I wondered if he was saving it all up to hold over me when it was more convenient, when I actually had something to offer, or if he was genuinely just being nice. *Was* Rich nice? I couldn't really remember.

'Stevie, you actually hate him,' said Mel, when she came over.

She'd brought flowers, which made me feel even more as if Callie had died. I'd looked from them to her, and she'd said, 'Oh shit, Stevie, no, I'm not buying into all of that. I just thought your place might need them.' We'd looked at each other and laughed, then. It was all so ridiculous.

She sat down next to me on the sofa and took in the chocolate wrappers, and then she took in me, a week without my skincare routine, in Rich's t-shirt and boxers. She said, 'What's up, huh? Why are you losing your mind over all this?'

'I don't know.' Just speaking to her was like breathing clean air again. 'I actually think I'm going insane.'

'I get that, Stevie-girl.' Her manicured hand pushed the hair back from my forehead. I told her about the Instagram page, and all the comments I'd been reading, and all the ways in which Rich had been pissing me off. That's when she told me that she thought I hated him.

'Maybe,' I said, in that way I did whenever anyone told me I should break up with Rich.

'I think you're deeply unhappy,' she said. 'Depressed, probably.' Mel had never had any qualms about diagnosing people. She'd told at least three of her ex-girlfriends that they had mummy issues and one that she was a sociopath. 'I don't know why you punish yourself by staying in this relationship.'

'You really think he's that bad?'

'*You* think he's that bad,' she said. 'It doesn't really matter what I think.'

She'd got another syringe in her lips, I noticed. She was beginning to take it a little far, not that there was ever much good in telling her those things. I'd always thought she was ridiculously beautiful, lithe and tan and glassy-blue eyed, the kind of girl I probably would have fallen in love with had I met her in a bar in my twenties and not in a playground when I was eight, offering to show her underwear to the boys in exchange for Digestives and twenty-pence coins. She tried to rope me into the business but my underwear had Disney princesses on it and I was too embarrassed to show it to anyone. My job was to keep watch next to the monkey bars or round the back of the PE shed or in whatever romantic spot she'd picked, as Mel looked around her and quickly lifted her skirt, with a business-like attitude. For my troubles, sometimes I would receive half a Digestive. She always kept the twenty-pence coins.

She had always been electric to me, bright neon in my life, dragging me into trouble whenever I would let her, responsible for most of the good stories I had to tell on first dates. Women fell in love with her at an alarming rate. The only person Mel ever had any trouble impressing was herself.

'What do you want to do?' she asked, putting her feet up on my coffee table. 'Eat? Drink? I'll go out and get you whatever you want.'

'I don't know.'

'There must be something that'll help.'

I shrugged.

'You should be on medication,' she said, 'I reckon. Sertraline, probably.'

'I'm not depressed, Mel.'

'Of course you're depressed. You've been depressed for years. It's why you won't let yourself be happy.' She turned towards me on the sofa, propped up on her elbow, resting her cheek on her hand. 'Do you want to go out tonight? Sarah has a table at that place we went for Huda's birthday. Remember? Where I got with that absolutely *stunning* girl but it was never going to work because she was going back to Nigeria?'

'Right,' I said, half listening. I was on Callie's Instagram again.

'Were you there that night?'

'I don't think so.'

'You should come out with us,' she said.

'Those girls don't like me.'

'They do like you. You just don't try with them.' She looked at me, exasperated. 'Why does it feel like it's getting worse again?'

'What?'

'The Callie obsession. It's getting worse again. Put your phone away, come on.'

'Everyone's obsessed right now.'

'It's different with you,' she said. 'Obviously.' I put my phone down on the coffee table. 'Just break up with Rich,' she said. 'Please? As a birthday present to me. And stop letting your mental health revolve around the well-being of your famous ex.'

'I'm allowed to be sad if she's dead.'

'Sure. But she's not. Stop being a nut.'

My phone buzzed.

@steviestone5 !!!

Multiple tags in the comments of a video. It wasn't posted by any of her official socials, but by some random page with no profile picture and no other posts. Mel watched over my shoulder. The video was taken from outside some mostly empty building, like a well-kept warehouse, with white floors and brick pillars. The camera watched through the window as people bustled around inside, conducting a photoshoot, holding big circles of gold foil and moving lights. They parted, suddenly, and in the centre of it all, there she was. Callie.

She did look different. There was no denying it. Her lips were a slightly different shape. Her jaw was a little swollen. She was covered in white paint, every inch of her coated in it, other than her hair, with big dark circles under her eyes, so it was hard to get a clear idea of her face. She was also leaning on a crutch, propping herself up on her left side. But it was her. She moved, she posed, she even laughed. Calista lived.

The comments were ecstatic.

OMG she looks so healthy!! So proud of her!!

Hardest working woman in the industry

not her already working on a new era? girl you were dead

'She looks good,' said Mel, her chin resting on my shoulder. '*Really* good, actually. How is she not in a full body cast?'

'She's lucky, I guess,' I said. 'She was always lucky.'

I scrolled further down.

thats not her

I paused on the comment. Just three words, no punctuation.

thats not her

I watched the video again. I examined the way she tipped her head back to laugh. I watched her pose. There was a stiffness to the way she held her arms that I had never noticed in her before. She was too smiley. I looked up at Mel.

'No,' she said. 'Stevie.'

'Maybe it's not her.'

'It *is*.' She jabbed a finger at the screen. 'You can see that too, right? I'm not crazy?' I scrunched up my nose. 'Where's her tattoo again?' asked Mel.

'Hip.'

'Okay, so look.' We waited. Calista – whoever she was – raised an arm, and the white drapery of her top rose just slightly. 'There,' said Mel triumphantly. There was a small black star on the woman's hip. The video cut out there and looped back to the start.

'Anyone could get a tattoo,' I said.

'Do you want her to be dead?'

'Of course not. How could you say that?'

'Because this is what I'm talking about, Stevie. You don't want her to be dead, and she isn't. So let it be true. Let yourself be happy.' She checked her phone – she had a flat to show. 'And break up with Rich,' she said, picking up her bag. 'Or – and you may think I'm joking – I will actually do it for you.'

'He's not that bad.'

'He's not,' she said. 'I actually feel sorry for him.'

◆ ◆ ◆

After she left, I watched the video over and over. In between watches, I would scroll down to look at that three-word comment.

thats not her

A couple of hours later, someone had replied to it.

It's not! Check my recent post!

It was *@whathappenedtocalista,* the page that Rosie had convinced me to follow. I clicked on the profile. Sure enough, there was a new post. It was a slowed-down clip of the video, a turn of Calista's head, zoomed in and grainy. Then it cut to a clip from seven years ago, during a promo for *Want Me Want Me.* A younger Calista turned her head and laughed.

I watched the two clips several times through. The knot in my stomach wound tighter. They didn't look like the same person at all.

Of course, these clips were taken seven years apart. A person might change quite significantly between the ages of twenty-two and thirty. They might almost be someone entirely different. Especially if they'd been in a significant accident – *especially,* as comments on the original video pointed out, if their face was still healing from bruising. She'd been in bandages not that long ago, after all. She might still have quite a lot of damage. She might have even taken the opportunity to have some work done. Maybe the fact that she didn't quite look like herself was the most natural thing in the world.

But my gut was sure, much as I tried to convince myself out of the feeling. One of these women was my Callie, and the other wasn't. It was as simple as that.

I liked the video.

A few seconds later, I had a new DM request.

> *@whathappenedtocalista: Hi Stevie! I'm so glad you found my page!! People like you who really know Callie are the ones who can help convince everyone of the TRUTH!!!!*

They sounded like a child. I immediately regretted the like. Another message pinged through.

> *@whathappenedtocalista: I have SO MUCH evidence*

I couldn't help myself.

> *@steviestone5: Hi. What kind of evidence?*

They wrote back immediately.

> *@whathappenedtocalista: I've been examining all the photos and videos going back since before Put This On My Headstone and I think they've had a body double ready to go for years. Did you ever hear anything about it when you two were together?*

> *@steviestone5: No, I didn't.*

Then, for my own sanity.

@steviestone5: That all sounds a bit mad.

@whathappenedtocalista: I know it does but there's no other way to explain what's happening. We all saw the fall. How could she be doing a photoshoot a week later?

I didn't know what to say to that. But I couldn't go on talking to whoever this person was. Rich thought I was unstable and Mel thought I was mentally ill. I didn't want to prove them both right in one fell swoop. I shut my phone. A few minutes later, I saw another message flash up on my home screen.

@whathappenedtocalista: Message me any time if you want to talk about this further.

The door opened, which made me jump.

'You alright?' asked Rich, coming through. 'You look spooked.' He crossed the room to kiss me on the cheek. 'Apparently she got papped. Told you she'd be fine.' He looked visibly relieved – he clearly considered the matter ended and his girlfriend cured. 'What do you want to eat tonight?' he asked, in a very particular way. Now that Callie was proven alive and healthy it was obviously time for me to start pulling my weight in the kitchen again.

The video split the internet. One side considered the matter resolved. The other – an increasingly vocal minority – took it in the same light that *@whathappenedtocalista* had. It was uncanny, flesh-tingling; it proved that all was not as it should be. Calista wasn't

Calista. Was it a deepfake? people speculated. A body double? Old footage made to look new?

Then *Time* did a phoner with Calista. No photos – she was still in 'both physical and psychological recovery' and the team 'just couldn't make it happen logistically' – but the interviewer made sure to confirm that yes, he had heard her voice on the other end of the phone, and it had very much sounded like her, other than a bit of slurring due to a still-healing jaw. No reason for concern, nothing to suggest that he was being duped. It wasn't a long piece. He spoke about the impact of the accident on her relationship with performing.

> **Calista:** *It hasn't changed a thing. I know that seems strange to say. But things you love can hurt you sometimes, and you just have to love them anyway. I'll definitely be more cautious moving forward. But it's also shown me just how much my fans love me.*

That last sentence didn't sit right with me. She never really used the word 'fans' – she'd been borderline allergic to it when I'd known her. The journalist asked if she was aware of the conspiracies flooding the internet.

> **Calista:** *Oh, I'm honoured to be the centre of a conspiracy. Celebrity conspiracies are always good fun.*

That did sound like something she would say. But the second part of the answer was strange.

> *I do think there are so many more important things for people to be worried about though. I fell and hurt myself, and now I'm taking it easy. Aren't there bigger things to be talking about in the world than that?*

That didn't sound anything like her. I couldn't even quite articulate why to Rich, who sat faux-patiently while I unpacked the interview out loud, sentence by sentence.

There's been a video of you circulating in which some people think you don't seem to look quite like yourself. What do you make of the speculation around that?

Calista: *I've aged, I've been injured, I was covered head to toe in paint . . . I don't really know what else I can say about it. The fact of the matter is that right now, I feel more like myself than ever.*

I read that last sentence out loud to Rich.

'Good for her,' he said.

I watched the video of her in the warehouse again, that sentence playing on a loop in my mind. '*Right now, I feel more like myself than ever.*'

It was far too much. Callie loved to keep people guessing. That line felt desperate, like she really did have something to prove. I read it again, and then I went back and read previous interviews. *Rolling Stone. Variety. Vogue.* I compared tones and phrasing. My head swam with her words. Just before I fell asleep, I messaged the conspiracy page.

@steviestone5: That Time piece isn't her. I'm sure of it.

Rich shook me awake the next morning. 'You're late,' he said, standing over me in his suit shirt and boxers.

'Shit.' I sat up. 'Did I sleep through my alarm?'

'Right through it. I thought I'd let you rest a little longer, though. I think that was the first good night's sleep you've had in a while.' He was smiling, as if he'd had something to do with it. 'You're feeling better, then?'

'Don't let me sleep through my alarm,' I said, scrabbling down the side of my bed for my bra.

'I will if I think you need it.'

I gave him a kiss before I left, because he probably was trying to be kind in his own way, and ran to the Tube station. My phone was going off again. More tags, likely extracts from her *Time* piece. I couldn't be the only one who had suspicions about it.

I was only twenty minutes late for work in the end. Rosie was halfway through an almond croissant. She gave me a grin as I sat down next to her at my desk, her chin covered in crumbs.

'There she is,' she said. 'You're famous!'

I stared at her, still bleary-eyed. Her grin wavered.

'You didn't see?' she said, and she held out her phone. One of *@whathappenedtocalista*'s posts had blown up. Thousands of comments, hundreds of thousands of likes. I squinted at the screen, and my chest went cold.

It was a screenshot of my message.

@steviestone5: That Time piece isn't her. I'm sure of it.

Rosie took her phone back. 'Do you really think it isn't?' she asked in hushed tones, leaning in. Her breath smelt like pastry. It was the first time either of us had acknowledged my relationship with Callie.

My phone rang. It wasn't a number I recognised. Possibly a journalist. Possibly a lawyer. *Shit.* I let it go to voicemail.

'I think it's weird too,' said Rosie. I was trapped in some nightmare where we were co-conspirators. Her computer pinged. She leant forward, her hand on the mouse, and I mumbled something about the bathroom and slipped away.

The toilets were empty, thankfully. I sat down in a stall, my hands sweaty, and held the phone to my ear.

'Hi, Stevie,' said a voice I didn't recognise. 'This is Harma, Calista's PR manager. I think we've met before? We'd love to invite you into the office to have a chat. Calista would really like to speak with you. Give me a call back and we'll arrange a time.'

I played the message again. My chest stung. I couldn't see straight. Was this what a panic attack felt like? Someone rapped on the door.

'Stevie?' came Rosie's voice. 'Are you alright? I didn't mean to upset you.'

I opened the door. She only came up to my shoulder, blinking her big eyes up at me sympathetically. Her fingers twisted around each other.

'I'm here if you need someone to talk to,' she said.

'I've got cramps,' I croaked.

'Oh,' she said. 'Um. Okay.'

I moved past her and headed back to my desk, taking my bag from the back of my chair. I hadn't even unpacked.

'You alright, Stevie?' asked Vera. I ignored her. I got back in the lift. Out in the street, I listened to the message a third time, just to convince myself that it wasn't anything to be afraid of. Every time I listened, Harma's voice became more threatening. I remembered her, from all the way back in the early days. She used to carry around a ludicrously big bag and wear gems on her nails. I tried to recall how Callie had felt about her. I think we'd laughed about her a little behind her back, made fun of her PR spiel and forced patter.

'Calista would really like to speak with you.'

On the street behind the office, I sat down on a wall with my bag beside me and rang Harma back, biting the skin around my thumb.

'Hello?'

'Hi,' I said. 'This is Stevie.'

'*Stevie,*' came Harma's voice. 'Great to hear from you. What's your availability looking like this week?'

'My— Um, I'm pretty free.'

'We'd love to bring you in. Do you have any time tomorrow?'

'Is this— What's this about?'

'Oh, it's just a general chat. I don't want to say too much over the phone.'

'With Callie?'

'Well,' she said, 'on her behalf, certainly.'

'Is this about the post on social media?'

A slight pause. 'There's just a few sensitive things to talk about,' she said, 'and it's better not to do it over the phone. I can book you in for tomorrow morning, then? I'm happy to send you the details.'

'Sure. Yeah. That's—' Asking again about Callie would have sounded desperate, especially when Harma had more or less implied she wouldn't be there. Still, I wished she'd give me a straight yes or no. 'I'll see you then.'

After we hung up, I sat on the wall for some time and wondered when it had all got so ridiculous. Which is funny to remember, considering where it ended up.

Calista (2016)

The Germans probably have a word for when your heart stops and it feels exactly as if you should have died, except you go on waking up, over and over and over, and your physical health feels completely incongruous with the lifelessness you hold in your body, and there is a little voice screaming at you in the back of your mind that you should be dead. That there is no way you can survive this.

'All of me is heavy,' I say to Mel.

'Oh,' she says, 'Stevie-girl.' She hugs me on the front step of her block of flats, her lighter held between two fingers over my right shoulder. I am newly twenty-one – as of yesterday, actually – and don't want a party. There is nothing to celebrate.

I have moved in with Mel because I've realised, two and a half years into university, that I don't really have any friends. Not real ones, whose doors I can turn up at in tears in the middle of the night. This never mattered so much before because I had Mel and I had Callie, two angels with a hand in each of mine. Now I can't go home to my flat and be there knowing that she isn't coming back.

Mel and I sit on her front step, her smoking, me clutching my stomach, being some long German word I don't know. She clicks her leopard-print sliders together like Dorothy and I wish that somebody would come take me home.

'Where's she playing tonight?' she asks.

'Vienna.'

'Boring. What's Vienna got?'

'I don't know. Opera?' I lean forward and bring my legs up, resting my chin on my knees. 'It's been a month today.'

'Stevie . . .'

'I know I shouldn't be counting.'

'No, you should not.'

'She's over it, Mel.'

'She's not over it,' says Mel firmly, tapping her cigarette on the step. 'Over what? Over you? Ridiculous, Stevie-girl. Nobody ever could be.'

We watch a McDonald's cup blow down her street, spilling drops of milkshake. It's a very windy spring. The fake ivy has blown off Mel's tiny, one-person balcony and is lying in the gutter a little way off from us. I wonder what the weather is like in Vienna. I hope her plane had turbulence, I think, and then feel guilty.

The worst part – well, maybe not the worst part, it's hard to pick a worst part, but the part that really kills me, that comes back to haunt me over and over – is how far off I saw it coming. I can pinpoint the moment. It wasn't when she got the deal – we were closer than ever then, legs tangled up in each other's as we sat on the sofa, her manager on speaker, and tried not to scream. Someone took a photo of us kissing outside the building after she signed her contract. I understood it was huge then, that they were going to take her places, but not that they were going to transform her.

Calista, as I knew her, always wore a guitar over her shoulders. She stood onstage in strange dresses that she found in charity shops and car boot sales, in accessories that she made herself, and sang her funny, bold, scrappy little songs that I'd watched Callie write on the floor of our apartment. She always wrote lyrics on her stomach and guitar parts on her back. Watching her work was sometimes like watching a beached seal trying to free itself – she would have a thought, and flip over to scribble in her notebook, and hum something, and flip over to lie with her guitar, staring up at the ceiling, singing under her breath. She didn't like me to watch her, but it was my favourite thing in the world. Cliché to say, but I have never seen anything as beautiful as Callie lying on her back with her guitar, staring up at our ceiling with single-minded focus.

She called me one day while I was working on an essay at the desk we shared and gave me an address. 'I'm at a fitting for my music video,' she said. 'Come! Come!' There were people talking in the background. I could hear in her voice that she felt beautiful. I put the address in my phone and went to South Kensington to meet her.

The place was on a private street, white terraced houses running all along it, a gentle curve of clean pillars and black iron fences. The paving slabs were the cleanest I'd ever seen in London. On the upstairs balconies of every single house stood perfectly round shrubs, trees in baskets with skinny trunks, leaves trimmed into green orbs. I walked the curve of it until I found the house number she'd given me. When I rang the bell, I felt a little like the oil on my finger was going to make it dirty.

'Hello?' said a voice on the intercom.

'It's Stevie.'

'Stevie?'

'Callie's Stevie.'

Some conversation that I couldn't make out. 'Oh, Stevie,' came the voice. 'Sorry!' The door gave.

I followed the sound of voices up three flights of white carpeted stairs. The walls were lined with photos of women in dresses. I recognised some of them – singers, actresses, reality stars. On the third floor, the double doors to a large sunlit room were open. There were eight or nine people in there, crossing the room urgently with arms full of stuff, whispering in ears and writing things down, or just standing around making wry observations about the proceedings to whoever stood next to them. I wondered what each person's purpose was, and why I didn't know any of them. In the centre of the room, Callie stood, dressed all in yellow. The bodice of her gown was corseted and behind her the skirt stretched over the floor, all feathers. Her blonde curls fell about her shoulders. They had her in yellow satin gloves up to her elbows, with a feather in her hair. She looked like some exotic bird. When she caught sight of me in the mirror, she turned. Her face was luminous.

'Isn't it amazing?' she said. 'I really wanted you to see the one I had on before. Maybe I'll try it on again, just for you.'

I circled the dress. 'You look incredible,' I said. There was a general air of fanatical approval in the room that I did my best to imitate. 'This is – this is for "Don't Save Me"?'

She nodded. The feather bobbed up and down. I ran my hand over the skirt, feeling the curve of her somewhere underneath it, and she giggled in a way that made me want to grab hold of her hips.

A woman in a white t-shirt came over to shake my hand. Her hair was tied back and her whole appearance was a little boyish, but in more of a 'too busy to care' way than a gay one. 'Stevie, hi,' she said. 'I'm so sorry about the confusion there. Harma.'

'Hi.' I tried to remember if Callie had told me about a Harma. Her team had grown massively over the last few months.

'So lovely to finally meet you!' It sounded genuine. She didn't look much older than us, in her ponytail and jeans. 'Isn't this so exciting? Don't you just love the song?'

'Oh, yes,' I said. 'I just love it.' Callie pulled a face at me in the mirror.

The lead single on her second album was not my favourite. Which was fine – I didn't have to love everything she did. Just seeing her do it all was enough. I already knew that she wanted to have a career where she tried lots of different things, put on different voices, became different people for different projects. When she'd played me 'Don't Save Me', I'd understood that she was doing radio pop her way, with the input of some buzzy Norwegian producer. It was a sound she was good at, and the song was objectively not bad, but I didn't like how unfamiliar she sounded. When she'd created Calista I'd had to get used to who she was as that person, and I had – to the point where I had fallen in love with Calista almost as a separate creature from my Callie. Now Calista's definition was changing. I saw that they wanted her to have mass appeal, to belong to big crowds, and I could see that Callie – who had never admitted to ambitions of going mainstream – wanted that too.

They were making her shiny, in her lemon-yellow dress. Callie isn't shiny. She sparkles in that way your skin does after a night out when the glitter from your outfit or other people's outfits migrates all over your face and hands. She's dazzling, but she isn't perfect. She struggles to regulate her emotions, and she's a terrible drinker, and she's made her fair share of really honestly god-awful decisions. She had a messy childhood, a messier adolescence, with parents who tried against all the odds to raise her Mormon in Brighton and to turn a stern blind eye to both her atheism and her queerness. But these are all parts of Callie that can't be excavated. They are fundamental to what is magic about her. They wanted to make her this untouchable thing. Callie isn't untouchable. You can reach out and put both your hands on her. And god, it's all I ever want to do.

'I think I'm going to wear this one in a swimming pool,' she said, and laughed. 'God, can you imagine ruining a thing like this? All because we think it'll look cool. Artists suck.'

Everyone in the room laughed. It was an over-eager sort of laughter, but she didn't seem to notice. She turned back to the mirror with her hands busy in her hair, repositioning the yellow feather. I watched her in the glass, and it was almost as if we were standing in entirely different rooms. Callie in one room, all in yellow feathers, made so beautiful I almost didn't like to look at her. Me in another identical room, only mine was empty, and nobody was there to notice me leave.

But she turned back before I could slip out. 'By the way,' she said. 'We're changing the name of the album.'

'Oh, really? How come?'

'They thought Love Shack *would remind people too much of B-52s.'*

'That's a shame,' I said. 'I liked that name.' The 'love shack' was what Callie had started jokingly calling our flat. The album title had convinced me that I was still in this record, somewhere, even when none of the songs felt that familiar.

'Actually,' she said, 'they wanted to do a self-titled thing. Just call it Calista.*'*

She said it casually but she was watching me for my reaction. I used to tell her she set too much store by my opinion. By that point, though, it was nice to feel any anxiety from her about what I thought. Everyone around her always seemed to know so much more about what she should be.

'Huh,' I said.

'You don't like it?'

'It does feel like more of a debut title.'

'Well,' she said, 'this is kind of a debut.'

'No, it isn't. Put This On My Headstone *was your debut.'*

'Yes, but this is my major label debut. Anyway, no one ever should have let me call it that in the first place.'

'I love that title,' I said. 'It feels like . . . forever.' I blushed, when I said the last word, but she reached out and took my hand.

'I just think this is the right move,' she said. 'This is the beginning, really. It all starts here.'

She pressed my wrist to her lips and smiled at me over my fingers. She looked like someone had designed a perfect doll of her. I wondered, if this was the beginning, what everything before this actually meant to her now.

I thought, I can't hold on to her.

I tell Mel all of this on her front step, as she rubs my back and tries to give me her cigarette. What I don't tell her is that last week when the album was released, I joined Callie's livestream for a few seconds just to see if she gave any indication of missing me. I left after a few minutes because it was so hard to see her so happy. I don't think she even noticed.

'You should block her on everything,' says Mel, as I open up Callie's Instagram again. 'There's no point torturing yourself like this.'

'She's big now, Mel. I'll see her in the fucking news. And I'll hear the album everywhere.' Only a few days in the world and Calista *is massive – far bigger than* Put This On My Headstone.

'Is the album about you?'

'I don't know what it's about,' I say. 'It's different from her old stuff.'

'Less heart on her sleeve?'

'It's a performance. Which is great. But there's some parts where I feel like she's . . . missing.' Mel is watching me. 'What?'

'You spend so much time thinking about Callie,' she says. 'You have ever since you met her. What would happen if you just stopped? Could you do that?'

The question makes my heart thud. It's one thing to lose her. It's another to let go of her. 'I don't know,' I say honestly. She finishes her cigarette and tells me that she wants to see me happy. I tell her that I'll do what I can.

Chapter Three

Harma hadn't aged, which isn't a compliment exactly. It was unnerving. I was aware, of course, that people in the industry had ways of slowing their visible aging even more effectively than those of the women around my office. But Harma had once looked as if she could have been an older sister to Callie and me, and now she looked younger. The skin on her face was taut and plump. Her eyes were slightly too wide. She was more or less how I remembered her – cordial, conspiratorial, like she'd been wandering the halls of this record label for god knows how long trying to find another normal person in all of this, and thank the Lord, *there I was.* In reality, I knew that there was nothing normal about Harma.

'God, you look wonderful,' she said. 'It's so good to see you. How many years has it been? Eight – or nine?'

'Something like that,' I said. We'd met maybe three times previously and had probably exchanged less than fifty words between us. I followed her up the stairs.

We were meeting in an office space near Old Street that I'd walked past too many times to count. Had they been inside all along? I wasn't even sure who 'they' were, whether I was meeting people from the label or just from Harma's agency – or maybe just Harma, who had rented a room in which to give me a stern talking-to. I wondered if she would offer me money. I wondered if I would take it.

Rich hadn't wanted me to go, which had surprised me. I'd thought he would be as intrigued as I was. 'They're probably just looking for a way to serve you papers,' he said the night before, ironing behind me as I sat on the sofa watching a show about paramedics in helicopters. I didn't like when he stood directly behind me with the ironing board, his quiet presence over my shoulder, the ominous hiss of the iron tickling the hairs on the back of my neck.

'I don't think you're allowed to invite someone over to serve them. Are you? Anyway, I haven't broken any laws.'

'No, but they can still sue you for libel.'

'I don't think so. I didn't speak publicly. At least, not on purpose.'

He made a kind of questioning hum, which was the sound he made when he was out of his depth in a conversation but didn't want to admit to it.

'Why wouldn't I go?' I said.

He didn't say anything for a second. On the TV, two paramedics rushed out of a helicopter in the Scottish Highlands, scrambling over rocks and thistles towards an injured dogwalker. The dog-walker sat very still in the grass, leg crushed under a rock, anticipating them. The dog yapped and spun in a circle. It had seemed quite high stakes, paramedics in helicopters, but once you'd seen one rescue, you'd seen them all. This one had a dog, at least.

'Do you think she'll be there?' he asked.

I turned around to stare at him over the back of the sofa. He was ironing with a great deal of focus, in his t-shirt and boxers, his hair stiff with mousse. 'Are you *jealous?*'

'Don't be vindictive.'

'You can't just evade the question by telling me what not to be.'

'You don't think it's unproductive to be vindictive?'

'Yes, Rich, everyone should not be vindicative all of the time.'

'I'm not jealous,' he said, delightfully petulant. I turned back to the TV. 'I mean,' he said, behind me. 'Who knows what really happened with you two?'

'Well, I do.'

The same little questioning noise in the back of his throat. He'd implied disbelief about my relationship with Callie before, but never that I was lying or exaggerating. I decided not to rise to it.

'I don't know if she'll be there,' I said. 'I mean, that's the point of all this. I don't even know if she is anywhere.'

'You can't really believe that.'

'I don't know what to believe.'

'But why on earth would you think she wasn't?'

'Because I knew her.'

The rustle of folding shirts. 'If you really thought that,' said Rich, 'and you really loved her once, then you'd be too distraught to even think about going. You'd be too distraught to even do anything.'

I turned around to look at him again. He was pressing the sleeve of his shirt down very deliberately, making a tight fold. 'Would you be that distraught if one of your exes disappeared?'

'That's different,' he said. 'My exes are crazy.'

He caught my eye. He scratched his neck, and I raised my eyebrows, and then he let out a little self-conscious chuckle. I found myself laughing with him. He leant over the ironing board and kissed the top of my head. 'Sorry,' he said. 'Go if you want. Obviously. Whatever you feel like you need to do.'

Okay, I thought, as he folded up the ironing board. *So, not tonight.*

◆ ◆ ◆

Harma led me up the stairs, past wooden office doors with big blue handles, signs that read '*PRIVATE*' and '*NO ACCESS*', like this really was some kind of hush-hush operation. My spine prickled. Then I pictured Callie, blonde hair tied back from her face, sat behind a boardroom table to greet me. *Hi, Stevie. God, what have you been doing? Did you really not recognise me? Did you really think I was dead?*

'Just in here,' said Harma, holding the door. I saw as she pushed on it that she was wearing an engagement ring.

There were only two other people in the room, and neither one was Callie. One was a man in a navy shirt, neutrally handsome, the kind of good-looking that guarantees relatively smooth sailing through life but without any particular privileges. The other was a woman, older and greying but so poised with it that you felt as if it must have been her choice to age. She wore a white shirt buttoned all the way up with a bird-shaped pin at her throat. They both sat at a glossy table, the only thing in the room other than themselves and their laptops. The man had his closed, his hand resting on it, but the woman was typing as I entered. She looked up briefly, nodded, and returned to what she was doing.

'This is Stevie!' said Harma behind me, with almost enough enthusiasm to convince me that anyone there was excited to meet me.

The man stood up to shake my hand without a change in expression.

'Well!' said the woman at her laptop. She didn't elaborate further.

Feeling suddenly as if this had been a mistake, I sat down in the chair that Harma pulled out for me. She was still over-enthused. I felt a strong wish to see this little gathering through her eyes.

'This is Charlie,' she said. 'And Stevie, this is Gene Parrison.'

Gene, eyes on her laptop, raised a brief hand. I didn't know Charlie, but I knew Gene Parrison. She'd been Callie's manager since 2018. We'd never met, but I'd heard her name many times over the years, not only in connection with Calista but many other huge stars as well. If social media was to be believed – which just then was still up for debate – she'd launched a hundred careers with a good word and ended five hundred with a bad one. Different internet subcultures credited her with everything from directing and releasing her clients' sex tapes to *heavily* influencing Anna Wintour's guest-list decisions at the Met Gala.

I sat down. Harma, from seemingly nowhere, produced a bottle of water and a glass and placed them in front of me. 'Thanks for coming in,' she said. 'We know you must be busy.'

'Yes,' said Gene, 'I'm sure the internet conspiracies are taking up a lot of your time.'

Harma's smile didn't move. She looked at me expectantly.

'I—' I started, but there was nowhere for the sentence to go.

Gene finally pushed her laptop away from her. She folded her hands – manicured peach – and fixed me with a look that made me feel like a naughty child. 'I mean *really*,' she said.

This seemed to be the moment where I was supposed to offer an apology, but I resisted. 'It was a private DM. I regret that it was leaked—' Was 'I regret' an apology? I paused. 'I've known Callie a long time, and I was just concerned.'

'No,' said Gene, 'you knew her a long time *ago*. Not quite the same thing, is it?' Jesus. I was starting to sweat. 'Have you seen how many tabloids have picked this story up?' she asked. 'Probably a very exciting thing for you.' I had seen, and I had been horrified. Rich kept bringing the articles up on his phone and asking me what on earth I'd been thinking. Most of the pieces had adopted a tone pitying of me and other self-deceivers, but a few questioned whether we should all be looking into this further. I'd been avoiding calling my dad back because I was so mortified. Mel had spent the morning texting me screenshots of her favourites with *You're a massive fucking idiot* written underneath.

'It shouldn't have gone that far,' I said.

'No,' she said, 'it shouldn't. Should it?'

Her condescension was unbearable. 'I was concerned for an old friend. I'm happy to post something saying—'

'Yes,' said Gene, cutting me off, 'we've prepared something for you, actually. Harma has . . .' She trailed off, absorbed in something on her screen. Harma cleared her throat and held her phone out to me.

> *I deeply regret the role I've played in furthering this discourse. Sometimes we forget that the people involved in these internet jokes are real people and that what happens online can affect their real lives. I want to truly apologise to Calista, her loved ones and her fans.*

Perhaps I should have been angry, reading it. I just found myself cringing deeply. Charlie watched me, fiddling with his pen.

'All good?' asked Harma brightly.

'I don't work for—'

'Inserting yourself in this way was deeply wrong of you,' said Gene, still engrossed in her laptop. 'It's not a matter of working for us. It's a matter of doing what's right.'

'I don't mind saying I'm sorry,' I said, and cringed even deeper. 'But— Look, if I could see her? Speak to her? What she went through was really scary, and I just want to know that she's okay.'

A look passed between Gene and Charlie, and all of me reacted to it, almost as if I already knew what it meant.

'Is she— Is she *here*?'

A slight waver in Harma's smile told me that I was right. Every hair on my arms stood up. The relief was overpowering – then she was okay, truly, she was fine and healthy and in this building – but so was the embarrassment. She knew. She'd seen my message to that headcase on Instagram. I must have imagined running into her again under a hundred different circumstances and this was one for which I hadn't prepared myself. It almost couldn't have been worse.

'Is she joining?' I asked, trying to keep the croak out of my throat.

'She hasn't decided,' said Charlie. His voice was very deep. He looked a little disdainful of me, like I was lacking some quality or other and, on the basis of this lack, never should have been let into this room. I resented the implication that Callie confided in him. 'I'll go ask her,' he said. 'See how she feels.'

So, she was angry at me. I sat in my chair, trying not to tremble, feeling smaller than small, as Charlie disappeared through another door at the far end of the room. Without another glance at me, Gene pulled her laptop back towards her and the tap of her peach nails resumed. Harma gave me a smile as if she was about to initiate friendly conversation and then picked up her phone and started to scroll her emails.

Charlie took his time. I gripped the underside of my chair, working my fingernails against the wood. The instinct to run came out of nowhere and overtook me. I thought, again and again, outside of my own control: *I can't see her. It will ruin everything.* I wasn't sure where the thought came from, or what it meant, only that I felt it worse than any feeling I had ever had to hold in my body and breathe through.

The door opened. I thought I might pass out. Charlie entered first. He looked back.

'It's okay,' he said, surprisingly tender.

When she walked in I thought, *It's her. That's her.* In the next second, I didn't know.

It looked like her. Her blonde curls were pulled back in a ponytail, exactly as I had imagined they would be. She wore a white jumper and brown shorts that hit the middle of her thigh, white trainers, no jewellery. Her face was open, earnest, a little shy. I'd thought she might walk in and be a pop star, but she wasn't a pop star. She was just Callie. And it hurt to see her, just Callie, and to know that she had gone on existing underneath Calista the entire time, out of my view. The next second, she crossed the room towards me, and it didn't look like her at all. I watched her coming towards me. I thought, *I don't know who this woman is.*

I still went to her. I was going to hug her, and then at the last second, I didn't. We just stood in front of each other, completely at a loss.

I said, 'Your jaw.'

She touched her fingers to it. It was swollen and a little yellow. It changed her face, not entirely, but distinctively.

'Is it still sore?'

'Not really,' she said. 'A bit. They say it might never look entirely the same.' She stared at me, searchingly. Whatever she was looking for, I wanted to draw it out of myself and present it to her with both hands. 'Do I still look like me?' she asked.

My Callie. 'Yes,' I said. 'You still look like you.'

She smiled.

'We're aware that there may be doubt about that fact,' said Gene. Gene had the voice of a woman who had never once had to clear her throat before speaking. 'An incident this severe – of this traumatic a nature – does invite a degree of speculation. And with the efforts of *certain* people on the internet—' She didn't look at me as she said this, but I still flushed. 'Calista's recovery has been miraculous. Her next project is going to be sensational. The worry is that all of this nonsense might overshadow whatever moves we make next.'

Callie's eyes were on Gene, nodding along. Her mouth was neutral – her brow was smooth. There was nothing in her manner to indicate that she hadn't wanted to see me. But she was Calista, even here. Always happy, always pleasant, always available. It was impossible to know what she really felt.

'It's obviously a long time since the two of you have seen each other,' said Harma, whose phone was now face down on the table, still buzzing. 'Must be strange! The fact is, Stevie, however long ago it was, you do still have a degree of . . .' She clicked her fingers twice. The engagement ring caught the light. 'Influence. Over the fans.'

'For better or worse,' said Charlie.

He really did look at me like he hated me. Maybe he was in love with her.

'So, you need my help?'

'We don't need you to help,' said Gene. 'We just need you to not hinder.' Somehow, this conversation had reached new levels of embarrassing. I felt like a primary-school child pulled into the head's office. I had only been pulled into the head's office once in primary school, for failing to hand in my big end of year five project despite being given a two-week extension. I had found it impossible to explain that the idea of even starting the project – a small family history book, for which we were supposed to trace back the lines of our parentage and interview our older family members – had filled me with such oppressive anxiety that it had paralysed me. The school couldn't understand this any more than my parents could. This had been the year before my mum passed away – she hadn't even been sick yet – and there were children in my class who were adopted, who had absent parents or a total lack of grandparents, and none of them had been unable to turn anything in. But there had been no logical reason for my behaviour then, just as there was none now. *I'm sorry,* was all I would have been able to offer them. *I don't know why I'm like this.*

'Of course, you don't have to post the apology if it feels inauthentic,' said Harma, unfailingly chipper. 'All we ask is that you're mindful of what you put online and who you interact with, just until this situation blows over.'

'Sure,' I said. 'Of course.' I hesitated. 'Would you rather I stayed off social media altogether?' I addressed the question to Callie herself, almost without meaning to. She was staying quiet, following the thread of the conversation as it moved between the rest of us, but not chiming in with any opinions of her own. She looked back at me, startled.

'I think that would be a bad idea,' said Gene. Charlie nodded, eyebrows low in his forehead. 'We don't want any theories popping up that Calista's team has "silenced" you in some way. You know how people are.'

I do, I wanted to say. I couldn't. I knew that I was people.

'It's just about being mindful,' said Harma. 'Post as normal, post about Calista even, but keep it positive. Well wishes, encouragement. It's lovely that you care, and people love to see that. Be authentic. There are just certain corners of the internet that we should all probably steer clear of.' She gave an exaggerated grimace.

'And keep this chat to yourself,' said Gene, 'if you can.'

I wanted to fall through the floor.

'Right,' said Harma, after a moment's silence. 'Well. That was nice and easy. Thanks for coming down, Stevie – we all appreciate you taking the time.' She stood up expectantly. I was still watching Callie. *Say something,* I urged her, but she didn't. She smiled back at me, polite, a little uncertain. For a moment I thought wildly, and with an urgent clarity, *That's not her. That's a total stranger.* The moment passed, again. How many people had she met and loved in the decade that had passed? I was a stranger to her. She wasn't one to me. There was nothing remarkable about that, given who she was.

I stood. Harma opened the door for me. I expected that she would follow and show me out, but she didn't. 'Thanks again,' she said. Gene had already returned to her laptop. As the door closed, I saw that Callie was still looking at me.

I took the stairs slowly. All those years of waiting, and that was what our grand reunion had amounted to. She had been pleasant to me, irreproachable, but she was essentially only there to ask me not to take part in vicious online speculation. The shame I felt was too much for me to manage, so I left the building and crossed the street to Sainsbury's to buy a carton of cigarettes, which I hadn't done in a long time. That was it. I would probably never see her again.

Only, when I emerged back out on to the street, there she was. Just as unassumingly beautiful, in her white jumper and brown shorts, except now she had a white cap on her head, pulled down low. I stood dead still on the pavement and stared at her for a second.

'Hey,' she said.

'Should you be . . . out?'

'No,' she said. 'Can you come back into the building? Just the lobby. Just so we're off the street.'

I followed, holding the carton of cigarettes in my hand, now wishing I hadn't bought them. We crossed the road quickly, weaving between cyclists. One stayed looking at us a little longer than the others, and I touched Callie's shoulder, urging her to move faster. I felt her start slightly, and was aware too late that this was the first time I had touched her in many years.

Inside the building, the reception desk empty and the lobby vacated, she took off her cap.

'Hey,' she said again.

One second she was my Callie, and the next she wasn't. Then she frowned, and I knew her again.

'Your face is going to take a little getting used to,' I said.

'For everyone, I imagine.' She pressed her fingers to her jaw, feeling along it. 'Is it really that different?'

'It's a little different.'

'But you still know me?'

'I still know you.'

Her features cleared. Sun broke. It had hurt her, then, my not knowing her instantly. I didn't ever want to hurt her like that again.

'Your voice is different too,' I said.

'Is it?'

'Deeper.'

'They said it might be affected,' she said. 'But also—'

'Time.'

'Yes.'

Her eyes moved across my face, sideways, then vertically. Then she took in the rest of me, my cuffed jeans, horribly out of fashion now, Mel's t-shirt that I had never given back.

'I can't believe you're really here,' she said. 'Did you come because you hoped you would see me?' I nodded. No sense in lying. 'You're different too,' she said. 'Your face has changed. Not in a bad way, but it isn't the same face. And you carry yourself differently.' I felt like a moth held under a microscope. I let her finish her examinations. 'Stevie,' she said. 'I've been thinking about you lately.'

I could have died right then. 'You have?'

'You heard me, didn't you?' she said. 'In Rio. Before I fell.'

'I didn't really know what to make of it.'

'Me neither,' she said. 'I suppose I found you on my mind a lot. Does that happen to you? Do you find that certain people come back to you, at certain times? Do you think about me?'

'Everyone thinks about you. The whole world thinks about you.'

She laughed. 'Yes. I suppose it must be different.'

The rhythms of her speech had changed. She was more considered in what she said, no longer the girl who would lie on her bedroom floor and rattle off entire paragraphs of her thoughts.

'I really want to see you,' she said. 'Properly. Catch up.'

'I'd love that,' I said, with the sensation of falling backwards.

'Coffee?'

'Can you do coffee?'

She grinned. 'Don't know. Let's find out. I know a place near Euston Square. They're pretty discreet.'

'Okay. Let's do coffee.'

She laughed. Before I knew what was happening, she had thrown her arms around my neck. 'Me and Stevie! Doing coffee! Harma has your number, doesn't she?'

'She does.'

'Then I'll send you the place,' she said, pulling away. 'Tomorrow? Can you do tomorrow?'

'I can do tomorrow.' Of course I could do tomorrow. I could have done 3 a.m. that morning for her.

'I'll text you,' she said, and she ran up the first few steps, quick and light. She was eighteen again then, to me. She looked back. 'All that conspiracy stuff,' she said. 'Did you really believe it? Did you really think I was gone?'

'I don't know,' I said honestly. 'I think I was just scared.'

'I understand that,' she said, with a small nod. 'It must have been scary for you.'

'I think it was scary for everyone.'

She nodded again, remorseful. Like she knew. Like she understood how scary the idea of losing her might be for all of us.

◆ ◆ ◆

Her text came through when I was already in the office the next day, eyeshadow palettes all over my desk. She didn't sign her name on it, just sent me the name of the café followed by *Midday?* It was less than two hours' notice and I wouldn't be able to make it there and back in my lunch break. I still said yes. I wondered if it was her real number that she'd texted from. She'd had the same one for years, early on, but she'd either changed it or blocked me in 2018, after my disastrous drunk call.

Rosie had been shooting glances at me all morning. When I put my phone down, she leant over her desk and said, in a voice that gave the impression of being hushed but was actually no quieter than her speaking voice, 'Are you doing okay?'

'I'm good,' I said.

She pressed her lips together, the most patronising version of a smile she could have given me. 'Just wanted to check in.'

'That message was fake,' I said. 'It wasn't me. Just a doctored screenshot.'

'Oh!' she said. 'Really? God, that's fucked.'

'Yeah. I'm trying to get them to take it down.' That was also a lie – I had blocked the page without contacting them further.

'You should sue,' said Rosie, with all the confidence of someone who had only the vaguest idea how that would work. 'So, you don't think that *Time* piece was suspicious?'

'God, no. It's all ridiculous. She's definitely fine.'

'Well, that's a relief,' said Rosie, disappointed.

◆ ◆ ◆

I redid my make-up in the bathroom before meeting her. My face was horribly sticky and it was a challenge getting any product to stay in place. My mascara slipped from between my fingers and rolled into an occupied stall. 'Shit,' I said. 'Sorry.' The flush sounded, and Dana from Sales emerged and handed it back to me with a pissed-off smile.

It was a half-hour commute to Euston Square and then a ten-minute walk to meet her. I picked up a pamphlet on meditation from a street preacher and used it to fan myself as I went. The day was not hot but deceptively muggy, the clouds gathering thick above us. I was horribly conscious of not being twenty anymore, of having more body to contend with, more skin to sweat from, more anxieties than I'd had before, far less cool. I had never been cool exactly, but when Callie had loved me I'd at least been able to fake it. I had been a rock-star girlfriend, up for whatever, whenever, a constant cheerleader, her connection back to real life, like one of those ridiculous grounding mats people sold online. Now I was a copywriter in a small flat I hadn't really bothered decorating, with few friends apart from Mel and a handful of girls from university I went for awkward drinks with now and then, and a boyfriend I was going to break up with, probably, in a few days. And Callie was Calista. Not only that – she was Calista reincarnated. Calista who had risen from the dead. Her legacy was cemented.

What was I *doing?*

I was there at midday exactly. She was early. She'd never once been early in all the time I'd known her. Date nights had always begun with a stream of apologetic texts updating me on her movements as I sat at the table in whatever restaurant she'd picked and tried not to look like I was waiting. Maybe that was something she'd had to train herself out of in her line of work.

The café was on the ground floor of a small but visibly expensive hotel, a white townhouse with a Union Jack flying from the top balcony. I was met at the front desk – 'Are you here to meet someone in particular?' asked the waiter in a conspiratorial manner. He had probably already been given my photograph. The inside dining area was darkly wallpapered, lined with bookshelves, although the volumes were turned around so that you couldn't see the spines, just the neutral beige of the paper edges. It was virtually empty – I looked for her among the scattered diners sipping tiny cups of coffee and cutting into elaborately plated eggs, but she wasn't there. The waiter led me straight through the room and out of a back entrance to a small walled garden. I was grateful for the fresh air. I willed myself to stop sweating.

There she sat, in a long black dress that had an appearance of looseness, only when she stood up to greet me I saw that it was designed to cling to her body in the perfect places, to give the impression of casual drapery when in reality it fitted her like a glove. She had dark sunglasses on, which she didn't take off, and her hair was down. She was a bit further into her world like this, a bit further out of mine than she had been in her ponytail and white jumper. I was tongue-tied, like we were at a meet-and-greet. She kissed my cheek.

'Hey, Stevie,' she said. 'Thank you so much for coming.'

The waiter pulled my chair out for me and smoothly vanished.

'Are you hungry?' she asked. 'I ordered us these pumpkin salads they do here.' She seemed very excited by the salads. 'And I got tea,' she said, and on cue the waiter reappeared with a teapot and two teacups, which he placed in front of us.

The garden was very small, with only three round tables in it, everything white metal, ornately warped. Ours was the only one occupied, of course. A small bird perched in the centre of another, searching for crumbs. We felt sequestered away, a secret hidden in plain sight, the sounds of traffic nearby. The walls around us were tall red brick, ivy-covered. Callie sat with her back to one of them, looking like an album cover as she poured my tea.

'Thanks,' I said.

'It's good,' she said, passing me the cup.

'What is it?'

'Mint and mango.'

'Oh.' I hooked my finger into the handle of the cup. 'You never used to like tea.'

'I've always liked tea,' she said.

We both sipped. Her sunglasses were still on but I was close enough to her now that I could make out her eyes through the lenses, watching me as she brought the cup to her lips.

'This is so strange,' she said.

I laughed, setting my cup down. The bird hopped closer. 'Nine years. I really thought I'd never see you again.'

'Did you?' she said. 'I always felt I'd see you again.'

I wasn't sure how to answer that. She reached across the table and took my hand.

'Besides,' she said, 'not nine years. Five.'

I stared at her. 'You remember that? On Carnaby Street?'

'I remember.'

'I wasn't sure if you even knew it was me.'

'Stevie,' she said. 'I'd know you anywhere.'

My Callie. Even then, on Carnaby Street, I remembered thinking that she seemed different. A total stranger to me. But she hadn't been then, and she wasn't now. I wanted to say that I'd know her anywhere too – but I couldn't, of course. My doubt was the very thing that had brought us back together.

'How's Mel?' she asked.

'Good. The same. I'm not even just saying that – she is exactly the same as she was nine years ago.'

'I'm glad. I always liked her.'

'Did you?'

'Maybe I had a funny way of showing it sometimes,' she said with a smile.

Our salads were placed in front of us, large colourful bowls of orange and green. She picked up her fork and dug in with a ferocity that startled me.

'What?' she asked, mouth full, when she realised I was watching her.

'Are they not feeding you?'

She shrugged, continuing to shovel food into her mouth.

'What does that mean?'

'I nearly died. Everything I do is pretty closely monitored at the moment.'

'Surely that means they should be feeding you properly?'

'They are,' she said. 'Don't worry. I'm just hungry.'

She carried on making her way through the salad, a little slower now, self-conscious. I picked up my own fork. She watched me take the first bite. 'It's good?' she said. There was something strange in the inflection. I hesitated, and concern crossed her face. 'What's wrong?'

'Nothing.' She carried on looking at me, fork moving through the food, still eating without looking down at her bowl. I realised what it was that had been throwing me off ever since yesterday – there was something erratic in her manner, something insecure, that had never been there before. 'I'm worried about you,' I said.

'I'm fine.'

'You don't seem yourself. You seem—'

'I had a big accident,' she said. 'Of course I'm not quite myself.' It was said a little sharply.

'Did they say that your personality might be impacted? By the . . . impact?'

'No,' she said. Her chewing slowed. 'Do you think it is? Impacted?'

'I don't know. Perhaps. You hit your head pretty hard – it can happen.'

'Do I seem that different?' she said. She was crestfallen. As if it were the only thing that mattered in the world, what I thought of her, whether she was still the same to me. Even when she had loved me more than any other person on earth, I could never remember her putting so much weight on what I thought of her. She waited for my answer.

'I suppose I wouldn't know,' I said. 'I don't really know you anymore.'

She chewed, eyes on her food again. 'I think you still know me.'

'You've lived quite a life. It must have changed you a lot.'

'But I never really let go of you,' she said. There was little emotion in it. It was just a fact. It sent my heart careening towards my tonsils.

'You didn't?'

She shook her head.

'Why did you ask me to meet you?' I asked.

'I just needed to see you,' she said. 'I needed you more than I needed anyone else.'

'But why? Why me?'

She looked at me frankly with those enormous blue eyes. A piece of rocket, fallen from her fork, lay on the table in front of her. 'I don't know,' she said. 'I just did.'

The way she was looking at me was far too intense. I watched the progress of the bird, taking small jumps along the paving slabs, over the moss growing in the cracks between. 'I thought you'd never want to speak to me again after that drunk call.'

She didn't say anything. When I glanced up, she was frowning.

'You don't remember?'

'When?'

'You were at your album release party. A couple of years before Carnaby Street.'

'I was pretty drunk too, that night,' she said.

'Callie, you blocked my number.'

'I wouldn't have done that.'

'Well, someone did. I could never get through to you after that.'

'Huh,' she said. 'I'm sorry.'

She went on eating. The bottom of her bowl was beginning to emerge. I stared at her. 'You really don't remember?'

'I mean, I remember you called. Nothing specific.'

I really couldn't have been as important to her as she was making out. That evening was still so fresh in my mind. But if I didn't matter like she said I did, then why was I here? Why was she saying all of this? Maybe her mind really had been damaged in the fall. Maybe something had shifted in her brain, intangibly, and she would never be quite the same. Or maybe the fall had knocked that call out of her brain entirely. There was something very strange about sitting here with her, eerie almost. I couldn't put my finger on what it was.

'I'd like more tea,' she said. 'Would you like more tea?'

She turned her head in search of the waiter. When I saw her side profile, I felt chills go up and down my arms.

She looked like a complete stranger.

It wasn't any one thing. She had all the right features – those huge blue eyes that sloped, slightly crooked nose. Delicate lips, a soft pout. Colouring so fair I used to follow her around in the summer begging her to wear SPF. She should have looked like Callie – and yet she didn't. Suddenly, from that angle, she didn't look anything like her at all.

She turned back to me. 'Are you okay?' she asked. She sounded afraid.

There was a click from behind me, loud enough that it made me start. I turned in time to see a long lens disappearing back over the brick wall.

'Oh, shit,' said Callie calmly.

I watched her shake her hair back, adjusting her sunglasses on the bridge of her nose. I didn't know what I was feeling. There was a dark muttering in the back of my mind that the woman I was sat with wasn't the girl that I'd once loved. Not just because everyone changes as they grow, not just because Calista had become something far beyond either one of our expectations.

She was a fake.

It was an insane thought. The internet, those people and their crazy theories, had poisoned me. Mel had begged me to let myself be happy, and here I was, with Callie, drinking tea. Maybe I was self-sabotaging.

The clicking started up again. She still didn't seem surprised. 'Is that why you invited me here?' I asked. 'So that they would get photos of the two of us?'

'Of course not. Why would I do that?'

She did look more like herself – or more like Callie – when she stared directly at me like that. But I couldn't shake the thought that Callie wasn't here at all. I looked at her, and I couldn't accept her face as Callie's face. The two didn't align. She was someone else entirely.

I felt like I was in a nightmare. I couldn't make sense of any of it.

'I was thinking about your first album, the other day, after I saw you,' I said. '*Put This On My Headstone.*'

'Yes. You loved that one.'

'Do you remember why I liked the title?'

A moment's hesitation. She scratched the side of her nose and laughed. 'It was funny,' she said. 'Why are you being so intense?'

'You lay on my bedroom floor one night and you wrote the title track while we ate takeout. Do you remember where from?'

'What?'

'The food. Do you remember where we got it from?'

'Honestly, Stevie,' she said. 'It was so long ago.'

'You don't remember?'

'Carla's. Wasn't that the place we liked? With the pastas?' She didn't say it like she was recalling an experience but a fact that she had memorised.

We stared at each other.

'I have to go,' I said, standing up so abruptly that my chair tipped over. I was all gooseflesh and pounding heart. 'It was good to see you.'

'Stevie—' She stood too, reaching for me. I took two steps backwards, nearly falling over the capsized chair. She looked startled. 'What's wrong? Why are you freaking out?' Her voice was tender and I felt the pull of it. It was a remarkable impression. But it wasn't Callie's voice. There was no saying exactly what was lacking in it. It just wasn't her.

'I'm not,' I said. 'I'm really late back for work. Sorry. I didn't realise how long the commute would be, and I—'

'You still don't believe it's me,' she said.

She looked like all the light had gone out of her world.

'I'm sorry,' I said.

'Why?' she asked. '*Why?*'

I opened the door back into the restaurant. The waiter sprung out of my path as I hurried through the main dining area and out into the lobby. Her question, the pleading tone of it, followed me out. She thought I was crazy. Maybe I was crazy.

Then, suddenly, I heard it differently.

Why don't you believe in me? I'm doing everything perfectly.

She didn't follow me. I didn't look back.

The cameras were waiting for me on the pavement. I kept my head down and walked quickly. So, that was the game. She hadn't wanted to catch up. The people in that room – Harma, Gene, Charlie, whoever else shared responsibility for the finer mechanics of Calista – had sent her after me so that I would appear with her in public. Photos would come out of the two of us on our coffee date. *See,* people would say. *There's no truth to it. Stevie didn't write that message. She knows that Callie is absolutely fine.*

I knew even less now than when I'd been blindly groping for clues on social media. As I walked, I replayed moments from our meeting in my mind. In some, she was herself, just older and with a face slightly changed from surgery and the trauma of her fall. In others, some other woman sat in her place, wearing her face like a mask.

But she knew me. She knew Carla's. She remembered Carnaby Street, the last time I had seen her in person, five years ago. She'd become separated from her security by a mob of fans and was lost in them. As if in a dream, I'd fought my way through to her, my arms around her, just for a second, before security reached her and took her away. The scene became less real every time I recalled it. But it had happened, and she had remembered. Only Callie would have known about that.

Still.

In my gut, there was a feeling I could not ignore. Gentle and persistent, almost a bleating. She was gone, she was gone, and I would never know her again.

I found myself at Euston Square. The Tube station wasn't busy mid-afternoon on a weekday, but the presence of strangers around me was suddenly alarming and uncomfortable. I didn't know them. I couldn't trust their faces. I didn't want to be around anyone else. I wanted to be alone with my own skin and flesh and face, the only things I could count on to be exactly what they were. If Callie wasn't Callie – out there, breathing, with her same mind and her same soul, and the hands that I had lifted to my lips and kissed on lazy Sundays, sharing her tiny sofa – then there was no longer any floor to the world.

It wasn't warm, and the Tube was airy, but I was sweating so much that I felt a droplet roll off my top lip. My legs suffered in M&S tights. The feeling of my hands in my hair was disgusting. No one asked if I was alright, of course – this was London, and no one ever did – but there were glances of concern. I was shaking. In another era, another place perhaps, or a Dickensian story, the jovial, red-faced man in the seat opposite mine would have leant forward and said, 'You alright, love? You look like you've seen a ghost!'

I couldn't go back to the office. I couldn't go home; Rich would return at some point, and I couldn't face his questions. I took the Tube to Liverpool Street. My legs carried me over the road, towards a twenty-four-hour diner that Callie and I had frequented following Wednesday nights out and Saturdays when the drinking started at midday. It was tall and skinny, and entirely empty. I went up to the third level and sat alone among the tables, and breathed out. When a waitress approached me, clearly resentful at having been made to climb two flights of stairs when there were plenty of available tables on ground level, I ordered nachos and a pizza and a falafel wrap, and a milkshake with two shots of vodka in it. The food came staggered. I spread it all out on the table and picked at it. My dad had always hypocritically hated my anxious eating habits, that need in times of stress to be constantly putting different foods in my mouth, but Callie had encouraged it. When I came to her, worrying myself over something or other, she would walk me around the supermarket and down the row of takeaway places behind our flat, and at home we would pass it all back and forth between us, wasteful and happy.

I was probably losing my mind for real this time. I watched the video of her again, posing, seen through the window, painted white. I could no longer trust anything my eyes saw. When I had watched it so many times that I knew the exact beats on which her chest rose and fell as she drew breath, I propped my phone up in front of me and put on some godawful vampire show that we'd watched together at eighteen. I gave it only half my attention, if that. I couldn't stop my mind from spiralling through theories.

She had a twin I'd never known about. Or, that had been her in the restaurant, but the fall and surgery had changed her beyond even my recognition and she would never quite be the same person again. Or, that woman had been a body double, someone they'd hunted down and found, like a miracle, to pretend to be her. Why? To give her privacy while she recovered? To meet and appease me, because Callie herself couldn't be bothered to do it?

I tried to give the teenage vampires my full attention. I tried to care about who they fell in love with and broke up with, and how difficult it was to finish high school while fighting off an intense craving for human blood. It worked, for a while. But I couldn't stop the question drifting to the front of my mind.

Was Callie alive?

This was what it felt like to go mad, then.

The hours drew on. The waitress came over to ask if I wanted anything else, but I said no – I was still gently picking at the plates of food in front of me. When it started to get dark, and the room began to fill up, I still didn't move. Eventually, at the end of Season One, I realised I had been there for seven hours. It was time to go home.

Where are you? Rich had texted.

I switched off my phone and went to Mel's.

'Shit,' she said, when she opened the door. 'What happened to you?'

'Can I sleep on your sofa?'

'Fight with Rich?' I nodded. 'I will dump him for you,' she said. 'Not joking. I'm giving you, like, three days now. And then I'm coming round and breaking up with him myself. I'll even pack his stuff up.'

'I know you will.'

She took me in her arms. I let my head fall forward, burying my face in her shoulder. 'Stevie,' she said, 'you are seriously not your best at the moment.'

'I know.'

'Of course you can sleep on my sofa. You can sleep in my bed if you like.'

'The sofa's fine.'

She pulled back, her hands on my shoulders. Her face was so beautiful, but I didn't like her new lips. I reached out and touched them gently. She raised her eyebrows.

'Are you hitting on me?'

'You should stop doing this.'

'Personal choice. You don't get to tell me to stop.'

'I just like your face. I always want to be able to recognise it.'

'Of course you can recognise it. It's just a tiny bit of filler.'

'I don't want your face to change,' I said.

'Well, I do.' Her arms were folded. 'Seriously, what is up with you?'

'Just tired,' I said.

'Do you need dinner?'

'I ate. I ate *so much*, actually.'

'Well, that's good,' she said, but she didn't sound sure. She watched me move past her and lie down on her couch. 'Are you going to sleep already? It's, like, eight p.m.'

'I told you, I'm tired.'

'Alright,' she said. 'Weirdo. Come in, criticise my face, fall immediately asleep.'

'I'm not criticising your face. I love your face. That was my whole point.'

'I love your face too,' she said. 'Talk to me in the morning, okay?'

◆ ◆ ◆

But I didn't. After a night of barely sleeping, I snuck out as the sun was coming up, like a douchey one-night stand. She would wonder why I'd done it, if I was mad at her, but I couldn't explain. I couldn't explain anything to anyone, just then.

The light was delicate and barely there, blueish and shadowy, enough to see my feet and hands as I walked but not to read the street signs from a distance or feel safe moving past the entrances of alleyways. The Tube had just started running, but I took the bus instead, even though it was a far longer journey, and distracted myself by breathing slowly and counting takeaways. Twenty-seven by the time the bus pulled up at my stop, and still not enough to let me switch off my mind. There was a mounting feeling of dread the closer I got to home. Maybe I could sense that she was waiting.

When I turned on to my street, I could see that someone was sat on the steps of my building. They wore all black, their hood up, and at first I thought that I was about to get mugged on my own doorstep, as if things couldn't have got more ridiculous. But of course it was her. Callie, or not Callie, or whoever she was.

She stood up.

'Sorry to ambush you,' she said. Her voice was different. I looked around me. 'No cameras,' she said. 'Just me. No one knows I'm here.'

'Why should I believe you?'

She spread her hands. The gesture was completely unfamiliar.

'How did you know where I lived?'

'Because Callie did,' she said.

I could have fallen to my knees. She stared at me, eyes wide and frightened under her black hood.

'You're not Callie?' I asked her, even though I already knew. Even though I should have known from the first moment I saw her.

'No,' she said. 'I'm not.'

Pointelle (2021)

When Callie appears on the steps of the Met, it is seemingly as if from nowhere. No one has footage of her walking up them. No cameras are on her at all until she is already established in front of the museum, in a white leotard and pink wrap-around cardigan. The thing that makes the image so striking is the pale pink tutu that sticks out almost horizontally around her waist and then falls, layers and layers of tulle encircling her, and Callie standing in the middle of it like a cake topper. Her hair is in a low bun. Her cheeks and lips are flushed. She raises her arms in an arabesque, and the building lights up pink, with a giant kiss projected on to the side of it. Everyone has stopped walking to applaud her. Surely nothing inside the Met could rival this.

I am doing my hair in the wardrobe mirror, my phone propped up on my nightstand, scrolling between videos as I go. When this one comes up, I stop. I have been holding locks of hair in place for an updo that I am attempting – now I let them fall. I stare at her, stood there calmly with her hands clasped as the noise around her grows.

It's a live video, I realise. That is where she is and what she is doing right at this current moment. I am here in my flat in London, doing my hair before my date with Leonora. And she is in New York, posed for some mysterious reason in front of the world, lighting the city up pink.

A cheer goes up. The comments let me know why – she has just put out a press release announcing her sixth album, Pointelle. *There hasn't been a single yet, or any artwork, no whisper of another project coming so soon after* Dry Ice. *It's a total surprise. Callie has always loved surprises.*

I should be leaving in five minutes, but instead I swap between social media apps, scroll post after post. I see a video of her calmly walking down the steps of the Met, smiling, security parting the crowd for her and guiding her into a black car. She doesn't even say a word. She must feel powerful beyond explanation. Right now, she is in a car driving through the streets of New York, pleased with how it's all gone. I wonder who she's calling first. Probably the tennis player that everyone says she's dating.

Leonora rings me as I'm walking down the stairs in my building, updo abandoned, hair loose and a little greasy. 'Where are you?' she asks. 'I'm here already. I've been here ten minutes.'

'Were you early?'

'Yes, but now you're late.'

'I'm on my way.'

'When did you leave?'

'Ages ago. Traffic's terrible.'

'God, you're such a bad liar,' she says. I laugh, but maybe she isn't being playful. 'See you when I see you,' she says and hangs up.

When I get to the bar, she's sat facing the door, but she still pretends not to notice me when I enter, scrolling through her phone instead. The place she's chosen is small and dark – all her favourite bars are. Leonora is five years older than me and has just entered her thirties, and our relationship, which was far less serious six months ago, has now become an adult relationship, in which we have adult conversations and go to adult bars. She's also just started getting Botox, which isn't something I've even thought about yet and has widened the age gap between us. Our relationship doesn't feel like my relationship with Callie, in which life was warm and bright and we were girls together. But then, I'm not a girl anymore. I can't expect to have that with anyone ever again.

I walk over and tilt her chin up to kiss her. She looks a little sulky, but still beautiful. Her hair is very dark, the raven-black of fairytales, with the red lips to match. Her skin is a warm brown and makes a great case for her £65 moisturiser being actually worth the price tag. 'Hello,' I say. 'Sorry I'm so late. You look gorgeous.' Normally I'd be unsettled by her sulkiness, but right now I feel giddy.

'Thank you,' she says. I sit opposite her. The menus in front of us are covered in red leather and the cheapest bottle of wine is more than I would ever choose to spend on wine, but I don't mind doing things I wouldn't choose to do to make Leonora happy. I do like her a lot. She has a good deal of what my dad calls 'direction', not that I've let him meet her. She loves film and music and knows exactly what she needs to make her happy and exactly what she wants in bed. It isn't love, yet, and maybe it never will be. Falling in love is hard-earned for me, in a way I never imagined it would be, but I'm beginning to make my peace with that. 'I've ordered the Riesling,' she says, pointing to it on the menu. It is the third-cheapest bottle.

'Lovely,' I say.

She smiles. 'You're so late. You have some ground to make up.'

'I'm sure you have some ideas how.'

She takes my hand in hers, turns it over. She's a more sexual person than I am and I used to think it would be hard to keep up with her, until I learnt what a reassuring thing it is to let someone else tell you exactly what you need to do and when in order to make them happy. With Jeremy, I would often get horribly in my head about the amount of sex we were having and whether he secretly wanted more. 'You seem . . .' she says.

'What?'

'I don't know. Excited. Bouncy.'

I shrug.

'Did you see the video?' she asks.

'Which video?'

'Oh, come on. You know what I'm talking about.'

I grin, looking up at her. She smiles, a little exasperated. 'Yeah, I saw it. Everyone's losing their minds over it.'

'Was that why you were late?'

'No, I watched it on the way.' She doesn't believe me. 'I mean, it's a cool stunt. Inventive.' I can feel that something is off. I try to dial down my excitement. 'She's good at stuff like that.'

'I don't know,' says Leonora. 'I thought it was a little obnoxious.' She lets go of my hand. I am no longer giddy, suddenly. I try to go on smiling.

'Obnoxious how?'

'To stand there? To not say anything?' Our overpriced Riesling arrives. It could be correctly priced, actually. I know nothing about wine. The waitress fills my glass as Leonora keeps talking. 'I guess I prefer when artists are more down to earth. I mean, to do that at the Met of all places . . . you have to kind of assume that everyone cares about you.'

'Everyone does care about her.'

'No, Stevie, they don't,' she says, in her measured way.

'Are you joking? It's Calista.'

'There were absolutely some people there who were like, who is this girl? Why is she just standing there dressed like a ballerina? Why is the building pink? Why is she not saying anything? Does she need help?' She picks up her wine glass with a smirk. There's a meanness to it. 'It's kind of funny to think about.'

'I don't think anyone was thinking that. I think that's just you.'

'Why do you care so much?'

'I don't,' I say. 'This wine is disgusting.'

'You're the only person I know who cares this much about their ex. It's weird.'

'Who else do you know with a pop-star ex, Nora?'

'Even that. The way you talk about her. Your pop-star ex. It's, like, such a status symbol for you. It's so immature.' Since she turned thirty, everything I do is immature, like it's my fault for being born five years after her.

'It's not a status symbol. But, okay, I'm meant to stop being a fan of her music? Just because we broke up? It doesn't work like that. I still love the art she makes.' I've had this conversation so many times by now, with so many different people, at so many different levels of inebriation. The speech is well rehearsed. 'She's a good person, and she's talented, and I think she deserves her success. If anything, pretending like any of that wasn't true just because we broke up would be immature.'

'Yeah, but you go way beyond that,' says Leonora.

'How?'

'You know you do,' she says, but she doesn't elaborate.

I sit and sip my disgusting wine. She watches me with sad eyes. I know, suddenly, what's coming. It's been a decent ten months – not magical, not electrifying, but nice. We met at a party for a mutual acquaintance – a co-worker of mine I was never that close to, the girlfriend of someone Leonora went to secondary school with. She complimented my jeans and helped me pour a glass of Pimm's out of the faulty canister, and later when we all went out, she fucked me in a club toilet with a rhythm so casually steady, like it was nothing, that I felt safe and taken care of. I will miss that feeling.

'I think you're being really unfair,' I say, and in my mind I watch the argument spiral and grow new heads, a premonition of what's to come, and I sit back in my seat and prepare to ride the roller coaster down, down.

Twenty minutes later, I storm out of the bar like I'm in a movie. We don't talk again. I see her once, seven months on, outside a jazz bar in Shoreditch. She's started smoking again, passing a cigarette back and forth with a blonde, pixie-like girl far prettier than me, and even younger. Pointelle *is my least favourite album.*

Chapter Four

The girl who wasn't Callie still took her coffee black with sugar, like Callie did. She didn't talk the same – her voice was raspier, with a hint of an accent – but sometimes she would slip back into Callie's voice, like when I handed her the mug of coffee and she said, 'Thank you,' sweet and high-pitched. I blinked at her, and she seemed to realise that she'd done it. She wore the little silver charm bracelet that Callie had worn since she was eighteen. It clinked against the mug as she took a sip.

She was really very convincing. You could tell she wasn't Callie when you knew and you really tried to see it, but you could also be fooled by her, if you let yourself. She moved like Callie. She spoke like her, when she tried to. She had almost the same face, and any differences could be explained away by time, by the fall, by plastic surgery, if they chose to make her admit to that. I watched the girl drink her coffee and I thought, in a strange moment of calm, *Good job. Good job everyone involved. Great effort.* They'd come about as close to a convincing clone of Callie as it was surely possible to get.

Was she a clone? Had we made scientific leaps that I wasn't even aware of? Was she a secret twin sister? A cousin with an uncanny resemblance that I had never known about? What was she doing here? How had this happened? The fog of panic that hovered constantly at the edges of my vision started to curl in around my eyes, and I did my best to blink it away. Answers, then panic, in that order.

Where was Callie?

She set the mug down. 'Thank you,' she said again, in her real voice. It was so strange to hear someone else's voice come out of Callie's mouth. 'It's very good.'

'Do you take it like that because she does?'

'No,' she said. 'We just have a lot in common.'

It was hard to even know where to begin. She waited. Eventually, when I didn't speak, she cleared her throat, a harsh sound. 'My name is Inese,' she said.

She waited for a question. I asked the first one that came to mind. 'Are you from London?' As if we were on a date.

'Riga.'

I had to laugh. It was all too ridiculous. 'What?'

'I was born in Riga, in Latvia. I've lived in London many years now—'

'I'm sorry, what the *fuck?*'

She sat staring up at me, both hands clasped around her mug. When she wasn't trying to be Callie, her top lip protruded over her bottom slightly. Her eyes were quick and discerning.

'No one knows I'm here,' she said.

'Like they didn't know you were with me yesterday?'

'I swear. They don't know I'm telling you this.'

I sat down opposite her, not in a chair, but directly on to the carpet, holding my knees to my chest. I felt exhausted.

'I don't understand. Who are you? How did they find you?'

'They scouted me years ago,' she said. 'I used to perform at open mic nights. Do local TV. Someone from the label found my social media and sent me a message. I thought it was a joke.'

'Saying what? What did they scout you for?'

'Because I looked so much like her,' said the girl. 'Everyone told me, after she got famous, how much we looked alike. They brought me in, explained the situation. Offered me all this money.'

I was shaking my head at the carpet – I stopped when I realised, as if there were a world in which she might think I was the crazy one.

'There were surgeries. Callie helped advise on those. She taught me lots of things.'

'*Callie* did?'

'She always told me I was doing an amazing thing,' said Inese. 'She said that Calista was bigger than both of us. She said I could stop any time I wanted. But I didn't want to.'

'You've done this before?' I asked. 'You've . . . been her? Before?'

She nodded. 'Yes. When it was needed.'

'Callie would never sign off on that.'

'She put it in her will,' said Inese. She had an odd, blank way of speaking. It took me a minute to understand what she had said.

'Her will?' I repeated.

'That I should carry on. Get her new project out in the world. If she wasn't well enough, or had to step back, or if – if something happened.'

She said those last words very quickly, like it was a relief to get them out, and then she waited, sat forward on my sofa so that her spine didn't touch it, hardly breathing. I understood what I should have understood the moment she turned her head to the side in that café garden, the moment I'd looked in her eyes and known that she was a stranger to me.

'Callie died at Copacabana Beach,' I said.

'I'm sorry,' she said. 'Yes.'

I couldn't speak. I felt her hesitate, then stand up, placing her mug on the table. She walked over to me. She didn't crouch down beside me on the carpet, but instead stood, looking down. The blurry shape of her in the corner of my eye was eerie. I could see the bracelet on her wrist, dangling just above my head. I reached out and slid it over her hand. She didn't stop me, just held her arm out and let me take it. I clutched it tightly between my fingers.

'I really would like for us to talk,' she said.

'I need you to go.'

She went on standing there. I could hear her breathing.

'Please go,' I said. My voice came out reedy and pathetic.

'I'll write my number,' she said. 'Where's a pen?' I didn't reply. I let her search for one. 'This is a better number to call,' she said after a minute. She must have spotted the pencil lying by the fridge. I could hear her scribbling on some scrap of paper. 'Don't contact the other number. Contact me here, and we can speak.'

I didn't reply. She waited a few seconds longer, and then her footsteps carried her quietly out. The door closed behind her.

Callie was gone.

The pressure of my knees against my rib cage was the only thing I could feel. I pulled them in tighter, squashing down the bottom of my breasts, expanding the ache and holding on for as long as I could. After some time, impossible to say how much, I took out my phone and watched her fall, and thought how stupid I had been to think she could survive it. I read her *Time* piece and thought how stupid I had been to think she ever could have given those quotes. Probably Inese had made the call, doing her uncanny impression of Callie's voice, but it was Harma who had written those answers for her. That had been Inese posing in the hospital bed, her head wrapped in unnecessary bandages, a team on hand to make it convincing. I watched the video of her at the photoshoot, taken through the window. The whole thing was ridiculously staged, now that I really considered it – some lucky individual stumbling on a perfect view of her through a window, like it would ever be possible to happen upon a Calista shoot like that. This was a woman who had appeared on the steps of the Met without anyone noticing. Inese had probably had some last-minute work done, final convincing details, and the white paint and blurry distance were hiding any imperfections.

Callie was dead, and they were carrying on without her, like Calista was a title. Like it was some torch that anyone could pick up and run with.

Callie was dead.

For an hour, or maybe more, I lay on the carpet and I cried – slowly at first, disbelievingly, and then with a howling, frightening viciousness until my head ached and my chest was on fire, and the carpet had left an imprint in my cheek.

Work had called me. So had Rich, and he had sent texts. The first few were increasingly concerned, and then his tone got sharper. *Mel says you're at hers. I'm going to the office, we can talk about this when I'm home.* He would be sat in his cubicle nurturing his injury and betrayal, practising the manner in which he would step through the door, disappointed in me but reluctantly forgiving. I would have to find a way to be out of the flat again that evening.

Instead of texting him back, I scrolled through Calista fan pages on Instagram. I knew what I was looking for now, and it took me surprisingly little time to find it – a paparazzi photograph of Callie from three years ago, but with her top lip jutting out just a tiny bit over the bottom and her jaw a slightly different shape. She was stepping in through the back door of a venue. *Calista heading into the Eventim Apollo to play a special one-night-only performance for fans.* I remembered that. I hadn't been able to get tickets. If I had, would I have gone and known it wasn't her? But surely Inese hadn't performed the whole show for her.

I searched for footage of the performance. There were iPhone recordings of her singing fan favourites with a small band. It was all pared back – not Calista's usual spectacle – but it was startlingly good. It was definitely Inese, but I really did wonder – had I never met Inese, never known of her existence, would I have been able to tell? She wore heavy, fantastical make-up and a hooded dress, all white drapery. A strange look for *Pointelle* and hardly a hint to *Grenadine.* When you knew it was a disguise, it was obvious. If you didn't, then it would have sounded ridiculous to say that out loud.

Inese didn't just have Callie's speaking voice down perfectly, when she sang, she sounded exactly like her. She must have spent hours practising. She had said that Callie herself had coached her, an image so strange and oddly upsetting that I tried to put it out of my mind.

'Okay,' she said, as Callie. 'This is one highly requested by you guys.' Couldn't the crowd hear the slight oddness of her phrasing, I wondered? Evidently not. They were screaming their love for her, just like always. Just as if she really was Calista. Behind her, the pianist began to play. The person filming tilted their phone into portrait mode, zooming in so that Inese filled the entire screen. She raised the mic to her lips.

It was the song she had been singing in Rio the night she fell. Or, rather, the song Callie had been singing. It was a fan favourite from *Put This On My Headstone,* a song that had only gained traction years after the album's release, long after Callie and I had broken up. She had only recently started to play it live again. Some had theorised – correctly – that it was a song about me.

The song was called 'Again, Again, Again'. She'd written it over a long period of time, unusual for her, lying on her back in the living room, picking out guitar chords among the takeout boxes, rolling over on to her stomach to scribble lyrics in her notepad. She wrote and rewrote it, scrapped whole verses, composed new ones on train rides and in bars, three drinks down. There was too much she wanted to say in it, she said, and eventually she had to stop somewhere and the song had to be finished. It was beautiful, one of the best things she had written up to that point, and still something special in a career of beautiful, excellent songs. It was about us, and Carla's, and long nights of dancing that ended in that late-night diner opposite Liverpool Street Station, and how she only had to play me a song once before I would go away and learn all the words like I was studying for a test. The lyrics read like a prayer to it all. She told me – just me, only me – that if I let her, she'd do it all with me again, again, again.

Fans fell in love with it slowly, as her star rose and people began to scour her back catalogue. Then people began to walk down the aisle to it, to use it for their first dances. Teenagers held each other tentatively at prom and swayed to it. But no one understood it quite like I did.

And here was Inese, onstage in front of Callie's fans. Pretending that she understood it too.

I wanted to cry for another hour. But there was another feeling coming over me slowly. What was I doing? I'd had her in front of me. I could have got all the answers I wanted. In my shortsightedness I'd asked her to leave. She'd been willing to confide in me for whatever reason, perhaps because she thought Callie had trusted me, perhaps because she thought that anything I would do for Callie I would do for her. There was still some chance that she was crazy, that I was seeing things that weren't there. If I wasn't, if this was all true, then I had to understand why.

I picked up the envelope she had left on the coffee table, her number scribbled on the back in pencil.

Hey, it's Stevie. Can we meet to talk?

She replied instantly. *I can come back to your flat?*

No, I'd rather be out when my boyfriend gets home. Can we meet at your place?

It's tricky.

A new thought struck me. *Are you living in her house?* I knew Callie had a place in London that she rarely used.

I will explain everything, she said. *I will rent us a hotel room. I will answer any questions you have. We will speak there.*

Half an hour later, she sent me the location of a Travelodge in Elephant and Castle. She met me in the lobby in a hat and dark sunglasses. She raised her eyebrows when she saw that I was carrying an overnight bag but said nothing. I followed her in silence up to the room.

When the door closed behind us, she said, 'Are you recording?'

'No,' I said honestly, showing her my phone. It only occurred to me when she asked that I probably should have been. I spread my hands, turned out my pockets. When she still didn't speak, I opened my bag and showed her the contents – a change of clothes, a phone charger, a washbag.

'Take off your shoes,' she said.

'Seriously?'

She raised her eyebrows again, so I took off my trainers.

'Happy?'

'Happy is the wrong word,' she said.

She sat down on the bed. I took a seat in the armchair. She pulled off her hat, blonde hair sticking up in odd directions. I felt a sickening rush of affection for her that died just as fast. She wasn't Callie, but there were still moments where Callie was all I saw. Brief flashes, before her face became unfamiliar again.

'You must have lots of questions,' she said.

'When did this start?'

'2019,' she said. 'Thereabouts. After her diagnosis.'

'Her diagnosis?'

She looked at me curiously. There were things that she wanted to learn from me too, then. 'I wondered if she'd told you.'

'We weren't in contact, by then.'

'She always spoke of you fondly,' she said. 'Sometimes I wonder if she was quietly reaching out.'

'No,' I said. The word was painful. 'She never did.'

'Ah.'

'How much time did you spend with her?'

'A fair amount in 2019,' she said. 'Early 2020, some, but she was locked down in the US after that, and then even when she moved back to London and things became more relaxed, she couldn't really have contact with anyone. That's when my job became more important, because people still needed to be reminded of her – she still had things to promote – but she had to be more careful.' Her features softened. She looked almost proud. 'I sometimes wonder if she'd have been able to carry it all on, without me.'

'But what did she have?' I said. 'Was it a mental-health thing?'

'No. Lupus.'

The word felt generically medical, something that I knew as a bad word without any specific sense of what it meant. It didn't belong with her, though. Callie as I remembered her was health and freedom.

'No one knew,' said Inese. 'She didn't want them to.'

'But why? I just—' It was distracting, how intensely she was watching me, clutching her black hat between her hands. 'I don't understand what's so shameful about a medical diagnosis. Why would she have to hide that? It's not like it's within her control.'

'We didn't really talk about why,' she said.

'You didn't talk about why?'

'She'd show up, and we'd talk about what was needed from me, and she'd give me pointers, let me study things. We talked about the meaning behind songs sometimes, but that was about as deep as it got. Then she'd leave. It was always management that I spoke to, really. Things often went through Charlie.'

Charlie, the man who'd sat beside Gene Parrison and looked at me like I was something he was considering stepping on. Who wasn't protective of Callie at all, but of the girl he'd been grooming to take her place.

Inese waited for a response. When she didn't get one, she leant forwards, blonde curls touching her knees. 'Callie saw Calista as this infallible thing. A pop-star archetype. Almost not human. She wanted to preserve the purity of that.'

'No matter what happened to her.'

'Exactly,' she said with a strange, sudden smile. 'No matter what.' Like she was thrilled I was finally starting to get it.

Strange to know how much Callie's view of music had changed in the years we'd spent apart. 'How sick was she?'

'I didn't know the details.'

'She didn't like to talk about it?'

'Well, definitely not with me. I think it was mostly the tiredness that made it hard for her. She would get these periods of intense exhaustion.'

'And then you would step in for her?'

'For performances, only a few times. I can count them on one hand. But often for interviews, and sometimes I went to premieres or fashion shows. Just to pose and leave. Her weight was fluctuating, with the lupus, so she looked different from photo to photo anyway. No one seemed to flag it, other than a few crazies online.'

'They weren't crazies if they were right.'

Taken aback, the colour coming to her cheeks, she said, 'No, I suppose not.'

'And pap shots? I know some of those are you. What's the point of you getting papped?'

'Oh, just so no one could ever think she was a recluse. So they could still see her everywhere, and be reminded of her, even when she was too ill to leave the house.'

Too ill to leave the house. My heart ached to think of her like that.

'And now?' I asked.

'Now is different,' she said. 'She— In her will, like I said. She left instructions that I should carry it all on, if I was willing to. She already had the new project lined up. The music is mostly written and recorded. The visuals are decided. It's all ready for me to just step into.'

'And you said yes.'

'I did.'

The absence of Callie's easy warmth was unnerving. It was like talking to a wax model of her, or a weird AI chatbot wearing her face.

'Why?'

'Because I believe in it,' she said simply.

'In what? In her?'

'In the art. In what she's created. If she didn't want it to die now, then I don't want that either.'

There was no obvious insincerity in the words, and when I stared at her, she stared back frankly, interested in what I would say next.

'Why are you telling me all of this?' I asked.

'So many questions,' she said, falling back in her chair.

'That's why we're here.'

'Yes, I know. It's good. I'm telling you because I want to make this work. You doubted her – me – and her biggest fans, they still like you. If you stand by her, they will all stand by her.'

'You,' I said. 'Stand by you.'

'Yes. Sorry. Me.'

She tipped her head to the side, her arms very stiff beside her, and waited. She was nervous – that was where the oddness in her manner came from. Of course she was nervous.

'I have to think about it,' I said.

'Okay. That's okay.' Another pause. 'Any more questions?'

'Probably. I just—' I couldn't take another second of her staring at me like that. 'I can't think about it right now.'

'I understand,' she said. 'The room is paid for. Would you like me to go? You can use it, if you want.'

I did want to. I let her slip out. The hotel room was comforting – the cleanliness of it, the lack of personality. I plugged my phone in. Rich had called, again and again. It occurred to me that I was treating him quite awfully, actually, and that I was giving him more and more leeway to make me a villain. When I was out the other side of all this, it would be crunch-time. I would either have to grovel or end it, and neither one seemed particularly appealing. Mel had called me too. She'd also sent me several messages, one of which ended:

> *If you don't get back to either me or Rich and assure us that you're not having some kind of psychotic episode I will literally call your dad on you.*

I'm nearly 30, I couldn't resist replying.

Okay but that worked!! she sent back. *Where are you?*

I'm safe, I promise. I'm just thinking some stuff through.

You're in deep shit with both of us for this behaviour, she said. *Love you. Have a good think.*

I went down to the hotel café for a sandwich and a packet of crisps and tried to have my think. There were too many things to consider at once and I sat staring straight ahead as I ate, trying to make myself understand it. A café worker came over to my table – 'Miss, are you okay? Do you want us to call somebody?' – and I realised I probably looked high out of my mind.

'I'm fine,' I said. 'Sorry.'

I finished my sandwich and went back to my room. A heaviness came over me again and I found myself lying on the bed with my shoes still on. Callie was dead. I tried to get the thought out of my body, to give myself a moment of peace, but I couldn't. Callie was dead, and what was worse, she was only dead to me. To the rest of the world, she lived. It didn't seem fair, not when I had loved her so much more. I cried again, curled up sideways on top of the duvet. Somewhere in the background, my body writhed, my trainers leaving faint grey marks on the sheets.

She had said my name on that beach. What if she'd run offstage and barked at her assistant for her phone, and dialled my number, and asked, *Were you watching? Did you see?*

Yes, I would have said, *I was watching. I'm always watching.*

I'd always imagined I would see her again. Maybe shopping in Liberty's at Christmas, surrounded by her security. She would have looked across the store and caught my eye, and maybe we would have spoken, or maybe we would have just shared a single nod, a moment of mutual recognition and respect. Even that might have been enough. Her death was a huge unanswerable question that I would never put to bed. *How* could I keep this secret? For the rest of my life, people would bring her up, and I would have to not cry. I would have to not show how heavily I held it, right in the dark, sticky, apricot pit of my rotting heart.

I googled *lupus*. I read lists of symptoms. They didn't make sense. The words rolled off and over my brain. My mind was greasy. Hours passed, but eventually I called Inese again, like we'd both known I would.

'More questions.' My voice was hoarse from crying. If she noticed, she didn't comment on it.

'Okay,' she said.

'The two of you didn't have many deep conversations?'

'No, not many.' It was easier to talk to her this way, her voice disembodied and distinctly different from Callie's.

'But you seem fairly certain what her wishes were.'

'I have her diaries,' she said. 'I was given them by Charlie.'

'She kept diaries?'

'They're thorough,' she said. 'They're more a documentation of her life than the inner workings of her mind. But her intentions are fairly clearly laid out in them.' I imagined holding those volumes in my hands. All the insights into Callie that I had been missing. 'Are you there?' asked Inese.

'I'm here.'

'You can have them, if you like. The diaries.' She said it casually, as if she were offering me a stick of gum. I understood, though, that she was trying to be kind.

'Thank you,' I said. 'I— Maybe, yes. Maybe that would help.'

She didn't reply. I could hear her breathing. 'Stevie?' she said.

'Yes?'

'I'm frightened,' she said flatly.

'What are you frightened of?'

'Consequences,' she said.

'What consequences?'

'The things they can do . . .' she said. 'I didn't even realise all the things they're capable of doing. I don't know what would happen if . . .'

She trailed off. I found that I was crying again. Maybe I was crying for her this time. She sounded achingly lonely.

'I can't fail,' she said. 'You understand that, don't you?'

We lay, breathless, holding phones to our ears, in different rooms, in different parts of the city. The lights were out. It felt as if she were lying next to me in the dark, her measured breaths in my ear.

'I think so,' I said. 'I think I do.'

I came home at three the following afternoon, overnight bag on my shoulder, hair unbrushed, no make-up on. Rich was standing in our living room when I entered, the sofa dented behind him, as if he had jumped up as soon as he heard my key in the lock. I closed the door behind me, wondering if he would take that as a cue to move towards me and hug me, but when I turned back he was still standing there. He had a white t-shirt on and these awful tracksuit shorts that did nothing for him.

'Why aren't you at work?' I asked. There was arguably no good way to open the conversation, but I'll admit that was definitely a bad one. He frowned at me with very wide eyes but said nothing. I put my bag down on the carpet.

'Where did you go?' he asked eventually.

'I just needed some time to myself?'

'Are you cheating on me?'

The question was so unexpected and so ridiculous that I let out a bark of laughter. 'God! Rich! No. Sorry.'

'Why are you laughing?'

'It's just – god, it didn't even cross my *mind* that you would think that.'

His features cleared, and I realised too late that there was a second question behind *Are you cheating on me?* In his mind, wrapped up in that question was an unspoken *Are you breaking up with me?* I had reacted with genuine astonishment. Mirth, even. I wasn't going anywhere.

'Well,' he said, scratching his neck. 'I don't get it. I mean, did you go clubbing?'

'Do I look like I went clubbing?'

'A little bit. I mean, you look like the morning after clubbing.'

'Great.'

'You look rough,' he said. 'Sorry, but you do. Stevie, what the *fuck?* I'm worried.'

'Look,' I said, 'it's not that crazy. I just had the urge to be on my own for a while. Don't you ever get that?'

'You had the urge to be on your own so you crashed on Mel's couch?'

'She told you.' She'd actually covered for me – she had no idea where I'd been last night. When all this was sorted out, I would buy her flowers. When all this was sorted out. What a ludicrous thing to think.

'Yes, she told me, because she's not a total fucking bitch.' I winced, and so did he. 'Sorry,' he said, 'sorry. I hate that kind of language. You get that this is weird, though, right? You get that this is weird behaviour?'

There wasn't really any point denying that.

'You can talk to me,' he said.

He sat back down on the sofa and patted the spot beside him. He managed a smile – open, hopeful – and my heart leapt towards him suddenly, this great big running leap, like it was penned in at the sides and barrelling towards the only possible exit it saw. I sat down next to him.

'It's Callie,' I said.

The smile vanished.

'What about her?'

'She's dead.'

No reaction for a minute. Then he leant forward and put his head in his hands.

'Stevie. Fuck.'

This was the moment that sealed it. If he'd tried, even a little, if he'd balked but then asked, *Why do you think that?* or if he'd looked at me like he wanted to trust me, I might have told him everything. But the judgement was immediate. I heard it in his voice. *Okay. She's crazy.*

I picked my overnight bag back up and headed to the bedroom. He let me go, still sat on the sofa, shaking his head. I thought he might stay there the entire time, but once he realised there was no one to perform to he moved down the corridor into the bedroom doorway.

'What are you doing?' he asked.

'Packing,' I said, rolling up underwear.

'You're leaving again?'

'I'm going to go stay with a friend,' I said.

'Mel's worried about you too, Stevie.'

'Maybe I won't stay with Mel,' I said. 'Maybe I'll stay with a different friend.'

'You are cheating on me,' he said, his voice small and sad, worming down the back of my neck.

'I'm not. I told you.'

'Then what's going on?'

I tried to push past him, but he caught the strap of my bag and pulled. There was violence in the gesture, but when I looked at him, his face was wet and wobbly, entirely pitiable. He just wanted to understand, said his shining eyes, his pouting lip. I wrenched my bag back.

'There's no point,' I said, and I could have elaborated further, but in the end it was easiest to leave it at that.

◆ ◆ ◆

I wasn't planning to leave forever. I sort of wanted him to think that I might, which I knew was terrible, but I couldn't take any more of Rich's wheedling doubt. It wasn't just his doubt of Callie's death – that I could understand, even if it nettled me. Rich seemed to doubt everything about me that felt most fundamental: my intellect, my queerness, my ability to rationalise a situation, the fact that I could be funny. All of that scepticism, and yet he never seemed to doubt himself for a second.

I didn't know Inese, and she didn't know me. But she had trusted me and turned to me with confidence, in a way that Rich never would. There was no one else either of us could speak to about this thing that we both knew. It was both terrifying and inescapably true that she was the only person I could go to.

I called the scribbled pencil number.

'I need to get out of my flat. Can I come to you?'

'*Yes*,' she breathed. It was the first time I had heard her speak in her own voice with so much emotion.

Back in 2018, Calista did an *Architectural Digest* tour of her house in Hampstead. She was generally praised for her interior décor – a modest mix of creativity and restraint, luxury items that were never too flashy, rooms that never bowed under the weight of their own try-hard grandeur, but announced how successful their owner was all the same. Her walls displayed local artists. All her chairs looked comfortable. Her kitchen and bathrooms weren't empty white voids, but covered in vintage tiles, with copper taps and soap dispensers she claimed to have found in a charity shop in Dalston.

Trust Calista to be the only famous person with any taste, read a much-liked comment.

We had broken up two years prior. I knew, unless her taste had rapidly developed in that time, that Callie hadn't decorated her own house. What a room looked like was barely of any consequence to her – she always left that kind of thing to me. When it came to music and all the surrounding, intersecting arts of pop stardom, her creativity was endless. Pull her out of that world and she was just as ordinary as the rest of us. It was a comfort. I didn't have to see her in every room.

Inese told me, as she toured me around Callie's Hampstead house, that she did love interior design. She was quite good at it, she said. At one point, for a little extra money, she had renovated Callie's closet for her. She showed it to me proudly, pulling out drawers and explaining how she had selected the small hexagonal handles. Her face was flushed and excited. She was younger than Callie and me, I realised suddenly.

'How old are you?' I asked her, as we moved upstairs to the guest bedrooms.

'Twenty-five,' she said.

'You were a teenager, then, when they brought you on board.'

'I've always looked older than my age,' she said. 'Look, this soap. I love this soap.' We were in the en-suite of the second guest bedroom. She had picked up a bar of green soap from the bathroom countertop; she brought it to her nose and sniffed. 'Divine,' she said, in an affected voice. I laughed, in spite of everything. She glanced at me, startled, like she had been funny by accident.

They had moved Inese into this house a week after Callie died, she said. She'd been in LA when Callie fell – she'd been pulled instantly into a series of different meetings, without even enough time to put a bra on. 'I just sat there with no bra, with all these different people talking at me.' Six hours later she was on a plane to London, holed up in accommodation sourced by management for a while, before she was given the keys to the Hampstead house. They'd done a sweep of the place first, tallying up and making plans for anything particularly significant or valuable. Then they'd left her there, to acclimatise, they'd said.

'Like method acting,' she told me, sat on the kitchen sideboard, legs swinging. She didn't seem surprised by the overnight bag sitting at my feet.

'They want you to start feeling like you *are* her?'

'I suppose so,' she said. 'It makes sense, doesn't it? A performance is the most convincing when it's not even a performance at all.'

She made me a strong coffee and an even stronger one for herself. We sat at Callie's oak kitchen table, beside her gallery wall of Robert Mapplethorpe prints, and drank out of her earthenware mugs. After a while, I noticed that Inese's hands were twitching.

'It feels like living in a ghost's house,' she said.

'Like it's haunted?'

'Yes, that's what I mean.'

'I get that.' She was staring at me over her mug, like I was the one with a famous face. 'What is it?'

'I always liked you,' she said.

'We've never met.'

'But the sound of you. How loyal you were. How you never said anything bad about her, never tried to get a headline or make a buck for yourself in all the years that followed. And how you looked at her, in all the pictures.' She was staring past me, like she wasn't even talking to me. 'Even before I was doing this job, I remember how I loved how you looked at her in all the pictures.'

The light on her face was soft, filtered in through the massive plants in Callie's back garden.

'She has a photo album with you in it,' she said. 'It's on the shelf in her bedroom.'

'I made that for her,' I said. 'She still has it?'

Inese went and fetched it. She was in a white tracksuit, her feet bare on the laminate floors. Gliding away from me with her blonde hair thick on her shoulders, she really did look like the ghost that haunted this house. I had half hoped that she would take me with her, to see Callie's bedroom, but it was her room now and maybe she didn't feel comfortable inviting me into it. The idea of this stranger sleeping in Callie's bed made my stomach turn.

She returned with the book held to her chest. It was a blue cloth-covered, hardback album that I'd made for Callie a year into our relationship. She laid it on the table and flicked through it, languidly, as if she were already familiar with it.

'This one,' she said, jabbing the picture with her finger.

It was a shot of the two of us backstage at her big gig in Brixton, circa 2015. We had our arms wrapped round each other, her hair covering my shoulder. Mine was cut short back then, stopping just at my chin, and my eyeliner was heavy. We were both red and sweaty, beaming. Underneath the picture, someone who wasn't me had drawn a heart. In a different colour was written, *This night was so wonderful.*

I slid the book towards myself. Inese watched, sipping her coffee. Many of the pages contained those little notes, written in purple or blue or pink, like whoever wrote them had been picking different pens out of a pencil case.

I remember this so clearly, under a photo of us dancing in a bright pink bar.

I wish I had more photos of this, under the two of us paddle-boarding, the time we went with Mel's brother and his friends to the Lakes.

She looks so beautiful here.

This one was scribbled in teal beside a picture of us lying on our stomachs in Regent's Park on a tartan picnic blanket. We'd set up the camera on a timer some distance away and prepared our pose – but I still appeared caught off guard, looking at her.

I touched the words with my finger.

She looks so beautiful here.

Surely written by someone else – Inese perhaps – about Callie. Not by Callie about me.

'Do you want to keep it?' asked Inese.

Flustered, I closed the book and pushed it back over to her. 'No, no. It belongs here.'

She shrugged. I picked up my mug again.

'Her new project,' she said. 'It's all about resurrection.'

I nearly spilt my coffee. 'What?'

'Oh, yes. It's quite eerie. Quite strange timing, they're saying. I have wondered if she knew. If—'

'If it was on purpose?'

'But I don't think so,' said Inese, 'because I don't think she was like that. This is just god's little joke.' She twisted her mouth to the side, staring down at her mug. 'But that's what it is. I have to resurrect her.' She saw that I was still looking at the photo albums. 'I have the diaries,' she said. 'All her diaries. They're in her room. I can show them to you.'

'Really?'

'You don't want them?' she asked.

'I do,' I said. 'Just—' There was no way for me to tell her that this was like a genie appearing to grant my most earnest wish. All of Callie's private thoughts heaped into my arms – it was a kind of deliverance I couldn't trust.

'You're worried what they say about you?'

I wondered what she'd read. Maybe I wasn't even in them at all. Her face gave nothing away.

'I'll make you up a bed,' she said. 'There's so many bedrooms in this place.'

'I came here to talk,' I said.

'I know.'

'There's so many things I still don't understand.'

'Do you want to talk now?'

'I—' There were too many possible first questions. 'I suppose—'

'Maybe I could get you a pen and paper,' she said kindly. 'You could get some rest and write down all your questions, and then in the morning I could answer them all. Yes?' She jumped up from her seat, checked in my mug to see if I was done drinking. It was cold. She looked up to find me staring at her. 'What is it?'

'You seem so different from her.'

'Oh,' she said. 'Well, yes.'

'Just, like, an entirely different person.'

'You're wondering how I ever fooled you?'

I couldn't help laughing, although it came out brief and harsh. 'I suppose so, yes.'

'Fooled you like this?'

She pushed her hair behind both ears, looked over at me with a slight smile. Her face was soft but there was a mischief in it. She walked over, her hands in her pockets, her head tipped to the side. I felt myself leaning away from her as she rounded the side of the table.

'Do you recognise me now, Stevie?' she asked.

There was a pause. I turned away from her. 'Stop that,' I said. I felt sick.

I heard her take my mug from me. She poured it out in the sink.

'You're not easily fooled, Stevie,' she said in her normal voice. 'Don't worry. I'm just very good.'

◆ ◆ ◆

The Hampstead house had five bedrooms. She toured me round all of them and asked me to choose. I told her to pick whichever one was most convenient, that it didn't matter to me where I slept, but she made me choose anyway. She seemed strangely proud of these bedrooms that she hadn't decorated, in this house that wasn't hers. I picked one far away from her room, on the floor below, with an adjoining green-tiled bathroom that smelt like cleaning fluid. On the wall opposite the bed, there was a piece of grey abstract art, another clue that Callie hadn't had much hand in decorating this place. Callie had always liked more outward-facing art – art that wore its heart on its sleeve.

'I'll get you pyjamas,' said Inese, when I set my suitcase down on the bed. She was gone before I had a chance to tell her that I had brought my own. She returned with two pairs of matching collared shirts and shorts, in grey and green stripes.

'Where did you get these?' I asked her, as she laid them on the duvet.

'She has a whole cupboard of them.'

'These are hers?' I asked, spooked. She looked back at me, nonplussed. But of course Inese was wearing her clothes. She had been ever since she moved in. 'I can't wear these. I'll just wear my own.'

'Okay,' she said, shrugging. 'I bet these are nicer than yours, though.'

'Probably. But I can't— I can't sleep in her clothes.'

'Hm,' said Inese. 'Okay. I understand.' She left them folded up on the armchair in the corner of the room – her version of a compromise. I stood by the chair for a second, stroking the collar of one of the shirts between my fingers. Phantom spiders crawled up and down my back. I put a pillow on top of the pile of pyjamas, so that I could forget they were there.

It was still very early, far too early to sleep, especially after the strength of the coffee that Inese had poured me. Still, she laid a blank blue notebook and pen on top of the bedside table and slipped out. I could feel this was a sacrifice for her. She wanted to hear my questions even more than I wanted to ask them. She wasn't exuberant exactly, but she had so much time for talk. The need to talk to me spilt out of her whenever she took the lid off. I still wasn't entirely sure what it was and why it was directed at me specifically – maybe because she had decided, for reasons only she knew, that I could offer some help beyond the help she had already. I wanted to understand why she felt so called to do this, why she was so happy to sacrifice whoever she was and fold herself up entirely in a dead woman's identity.

I turned my phone back on. Rich and Mel had called me several times, and now they seemed to have got my dad involved – he had rung twice, which was practically obsessive for him. I wondered what they had told him. I would have to do damage control now – Rich was the sort to call paramedics on me and claim I was having a psychotic break, all for a few hero points.

I put them both in a group text, and then added my dad, on the off-chance he was worried.

I promise you all that I am fine and healthy and just working through something privately. I'm an adult and I deserve to be given the space to do that. Don't contact me for a little bit and I swear soon I will explain everything.

I meant it. I just needed to find a version of the story that made sense to say out loud.

Inese's footsteps came down the corridor, past my door, and then up the next flight of stairs. When I was sure that her door was closed, I slipped down to the kitchen. The photo album was still lying on the table, closed. *For Callie,* read a small square of white on the blue cover, written in my own sloped black handwriting. It was silly, but on the way back up I held the book under my pyjama top, close to my skin, just in case I ran into Inese. I knew she wouldn't have minded me looking at it – she had offered it to me, after all – but I felt protective of my history with Callie and wanted to guard it from her, even though I knew she had been leafing through the pages of our life together for months, maybe even years.

The multi-coloured annotations were all over the book, a small observation beside almost every photo. The handwriting might have been Callie's, but truthfully – horrifyingly – I couldn't actually remember too well what her handwriting looked like. The annotations were too generic, no specifics, nothing overly personal, and eventually I put the book on the floor and lay back down. I picked up the notebook and pen that Inese had given me. The notebook was familiar – it was the blue spiral kind that Callie used to buy and fill obsessively with lyrics. She still had a stockpile of them then, somewhere in this house. *Oh god.* She had a stockpile of those same blue notebooks that she had piled on top of the desk in our bedroom, that she had stained the pages of with takeout and lipgloss. They were languishing in some cupboard somewhere. She would never fill them.

Why couldn't I actually understand that she was dead? Why did her death still feel like an open-ended question? Maybe it was the fact of Inese, sitting in her kitchen, wearing her clothes, walking towards me with her walk, speaking in her voice. Maybe Inese was standing between me and my grief, holding the tidal wave of it on her shoulders, smiling Callie's smile.

Or maybe this was how you felt, when somebody died who you didn't really know anymore.

But I had known her. I had known that Inese wasn't her. She had spoken to me, on that stage.

There's this person who was there for me, right at the start. She's someone I've been thinking about a lot lately.

Why had she been thinking about me? Why say that to me, there, then, in front of everyone, after all these years? Had she wanted me to pay attention to what happened next?

I opened the notebook. At the top of the page, I wrote, *Questions.* It felt ridiculous as soon as I'd done it. I added a colon after it, which felt even more ridiculous. This wasn't a school report.

Questions:

How does the legal side work? Has her death not been registered at all? Have you assumed her legal identity as well as her professional one?

What do her parents know?

Have you always been prepared in case this happened? Have you ever thought that you might say no? Do you miss being yourself? Do you think you will, one day?

What happens if people work it out?

What happened to her body?

That last one made me feel sick. I dotted the question mark and stared at it.

> *Why are you telling me all of this? Why are you so sure you can trust me?*

That was all I could think of just then. I closed the notebook and lay the pen on top of it, and then I burrowed down in the bed and put my headphones in. I felt that maybe *Put This On My Headstone* might bring me some comfort – her young voice, the immortality of it – but I couldn't even make it past the first song. I cried again. In this house, with all the things that weren't really her things and the writings I couldn't find her in, I felt closer to her than I had in years. And she felt further from me than ever.

I slept for a long time, dreamt intensely and forgot the entire thing within seconds of waking up. I got up and dressed mid-morning and went down to make myself breakfast, my notebook of questions in my hand. The kitchen was well-stocked – Inese with an Ocado account, or someone shopping for her? I added it to my list of questions and took my time over my eggs, but she didn't appear. Eventually I went looking for her upstairs, but there was no reply when I knocked. On my way back down, I bumped into her.

'Oh,' she said, 'there you are.' She was fresh-faced, no make-up but very awake in her jean shorts and t-shirt, as if she'd been up for hours. I was starting to notice that she always looked the most like Callie when I first saw her after some time apart. It was as if my eyes needed a second to adjust to her face in the light.

'Where have you been?'

'In the music room,' she asked. 'At the end of the garden.' She pointed out of the window. The garden wasn't large by regular standards but it was large for London, with high fences and a separate unit at the end. 'All her music stuff is in there,' she said. 'I practise every morning.'

The video of her onstage at the Apollo came back to me. I still didn't like the idea of her singing Callie's songs.

'Did you sleep well?' she said. 'It's a comfy bed. All the beds here are comfy.'

'I did. Thank you.' It had been a while since I'd slept that well, either because the crying had worn me out or because Rich hadn't been there to wake me up every few hours and ask me to breathe more quietly.

'Good,' she said. We stood on the stairs for a minute, looking at each other. She nodded at the notebook in my hand. 'Questions?'

'If you don't mind.'

'I don't mind,' she said. She was holding back her enthusiasm. 'Kitchen?'

We sat at the kitchen table. She started making tea, but I said, 'No, no, I'm fine.' She paused, her finger on the switch of the kettle, and then she came over and sat down.

'She loves tea,' she said. It was strange that she was talking about her in the present tense – it gave me hope for a second, but then she played the words back to herself and I saw her realise her mistake. My chest deflated. 'You ate?' she asked.

'I did.'

'Good. I'm sorry – I should have made you something. I'm not a very good host.'

'It's fine,' I said, as she grimaced. She gestured to the notebook, and I opened it, clearing my throat, already feeling self-conscious. The first line – my list of legal questions – seemed intense and interrogative. 'So,' I said. 'Um. Legally?' She blinked at me. 'How does it all work?' I asked weakly.

'Legally, I am her.'

'How?'

'I just am. All the documents and everything . . .' She waved a hand. 'There's like, four, maybe five people that know,' she said. 'I think. Unless there's more. They don't tell me everything. I'm just supposed to *schwoop*—' She made a little motion with her hand like a fish swimming. 'Slot in.'

'As if she never . . . as if nothing ever happened to her.'

'Yes.'

'Which is illegal.'

'Yes,' she said. I supposed that answered my question about whether anyone had actually been notified of her death.

'So, at the hospital . . .'

'No idea,' she said.

'There would be . . .'

'A body?' she finished. 'Yes. There would be a body. I don't know how they would have switched it. I thought maybe they would have said it was my body—'

'Are you dead?' I asked, surprised.

She grinned, like it was funny. 'Missing, technically,' she said. I gaped at her. 'Insane, no?'

'And your family? Your friends?'

'I left all that behind a long time ago.'

'But they aren't looking for you?'

'No.'

'Why not?'

'Charlie's money.' She nodded solemnly at my expression. 'It's all crazy. These people and their money – it's crazy what it can do. No, I don't know how they explained the body or where it went. I can ask Charlie, but I don't know if he'll tell me. She worked with a medical staff who were under a strict NDA with all her health issues, so maybe they know?'

I looked down at my list of questions, feeling increasingly out of my depth. The neat question marks at the end of each line now seemed like an effort to impose order on the inexplicable.

'What do her parents know?'

'Nothing,' she said. 'Well, just what the rest of the world knows. They seem fine.'

'Have you spoken to them?'

'Only on the phone. And only once. To confirm I was okay.'

Only once was cold, even for them, but they were hardly even her parents anymore. They hadn't been since I'd known her, since she had begun to pull away from the church in her early teenage years. It wasn't a normal church that Callie's parents were involved in, but some weird branch of Mormonism that they'd brought over with them from the States and that had never quite caught on among the sinners of Brighton. Callie's teenage years, as she described them, had been great adventures followed by long confinements in her bedroom, the cycle repeating over and over. She'd left at sixteen and hadn't looked back.

'What about Luke? Her tennis guy?'

'They're broken up,' said Inese. 'They've been broken up for three months. He was cheating on her. It just hadn't been announced yet. Harma has a statement ready, for when the time is right.'

'Poor Callie.'

'Oh, I don't think she ever really liked him all that much. It was just nice to have company when she wanted company.'

'Did she tell you that?'

'Her diaries did.' A small thrill came over me, at hearing those words.

'Her friends?'

'She's recovering. Not socialising much. But also, with her illness, she's become a lot more isolated in recent years.'

'I see,' I said, my heart breaking for her.

'You know, she didn't want to tell anyone, so they all thought she was cancelling plans and becoming a recluse for no reason.' Inese waved a hand. 'Makes my job easier.'

I felt suddenly furious at her callousness – at all of them, for reanimating Calista while Callie languished in the ground somewhere, if she even was buried. Who knew where they'd taken her or what they'd done? And here was Inese, taking phone calls with Callie's parents, posting selfies to her Instagram account. It was disrespectful. It was macabre.

She saw the change in my face. She leant forward. 'She wanted this, Stevie. Read the diaries – you'll see.'

I looked back down at my questions. 'Didn't you ever think about saying no? Being yourself again?'

'I can't really,' she said.

'You can't?'

'They can do all this with their money. Their money can do lots of things.' I waited for her to voice exactly what it was she was scared of, but she didn't. 'I love it, though,' she said. 'I love being her.'

'How can you love being someone you aren't?'

'Calista is a character,' she said. 'That's what Callie used to say. Just a character.'

'But you're not just being Calista. You're being *her*.'

'Only in private. Everything in public is Calista. It always has been. I think she was only ever really Callie when she was alone.'

'She was Callie with me,' I said.

She crossed her legs. 'More questions?'

'If no one can know, why are you telling me?'

'I had to,' she said.

'Why?'

'Otherwise, I'm alone.'

I looked down at the page. 'I don't understand what you want from me.'

'This is what I want from you,' she said.

She touched my hand. She was tanned in her jean shorts and ponytail, flip-flops on her feet, like some sister of Callie's just returned from the beach. Callie had always wanted a sister.

'Is that the whole list?' she asked, pulling away.

The last question seemed stupid now, but I asked it anyway. 'Who does your food shop?'

She burst out laughing. 'Really?'

I shrugged, defensive.

'Charlie,' she said.

I closed the notebook. 'That's it.'

'Nothing else?'

'The diaries?' I asked, my voice coming from somewhere so high in my throat that I couldn't prevent a squeak at the end of the question.

She brought them to my room in a wicker washing basket. There were about fifteen of them, varying in size, in thickness, in the wear and tear to their covers. Inese unloaded them and stacked them on the carpet in order as I watched from the bed. I recognised a thick, battered blue one – she'd written in it since I'd met her. It used to live on her bedside table with the broken leg. The rest were all unfamiliar. She'd lived so much, since I'd known her. We were just one of fifteen volumes in her life, if that.

Inese finished stacking the books. She stood in her flip-flops on the carpet, hands clasped behind her back.

'The thing is,' she said, 'they can't leave this house. Very sensitive material.' She said it so solemnly that under different circumstances it might have made me smile. 'You'll have to stay here, if you're going to read them.'

'I'm a fast reader,' I said.

She nodded. I couldn't tell from her face if this was what she wanted to hear.

'Well,' she said, with what was clearly great restraint, 'let me know if you need anything.'

'I will. Thanks, Inese.' We were both aware that I had never addressed her by name before. The moment I did, she looked like Callie again, and then the moment passed. She nodded and disappeared out of the door. The waistband of the shorts was slightly loose around her waist. Maybe Callie had bought them like that, or maybe Inese was just a little bit skinnier.

I crouched down on the carpet by the pile of books, and opened each one at the title page. *Feb 2013–June 2016,* read the battered blue one. She hadn't been a particularly disciplined diary keeper when I'd known her, putting it down for weeks at a time, writing only when the mood struck her. She'd clearly started to take it more seriously at a certain level of fame. The rest of the diaries encompassed much shorter periods of time, and her writing was more densely packed – a tight, sloped hand, always in black pen. I opened one at random.

18/10/21

Very tired today. Called Gene and told her there was no way I was doing Fallon. She suggested we throw Inese out there instead but couldn't do that to the poor girl. Live TV is far too much. Happy to be seen as a little flaky rather than put her through that.

Gabbie has passed my number to one of her co-stars who has apparently always had a crush on me. Hard to explain why I'm not dating too much right now. Harma pushed again on a statement. Apparently lupus is having 'a moment'. (??) Explained again I don't want the world to know my medical history. Don't want them all speculating on my health. I don't have much that's just for me.

Had the dream again. Too tired to write anything about it.

I closed the book. It hurt to read – not because it was hard to think about her being so ill in secret, although that was true, but because I could hear her so clearly in it. It was so distinctly her voice, down to the bracketed double question marks. I felt suddenly that I'd been delusional to think that Inese had ever been a good copy. *This* was Callie, just living, just by-the-numbers relating her day, too tired to try too hard or hold the pen for long. You couldn't recreate her.

I laid the volumes out in front of me in chronological order and then picked up the first one and opened it.

2/2/13

Well, I finally have a diary. Isn't it funny that it's taken me this long? Everyone who's ever known me imagines me as the kind of person who sits and writes long essays in their diary every night, and it's a lovely image but it just isn't a true one. I've never had the sticking power needed for a diary. Well, I'm going to try to. And I'll do my best to make it interesting, for when it eventually goes up for auction.

That brought me back to all the jokes we used to make about *when she was the most famous woman in the world . . .* She'd actually done it. I felt so proud of her I could have cried.

It's way too cold in this flat, concluded that first entry, *but Dora won't let me put the heating on for money reasons, so I'm going to go sit in bed in my winter coat.* By the end of that year, she would be moving into her own place. Dora was the roommate she'd had when I'd met her, the one who brought Callie along to the flat party in Brixton where we'd met. I remembered her as a sour-faced, chronically jealous brunette, although I'd had a habit of assuming everyone was jealous of Callie.

There weren't many entries in those first few months, just sporadic scribblings about small open mic nights and trying to find someone to help her record a demo. *I know I've got so many good songs,* she wrote, *if I could just find someone to help me make them sound good. They say you just need to keep going almost like you know you'll make it, no back-up plans, no safety nets. I've never had a safety net to speak of and any back-up plan I come up with makes me miserable to think about, so I suppose I'm following that advice without even trying. I want this so badly. It's terrifying to want something this much.*

She was just seventeen here. A girl who had passive-aggressive conversations with her roommate about her late-night guitar-playing habits and who hadn't yet found a good hair routine for her curls. She had one pair of trainers, one pair of boots and one pair of heels. She went to the reduced section in Tesco every day to find something for lunch, and if you told her that you liked the way she dressed, she'd tuck her arm through yours and offer to give you a tour round all the best charity shops in South London, even if you'd only met her that afternoon. She thought that you could survive on music and love and optimism, if you were willing to sacrifice a few nice things. She still hadn't lost all the baby fat from her cheeks and her gums still showed when she smiled. The biggest achievement of her life so far was leaving home and getting a job in a bakery. The biggest heartbreak was the fact that her parents would rather she were someone else. She sliced her fingers restringing her guitar on her own and practised her piano playing on an electric keyboard that she had to tuck down beside her wardrobe when she wasn't using it, because her room was so small. She didn't know where she'd go from there. She didn't know that she only had eleven years left. I missed her so much then, that I knew I would have died for her if someone had given me the chance.

8/7/13

I think if I'd told the girl at the party tonight that I was going to go home and write in my diary about her, she would have laughed at me. But she would have laughed in a nice way, not in a mean one.

Thank you, Dora, for dragging me to uni parties with you!! I swear I will never complain about going to one ever again, but only if Stevie Stone is at all of them. Stevie Stone. That's a name you don't forget quickly. She sounds like a character in a classic country rock song. Is it too early to write a song about Stevie Stone, when I just met her tonight? Definitely. But I'll do it anyway. I don't even know if she likes girls. I think she likes me, because we sat and talked for two hours, about I don't even know what, and she told me I was pretty. But liking me isn't necessarily the same thing as liking girls.

I'm writing down that I met her because I think I'm going to fall madly in love with her and I want a record of the fact that I predicted it. I'm going to text her now, actually, not to say the falling madly in love bit, obviously, but just to say that it was nice to meet her and I'd like to get coffee with her sometime, if she'd like that too.

From Stevie: It was lovely to meet you too! I would absolutely love to get a coffee

And she put a little heart. Like this: ♥

I was absent from the next few entries – she didn't write about our date, just picked up her diary randomly over the next few weeks to talk about songs she was writing and gigs she was playing. Then, two months later, halfway through an entry:

Stevie asked me to be her girlfriend last week. I didn't write about it because I haven't even had time to. We've been with each other nonstop – I even come with her to her lectures sometimes, just slip in with her and sit down and write lyrics while she takes notes. She stays in my flat now and then, but mostly I stay with her and Mel at their place. I think I'm already in love with her. It's all happened so fast that I can't even really say how or when it happened. Actually, that's a lie, I can. I was playing her a song the other day. She sat and watched me from the sofa, holding a cushion to her chest. Her eyes were so wide, and I could see the lamp in them, so they were almost glowing. I forgot all the words, the way she was looking at me. I stopped and stumbled a bit, and said, 'Sorry, sorry,' and she said, 'You can start again, if you like. I want to hear the first verse again.' I think that's when I knew that I loved her.

I had my sleeve pressed beneath my eyes as I turned the pages, so that I wouldn't get them wet. The entries were short, irregularly spaced, but torturously vivid. The two of us winding away the winter together, warming each other up in our small beds in our small bedrooms, taking the bus between our two flats, wandering down Oxford Street to look at the lights, cooking dinner for each other, lighting candles, being young. She mused about what to get me for Christmas, and then on the very next page mused about spending Christmas together. Elation when I invited her to come home with me for the holidays. I was so nervous about introducing her to my dad, but she handled him well. She was no stranger to distant parents.

In the new year, music took over again, but there I was, still. Consoling her when things didn't go to plan, cheering in the audience even when she was playing to less than ten people. Listening to her songs on repeat, telling her how much I loved them. When she got her record deal, she wrote more about my reaction than she did about her own.

> *Stevie cried, she was so happy. When I came over to hers, she'd blown up balloons and covered the floor with them. She made a cake. She's not a very good baker, but that's okay. I lay in her bed with her arms around me that night, after she fell asleep, and I realised that I basically had everything I had ever wanted.*

It was like living it all again – the release of her first single, the writing and recording of the album. The nights she spent flipping between her guitar and her notebook as I read on the sofa and pretended not to be far more interested in her than in my book. The first time she played me 'Again, Again, Again', the sex we had that night, slow and lazy and loving. The new people around her, all there to help her music on its way to success. Moving her into her own place. How fast it seemed to unfold after that, the way it ramped up, from the album to her first headline shows to the first time she went to the US, how I skipped my classes and bought my own plane ticket to go with her, even though I could barely afford it. I loved her through the pages. Touching them was like touching her skin. She poured her love out to me in her neat, sloping handwriting, like she had chronicled it all specifically for me to read and be reminded. Her Brixton Academy show was a joyous climax, a slightly tipsy outpouring of adoration, for the music, for the experience, but most of all for me.

> *I can't believe how much I love her. I can't believe how much she loves me. It feels like carrying around more love than my body was ever designed to handle. There's some regulatory mechanism that I'm meant to have that I just don't, and so I'm feeling way more than I ever should have been able to feel. It's almost uncomfortable, but I still like it.*

I read on. By halfway through 2015, though, my stomach started to turn. It wasn't anything specific, at least not at first. The mentions of me weren't less frequent exactly, but they were more matter-of-fact. *Went out with Stevie. Stevie came along. Stevie can't come on the European tour with me, which is sad. Stevie called, said she missed me.* She didn't say that she missed me too.

I could sense something in the remaining pages, something coming towards me that I knew I wasn't ready to face just then, and I closed the book. I scavenged in the kitchen for toast and butter, and then I watched Inese out of the window for a while as she sat in the garden and scrolled on her phone. She didn't really seem to have much to do. At seven, she knocked on my door and asked if

I wanted to eat dinner with her. She asked it in the manner of one friend hosting another. I was angry with her all over again.

'I'm not hungry,' I said, even though I was.

She looked crestfallen. I tried not to feel guilty. She left and didn't reappear. I went to bed without the two of us crossing paths again.

◆ ◆ ◆

It took me a long time to fall asleep. I was sure I would dream of Callie, and I wondered which of the memories looping around in my brain would appear behind my eyes. I was afraid that it wouldn't be any of them, but just the image of her falling, plummeting, trailing white, no one to catch her.

So, Stevie. This one's for you.

It feels like carrying around more love than my body was ever designed to handle, she'd written. How are you meant to sleep, knowing that someone once wrote those words about you and then stopped feeling them?

When I finally did fall asleep, the only dream I had was of me awake, in my flat back home, sat beside Rich on the sofa, knowing that she was gone from the world.

◆ ◆ ◆

When I woke up, I checked my phone to see that they had all replied to my group text.

> *Mel: Stevie I don't know what's going on but we're all just really worried.*

Dad: Hi stevie people are worried about you give me a call or them when you can dad x

Rich: We love you

Rich hadn't told me that he loved me in weeks so to do it now in the plural was, I thought, an interesting choice. My dad had backed off after that, parental duties performed, but Mel and Rich were still calling. I was about to turn my phone back off but, perversely, I rang my dad instead.

'Hi, Stevie,' he said, surprised.

'Hey.'

'Are you okay? Mel's been texting. Says you ran off and no one knows where you are.'

'They know where I am. They're just being dramatic. You shouldn't worry.'

'Ah,' he said. 'Well, Mel always was dramatic.' Mel was the only one of my friends' names that he'd ever really been able to consistently remember and as such he liked to use it as much as possible, to remind us both that he did pay attention to what went on in my life. 'You're okay, though, Stevie-girl?'

He hadn't called me that in years, not since Mum had died and Mel had picked up the mantle instead. I found myself suddenly choked up. 'I'm okay, Dad.'

'Good,' he said. I could hear him shifting in his chair, rearranging his body. 'Good.'

'I need to go. Just wanted to tell you that, in case you were concerned.'

'No, I wasn't. Never need to worry about you.'

'No,' I said. 'Never do.'

I could hear Inese moving around downstairs. I sat up in bed and opened the diary. I was afraid of what was coming.

9/8/15

We're planning our anniversary, and Stevie wants to go away, but I feel like I've hardly been in the city this year and I want to stay here, see people, do things. She has uni, anyway, and she can't just skip out for a week, or she shouldn't. She doesn't get it, though. She always says she'd drop anything and everything for me, but I don't feel like she should. I wish there was a little bit more to Stevie's life, sometimes, so that I wouldn't feel so guilty about having so much going on in mine.

2/9/15

Pretty shit anniversary, all in all. Started arguing pretty much as soon as we got to the restaurant. She always says I try to argue with her, that she never wants to argue with me, but then I don't really get what she thinks I'm doing – arguing with myself? She says I never prioritise us, that she doesn't feel important anymore, because I took a work call. Wasn't even a work call, really – Tamzin rang just to say she's excited about our session together and I picked up and spoke to her for all of five minutes. I know the real issue is that she's threatened by Tamzin, but she swears that she isn't. I just don't think it's fair that she puts so much pressure on me to be 'present' with her, whatever that means . . .

That entry went on for a while, in much the same vein. I skimmed it, horrified to know not only that she'd written it and probably meant it, but that Inese had read it. The entries were lighter for a while after that – she'd started work on *Calista,* and she was happy, but I could tell that she wasn't happy because of me. I got passing mentions again. *Stevie dropped by to see me for my fitting. Pretty sure Stevie isn't a huge fan of the single, but she refuses to tell me why.* Then, in January 2016, she wrote this:

> *More and more these days, the main thing I feel around Stevie is guilt. I think she loves me too much. She gets so mad if she feels like anyone else comes before her, and then she'll be so ashamed of herself for starting an argument that she just cries and cries, and we can never just have a nice evening.*

A few entries later, this appeared halfway through a recounting of a songwriting session:

> *Probably won't go on the album, but was nice to get out all the stuff I can't say to Stevie. Really on eggshells around her these days. I do love her and hope it gets better. Think maybe this is just growing up – you outgrow that teenage obsession with someone and you realise they're just a flawed human being, and maybe that's okay.*

Almost the very next day, she wrote this:

> *Have probably just avoided an argument that would have led to a break-up. I'm just choosing not to rise to it when she makes little digs about shutting her out. I don't see how I could be shutting her out, when we're always together and I tell her everything I do and everyone I see when we're not. I'm holding my tongue because I don't want the drama while I'm so busy generally, but not sure how sustainable it all is.*

On and on, it went, for months. Arguments we didn't have, things I was doing wrong that I didn't even know I was doing. I skipped the entry in May where she wrote about our break-up – I couldn't manage that one – and read the book all the way to its abrupt end. She met someone else, this drummer called Bruno from some shitty band. People had always speculated that *Loser* was about their break-up, even though the relationship was never confirmed. They were introduced through her stylist. What a clichéd celebrity way to meet.

> *I used to think I would never meet a man I could love like I loved women, but I need to stop basing my whole idea of what love is on Stevie when that was never right anyway. I still don't know if he's someone I could love – I just met him – but I'm starting to think there are versions of love that I'm going to feel in my life that I don't even have any concept of yet. It's such an exciting way to feel.*

I hated her for that one. I'd been grieving, deep in it, still sad every time I left the house, sad every time I lay in bed all day, wondering if I'd missed my one great chance at being known and seen. And she'd been running around meeting men who played in bands, excited at the chance to feel different kinds of love.

She stopped writing when she ran out of space. The last entry was a description of her second date with Bruno, a private dinner in a restaurant that his friend owned. She described the luxury of it, how special it was to have the candlelit place to themselves, eating tiny plates of food and strangely flavoured sorbet. I'd loved her when she'd had to unfold her keyboard stand from the side of her wardrobe to play me a song. I'd loved her when I'd had to pay for her Carla's takeout because she didn't have enough in her bank account. I'd loved her when no one else cheered for her. I'd loved her when no one else even knew her name.

I closed the book and tossed it to the other side of the room. What I really wanted was to rip it down the spine. Inese opened the bedroom door right as the diary hit the ground. I'd been so engrossed that I hadn't even heard her come in.

'Ah,' she said, 'you finished it.'

I didn't answer her. Today she was in a blue dress with fluttery sleeves that I had seen pap shots of Callie wearing before. It was eerie how all of Callie's stuff fit her perfectly.

'Are you okay?' she said. She was carrying a yellow ceramic plate with a croissant on it. 'I brought you breakfast.' Her eyes were very clear and curious. Between the dress and her soft voice and the earnestly plated croissant, she was like a children's cartoon character.

'Thank you,' I said, sitting up. My anger levels fluctuated – appeased slightly by her wide eyes, riled again by the sight of her in Callie's dress.

She eyed my oversized t-shirt, and her eyes flickered to the folded pyjamas under the pillow, but she didn't say anything. I took the plate from her.

'Surprised?' she asked, nodding at the book.

I shrugged, sat against the side of the bed.

'You're not surprised,' she said. 'You knew what it would say. That's why you didn't want to read it.'

I wished she would leave. Instead, she sat down on the end of the bed and watched me. I took a bite out of the croissant to appease her.

'You're better than what she wrote about you,' she said, her voice suddenly gentle. 'I know you were good to her.'

'How do you know that?'

'You haven't read the other diaries.'

'I'd rather not, if they're anything like that one.'

'You were the only one who didn't hurt her,' she said. 'She decided that she didn't love you anymore, and that was it. You never broke her heart or cheated on her or wanted her to make herself less than she was for you.'

'I never would have.'

'I know,' she said. 'I know that, Stevie. I could tell, when I read the diaries. I could see it in the photos.'

She looked at me with such genuine trust and admiration that it almost made me uncomfortable.

'The photos are out,' she said.

It took a second for this to connect. When it did, I reached for my phone and switched it back on. A bombardment of messages from Rich and Mel, along with a bunch of other people who barely ever texted me. Rosie from the office was among them.

Stevie no way!! Call later? I had never once called her.

Calista reconnects with rumoured former flame Stevie Stone at upscale Fitzrovia café, read the first headline I saw.

There were the photos of the two of us, taken from over the wall. Her management had wanted this, of course, but had likely imagined it would end there. For the first time, I felt a wicked thrill at the idea of them finding me here in this house leafing through these volumes, watching Harma's assured smile slide from her face.

rumoured former flame

Different publications referred to our relationship in different ways. Very few had ever outright called me her girlfriend or ex-girlfriend, but this was especially insulting. *Rumoured.* In the early days, Callie had never been coy about her sexuality or about the nature of our relationship. There were multiple videos of her onstage at her *Put This On My Headstone* shows talking about me. Of course, by *Want Me Want Me* her team had started to redirect any kind of narrative about her queerness, and she hadn't publicly confirmed a relationship with a woman since. She had talked about her bisexuality in recent years, since queer artists had begun to dominate mainstream pop, but many called it performative. The queer community hadn't felt represented by her for a long time and the damage was done. It was Calista's queer fans, actually, that loved me the most. They saw me as a victim of her management and PR team, cast aside as soon as it was decided that they would push her as a pop star for straight people, and even though this story wasn't real, I liked how they told it.

Another message from Rich popped up.

STEVIE CALL ME

I didn't call him. Instead, I sent a message. *Just a coffee. Her management set up photos without me knowing. Just figuring some stuff out, will talk properly soon.*

r u getting back together?? he wrote back immediately.

No, definitely not, I typed with confidence.

coming home??

I will, just need time, I sent, then turned my phone off. I didn't want to feel guilty over Rich, but I couldn't help it.

Inese hadn't taken her eyes off me. 'Did you know they were coming out?' I asked.

'Yes,' she said apologetically, 'at some point.'

'People in my life have a lot of questions now.'

'Do you have to go?' she asked.

I looked at the pile of notebooks on the floor. 'Not before I've read those.'

She nodded, brightening. 'I was going to watch a movie,' she said. 'Do you want to watch a movie?'

'Well, like I said—' I gestured to the diaries.

'Oh,' she said, disappointed. 'Of course.'

Even when she wasn't being Callie, their faces were similar enough that disappointing her felt fundamentally wrong.

'I guess I could take a break,' I said.

She smiled.

'Are you not . . .' I considered how to phrase the question. 'I mean, I assumed you'd be super busy.'

'Mostly,' she said. 'I had three days. Then some meetings tomorrow, then I have a photoshoot, then some promotional stuff . . .' She made a motion with her hand as if to indicate that something would soon be rolling and rolling with no discernible end.

'So, this is your time off?'

'Yes,' she said. 'But I don't like time off. I mean, I don't really go anywhere or do anything. It's just me, in this house.' I wiped croissant crumbs from my chin. 'And now you,' she said.

'Until I finish the diaries,' I said.

'Yes,' she said, 'until then.'

I was still angry at all of them, the people who had sat around that table and lied to me, the faceless however many of them, who had performed this awful sleight of hand, but I couldn't help feeling a little sorry for the girl in front of me, trying to conceal a new bounce in her step as she led me downstairs. Whatever her life had been before this, it couldn't have been much, for her to be so willing to give it all up. I didn't want to pity her, but they had made it hard for me. She felt too much like someone I already loved.

In the living room, she selected *Burlesque* and frowned at my face.

'You don't like this film?'

'Did you pick it because Callie loved it?'

'Everyone loves this film,' she said. I wasn't sure if I believed her. Who knew how much she knew about Callie now, after reading those diaries? Likely much more than I did.

We sat and watched in silence. Halfway through, she paused it and said, 'Did you ever think she wouldn't make it big?'

So that was how long her patience could hold out.

'No,' I said truthfully. 'I probably should have. But I was a teenager, and I thought that everything she did was wonderful, so how could it not work out?'

She nodded and pressed play, but I could see that she wasn't paying attention. Instead, she sat there with her lips slightly pursed, thinking up her next question. Another ninety seconds passed before she paused it again.

'Are you going home?' she asked. I wasn't sure how to answer. 'Soon, I mean,' she pressed.

'When I've finished the diaries.'

'But will you have finished them soon?'

'Do you want me to leave?' I asked.

'No,' she said, 'I don't. I want you to stay.'

'Why?'

'I want you to help,' she said. She twisted her hair around her hand, like she was preparing to tie it up. Then she let it fall again. She smoothed the hem of her dress over her knees. It wouldn't have been hard to imagine it was Callie who was flustered around me, nervous, who wanted something from me. It was a dangerous game to start playing.

'I don't get it,' I said. 'I don't see how I can help you. I think you probably knew her better than I ever did, by the end.'

She shook her head, shifting on the sofa to turn her body towards me. 'It's not about that. It's— Everyone around me is under many, many NDAs. This is their job. They believe in what Callie was trying to do, of course, but they're helping me because it's their job.'

'Right.'

'I need someone like you,' she said, eyes earnestly scanning my face. 'When those screenshots got leaked, and they wanted to bring you in, I begged to be there. I think I just wanted to see if you would think that I was her. You did, for a bit.' I flushed. She seized my hand suddenly. My arm went tense. She pressed my hand into the sofa cushion, her fingers pushing themselves between mine. 'You're more than just a fan,' she said. 'You love the music, and you know all about her, but you also really *knew* her. If you can help me make it convincing, then everyone will believe it. I'm— I don't know what happens to me if this doesn't work.'

That chilled me. She said it so frankly, a fact she'd accepted long ago, but she hadn't quite been able to convince herself or me that she wasn't afraid. 'You'd go home to Latvia,' I said. 'Wouldn't you?'

'I don't know,' she said again. 'I just don't know. It could be something bad.'

'How bad could it be?'

'*Please,* Stevie. Stay.'

She was pressing my hand to her chest now, my thumb against her clavicle. Her eyes filled my vision. I didn't know what to say. I was still fractured, set adrift by the loss of Callie. But with Inese in front of me, her loss didn't seem so definite. Those were almost her eyes. This was almost her hand, in mine. On stage at the Apollo, she'd angered me because she'd been so close, almost Callie, almost magical. I'd never imagined Callie's death, but if I had, I would have imagined an aching hole in the world – not some silent black absence, but a hole like a rip in the side of an aircraft, the air getting pulled from the cabin. This wasn't that. This wasn't like she had vanished, but like she had only grown faint, almost see-through, and Inese was promising to breathe her back to life, blowing gently on the flame.

I would never not know that she was gone, even if now and then I could forget. I'd lost her. But maybe the rest of the world didn't have to.

'I have—' She clutched my hand tighter as I started to speak. 'I have a job. A boyfriend.'

'I know,' she said.

'I have to go at some point. I can't—'

'I know that. But you can stay for a while, can't you? You could just stay for a while. While you read the diaries. You don't have to read them all at once. There's lots of them. They're long, you know. You can stay for a while.'

I put my other hand over Inese's, lowered it slowly. She looked near tears, the furthest her calm had come to cracking. I nodded.

'Yes?' she said quietly.

'A little while.'

'Thank you,' she said. 'Thank you.'

'I don't know how long. I'm not promising anything.'

She nodded. Her lip quivered, and there was a queasy feeling in my stomach as I saw her turn away to wipe her eyes.

'Inese,' I said. 'You want to be here, don't you? You want to be doing this?'

She nodded, rubbing her eyes with the back of her hand. 'Of course,' she said. 'There isn't anywhere else I want to be. This matters.' I believed her, despite the tears. 'I like it when you say that,' she said.

'Say what?'

'My name.'

That was what she needed me for, really. She wanted someone to know her name.

Want Me Want Me (2018)

Mel's new girlfriend is six foot one with tattoo sleeves up both arms, and she is outrageously hot. Mel doesn't often date outrageously hot women, or masc women, or women who are taller than her and more confident in conversation. Maybe this is what she's been missing, she tells me, sat against the bathroom door with her beer held between her knees, watching me piss. Maybe she's been dating all the wrong sorts of women and this radical change is perfect for her.

'Maybe,' I say, pissing. She crawls on her hands and knees over to me and kneels up to tip the last of her beer down my throat.

'It's just been shit out here,' she says, setting the empty bottle on the tiles. I flush, wriggle my jeans back up over my hips. I've had these jeans since I was eighteen and they no longer fit like they used to. 'Finding someone is shit.' She still hasn't got up off her hands and knees.

'How drunk are you?'

She shrugs. She has to pull her neck in to do so, like a turtle going back into its shell.

'Do you need to throw up?'

She kneels over the toilet bowl and lets me hold her hair back. We are both twenty-three, her as of six months ago, me as of two. Four or five years ago, throwing up was messy and night-ending. Now we manage it as calmly as tying our hair back. I listen to her gag, over and over, until her stomach is empty.

'Shit,' she says, sitting up. 'Is my make-up ruined?' I help her touch up the mascara that has collected under her eyes. She dabs the sweat from her face with the hand towel. 'She's going to think I'm a disaster,' she says. From outside the door comes her girlfriend's loud laugh. 'I should never have brought her.'

'She's having fun.'

'She always has fun,' says Mel. 'God, Stevie, she's such a good one. It's so hard to find a good one. You know?'

'I know.'

'You don't know. You haven't dated women in ages.'

'Of course I know. Men are trash.'

'Yes,' she says, rolling her eyes, touching up her concealer in the mirror, 'obviously, but everyone knows that. They can't surprise you. Women are trash too, that's what they don't tell you. But they're trash in this really manipulative, emotionally intelligent way. They're shitty in a way where you can't even be mad at them or you're the arsehole.'

'I think you're projecting.'

'You and Callie weren't exempt,' says Mel. She sheathes the concealer wand. 'You forget. Because you were fucking besotted. It wasn't all sunshine and rainbows there.'

I don't reply to this. Truthfully, I'm disbelieving. All my memories of Callie are good. She smirks at me in the mirror, and I realise how sulky I look.

'Sorry. Not trying to shit on it. I know how upset you get.'

'I don't get upset.'

'It's fine, it's great,' she says soothingly, coming over to me to stroke my hair. Her breath reeks. I should tell her, before she embarrasses herself in front of her outrageously hot girlfriend, but I stay quiet. 'Because now you have lovely Jeremy.'

Jeremy and I have only been seeing each other for a few weeks. We met on a dating app, a story I swore would never be mine. Callie and I used to make fun of dating apps. We would always say that if you couldn't meet someone in real life, magically, in an honest, fateful moment, then what was the point? We'd rather be single forever, we said smugly, from the safety of our shared bed.

Two years after our break-up, and I would rather not be single forever.

Jeremy was my first dating app date, which Mel says is ridiculously lucky. I've never dated a man before, not unless you count the handful of half-hearted Starbucks and sixth-form common-room dates I went on with boys from school, and truthfully 'handful' would be a generous term. Jeremy is twenty-four and has a good job at a start-up doing something I don't really understand even though he's explained it to me several times. He is saving for a flat deposit and he can make his own pesto. He is kind, and funny, and safe. He is much better than being single forever.

He's somewhere at this party for Mel's brother's flatmate, talking with the strange handful of people assembled in this tiny East London living room, likely wondering where I am. I move towards the bathroom door, unlock it.

'Lovely Jeremy,' says Mel. 'Thank god Callie dumped you. See? These things always work out.'

I fling the door open and leave her prodding at the corners of her eyes with her liquid eyeliner. When I rejoin the party, Jeremy puts a sweatered arm around my shoulders and says, 'Where were you? You've been ages.'

'Sorry,' I say. 'Mel's a mess.' I say it loud enough for her outrageously hot girlfriend to hear. All six foot one of her sidles out of the room to go look for Mel, and I smile up at Jeremy. 'Get me drunk.'

He laughs. 'Whoa, okay. This is a new side of you.' He says it like I've asked for directions to a swingers' party and three tonnes of crack. He pours me a whisky.

I drink it, and then I drink another. My stomach curdles, like my organs are shrinking away from it, but I keep dousing them. Mel comes up to me, looking a lot more sober, and gushes about how tender her new girlfriend is being with her, how sweet. Then she looks in my eyes.

'Uh-oh. Maybe it's your turn for a tactical.'

'Leave me alone,' I say.

'If this is about the Callie comments then you're being a baby,' she says, but she leaves me alone.

Just past midnight, someone puts on some music I don't recognise. But it stops me in my tracks, because that is definitely her voice over that energetic pop beat. I hurry over to the cheap red speaker and pick it up, staring at it like it can give me answers.

The album is out.

Mel is on the other side of the table. She wrinkles her nose. 'Pretty overproduced,' she says.

'It's so new for her,' says someone else.

'Hey, dickheads,' says Mel's older brother Jack, who I have always liked. He leans over the table to turn the speaker off. 'You guys are so dense. You know that's Stevie's ex, right?'

Disbelieving faces turn towards me. Someone laughs.

'She is,' I say petulantly, which is how I always sound when I have to defend my history with Callie. Jeremy is suddenly beside me, rubbing my arm soothingly.

'Damn,' says one of Jack's friends. Most of them still don't believe it.

I tell Jeremy that I'm going to the toilet. On my way out of the room, I grab the whisky bottle. No one notices. I carry it with me upstairs to Jack's bedroom and sit on the floor, my back against the door, wanting to cry. How had I managed to forget that tonight was the release?

Her social media pages are full editorial, the kind of effortless cool it surely takes the effort of an entire team to achieve. She's posted something a few minutes ago, from what must be her album release party. Her hair is down and she's grown it very long, so that it tickles her midriff as she spins. She has glitter all over her eyelids. She and a group of girls that look like models are jumping around and screaming the lyrics to Want Me Want Me*'s lead single. She looks wild with excitement. I take another sip of whisky, and then another. I wonder if she's even thinking about me at all.*

If I called, would she answer?

I find her contact. I hold the phone to my cheek. I'm starting to feel sick, so I pitch forward and curl up on the carpet, next to a brown stain. The phone rings and rings. Nothing. I don't want to leave a voicemail for her to have forever and listen to with all her beautiful new friends. I call again. Finally, the ringing stops.

'Stevie?'

The party is loud in the background. I swallow back bile.

'Hey.'

'Hey!'

A pause. She laughs.

'You okay?'

'I just wanted to say congratulations,' I rasp.

'That's so nice, Stevie, thanks.' I nod. 'Are you still there?' she asks.

'Yes.'

'Are you okay?'

'I just wanted to congratulate you.'

'Yeah, you did already.' The party noise dies. She's taken herself somewhere quiet to talk – in my whisky-soaked mind, this is a good sign. 'Where are you? Is there someone with you?'

'You're with me,' I say.

She laughs, a little uncertain now. 'Well, yeah, I guess. Kind of. I'm at a party right now, though, for the album, so I probably can't be long.' Another pause. 'It was so nice of you to call, though. I really appreciate you reaching out.'

'You're using a different voice,' I say.

'What?'

'Your voice. It's not your real voice.'

'I don't know what you're talking about. Listen, I have to go.'

'It's, like, this press voice. You're like this press person who does press. You're not even like a real person anymore.'

'Wow,' she says. 'Nice, Stevie, thanks.'

'You went so far away. I don't understand how you went so far away.'

She's quiet. Somewhere beyond where she currently stands, the muffled noise of the party continues.

'It's supposed to be like this,' she says.

'Not for me.'

'It's not about you.'

'Why not? It used to be.'

'I know,' she says gently, 'but things are different now.'

'Because you're Calista.'

'Because I'm Callie, and you're Stevie, and we are two people on different paths.'

I just about manage to hold myself back from saying that I don't want to be on a different path, that I would have walked her path forever, if she'd let me. I would have followed her into this world and, decades later, out the other side of it. I loved her before I loved Calista, and I would have loved her long after. I will never understand why she stopped loving me back.

'Listen, you should call someone else,' she says. 'Don't be on your own. I'm sorry you're having a hard night. I really have to get back, though. I hope you understand.'

'I don't understand,' I croak.

'I know, Stevie,' she says. 'I'm sorry.'

She hangs up. I call back, but she doesn't pick up. The brown stain on the carpet seems to have moved closer to my nose. Some far more sensible facet of myself has stepped out of my body and is now staring down on me, curled up on Mel's brother's carpet hugging a nearly empty whisky bottle to my chest. She is tutting and sighing. However big a part of me she is, she wasn't strong enough tonight.

There are footsteps on the stairs. Probably Mel, possibly Jack coming up here to hook up with the female co-worker he fancies. I panic, sitting up and shuffling away from the door.

'Stevie?' says someone, pushing it open. It's Jeremy, lovely Jeremy. He takes in the sight of me, phone in one hand, bottle in the other. Tear-stained. 'Oh dear,' he says, with a small smile.

'You're not meant to be up here.'

'Neither are you, I don't think. What are you doing?' I place my phone down on the carpet and start to bite my nails. 'Did you call her?' he asks.

'Who?'

'You know who.' He sits down beside me, making a little 'oomph' sound that ages him.

'How did you know?' I ask.

'Just a hunch.' I offer him the whisky bottle. He shakes his head. 'I wanted to ask you something,' he says.

'Okay.'

'Are you still in love with her?'

'It's been two years.'

'That's not an answer.' He nudges me. 'It's okay if you are.'

'How can it be okay? I'm dating you.'

'I know, but it's early with us. We've got time to fall for each other. If you're still healing from something, that's okay. I can wait.'

He is astonishingly nice. I'm not sure that I've noticed him being this nice before. But I also feel a degree of pity for him. Is it not a little pathetic, waiting around hopefully for someone to love you?

'You don't have to decide right now,' he says. 'But if you want to give this a proper go, then I'd like that too. I really like you, Stevie. And I think if you just give yourself permission to move on from her, then you might be surprised how easy you find it.'

I look up into his confident, smiling face. There is red stubble on his chin. His eyes are a bright blue. He looks like a friendly fisherman who has just pulled me from choppy waters. Don't worry, *his eyes say,* you'll warm up in no time. Let me put this blanket around you. Let me hold your hand. It's all going to be okay.

'Do you really think so?' I ask.

'I really think so,' he says.

We will break up six months later.

Chapter Five

Inese couldn't cook, but she liked to arrange things on toast. She made all kinds of things that way. Elaborate breakfasts of packaged smoked salmon, capers, olives, lemon rind, cream cheese. Melted chocolate and summer fruits. Expensive tapenade and smoked meats. Sometimes she would heat marshmallows in the microwave and smear them on to her toast, then make pictures on top out of chocolate chips. A butterfly, or a musical note, or a smiley face. Once, a ghost. She gave it to me, grinning, and didn't seem to mind that she found it a lot funnier than I did.

I had still never seen her do a grocery shop, but I was beginning to understand how things worked. The day after we watched *Burlesque* together, I came downstairs to find her working on a long shopping list, writing in pencil on a blank sheet of A4. 'Oh no,' she said, when she noticed me. 'You can't be down here.'

'Why not?'

'Charlie is coming. You'll have to go upstairs.'

I peeked through the curtains of my room and watched Charlie arrive with three men I didn't recognise. Inese greeted them at the front door. A few minutes later, one of the men left, folding Inese's list up on the way to his black car. I listened at the door but couldn't hear them all the way down in the living room. Instead, I waited on my bed until I heard the engine of the car again. The third man parked up and began to carry several enormous shopping bags towards the house, which he had to do in several trips.

The men seemed to be there to stay now, so I opened the next diary. It began where the other one had left off, the early days of her relationship with Bruno, who sounded like a bit of a sleaze. Callie was more impressed than she should have been by the way he put his card down everywhere he went without checking the price – I was disappointed in her. *It's nice to be treated like this,* she wrote, a sentence that made my stomach squeeze. They'd been together about six months, and she'd fallen hard. *It doesn't feel like it did with Stevie. I read those entries back and they're so pure, and so earnest, but I don't think love is really pure and earnest. First love, maybe, young love, but not adult love. Adult love is complicated and uncontrollable, especially in our world.* Our world, a world that I wasn't part of. She seemed to have forgotten loving me so hard it made her sick. It was like she'd been hit over the head. But it was easy to see how this relationship had given birth to *Loser.* There were sentences that had been turned into lyrics almost word for word. She did seem like a loser in these pages, trotting happily after him, blinking up at him from under heavy lashes, so distraught when they fought but then crossing half an entry out afterwards, explaining away his poor behaviour. I did my best to decode the words underneath her thick scribbling. My love for her had been so wholesome – how could she have preferred this man who dismissed her, who barely seemed to understand who she was?

The biggest surprise was that she and her mum had reconnected briefly during this time. There were a few mentions of them exchanging messages, and then this entry in October:

8/10/16

I'm stupid. Thought that going home for Mum's fortieth might be the start of something better. Obviously bringing Bruno was a mistake – musician boyfriend with no filter and an earring, strike one. But the whole thing was an ambush anyway. Mum might have been softer if Dad hadn't been there. I guess it doesn't matter in the end. They think that coming back to them means coming back to the church. Trying to bring me back is their version of loving me. I tried to explain this to Bruno.

'Fuck that,' he said. 'You're your own person.'

He's right. I am my own person. No one knows me like I do.

I bought Mum a Louis Vuitton purse. I know she's always secretly wanted one. She'll never be allowed to use it, of course, but I thought it might be nice for her to know that I tried to give her one all the same.

I realised that Inese was calling my name. The driveway was empty – I'd been so engrossed that I hadn't heard them leave. She was waiting for me in the living room in a red jumper and brown corduroy jeans. I was beginning to notice that while she wore Callie's clothes, she didn't wear them exactly as Callie would have. The rolled cuffs on the jeans and the low ponytail in her hair were small tells. I had started to make a mental note of all of these things, so that when she asked for advice I would be ready to give it. Against my better judgement, I was beginning to feel a little fond of her, and her toast creations, and the way she was all nervous excitement whenever I walked into the room. I still thought of her as an imposter wearing Callie's skin, but there were times when she was just Inese, in borrowed clothes, waiting impatiently for me to sit and hear her news.

'You look excited,' I said, sitting down beside her.

'I am. I'm ready to get out of this house.'

'They're taking you public already?'

'No, no,' she said. 'I'd be much more afraid of that.' She tightened her ponytail. 'We're filming the first promo soon. Just a teaser, to go out on her social media channels.' This was something that Callie liked to do, just drop a few seconds of the visuals and watch fans start to guess.

'Did they tell you much more about it?'

'They have a whole folder,' she said.

Despite myself, despite everything, I was excited. It hurt to feel. It was wrong to be excited about anything, especially art that would be released disingenuously, under Callie's name. 'Can I see it?' I asked, as lightly as I could.

'Charlie took it with him. But it's all there, in her handwriting. She always worked on paper.'

'I know,' I said.

'Right. She's planned the whole thing. The concept is that she's resurrecting her shiny pop persona from *Want Me Want Me,* except it's slightly off. Slightly wrong – zombie-ish almost. The music is going to be a little unsettling but in a way that makes you want to dance.'

I couldn't help myself. 'That's amazing.'

'Isn't it?' she said, delighted. 'It's called *Haunt Me Haunt Me.* She's parodying herself. It's genius. People are going to lose their minds.'

I could see the vision immediately. It was alarming how good it felt to be in on the very first stages of a Calista project, to know things that no one else knew. It hadn't felt like this in the early days. I'd always been excited by everything she did, of course, but it was different to feel there was a whole world outside leaning in, trying to catch Inese's words.

'What's the promo?'

'It's just a picture. It sounds cool. Then we're doing this video teaser in a couple of weeks. There's going to be these men, digging into a grave. When they open the lid of the coffin, there she is, in all her sparkly *Want Me Want Me* stuff, only she looks wrong. Like, a bit scary. They all rear back. They're spooked. She looks into the camera and she winks.'

'Oh my *god*. The internet is going to freak.'

'Except, it won't be her,' said Inese, and her expression became neutral again.

That brought me down to earth. She intertwined her hands, a crease appearing between her eyebrows.

'Do you think you can do it?' I asked.

She shrugged. 'Maybe not.'

'Isn't this what you've trained for?'

'It is,' she said. 'But maybe the training isn't enough. I don't know. I suppose we'll just have to see.' The words were calm, but her face was twisted, and her hands were trembling like they had been the first day I'd arrived.

Inese talked about the diaries like they were her favourite series of novels. Over the next couple of days, as I slowly worked through them, she would come up to my room and grill me for my thoughts, elated. *I loved that part! That bit is so sad. Did you see that coming?*

Some of it I didn't see coming. There was a final attempt to reach out to her mum, just before her and Bruno broke up for good. Callie's relationship with her parents made me and my dad look like leads in a heartwarming 1980s sitcom. Selfishly it made me feel a little better that it had all gone to shit again and I hadn't been the only reason Callie never went home for the holidays. She'd also briefly dated another girl, a model called Fi that I had never known about, for six months in-between *Want Me Want Me* and *Dry Ice.* These surprises stung sometimes, but for the most part, now that I wasn't in them anymore, the diaries were wonderful. She made biting observations about people in the industry – *Sex toys seem to be the new trendy business to go into but I wouldn't trust such a miserable woman to design a good vibrator,* she wrote of an American pop star I'd never much liked – and offered a magical insight into her creative process.

People thought Want Me Want Me *was too commercial,* she wrote in late 2019, *like I was just trying to get radio play and not actually giving them artistry, because god forbid pop and artistry might go hand in hand. So, my vision for* Dry Ice: *self-aware commercial pop that mocks its own self-awareness. Over-the-top showmanship. I'll be almost this camp figure, this ridiculous magician's assistant in a sparkly dress and a top hat. Can that be done how I envision it? I don't know, but either way I think it'll appeal to them. Or they'll hate it, but at least it'll be polarising enough that they'll have to admit I've done something other than try to appeal.*

This was one of her more energetic entries in 2019. Mostly they came slower. She'd got her diagnosis at the start of the year and was terrified at the prospect of having to sacrifice her productivity for her health.

I feel like I have so much energy and at the same time none at all, she wrote. *Or, I suppose, far too much creative energy and not enough physical energy to actually see it through. My body hurts after dancing, even if I don't dance for that long. I haven't told anyone yet, but the other day I took a shower and a whole clump of hair came out as I was washing it. Luckily it was underneath, near my neck, so I can cover it, but I hadn't even considered that I might lose my hair.*

It's such a strange thing, she wrote a couple of weeks later, *to feel completely healthy for weeks at a time, and then suddenly be so heavy that I hardly want to move. How can I have a career like this? Sometimes I don't really care what happens to me, but I want Calista to live. She's like my sister, or maybe more my daughter. Some wonderful, unreal being that I'm responsible for and that I want to take good care of. The world loves her. With her, I'm making art that I truly love. I don't want to lose her forever.*

When I hit February 2020, I held my breath, but she didn't write about Carnaby Street. She skipped over the month altogether, and picked up the book in March, in lockdown, when she wrote about feeling lonely. I wanted to scream.

◆ ◆ ◆

'I wish you could come with me to the shoot,' said Inese over dinner, a couple of nights after Charlie's visit.

When her hair was tied back, she was noticeably younger than Callie. It wasn't hard to imagine why Charlie might have become protective of her.

'Why?' I asked.

'For support.'

'Yes, but why me? You don't know me.'

'I just want you there,' she said. 'You feel safe.'

She wasn't doing Callie's voice, but she sounded a little like her all the same. I had begun to notice that she slipped into aspects of Callie sometimes without seeming to know that she was doing it, and I couldn't work out if this was because the two of them were naturally similar or because she was becoming so absorbed in her character that the lines between them were starting to blur.

My reading of the diaries had started to slow. I still needed to absorb them, craved that insight into Callie's mind, but I had begun to dread the moment that I closed the final book and knew that there was nothing else. Equally, the moment when there would be no excuse to linger in her house anymore, surrounded by her things, getting to look behind the curtain that divided her from Calista. There were plenty of reasons I should have been in a hurry to leave – work, for one. My boss, Kiera, had messaged me several times to ask why I wasn't in the office, then why I wasn't online at all. I thought about going back to the flat to get my laptop, but I couldn't face it. I knew that Rich had probably been practising how he would play it when I walked back through the door: he would be compassionate, sympathetic – a modern man who understood that mental health was complex, a radically empathetic partner who would stay and work through this with me, just so long as I could accept that everything was entirely my fault and I was crazy. I could hear the performative tone of his voice. I couldn't go back yet, not until I had everything straight in my head.

I messaged Kiera back and told her that I needed to take compassionate leave.

I don't mean to be insensitive, she wrote back, *but I don't think this situation meets the criteria for compassionate leave.* About an hour later she told me that she was setting up a mental health screening with HR and that they could possibly grant me a leave of absence if I was able to get a note from a medical professional validating my inability to work. I told her that I would, knowing full well that I wouldn't. Losing my job wouldn't be the worst thing in the world, I thought. I could take a month off and then find something else inane to write copy about. People said the job market was tough just then, but people were always saying that. I could stack shelves or clean carpets for a while maybe. It didn't matter. Very little outside of the Hampstead house mattered just then.

If Inese noticed that I wasn't making progress with the diaries as fast as I had been, she didn't say anything about it. She made me things on toast. She asked me, half shy, to watch movies with her. One morning, she told me that Callie had granola, in the voice of someone imparting important information. I went into the pantry and stared up at a box of orange and cranberry granola.

'She said you liked it,' Inese told me.

'She did?'

'She made me a bowl of it once, when I was here learning a song, but I didn't like it. So much cinnamon.' She wrinkled her nose. 'She said, "My ex – she was the only other person I've ever met who liked this stuff."'

'How did you know she was talking about me and not Fi?'

'Fi,' Inese said, wrinkling her nose again. 'Fi was nothing.'

If Callie's diaries were Inese's favourite novels, then I was her favourite character. It was a nice thing to feel. No one had been that interested in me in a very long time.

'Maybe I could,' I said now. 'Come with you.'

She looked across, her eyes wide. 'Really?'

'Callie used to bring me to this kind of stuff, sometimes. If you asked them to let me in I'm sure they would.'

'They can't know that you know.'

'So don't tell them I know. I mean, they've already reintroduced us. Maybe we're just reconnecting, Callie and I. The album's about resurrection, isn't it?'

She laughed, her hands settling. I found myself smiling.

'Okay,' she said. 'Thank you, Stevie.'

When the day came around, about a week after Charlie's visit, I found that I didn't actually feel so enthusiastic at the idea of leaving our little bubble. We had been getting on quite well together. I had mostly kept my phone off and any texts or missed calls I did see didn't quite seem to reach me, as if Mel and Rich were shouting through a window into a soundproofed room. Anxieties about my job status – *This is getting quite serious, Stevie, I need a response from you,* wrote Kiera – were just background noise. The grief couldn't tackle me sideways anymore either. Sometimes it did reach out for me, especially late at night after I'd read a few paragraphs of her writing and set the book down knowing that the story had an end, but she was also wonderfully present in this house. She didn't follow me around like heavy cloud but peeked cheekily at me around corners or beamed down on me in the back garden. My dreams were full of her. She had drawn a map for me, and here I was, following it. There was nothing dead in that. It was all life, all possibility.

Of course, I couldn't know what would happen when I walked into that studio and saw Inese pretending to be her. The grief might worm its way through the illusion, run me down, get its staining hands all over me again. I almost told her that I wouldn't go, but when I found her in the living room, sitting on the sofa with her hands twisting in her lap, she looked up at me like I was the only thing around her that remained on solid ground, and I found that the words just wouldn't come.

She sent me out of the house before they came to get her. 'You'll have to meet us there,' she said. 'I don't know what they'd think if they found you here.'

So, I got dressed in the last clean clothes that I had brought with me, and I turned my phone back on, ignoring the choir of buzzes that followed. I'd sent Inese to the kitchen to eat something, despite her churning stomach, and when I walked in I saw that she'd made herself toast with peanut butter and slices of pear, small half-hazelnuts positioned in-between. She paused mid-bite when she saw me.

'I'll see you there,' she said, as Callie. My spine prickling, I closed the door behind me.

I walked some distance away from the Hampstead house down the street and called an Uber to the Tube station. The driver wasn't feeling talkative, which I was grateful for. Callie always used to complain about the unfriendliness of London. She wished people would open up on public transport, share their life stories. At the time I nodded along with her, but I have never wanted London to be less anonymous. It is a city in which no one bothers each other, in which we all just let each other be.

Something strange was happening on public transport that day though. For every three or four people that ignored me entirely, one raised their head. One kept their eyes on me longer than the rest. I saw a young girl shooting glances at me the entire way to Leicester Square. After that, on the Piccadilly line, a woman in her thirties nudged her friend, whispered something. The friend stared in my direction.

At Gloucester Road, a woman turned to me at the ticket barriers and said, apropos of nothing, 'I think it's *so nice* that the two of you are reconnecting.'

'Thanks,' I said. She smiled and passed through. It was extraordinary. Suddenly people remembered me. I had never been with Callie at this level of fame. I had been approached a handful of times in the run-up to *Calista,* but mostly outside concert venues. Now I was known, and known in the best way – not by everyone, but by the people who truly adored her.

On the street, I texted Inese.

How's it going?

Just in the car, she sent back. *Give me twenty minutes.*

People are recognising me from the photos, I told her.

Good, she said. *Gene will be happy.* I didn't care about Gene, but I did wonder if Inese was happy.

I went and sat in a local café over the road, where no one gave me a second look, and drank a mocha. When Inese messaged to give me the go-ahead, I crossed the street. She'd sent someone outside to get me – a relatively young blonde girl with crooked teeth.

'Stevie?' she asked.

'That's me.'

'Amazing. She's expecting you.'

She led me inside. I wondered if, to this assistant, 'she' was Inese or Calista. How many people on this set today actually knew who they were working for? I wondered if any of them would guess, over time, whether they would go to the papers or ask for a payout, or just hold their tongues and carry on.

'Do you work for her?' I asked, as the girl held the door for me. 'Or for the label?'

'No, I'm her assistant. Just took over from the last girl, although I've been on Gene's team for a while now.'

'What happened to the last girl?'

'Oh,' she said, gesturing down the corridor, 'there's been quite a few personnel changes lately. I suppose it makes sense, what with the trauma she's been through.'

'Yes,' I said. 'I suppose it does.'

Inese waved to me as I entered the studio, and I felt a rush of affection for her.

'You're here!' she said. She was Callie again. It was strange to see, after spending so much time around her when she was out of character. She had so much talent, to be able to enact the change in the way that she did. There was still something distasteful in it, but I couldn't help being fascinated by it as well. It was the first time I felt an intense interest in who Inese was as a person and not just her role in Calista's story. Perhaps she had grown up doing impressions, putting on different voices, making her classmates laugh. She might have spent hours poring over her laptop and her phone, listening and repeating, practising facial expressions in the mirror. I wondered when she had first been told that she looked like Calista. Callie had achieved far-reaching international fame at about twenty-three. Inese would have been nineteen. She might have practised doing her hair like Calista's in the 'Want Me Want Me' music video, saved up for a gold halter-neck dress. According to her own timeline, she'd been recruited by Callie's team the very next year. Such a sudden swerve from her own path into Callie's. Beautiful, if she was to be believed, fateful, but violent all the same.

I gave her a hug. There was no small wink or secret smile when I pulled away – she was fully absorbed in her role, like Inese wasn't even in there anymore. I could feel that everyone in the room was looking at us. She stood up on her toes and kissed me briefly on the lips, like we did it all the time. I was too stunned to do anything except let her take my hand and lead me over to the make-up area.

'I have to get beautified,' she said. In the background, against the opposite wall, they were setting up a giant green screen. There was no sign of Harma or Gene Parrison, but Charlie was there, in a green shirt with a neatly ironed collar. He was pacing back and forth, pretending not to look in our direction.

We didn't talk while she was getting her make-up and hair done. I sat on my phone as she made polite conversation with the team. It seemed that the glam team had recently been replaced as well. Which of them knew what was really going on? Which of them had guessed? The only person whose mind I had any insight into was Charlie's, not that I could speak to him about it all. He caught me looking and continued to ignore me, sat on the other side of the room in a folding chair, his phone in his hands.

After a while, the blonde assistant approached to ask if Inese wanted anything to eat or drink – they had a craft services table set up, or she could run out and grab something.

'I could murder a burrito,' she said, exactly as Callie would have, 'but I can wait until after. I'd love a coffee, though, Mandy, if you could.'

'Local is probably safer than craft services for that,' said the girl apologetically. 'I'll step out and find some.'

I asked her to let me do it instead – the whole atmosphere was nerve-wracking and I wanted a breather. I couldn't imagine how Inese was feeling. When I returned, a coffee cup in either hand, her hair and make-up was done and she was standing over an iPad with the shoot director, having something explained to her. I passed her the cup and she kissed me on the cheek. Her curls against my skin made me shiver. When I pulled back, I saw in the edge of my vision that Charlie was watching us.

I sat back down on my chair for a while and waited until she emerged from Wardrobe. She ran over to me and took my hand, leading me to the other side of the room.

'Look,' she said, placing herself in front of the green screen and getting me to step back a few paces. She was wearing that gold halter-neck dress, but the hem was fraying and the stitching on it was strange and jaunty. Her make-up was smudged, her hair half undone. 'So, the idea is that I'm standing in this nightclub, but I'm kind of not quite in the picture. Like, I look wrong. And when you look closely, the club behind me looks wrong. No one's having fun. And one person's noticed me, in the corner, and they look absolutely horrified. White as a sheet.'

'Because you're a ghost,' I said.

She laughed. Callie's laugh. 'Or a zombie, or an apparition, or a hallucination, or whatever else. It's cool, right?'

'It's so cool,' I said. 'Honestly. It's going to be such a moment.'

She beamed. The photographer raised his camera again, and I went to stand at the back of the room. Someone beside me coughed, and I turned to see that it was Charlie. He gave me a brief nod, without bothering to look in my direction.

'Hi,' I said.

He lifted his eyebrows and said nothing.

We stood side by side in silence and watched her, standing very still with her shoulders slightly hunched. She could look very intense when she tried, but the problem was that when she did, she looked far less like Callie and far more like Inese. Between shots, when taking notes from the photographer and shoot director, she played her part to perfection, but she had no model for this cold, slightly creepy version of Calista.

'It's very different for her,' I said lightly.

Charlie looked at me with nothing behind his eyes and for a brief moment it felt as if he were considering whether or not to have me shot. 'Very,' he said after a few seconds. My breathing resumed. 'What do you think of it?'

'I like it. I think it's a great move.'

He didn't say anything. He kept his eyes on me.

'I don't think we ever met, back in the day,' I said. 'When did you start working for her?'

'I don't work for her,' he said, 'really. I work for her team.'

'Don't her team work for her?'

'It's complicated. Boring industry stuff.' He said it with the vaguest attempt at levity, as if to show that he was capable of being polite with someone a little more worthy of the effort.

'Huh,' I said. He was standing with his feet shoulder-width apart, hands clasped in front of him, like he was in formation. His aloofness was maddening. Just then, it felt as if he'd killed her with his own hands. 'What's your role exactly?'

'I'm a consultant.'

'A consultant on what?'

He smiled tightly. 'A few different things. More boring industry stuff.'

I took a sip of my coffee. It was still too hot. 'Her team is so big now. I can't keep track of it.'

'Well, she's an important person now,' he said.

'She was always important.'

'To you, maybe,' he said, so casually that it didn't sound like a dig until he'd already walked away.

I left the shoot a little before the end, to give me time to travel back to the Hampstead house on the Tube before Inese was driven home. When I heard the car rolling in, for a second my legs wanted to carry me downstairs and out of the door, to pick her up in the driveway and spin her round and tell her how well she'd done. The feeling passed, and I spent a few seconds trying to understand it. When I was sure no one had come into the house with her, I went downstairs. She was peeling her coat off. Her energy was flat.

'What's wrong?' I asked from the third step.

'I'm tired.' I watched her hook her coat up slowly, with both hands. When I didn't speak, she turned towards me. 'How was I?'

'Good. Really good. I thought you knew that.'

She shook her head. 'No one ever tells me.'

'You did great.' I regretted the words, even though she brightened at them. They felt like a betrayal.

'It's hard to know,' she said. 'This project is so new. I don't know how to be a version of her that's never been.'

'It's better this way. People won't notice the differences so much.'

She turned towards me, horrified. 'The differences?'

'Small differences.' She was still wearing her make-up – glittery eyelids, but hollowed cheeks. 'Hardly anyone would ever notice.'

'But you noticed.'

'I'm not anyone.'

'You,' she said. 'You who haven't seen her in years.'

She was still standing right by the door, leaning on the console table with one hand. I sat down on my step. I watched her turn towards the hallway mirror and take herself in. She pressed a finger into the glitter on her eyelid.

'Need to take this off,' she said.

I followed her up two flights of stairs to her bedroom, which spanned the entire top floor. I remembered it from the *Architectural Digest* tour as a warm, lemony yellow space with wood floors and a canopy bed, but it looked different now. The floor was carpeted lushly. So she'd still been lying on her back to write songs, right up until the end. There were plants everywhere, not tastefully dotted around the room, but piled in so densely it made the room feel like a garden shop. Fake ivy and strings of paper lanterns were spun across corners like spiderwebs. She had one wooden shelf above her bed, on to which was crowded a few photo albums and a collection of colourful notebooks. All her other books and magazines were dotted in piles around the room, in-between the plants, with no clear organisational system. The walls were covered in pictures, none of them framed or even particularly neatly displayed, but cut out from magazines or printed on paper and stuck to the paint with Blu Tack. Some of them were club scenes, women laughing in sparkly dresses, high-heeled shoes with the edge of a price in white text chopped off. Others were darker. Pale women. Women dancing frenetically. Witchy symbols and recipes for spells. Graveyards. Faces screaming.

Inese was in the bathroom, stood over the sink, scrubbing at her face. I walked around the room slowly, studying the things on the walls. She emerged, drying her face with an orange towel. 'Was this you?' I asked.

'No. Her.'

'It was like this when you got here?'

She nodded. 'She was working on visuals, I suppose.'

A spell to resurrect an old love, read one of the scraps, on the wall under her shelf. Callie had chopped off the rest of it. The title now sat above a picture of two hands clasped together in the dark. A big stage. Two girls, one with her head on the other's shoulder. I stood in front of the collage for some time. Inese rinsed her face again, then re-emerged with a pot of expensive moisturiser.

'You're using her products as well?'

'Until they run out,' she said. 'Then Charlie will probably get me more.'

'Charlie scares me.'

'He's a good man,' she said. 'He cares about me.'

'I think he knows I know.'

'It's okay if he does. You must just never say so. Don't open your mouth about it, and you and Charlie will get on fine.'

'What does he actually do? What's he in charge of?'

'Me,' she said. 'All things me. I think he used to be a spy, or whatever the real word is for spy.'

'He seems more like a soldier to me.'

'Well, something like that. Something secret and important. I think he's probably killed people before.' She sat down on the carpet, among the plants. I'd noticed as well that she did her make-up in a very particular way, to appear more like Callie. When she was barefaced you could definitely tell that she was younger. 'I think Charlie paid her parents off too,' she said.

'Jesus. So they know? You didn't tell me that.'

'They probably don't know for sure. He probably gave them money – *here you go, your daughter would like you to take this and never contact her again*. Great deal for them, since they don't contact her anyway.' She crossed one leg over the other. 'They'll still go to the press at some point, probably, but everyone will think they're just doing it for attention.'

'Doesn't that scare you?'

'A lot of it scares me,' she says. 'I have to not think about the scary stuff or I'll never be able to do it.'

She had wrapped one of Callie's cardigans around herself – she pulled it tighter.

'Is it just this project?' I asked.

She frowned. 'What do you mean?'

'Is it just this project they want you for?'

'I don't know,' she said.

'How long will it go on for?'

'As long as it can, I suppose. Until it's not worth it anymore.'

'And then what happens to you? Do you play her in retirement? Do you play her forever?'

She fiddled with the hem of the cardigan, her face impassive. She looked up, like I hadn't asked her anything. 'Did you ever meet them? Her parents?'

'No,' I said. I had moved to stand in front of a nightclub scene, a full magazine page. Callie had drawn strange dark figures into it in black biro, not obvious at first, but unsettling once you spotted them. 'They didn't want to meet me. I saw them from a distance once, though.' At the time I hadn't been sure it was them, but over the years I'd become certain. They'd been over the road from Brixton Academy, staring up at the sign that bore her name. Her mum had looked just like her.

She nodded. She'd tried to deflect my question, but it hadn't worked – it still hung there. Eventually she uncrossed her legs and said, 'It's one day at a time. That's what it is right now.'

'I'm going to go and do some reading.'

'How far through are you?'

'Not far.'

'Okay,' she said, relieved.

◆ ◆ ◆

In October of 2019, Callie met Inese.

They've done a remarkable job, she wrote. *It terrified me, to meet her – she seemed so pleased to be there. It's hard for me to recognise if she really does look exactly like me, because I don't think I have an accurate picture of what my own face does look like in my mind, and she's still recovering from surgery. I felt so guilty, when I saw the bruising on her face. But she's so honoured, she says. It all gives me such an eerie feeling, but I can't help but be grateful to her, even if I'm scared to trust Calista to her when it's just been the two of us in this bubble for so long. Me and my magical twin. I suppose we're sort of triplets now. I hope I'll learn to feel alright about it. I never was very good at sharing.*

She didn't write about Inese much, which was a surprise to me. Actually, over the next few years, the diaries became less about her career, less narrative driven altogether. She would spill her mind out on to the pages instead, hardly stopping to explain context or clarify who she was talking about. I saw a bit of Luke in there – she had liked him at first, and then less so, and then they became very casual, only seeing each other when they wanted to, not progressing the relationship forward. She seemed to pull away from her friends.

I prefer to be alone, she wrote, *these days. I want to throw myself into writing and nothing else. Maybe at some point I'll let Inese do all the performing for me, if she wants. God knows she'd be better at it than me, if she practised. But no one could be better than me at creating the things that I create. That's all I want to do now, just sit in a room with no windows and make things and hear the response from a distance.*

A few months later, she wrote, *No one can really understand who I am or what I've become. And it's not just feeling sick and feeling tired, and it's not burnout, no matter what they might think. It's the knowledge that everything I have now has to go towards Calista, and Callie is secondary. I'll save all my energy up for Calista, and when I'm Callie, I'll just be Callie in my own company. Maybe it'll drive me mad, to live like that, but I don't think so. I don't much want intimacy or to be known, not the way I used to. I think I'm very accustomed now to living with just myself.*

Just a few nights later she contradicted herself. *I'm so lonely it makes me sick, but I won't let myself do anything about it.*

Off and on for over a year, she hurt, and she healed, and she hurt, and she healed, but never, it seemed, by letting anyone get too close to her. I wondered what the real story was, if she'd been depressed, if something had happened that she couldn't bring herself to write about. Even now, when I was further inside her mind than I had ever been, it still wasn't enough. There were still parts of herself that she hid from me.

Inese passed my bedroom door later that evening, as I was folding my clothes from that day. 'Are you packing?' she asked, alarmed.

'No,' I said. 'Just putting things away in drawers.'

'Did you get to me yet?' she asked.

I nodded.

'And?'

'It's interesting.'

'I love how she writes about me,' she said, smiling to herself.

Charlie arrived with the first mock-up of Inese's images a few days later. He gave her ten minutes' notice – I ran with my French toast up to my room and freaked out when I realised that I'd left my fork on the table. Then there was a pattering of footsteps on the stairs, and I opened my door to find her standing there, holding it out, grinning nervously. I took it. The sound of a car engine had her racing back downstairs so fast I thought she was going to trip. I heard the door open and closed mine, quickly.

There were only two volumes left. I began the next, which became more career-focused again. Callie spoke less about her mental health and more about her day-to-day commitments. She detailed a lot of rehearsals with Inese. I could see why she'd been flattered by her portrayal – Callie wrote about Inese tenderly, admiring her dedication, worrying in a motherly sort of way whether it would one day all prove too much for her, but with plenty of faith in her all the same.

> *I've told her to tell me if she ever starts to hate it. She's a remarkable thing, that shapeshifter they've found. She must be far more talented than I am, to be able to do it at all. Sometimes I lie awake at night and worry about her, and sometimes I am so proud of her I want to cry. It's gratitude too, I suppose. She says she loves it. She says she wants it. I have to trust that, if I want Calista to carry on. And I do. Desperately.*

When I was able to join Inese downstairs again, she showed me the prints he had left, a few different variations of the image. They were incredible – she looked otherworldly, ringed slightly in white against a backdrop of moving bodies, one woman in the corner staring at her with a haunted expression. The woman had brown hair like mine and looked to be about my age and build. It couldn't have been deliberate, but part of me still wondered if it was.

'They're going up on social media on Friday,' she said.

'What's the caption?'

'None. We're just starting the speculation.' She gripped my hand, brought it under her chin, as she sat there staring down into her own eyes. 'I'm scared it just looks like me.'

I realised that I hadn't even been trying to see her as Callie. She was just Inese to me, in that picture. I looked again. 'It's convincing enough,' I said. 'And you're supposed to look slightly off. No one will question it.'

'Yes, but what about all the times in the future? When I'm not supposed to look slightly off? What then?'

She lifted her leg, placed her foot on the sofa, her knee level with her cheek. I touched her shoulder, cautiously. We never really came in physical contact with each other when we were alone. 'What's the point in worrying about that now? One day at a time, you said.'

'It's exhausting.'

'Well, I'm sure Callie was exhausted too.'

She shook me off. 'I'm fine, Stevie.'

I went to the kitchen to make lunch. Through the window, I watched her walk down the garden path to the music room at the end. She had the throw from the sofa wrapped around herself, the end of it trailing in the grass beside her bare feet. She closed the door to the music room. I strained my ears, but I couldn't hear her playing.

When the pasta was ready, I brought a bowl down to the bottom of the garden. From just outside the door I could hear gentle piano, a song I didn't recognise. She was singing too softly for me to make out any of the words. I pushed on the door. She turned, dropping her hands abruptly. I held out her bowl. We sat in silence, me against the wall, her on the piano stool, pushing her pasta around.

'What were you playing just now?' I asked.

'Oh,' she said, 'something of my own.'

'You write?'

She shrugged, more embarrassed than I'd seen her previously. 'Just a little.'

'Can I hear it?'

'I shouldn't even have been playing it.' She put her bowl on top of the piano and turned towards the keys. 'I could play you something of hers.'

'I actually watched one of your performances already,' I said. 'The Apollo.'

She paled. 'Really?'

'It was good.'

'No,' she said, 'I was awful that night. It wasn't right. It wasn't authentic. I was so terrified, afterwards, that everyone would know.'

'It made me angry.'

She dusted the keys with her sleeve, even though they were perfectly clean. 'Because I wasn't good.'

'You were very good. That's what made me angry. That song – you sang it like you had written it, and it made me angry because you didn't know any part of what me and Callie had been. It was like you were taking our thing and spoiling it.'

Her face didn't change. 'And now?' she asked. 'Do you still feel that I am spoiling it?' I couldn't reply. I didn't know. After a few seconds, she dropped my gaze and turned towards the piano once again. 'That song,' she said. 'I think I know the song you mean.'

She started to play. I'd never heard the song on piano before. The opening riff on guitar was so familiar to me – Callie had played it over and over when she'd first started writing the song, lying in the middle of our navy-blue rug, her feet under the coffee table, humming possible melodies. It sounded sadder on piano. Inese played it higher, gentler. But when she started to sing, I had to close my eyes and put my head on my knees to keep from crying.

'I'd do it all again, again, again.'

She was Callie. Callie in the early morning at the piano, her hair still messy from the night before, pressing bare feet on to the pedals. Callie singing into her desk mic, her headphones on, a crease between her eyebrows. Callie onstage at open mic nights, and Camden basements, and Brixton Academy, playing to her first few thousand fans. I listened in darkness, and I could feel her in the room with me, and in my mind I stood just offstage and watched a sea of lights sway back and forward. Callie stepped away from the piano and looked at me, beaming.

'Was I good?' she asked.

I opened my eyes. Inese had crossed her legs on the piano stool, her body turned towards me.

'Was I good?' she repeated, in her own voice this time.

Impossible to find the words to tell her that good or bad had nothing to do with it – this was magic and couldn't be so easily quantified.

The last of my anger disappeared as she watched me, hoping for an approving word. She was like an old photograph come to life. I knew then that in some strange, twisted way, this was a gift. As long as Inese lived, Callie lived. I would never have to lose her again.

Inese had actually started off doing impressions of Judy Garland, she told me. We lay on top of Callie's thick duvet in her canopy bed, staring up at the fake ivy and paper lanterns draped across her ceiling. She moved her hands above her as she talked, her nails still gold and sparkly. My eyes trailed after them. As a young girl, she had stood in front of the TV as her mum played *Wizard of Oz* and recited Judy Garland's lines along with her. She realised that she could make her singing voice sound like Judy's – or just a little higher – if she closed her eyes and really tried. 'Of course,' she said, 'my English wasn't very good, so the accent wasn't right.' When she was a little older, she pirated *Friends* and *Skins* and spent hours practising all the voices. She could switch between her English and American accents fluently and her grasp on the language grew very strong. She would do impressions at school of her friends, or the teachers, or people on the TV.

'It was fun,' she said. 'Everyone has hobbies. That was mine.'

She learnt to play guitar on her dad's old instrument and piano on the school piano that she would sneak into the music room to use. She told me this casually, but it impressed on me how extraordinarily bright she must be, to have taught herself everything she knew. After a couple of years of this, at the age of fourteen, she went to a bar in Riga and asked the owner if he would like her friend Judy Garland to play.

'He laughed at me,' she said, with a dismissive wave of her hand over our heads, 'of course. But then I pushed past him and sat down at the piano and began to play. Then I picked up my guitar and sung as Britney Spears, even though of course Britney Spears doesn't really play guitar. I did Madonna. Cher. Local celebrities too.'

'Could you really do impressions of all those people?'

'Not well. Passably. But, of course, it got some attention. I started to play at lots of different bars around the place. Some festivals. Then when I was eighteen I had a segment on this TV show, sort of a talk show, but I had a short entertainment section where I would do lots of different impressions. I still did Judy Garland and all the old favourites, but people really liked to see Calista, because she was so trendy, and because that was the one I was really good at.' Another dismissive motion of her hand. 'And then someone must have sent it to Charlie, because he just showed up.'

'They came to your house?'

'Oh, yes. Him and this other woman, Bo. I never see her anymore. They offered me all this money to go away with them.'

'Weren't you sceptical?'

'No. I jumped at the chance. My father was mean and my mother was the most ineffectual woman you'll ever meet. She knew he was a mean man, but she couldn't be bothered to leave him or turn him out. Can you imagine? Not even being bothered?' She kissed her teeth. 'I couldn't wait to go.'

'Do they know what you do?'

'No. Well, yes, probably. They will. At least, they'll recognise me. I think. I'd hope they would. Maybe it's better if they don't.' She was genuinely perplexed for a second. Then she grinned. 'Who knows what they think?'

'Do you think they might think you're . . .'

She caught my meaning. 'Dead?' she asked, in a very deep voice. 'No, because I send them money.'

'Oh, right. I remember.'

'Charlie sends it,' she said, 'really.'

'And they don't ask questions?'

'They're not allowed to. Those are the conditions of the money. When I left, Charlie gave them documents to sign, which means they have to be silent, I think, about anything they might know. Charlie takes care of that stuff.'

'And they're just okay with it? Letting you go like that?'

She giggled softly. 'I think of it like I'm a spy. But they get money, so they don't want me back. As long as they're getting money, they don't want me back.'

I rolled over on to my side to look at her. 'I'm sorry.'

'Don't be sorry,' she said. 'They get money. I got out. Don't be sorry.' Her face became very serious. 'It's a good thing to do,' she said. 'I would never stay like my mother. But she is who she is, and the money makes it easier. It's a good thing, to be able to make it easier. They'll always be fine now, both of them, with me doing this. That's something to be proud of, I guess.'

Her hands lowered, folding on top of her chest. Her hair was fanned out around her on the pillow like Ophelia in the water. Funny how to look at her from the side had always been unsettling, almost frightening, and this was the first time that it was quite nice, to look at her from an angle that revealed her and only her. Inese, who had grown up in a flat in Riga doing impressions of Judy Garland, whose talent and quick mind, along with some fluke in her genetics, had carried her all the way here, to London, to me.

'Don't you miss being yourself?'

'I never loved being myself,' she said. 'I never loved the person that I was.'

'Why not?'

She shrugged. Her hair moved under her shoulders. 'Some people don't. Sometimes you're just born not fitting right in your skin, I think, and there's not much you can do about it.' She was too young to have decided that, I thought, but I didn't say it. 'I'm very lucky, really,' she said, 'because it used to panic me, not being able to outrun myself. I used to think I might hurt myself – I used to think I might do something drastic—' She glanced over and laughed at my face. 'Really, Stevie,' she said. 'You don't have to worry. This is the best way to lose myself. This is the best job someone like me could have.'

'The surgery?' I asked. I wanted to go on asking her questions forever, hearing the musical way she answered, even when the words themselves weren't happy.

'Hurt,' she said. 'No, it wasn't too bad in the end.'

'You just . . . did what they asked?'

She touched the bridge of her nose. 'Mine was crooked,' she said, 'here. They said they'd pay to fix it. I thought, brilliant. I'd wanted it fixed for ages. Callie has a perfect nose. I wanted her nose. That felt like a present.'

'And then?'

'Fillers. Everyone wants fillers. She's got these really beautiful cheeks, and mine weren't so beautiful. Then my teeth – they realised that my teeth were a big problem, so that got added to the list. Mine were sort of yellow, so I really didn't mind that. And so—' She made a snowballing gesture, her wrist circling frantically.

'What else?'

'My brow. So that my brow line would be more like hers. Mine was lower.' I examined it. I tried to picture it differently.

'And your jaw.'

'My jaw.' The bruising was going down, but it was still swollen. 'That was tricky, because the idea was to make me look more like her by sharpening my jawline slightly and also to use the accident to explain why I didn't look exactly like her. They sent me in for it the day after she fell. I don't know how on earth they pulled everything together in time.' She traced her finger along it. 'There were other things, in-between. I forget some of them.'

'Didn't you ever miss looking like yourself?'

'People had been telling me I looked like her forever,' she said. 'But then they would squint and put their heads on the side and say, *Mm, no, not so much here. Not so much there.* It would always feel like they were telling me to fix things about myself. I always wanted to look more like her. Maybe it was weird, sometimes, but it was worth it.'

'You didn't ever worry about losing yourself?'

'That's what I'm trying to say to you. I spent my life trying to lose myself. That's the art of it. I like the idea of disappearing into someone else.' She pointed to the club scene on Callie's wall, the one that she had drawn the dark figures into. 'You see those? That's what I am. I'm a shadow person. And Calista, she was the opposite. I'm supposed to fade away and let her live through me.'

I was suddenly chilled. 'You're saying you'd let her overtake you like that?'

'If I get it right,' she said, her face peaceful, 'then one day it'll be as if I can hardly remember who Inese was at all.' I lifted one of her hands from her chest and held it in my own. She looked across at me, with a confused smile. 'You want her back,' she said.

'You play her very well, Inese. That's all it has to be.'

'That's all I'm describing,' she said.

We stayed looking at each other. She took her hand back and rolled on to her side, mirroring me. 'I think about things sometimes,' she said.

'What do you think about?'

'The body.'

I looked away from her. 'God, Inese.'

'How they got rid of it. What kind of people they must be, to be able to do that, and nobody knows. How many doctors they had to pay off. How they can really make sure that the doctors don't say anything. What would happen if people knew about me.'

She recited these things like they were an established list. 'Don't you talk to Charlie about all that?' I asked.

'No, Charlie wouldn't answer. They don't really like me to have questions anyway, Charlie and Gene – they just like me to show up and do my job.' She paused, her eyes to the ceiling, thinking something through. Perhaps she was figuring out how to phrase what she wanted to say exactly right in English. 'This is a very rare thing that I get to do,' she said. 'I have to be a certain level of grateful.'

I was watching her again. I couldn't look away for long. 'I wish you hadn't said that. About the body.'

'I'm sorry,' she said. She really did sound apologetic. 'These things just come into my mind. Let's distract ourselves. What about you?'

'Me?'

'Your family. How you grew up.'

'You know about me.'

'Only you after Callie. I don't know about you before.'

'Sometimes it feels like there isn't any before. Not really.'

She nodded. 'For me as well.'

'I grew up with my dad. My mum died when I was ten.'

'I'm sorry,' she said.

'Yeah, it was hard.'

'How?' she asked.

'How did she die?' Inese nodded. 'She had a stroke, and then she was sick for a bit and couldn't get out of bed much, and then a few months later she had another one, and that one killed her.'

'That's horrible,' said Inese.

'Yes.'

'You say it so—' She waved a hand. 'I suppose I'm the same, with what's happened to me.'

'I don't remember much about it.'

'How can you not remember?'

'I blocked it out, I think. Therapists say that can happen.'

'You've had therapists?'

'Of course.'

'I never,' she said. 'I always wanted one. They looked so nice and understanding in American movies. They offered me one, when I started doing this, but I would have had to lie in the sessions, so what's the point? No point doing therapy pretending to be someone else.'

'Probably not,' I agreed.

'You remember her, though?'

I shook my head.

'You do,' she persisted. 'You were old enough.'

'I try not to.'

'Why?'

'It's easier not to.'

'What do you remember?'

'Please leave it,' I said, hating the way it sounded.

'Don't you think it would be better—'

'No.'

She was quiet for a few seconds.

'How did your dad deal with it?' she asked.

'Not amazingly.'

'And now?'

'We aren't close. Never have been. He got quite distant afterwards. We didn't really worry about things like closeness, just getting by.'

'Do you still talk to him?'

'Yeah, but we don't ever talk about anything real.'

'I can see why,' she said, in a tone that forced a smile from me. 'Funny, isn't it? Me, you and Callie. All of us alone. But the two of you had each other, I suppose.'

She glanced across at me again, like she was waiting for something.

'And now you have me,' I said carefully.

When Inese beamed, it wasn't like when Callie used to beam. Callie's widest smiles still looked like catalogue spreads. She was luminous. Inese beamed like kids beam, when they show you all their teeth. Her widest smiles were inelegant. Pretty wasn't the right word, but I could have stared at her forever.

◆ ◆ ◆

We awoke the next day still on top of the covers in Callie's room, groggy. I had slept in my bra. Inese's phone was ringing. She picked it up and croaked a greeting as I negotiated my tired body into a sitting position, and then a standing. I left her on the phone and went downstairs to find my glasses. When I returned, she was sitting on the middle of the bed expectantly, waiting for me.

'What?'

'Interview,' she said.

'Today? Why does Charlie not give you more notice for these things?'

'He's going to share my full schedule soon. They just don't want to overwhelm me right now, he says.'

'It's a way of keeping you more controlled. You see that, don't you?' She shrugged, like she didn't really care whether they kept her controlled or not. I was beginning to believe she honestly didn't. What mattered to her was that she gave a good performance – the rest was secondary. 'Where is it?'

'At the label office in Coal Drops Yard. The journalist is meeting us there.'

'Do you want me to come?'

The tension left her shoulders. 'Could you?'

'I don't know that I'll be much help.'

'It helps just that you're in the room.'

'Well, if it helps you.'

'Not just me.' She reached for my hand, pressed it to her lips. I was too startled to stop her. 'People believe in you, Stevie. So they believe in me.'

◆ ◆ ◆

She looked wonderful when I rejoined her later. I was sweaty from the Tube, but she was poised in an oversized, strangely fitted black blazer and black kitten heels, her hair tied back and covered by a black hair net. The same blonde assistant with the crooked teeth showed me in, this time with a smile of recognition. Charlie was already there, touching up her lip-gloss himself, talking to her in a low, earnest voice. His manner with her was unexpectedly soft. She whispered something back, barely moving her lips as he dabbed at them with the wand, and he cracked a very small smile. Harma was also present, stood among a small group of label execs, and Gene Parrison hung to the side of the room talking to an assistant. I felt my face go red as I passed her. I wished I didn't react to Gene like a child to her scary headmistress.

Inese noticed me and beckoned me over, smiling as Callie. 'Hey, Stevie,' she said, air-kissing my cheek. She sat on a white stool, the sleeves of her blazer draped very deliberately over her knees. The wall behind her was white brick.

'I love this,' I said, gesturing to the outfit. 'Is this filmed?'

'No, just audio, but we're going to shoot a small snippet for their social media, hence the glam.'

'It's awesome. Very vampy.'

'You two are so cute,' came a voice across from us.

The empty chair opposite Inese had been filled by a woman with auburn hair and a notebook. Her legs, in shiny brown tights, were crossed over each other, and she had placed her phone on her knee. She was looking at us with a bright expectancy, like she was waiting to be let in on the conversation, as if the three of us were already friends.

Inese put a hand around my waist. 'We get that a lot.' I laughed, but I gently pushed her off. She glanced up at me, a little hurt, only for a moment.

'I remember you from the early days, Stevie,' said the journalist. One hand on her phone, keeping it in place, she leant forward a little and offered me the other. She said her name and the publication she was from – I didn't register either, busy wondering what she might remember. 'So magical, how you've reconnected.'

'Stevie's always been my saviour,' said Inese. 'I knew it when I fell. I just wanted her. When you have a thought like that, in a moment like that, you don't ignore it. You follow it.'

In an instant, the room had gone quiet. It was powerful, the way she was able to do that. The journalist pressed record with one discreet, manicured finger, and asked if Inese could repeat herself. 'That was just such gorgeous phrasing,' she said. Inese complied. 'Let's go back to that moment, if you don't mind,' said the journalist. 'What was that like from your perspective?'

'Awful,' said Inese. 'There's no other way to put it. I couldn't have been happier, coming out to start that show. And then it was the stupidest slip . . . I really did think that I was going to die.'

I had pulled back to the edge of the room, to give her space to answer these questions, but her eyes still sought me out for approval. I nodded, just a little.

'What was the slip?' asked the journalist.

'Oh, I was supposed to attach a harness around myself, and I didn't – so stupid – and then I wanted a better look at the crowd, so I leant too far forward. It was entirely my own fault. No blame at all lies with the crew at Copacabana Beach, and I do want to make that very clear.' The atmosphere in the room was one of approval. 'I do take unnecessary risks sometimes.'

'Have you always been like that?'

'Oh, yes.' Her eyes found me again. 'Stevie remembers better than me.'

I realised that she was panicking. She was hiding it well – extraordinarily well – but this was her first in-person interview, and she was so afraid of going to pieces.

'I remember you trying to crowd-surf in fifty-cap venues,' I said, raising my voice.

Laughter ran around the room. Charlie remained stern, but the execs were smiling, and Harma even clapped her hands together.

'Yes,' said Inese, with a laugh and a pretty blush. I would need to tell her not to do that later. Callie wouldn't have blushed. 'I've always had this real desire to be in among the crowd. There's something a little unnatural about sharing this experience of live music with them, only they're all together, connected, and you're apart from them on your stage. I would definitely do unsafe things a lot in the early days, trying to get close to them.'

'And have you accepted that separation now?' asked the journalist.

'Oh, yes. I've had to. But I still miss them sometimes. There's times where I still feel too far away from them.'

Her answers were good, but she was hardly looking at the interviewer. Her eyes kept finding their way back to me.

'That's why I used to get Stevie to stand in the crowd for me. Then, whenever I wanted to experience it, I could find her eyes and it was like I was reading her mind. In a way, a part of me was there with them.'

I can't believe she remembers, came the thought, instinctually, before my rational mind caught up.

'That's beautiful,' said the journalist. To my surprise, she turned to look at me over the back of her chair. 'How did it feel for you, Stevie, when you did that?'

Inese took slow, controlled breaths, Callie's smile plastered firmly across her face.

'It was the greatest feeling in the world,' I said.

◆ ◆ ◆

As Inese was shaking the journalist's hand and thanking her, Harma made her way over to me. She was in a navy jacket with slits in the sleeves that went all the way to her elbows, so that her hands could still punctuate every point she made without the shoulders of the jacket shifting.

'Stevie!' she said. 'So lovely to see you again.' It was impressive, how she managed to make the words so effusive, and yet still cut through with a vein of *Girl, what the fuck are you doing here?* She gave me a brief hug. Her back was bony and I didn't like touching it. 'I had no idea you were coming!'

'Yeah, it was kind of last minute. We were hanging out anyway.' She moved a piece of hair out of her lipstick, diamond flashing. 'That's a beautiful ring,' I said.

'Oh!' she said, looking down as if she'd only just noticed it. 'Isn't it? I wasn't settling for anything smaller than a knuckle.' She laughed like she was expecting me to join in and I did, unconvincingly. 'You know,' she said, 'I think it really helped, having you in the room. I know you were always *such* a comforting presence, all the way back when. Of course, that's not to say she's not a pro.'

'Yes,' I said. 'Of course.'

We smiled at each other, warmly and suspiciously.

Inese joined us and put her arms around my neck, laying her head on my shoulder. She smelt like Callie's Pointelle perfume, and underneath that, faintly of toast.

'You did so well,' said Harma. 'I know you felt rusty, but really, I think it's going to read so well. And the quotes you gave about the new album were absolutely spot on.'

'Do you think I did well, Stevie?' asked Inese, almost as if she hadn't heard.

'I think you were perfect,' I said, and felt her relax against me.

Harma put a hand to her heart. We had managed to hold her focus for long enough that the screen on her phone had gone black. 'You two are so sweet,' she said. 'Callie, honey, we're borrowing that headpiece so you might need to go and get it taken out.'

'Oh,' said Inese, her hands going to it. 'Of course.' She went to put her own clothes back on. Harma's nails tapped the screen of her phone as she unlocked it again. I made some polite noise about heading off, but she touched my arm.

'Stevie,' she said. Her eyes were still on her phone screen. 'I wonder . . . She's been cooped up preparing for so long, and it really might be nice for her to actually go out and *do* something, you know? A little shopping, maybe, on King's Road?'

I stared at her. 'Is that . . . possible?'

'Well,' she said, looking up, 'we have her security ready to go. I can call ahead and sort of . . . get things ready. Make sure people know she's coming.'

'Like, the shops?'

'Yes,' said Harma, and hesitated in a way that made me realise 'the shops' was the start of a list. I understood what she was getting at.

'And that would be . . .' She raised her eyebrows at me pleasantly, but with a slight hint of a warning. 'Helpful?' I finished.

'Very helpful to her, I would think. And probably nice for people to see her out and about.'

Did I want to be helpful to these people? I thought about refusing. It was one thing to hold Inese's hand through these interviews – it was quite another to be a willing prop in Harma's staged candids.

But I wasn't just helping Inese for Inese's sake. As much as the rest of the world, as much as anyone, I wanted Calista to live forever. Whatever was really motivating them all – respect for Callie's final wishes or corporate greed – the result was the same. Calista survived. Calista continued. In some way, Callie did too.

'What if it gets crazy?' That day on Carnaby Street came to mind.

'It'll be fine. We'll have people to pull you out if it's needed, but I'm sure it won't be needed.' She paused, both thumbs hovering over her phone. Her eyebrows were about to disappear into her hairline. 'Yes?'

'If she wants to,' I said. 'Yes.'

'Amazing. It's *so, so good* to have you around again, Stevie. I can't tell you how pleased everyone is about it.' Inese reappeared, still in her make-up but dressed in jeans and a loose white shirt, her dramatic hairpiece gone. 'Speak of the devil!' said Harma, and moved away without addressing her further. She walked over to Charlie and said something to him in a low voice. He looked over at us, in that way he did – blank, but somehow still ominous.

'What's going on?' asked Inese, still as Callie, but with an undertone of stress.

'We're going on an outing.'

'An outing?' She realised she was supposed to be excited and laughed uncertainly. 'Anywhere in particular?'

'Callie?' Charlie was beckoning her over to the side of the room. Harma moved away to give them space. I watched him bend over to whisper in her ear, and once again I was struck by how gentle his manner was with her. There was even a hint of a smile. He pulled away and raised his eyebrows at me. She rolled her shoulders back and turned towards me, surprised.

'I hear you're taking me shopping.'

'That's what I hear too.'

'What a nice thing to hear,' she said.

I had to wait for an hour or so while they brought in new wardrobe options for her and redid her hair and make-up to look slightly less 'considered', in Harma's parlance. I went for a walk around Coal Drops Yard and tried to absorb what felt like the last few minutes of normal life. When these photos came out, Kiera would know why I had been ignoring her emails. Rosie would probably flip her desk. Thinking about the office was funny – thinking about Rich was less so. I put him out of my mind, like I had become accustomed to doing. I hoped Mel would understand. I hoped she would be happy for me.

When Inese was ready, they drove us to Sloane Square and let us out around the corner. She was wearing sunglasses. I reached over to take them off, gently, but she held them on with both hands. When we arrived, I went round to her side of the car and helped her out, my fingers laced tightly through hers. I could practically feel her heart thudding through her hand. I rubbed my thumb gently over the inside of her wrist and breathed slowly with her, in and out. I let her take the first step.

It took only a few minutes for us to be noticed – probably because of the two security guards flanking us, actually. But once it happened, it swelled, like people were riding in on waves, like they were plankton brought in on a high tide, a surge of them in every direction, and cameras waiting all the way up the road to take pictures. Security kept the worst of it from reaching us, but we had phones shoved in our faces, flashes going off on our left side and our right. People touched our shoulders. A woman in a scarf patterned with birds stood on her toes to tug my arm towards her, lowering my ear to her mouth, and said, 'I'm *so* glad you're back together.' I smiled at her and wrenched my arm free.

We only went into one shop, some Scandinavian boutique. The manager had already spoken to Harma on the phone and had the place closed off for us. We wandered around the store in near-silence, Inese clutching my hand tightly, her other hand on her sunglasses. It was a strange, between-worlds feeling. Facing forwards, everything was beige minimalism, a few store assistants keeping a respectful distance, beautiful clothes in neutral colours displayed sparingly. Whenever I made the mistake of glancing over my shoulder, though, I felt my stomach twist. People were pressing themselves up against the glass doors, banging on them with fists. They screamed and cried. A woman near the front convulsed with full body sobs, two flat hands pushing into the glass like it might give way and let her fall through and drag herself over the carpet to Inese's ankles. Cameras were raised over heads. Phones were held in front of people's faces, recording every movement with glinting, greedy eyes. I kept my eyes on Inese. She chatted quietly and politely with the sales staff, touched the sleeve of a jumper and told me how lovely it was. She acted as if the second world behind us didn't even exist.

I pulled her close to me. 'You should wave at them,' I whispered.

From this angle I could see her eyes behind the sunglasses, full of fear. 'I can't.' She said it with a smile, very softly.

'You can. They'll love it.'

Still smiling, she squeezed my hand and very slightly shook her head.

'Do it,' I said. 'Just see what happens.'

She closed her eyes. Then, still holding my hand, she turned and gave the crowd a small, hesitant wave.

Even from the other side of the glass, the roar was terrifying. I felt her flinch, and then she waved again. They were even louder that time, uncontrollably joyous. The crying woman near the front nearly fell to her knees. Inese took her sunglasses off.

I love you, I watched her mouth to them. *I love you.*

We love you, they roared back, in a chorus of pleas and sobs and shouts and camera clicks. *We love you more.*

She shook the whole car ride home. She draped herself across me in the back seat, her seat belt off, and I held her in my arms and stroked blonde curls back from her forehead. I didn't tell her to calm down. It wouldn't have done me any good just then, to be told that. We both of us sat there and processed it, me very still,

Inese trembling all over, until the car pulled into the driveway and we realised that no one had even had to be told that I was going home with her.

◆ ◆ ◆

There was an enormous response to the pictures online. Our coffee date might have been any number of things, but here it was obvious that we were together. Try as I might, I couldn't help picturing Rich's face when they came up on his phone. I had been telling myself for days now that I would go home very soon, even if it was just for a while – I just had to come up with some kind of explanation. I would break up with him properly. He deserved that much.

Harma sent Inese the statement that they were releasing on Instagram:

> *Thank you all so much for the love. As many of you have guessed already, Luke and I haven't been together for a few months now. I'm not going to be answering questions on my relationship at this time – it's all just between me and the person I'm with – but all you need to know is that I'm exactly where I need to be after everything that's happened, with exactly who I need by my side.*

'That's beautiful,' I said, reading over Inese's shoulder on the sofa and feeling another twinge of guilt.

'She is quite good at her job,' said Inese, taking another bite of her toast. Today she was eating chicken pâté with chopped cornichons and grated carrot.

With Harma's blessing, Inese had been posting on Instagram herself. Photos of two plates at the kitchen table, or our socked feet touching with some old musical playing on the TV in the background. Just a little here and there, but enough to dominate headlines and feed the fan pages.

> *loving Calista's oversharing era!!*
>
> *Says soooo much that she feels comfortable posting like this. Real ones remember how good Stevie always was for her.*
>
> *Is no one else finding it weird how much her social media activity has changed since the accident?*

For a second I thought that the last comment was from @*whathappenedtocalista,* but I had blocked them long ago. It was a new one, *@calistatruthh.* They'd posted the photos from King's Road already, placing Inese's face alongside old pap shots of Callie. I blocked that page too, before reading the comments, and moved my phone away from me.

But I would find myself returning to these pages more and more frequently, unblocking and blocking them again, monitoring their followings, checking their latest posts. I was never brave enough to scroll through the comments, but sometimes I would accidentally read a couple and my peace would be disturbed for a couple of hours. I never spoke to Inese about these pages. I hoped she wasn't seeing them as well.

I was scrolling through a new one – *@whitebench8080* – on my bed one morning when the doorbell rang. It was the day after the King's Road photos had been published online. Inese was in the music room practising, gearing up to start all the real work on the album release, and I should have been reading the diaries but couldn't bring myself to pick the book back up. I was getting dangerously close to the end. I had received a new influx of messages from Rich and Mel since the photos had come out but had swiped them away, still frozen, knowing that I was unable to explain myself.

Charlie had already been to the house that morning and I was surprised that he was back so soon. But when I looked out of the window, his black car wasn't parked on the driveway. There wasn't any car at all. The bell rang again, twice.

I ran downstairs to find Inese hesitating in the hallway. 'Don't open it,' I said.

'It might be Charlie,' she whispered.

'If it's Charlie, he has a key.'

'Is our address online?' she asked.

'Possibly.'

'Shit.' She backed away from the door.

'Stevie?' called a voice from the other side. Inese turned panicked eyes on me, suspecting betrayal. 'Stevie, I just want to talk to you.'

'It's Rich,' I said. '*Shit.*' Inese put a hand on my shoulder. 'Listen, just go into the kitchen.' She hovered in the hallway, frowning. 'I won't let him in, I promise.'

When Inese was safely in the kitchen, I opened the door. It wasn't just Rich, in his most unflattering pair of jeans and an overpriced white t-shirt. Mel stood a few paces back.

'Stevie,' she said. 'Shit. You're okay.'

'Obviously I'm okay.'

'It's not obvious,' said Rich, standing just a bit too close to the doorway. 'It's not obvious *at all,* Stevie. We thought you'd joined a cult or something.'

'I didn't think that,' said Mel.

'Well, what other explanation was there? I mean, you've cut *everyone* off. You've basically gone radio silent, and then there's suddenly these pictures everywhere of you shopping in fancy shops with your pop star ex-girlfriend? What *is* that, Stevie? We lived together. The contract's up for renewal on the flat, by the way, and I'm going to have to find somewhere else to live if you don't come home. Are you coming home?'

'Maybe,' I said.

'Maybe?'

'I wanted to explain all of this properly—'

'Explain now,' he said, arms folded.

I looked from him to Mel, who gestured for me to speak.

'Fine,' I said. 'I think we should break up.'

He unfolded his arms, stuffed his hands in his pockets and let out a laugh in the direction of the sky. Again, I looked towards Mel. She shrugged. She looked angry.

'I wanted to do it in a better way—'

'You swore you weren't cheating on me, Stevie.'

'I wasn't. I— I'm not.' I was still looking at Mel. 'It's hard to explain,' I said weakly.

'Stevie, what the *fuck?*' he asked, with a small bounce of his knees that I would have found funny under different circumstances. 'We've been so chill for ages now, and I get that all that shit with Callie threw you off – I was really fucking understanding about that, actually – but then you pack a bag and leave and don't mention you're going to live with her? I mean, are you one of those people who has some sort of Florence Nightingale kink? Like you just *had* to rush to her side and care for her? You've never been that fucking caring towards me.'

Mel had her hands in her pockets, watching Rich rant with raised eyebrows. 'You're with him?' I asked.

She held up both hands. 'What was I meant to do? He stormed over and asked if I knew where you were. I wasn't going to lie.'

'How did you know?'

'I have you on location services from that night you got in the world's sketchiest fucking Uber. Knew you'd forgotten. Dickhead.' She was in her grey tracksuit, barefaced. She looked like she hadn't slept.

'You knew I was here the whole time?'

'Of course. I was letting you work through your shit or whatever you needed to do. Didn't realise this was a full regression, though.'

'It's not a regression.'

'You and Callie broke up for reasons, Stevie.'

'We've changed.'

'You haven't.'

'Well, she has. She's changed a lot, actually.' I nodded towards Rich, who was waiting for his moment to interject and continue his monologue. 'I don't understand why you brought him here. You hate him.'

'*You* hate him. I'm indifferent.'

'I don't hate him. I don't hate you,' I told Rich, who didn't look particularly appeased. 'But we should talk another time. You shouldn't be here.'

'I'm here because I care about you,' said Rich. 'I want to get you the help you need.'

I looked back at Mel. 'Seriously?'

'His heart's in the right place, Stevie.' Her face, paler than the rest of her body, softened. She looked unfamiliar like this. Make-up used to look like dressing up on her, and now I wasn't used to her without it. 'We're worried about you.'

'I'm fine. I promise. This is . . .' I waved a hand. 'She's going through a lot right now.' I saw that Mel was staring at my wrist. 'What?'

'You're wearing her bracelet.'

'Yeah,' I said. 'And?'

'Stevie,' said Rich, 'you came home a couple of weeks ago and told me that you thought she was dead. *Dead.* And now you're back with her? Does anyone else think that's really disturbing?'

Mel raised a hand. I rolled my eyes. 'This is embarrassing for you, Mels.'

'Embarrassing?'

'I get Rich showing up here and making a scene, but not you.'

She took a step forward. 'Alright, Stevie, I love you, but you can dispense with that fucking attitude. You can't cut off everyone you're closest to and disappear into some mansion in Hampstead and act like it's our problem for being upset by it. I've been crazy worried about you.'

'I'm happy,' I said. 'I'm happier than I've been in years.'

'Then why couldn't you share that happiness?'

'You wouldn't understand.'

'Jesus. Fine. Fuck you, then.'

'Fuck you too.' My voice was hoarse.

'Stevie,' said Mel. 'I love you. Even if you're being an absolute arsehole right now. And I really, really think that you are putting yourself in a bad situation here, even if you don't think so in all your fucking wisdom. So, whatever, I'll go. But I'm *here,* okay?'

A lump rose in my throat, but I swallowed it down again with a shrug. She kept her eyes on me for a minute, almost pleading, or as close as I'd ever seen Mel come.

'You just have to trust me,' I said. 'There's a lot going on. It's not— It's fine. I'm fine.'

She mirrored my shrug, and turned to go, walking off down the drive. Rich cleared his throat.

'I think we should give it another go,' he said.

'Rich, fucking hell,' called Mel over her shoulder.

My patience ran out. 'I actually think we should stay broken up forever.'

He blinked at me. 'I think you're a pretty miserable, awful person, Stevie. I tried really hard to love you.' His mouth twisted. 'And I'd try again, that's the crazy part.' He waited for a response, but I didn't have any for him. There was nothing to disagree with or be surprised by. I watched him follow Mel down the drive.

Inese waited until they were out of sight before she appeared in the hallway behind me, the cuffs of her sweater falling over her wrists. We looked at each other for a second, before I turned back towards the empty driveway. I felt her come up behind me, slide an arm around my waist and another around my shoulders. I let her hold me there for a moment, breathing as I breathed.

Dinner At Mine (2024)

I keep a space for Callie on the wall beside my desk, in-between the photo of Rich and I at the Haunted Orchard and the one of me and my dad standing in wellies in the river outside my aunt's house in Wales. In both of these pictures, I am in a big coat, although obviously not the same coat since they were taken twenty years apart. In the photo of Callie and I that I keep in my desk drawer, I am wearing almost nothing. Just one of her bras, red, which I took from the drawer in her room without asking, and a very small pair of black shorts. Callie is in a short white dress cut down to her navel, completely open at the back. We have our arms around each other, drinks in our hands, giggling. You can tell that we think we're not only the most provocative people at the party we're at, but the most provocative people to attend any party ever. We are cute, conspiratorial. We don't even realise how young we look.

When Rich moved into my flat with me I took the photo of Callie off the wall. He didn't ask me to. I don't think he even noticed. It leaves a lopsided gap in my collage, though, which he's sometimes suggested I fill with us on a night out, us at his uni friend's wedding, us outside Buckingham Palace like two tourists. I never have. Maybe I am waiting until the day he is gone to put the photo back up again. I won't have any trouble replacing the one of us at the Haunted Orchard. I don't like how I look in it anyway.

He comes into the living room as I am staring at the wall and puts his hands on my shoulders. 'How's it going?' he asks. He is currently unemployed and here all the time, which has forced me to pretend that my job is much busier than it actually is. I don't like to be domestic with him in the day, only in the evenings, when it's easier to curl up on the sofa with him and watch something mindless. He kisses my cheek.

'I'm swamped,' I say. I am writing copy for moisturisers. Our in-house ones are easy but every external retailer has sent me a list of talking points that read like things a sea-witch might promise you in exchange for your voice. 'Could you make me a coffee?'

'Oh, I'm busy too,' he says, even though he isn't. He says this not out of laziness, but because he has decided that I drink too much coffee and it is up to him to gently nudge me into better habits. He will no longer make more than one coffee for me a day, even when he is already making one for himself and being a ginormous hypocrite, and if I go over to use the machine, he will say things like, 'Remember, caffeine is a drug. Are your hands shaking? Hold them out so I can see.' I have started to look for jobs for him myself because Rich means very well but being around him all day every day is a waking nightmare.

'You're not meant to feel like that,' said Mel, when I went to hers for dinner.

'Oh, I always feel like that eventually.'

'Yeah, which is why you've broken up with everyone you've dated before.'

'But eventually I have to see it through, right? I have to actually live with someone and adjust to their habits and just choose to love them. That's what they always say – love is a choice.'

'Love is a choice when you're fifteen years into marriage with someone and you're going through a rough patch but you still – baseline requirement – like them as a person.'

'You used to like Rich,' I said, tearing off a piece of naan.

'I used to like that he made you happy,' she said. 'I've always been lukewarm on his personality.'

'I'm still happy,' I said.

'Being happy isn't just not being violently unhappy.'

'I think it is,' I said, 'for me.'

'No, Stevie-girl,' she said gently, 'it isn't.'

But here we still are, Rich and I, sharing space. Sharing walls. His face in frames and cheaply Blu-Tacked to the space beside my desk. He hums Guns N' Roses around the flat, but only the guitar solos. When he cooks, he pretends that he doesn't want credit, and then wants credit for not wanting credit. He won't leave me unless I chase him out with a broom, and the only deep examination he will do of our relationship is whether I am being entirely fair to him when I tell him that I don't like his tone sometimes. I feel the absence of crushing sadness, so I suppose that must be good enough.

We don't talk about Calista's new album. He doesn't like it. He doesn't get it. He thinks pop can be pop, and it's not for him and that's fine, but that there's no point trying to get all pretentious about surface-level lyrics. I love Dinner At Mine. *It's baroque pop; it's performance art; it's self-aware and self-indulgent all at once, as so many of her projects are becoming. Rich will never understand Calista like I do. And he will never know Callie's mind like I know it, even though he often doubts whether I know it at all.*

'People change so much between the ages of twenty-one and twenty-nine,' he told me once over some of the worst Chinese food I have ever had in central London, at a place around the corner from Euston Station. 'That girl you knew is probably gone forever.'

He said it so casually, sweet-and-sour sauce on his lips, like he hadn't just killed and buried her. I walked out of the restaurant. Later he acted confused about why I'd reacted so aggressively, and I said, 'I don't know, I'm probably hormonal,' to avoid an argument.

'Isn't it weird,' he asked another time, at an awful whisky bar in Bishopsgate, 'just being a fan now?'

I was weary. Dinner At Mine *had just come out and all I wanted in the world was to tell her how much I loved it. I had called her number a few times over the years, since the disastrous drunk call at Mel's brother's party back in 2018. She had blocked me after that party and I had remained blocked ever since – actually, by now she probably had a new number that I would never know. Still, I rang. Listened to the beep that I couldn't leave a message at. Sent texts that didn't go through.*

The album is incredible, *I told her, the day after it came out.* I cried my eyes out. I'm so proud of you. *I watched the small red exclamation mark appear beside it and closed my phone.*

'It is,' I told Rich in the whisky bar in Bishopsgate. 'So weird.'

He comes into the living room and informs me that he has made me sleepy-time tea instead, which he believes will counteract some of the effects of the caffeine. I say thank you and set it down beside me, with no intention of actually drinking it. He is pleased.

'I'm just looking out for you,' he says. 'You know that, right? It's because I care about you.'

'I know,' I say. 'Thank you.'

You're so perfect, Stevie, *Callie had whispered in my ear that night, in her short white dress, her hands playing with the straps of my red bra.* You're so fucking perfect it's unreal.

Chapter Six

The photo of Inese standing in her gold halter-neck dress in the middle of the nightclub went nuclear.

CALISTA 9 IS COMING OMG!!!!

GIRL I swear you don't sleep and we love you for ittttt

The self-reference! I can't! This is literally going to be the best album of her career

On a different corner of the internet, one that I kept getting drawn back to, the comments looked like this.

They literally aren't even trying to hide it anymore. Scary.

So evident that this girl is reaching out for help through her artwork and probably the music as well. Why isn't anyone listening??

Who tf is this

In all of their replies, the truther accounts flocked.

She's a clone, said *@calistatruthh. This project has been in the works for a while. Check my page for more info.*

It's an AI image, said *@whitebench8080. All the pap photos are AI too – my friend was on King's Road that day and swears it was super quiet and empty.*

They've literally been working with Calista lookalikes for years – it's so easy to spot, said *@0nmyheadst0ne*, a new one. *Look at the side by sides. They probably have a whole lot of them ready to go. Just wait – we're going to start seeing her everywhere.*

Charlie had told Inese not to read her comments, so she didn't, at least as far as I was aware. Her relationship with Charlie was strange – she looked at him almost as a guardian angel, someone who had plucked her from her old life and the house in Riga she didn't want to live in anymore and chosen her for some higher purpose. She trusted him implicitly. I wasn't sure how he felt about me, but I had decided to trust him too, at least where Inese was concerned. His care for her was apparent, even if everything else about him was shady. And I had to agree with him – reading the comments wouldn't have done her any good.

Still, she knew that the artwork had made an impact. The phone and Zoom interviews started in earnest. I was always in the room for them, sitting off-camera, nodding my encouragement, circling my hand if I thought she should elaborate. At her request, I had started to give her notes.

'Don't say "fans",' I told her, after one call. 'She never said "fans". She felt that it created too much of a barrier between her and them.'

'Really?' she asked. 'I think she might have changed her mind on that.'

'Did she?'

'Finish the diaries, Stevie,' she said. 'Why won't you finish the diaries?'

I just had one volume left. It had been sitting by the side of my bed for a month and I couldn't bring myself to open it. Now that Inese seemed less concerned about the possibility of me leaving, she was impatient. She wanted me to have the complete story, like she did, so that we could talk about it all like we were doing a book report.

But I couldn't finish the diaries. It would have felt like losing her all over again.

Besides, there was no time for reading. We were far too busy. We shot the album cover by a curtained-off section of the South Bank by the Thames, Inese standing in a monstrous party dress with a huge bunch of black balloons, her under-eyes shadowed, the ends of her hair dipped in something black that dripped down her bodice. When she saw the final shot she threw her arms around me and stained my t-shirt, but I didn't mind. The shoot was done as quickly as possible in as private a way as could be managed, but of course fans found out. Those travelling down the Thames via boat could just about see us from certain angles – whenever they did, they would break out in cheers and call her name – *Calista* – over the water. When a drone started flying overhead, everyone cleared out as quickly as they could.

The vocals were the part that scared her the most. The album was mostly recorded, but Inese still had to put the final touches to it. I would sit on the floor of the music room to listen to her, singing over choruses, ad-libbing, occasionally re-doing a whole verse. It was always strange, to hear her voice alongside Callie's. The first time that we got a file from the producer to listen to, I cried before we'd even opened it. It was the knowledge that I was about to hear something new, in Callie's voice. When I looked up at Inese, tears in my eyelashes, she was pale.

'Play it,' I said.

It was an incredible song, distorted techno in places, dissolving into strings as the protagonist emerged from the club into daylight and realised that the night was over. It sounded radically different from anything that Calista had done before.

'Oh, god,' said Inese when it was over, her voice thick.

'What's wrong?'

'She's a genius. What happens after this album? I can't do what she can do.'

'Don't worry about that,' I said, setting up her desk mic for her. 'Just focus on this album.' Charlie called in remotely to talk her through it, but Inese had been practising recording her own vocals and was surprisingly adept. Her voice blended with Callie's, her vowels melting into Callie's vowels, the hiss of her 's' slithering into Callie's 's', until you couldn't distinguish the two of them, just one woman singing about dancing and decaying and stepping into the morning.

'When did you realise that I could really do it?' she asked me late that night in the kitchen, the two of us cleaning it together. She gripped her cloth and waited.

'When you sang to me,' I said. 'When you sang to me and I closed my eyes.'

She beamed in that way that was so distinctly Inese.

Once the album was finished and ready, our trips out into the world became more frequent. We never walked the streets for long, but we became braver at facing the quickly accumulating crowds. Restaurants were better; we could sit undisturbed for the most part, with only an occasional interruption from a fan at our table, asking for a napkin to be signed. These were always fans with access to the same exclusive places as us and so they were never as confronting as the fans we met out in public. They didn't cry or scream but asked politely, played it cool. They wanted us to think they were cool, but we didn't. We only thought that we were cool. We would tell each other this afterwards and laugh.

My dad didn't call anymore – we went through periods like this. When I stopped putting the effort in for a while, he would follow suit. Rich left me one drunk voicemail that I couldn't really hear because his signal was so bad. Mel still texted. I never replied. I was part of something sensitive now – I was a component in a magic trick. I couldn't reveal myself. Calista mattered more than everything else. Increasingly, so did Inese. Her hours in the music studio, the lemon and honey on her breath, her love of silky pyjama sets and movie musicals. The way she smiled when I entered a room, the way her eyes followed me out when I left.

About a week after Inese finished vocals for the album, we went for a walk through Regent's Park with two security guards and tried to ignore the cameras. They hadn't called paparazzi this time, but we had become used to staring down the lens of someone's phone. Heads turned as we passed, picnic blanket conversations ceased, but security kept them from approaching. Our names were called, and we smiled vaguely, but we didn't acknowledge individuals. We were untouchable. In a low voice, Inese played her favourite game, trying to guess the tabloid headline.

'*Calista and girlfriend Stevie Stone step out for a jaunt around the park.* No, *Calista and girlfriend Stevie Stone are blissfully loved up during Sunday morning walk around Regent's Park.*' She giggled.

'Blissfully loved up?'

'I could look at you once,' she said, 'like this.' She held my eyes for just a second, with a smile, and then looked away. 'And they will say that we're blissfully loved up.' She took my hand. 'What did they write about you back in the day?'

'They didn't, really.'

'No?'

'She wasn't that big for the first couple of albums, and if they did write about us it was always "and friend". *Calista and friend get lunch in Soho. Calista and friend take a visit to Oxford. Calista and friend make out in front of Nelson's Column.* Isn't friendship a wonderful thing?'

'Did you really make out in front of Nelson's Column?'

'No one took pictures of it.' I grinned, and she laughed.

There were ducklings in the pond, seven of them, following their mother in a line. We stood and watched them for a while, as people took photos of us from the other side of the pond. I had become accustomed to the click of cameras and calls of Calista's name, as much a part of autumn as the hiss of wind or the crunch of leaves. Inese swung my hand, leading me on from the ducklings before I was done looking. I kept my eyes on them as we went, until I felt her stop suddenly.

There was a person in our path, a man of about thirty-five, with big eyes and stubble on his chin. He looked at us expectantly, but he didn't ask for a picture.

'Hi,' said Inese, as Callie. The security guards moved in behind us. Rodney and Chris were their names – quietly commanding presences that circled us like orbiting moons when we were in public, ushering people out of our space. Even though I couldn't see them, I could feel that something about the man had them on alert.

'Pleased with yourselves?' asked the man.

The moment he started to speak, I felt it too. There was a quiver in his voice that gave him an air of instability. He looked at us both with real hatred. Inese maintained her smile, but she gripped my hand tighter.

'Where's Calista?' he asked. 'Where's Calista, you bitch?'

She let out a short gasp at the word, and then a scream as he lunged towards her. Rodney stepped in the way and caught him, the man's limbs flailing in strange patterns like a weird wind-up toy. Chris began to hurry us along the path, towards where the car was waiting outside the gate.

'THAT'S NOT HER!' screamed the man, behind us. 'THAT'S NOT THE REAL CALISTA!'

Heads turned towards us as Chris ushered us back towards the road. People leant in to whisper to each other. Some laughed, but some stared at Inese with a scrutiny that made me light-headed.

Once we were safely in the car, she burst into tears. I took her in my arms and let her cry into my shoulder as the car sped towards the traffic lights. 'Where's Rodney?' I asked Chris.

'He's dealing with the situation,' said Chris. 'Don't worry.'

We passed two police cars, sirens blaring, driving in the opposite direction. Later, we learnt that the man – Martin Howard, age thirty-four – had been arrested for attempted assault.

Inese was shaken for a while after that. Charlie visited and brought her a box of her favourite chocolates from Fortnum & Mason – for someone who ate mostly stuff on bread, her tastes could be quite randomly extravagant. While he was there she talked about the situation very calmly, but as soon as he left, she collapsed into my lap, spent. I stroked her hair. I liked being the only one who saw her like that, but I also wished that I could take her fear away.

That night, after we had already separately gone to bed, she knocked on my bedroom door and then pushed it open. We were both wearing a set of Callie's pyjamas, mine grey stripes, hers a pale, delicate green.

'I can't sleep,' she said. 'I keep thinking he's going to come in through the window.'

'He's been arrested, Inese. You'll have a restraining order against him soon enough.'

'Callie will have a restraining order against him. I'll have nothing.'

I pushed back the duvet. She was still for a second in the doorway, and then she walked over and slipped into bed beside me. Neither of us commented on it.

'There will be more of them,' she said, pulling it over her chest. 'I've seen it online. I know you all don't want me to look, but I do.'

I thought of the countless posts and pages that I'd scrolled through, the sick feeling that accumulated in my stomach when I did. 'Oh, Inese,' I said. She burrowed down in the covers, her face in the pillow. I stroked her back for a while, until her breathing evened out. After that, we never slept apart.

Two weeks after the incident in the park, Inese was supposed to give her first live performance since the accident. It was a label event, just a small crowd of professionals, a chance to debut the album. They would mostly be playing the pre-recorded tracks, but the label thought it was a good idea for her to perform a couple of songs live, just to quell any 'chatter', they told us, through Charlie.

'I can't do it,' Inese said, the three of us sat in the living room. I was no longer excluded from her meetings with Charlie – I had just begun showing up, and he had accepted it. He still mostly acted as if I wasn't there, his attention always on Inese, but he never called her by her real name.

'You can,' he said, not in a tone of reassurance – Charlie didn't really do reassurance – but as a matter-of-fact. 'I know how hard you've been practising. And you still have two weeks to prepare.' It was the wrong time to tell her, the evening after she'd been accosted by some crazy person. Charlie thought of Inese as stronger than she really was, I'd noticed. No one knew her quite like I did.

'They'll all know,' she said, biting her thumb. I lifted her hand slowly from her mouth and placed it on her knee. Charlie watched, his eyes flickering between us. I squeezed her knee, my nails pushing into the skin just a little.

'They'll know that you're a star,' said Charlie carefully. 'They'll know that Calista's legacy is secure. That's all anyone needs to know.'

He visited most days in the lead-up, sitting and listening to her play and sing for an hour or so, in what he clearly felt was his designated seat in the music room. But it was me who sat with her when he was gone, from morning until afternoon, listening, absorbing, feeding back. Callie would sing it lighter. She would sing it breathier. She would play this line like a joke. She would deliver this line like a prayer. Inese sat, nodding, drinking it in. Then she picked up the guitar and went again.

'Stevie,' Charlie asked me once, while Inese was in the kitchen making coffee, 'do you not work?'

'Not currently,' I said. I'd received an email from Kiera letting me know that my contract was void. *I'm sorry it's come to this,* she'd written. I wasn't, particularly.

'You weren't renting a place?'

'Yes, with my boyfriend. We broke up.'

'Are you still paying the rent on it?'

'No. He might be. We only had a couple of months left on the contract anyway.'

'So, you really just abandoned your entire life for this,' he said. 'You must really love her.'

Inese came back into the room carrying two mugs. She set them on the table and disappeared back inside to get the third. She'd used Callie's *Don't Be A Dick* mug for Charlie, and I had one that Inese herself had painted, black and stripy like a mint humbug.

'It's not about me,' I said.

'What do your parents think?'

'They just want me to be happy,' I said, but as I was still talking, Inese said, '—Stevie's mum died when she was little. She doesn't talk to her dad much.'

He looked at me, and his face was unreadable. I flushed. Later, when Charlie had gone, I confronted Inese. 'I don't want Charlie knowing my business.'

'I didn't know it was a secret.'

'It's not. I just don't talk about it.'

'Maybe you should,' she said. I was furious with her for an hour or so, and then I heard her singing through the kitchen wall, her voice low and mournful, and the fury dissipated. When Charlie came over the next day, the two of us didn't speak at all.

I never quite got up the courage to ask Charlie how much of what he was doing here was essential work, in his job description, whether he was supposed to be with her for all of this, whether he was meant to be delegating, or whether sitting and listening to her play wasn't required of him at all. I didn't want to hear him tell me that he loved her. Crowds could love her from afar, fans could love her through the internet, but no one got to love Calista up close except for me.

We had begun to argue a little lately. She felt that I had been hard on her, at points, when her fingers were tired from playing or her voice became raspy. When she pointed this out, despite knowing that I had only good intentions, I would always feel instantly guilty. Then we would need some space from each other, retreating to lick our wounds. These moments always filled me with a sense of dread, as if my body sensed something looming on the horizon that my eyes couldn't yet make out.

◆ ◆ ◆

The day of the label party, hair and make-up turned up to the Hampstead house at midday, even though we didn't have to be there until four. I busied myself making teas and coffees as Inese sat at a station set up in the middle of the living room and was beautified for hours. Charlie wandered between rooms, looking a little lost. Occasionally we would meet in the corridor and each moved past quickly without making eye contact. Inese never broke character, but she was tense. Callie's easy chatter didn't come so easily to her and there were moments of silence in the room that I would have to step outside to escape. My heart wouldn't beat normally. I was terrified for her. Charlie, who I had never seen smoking, was constantly coming in and out of the garden with the smell of it on his hands.

I went upstairs for a while to try to calm myself down, and ended up scrolling through Mel's texts. She had stopped asking if I was okay and was instead sending me small, regular observations, details about her day.

Hey dickhead. Moon's fucking massive tonight. Miss you.

I bought the floppiest sunflowers from Sainsbury's today. Thought how good you are with flowers. I'm useless with them.

Just seen you on the Daily Mail's socials going for a jaunt around Kensington. Aren't we fancy? Hope you're good.

Watching A Star Is Born just feels wrong without you.

I usually ignored these messages. They chilled me. Other than the references to pap shots, they could have been texts you sent to the phone of a dead person, down to the perfect punctuation. At that moment, though, hearing her voice in them was a comfort. I lay on my side and scrolled, reading each one twice.

'Stevie,' came Charlie's voice up the stairs.

When I re-entered the living room, she was stood in leather shorts and a deconstructed black top with a trailing hem, with dark eyes and a head full of messy waves. Blinking was like running my thumb over the pages of a flick-book, watching her change. *Callie. Inese. Callie. Inese.*

'Where were you?' she asked, coming towards me, still flickering like a strobe light. Her fingernails were long and white, with silver moons on the ends of them. They dug into my arm as she gripped it. 'I need you here.'

'I'm here,' I told her.

In the car, she hummed the whole way, to warm up her voice. At first she hummed scales and octave jumps, but after a while she settled into humming one long, continuous note, like a refrigerator or a very gentle cicada. I closed my eyes and let to it stir the contents of my brain. As she hummed, she kept checking her face in her phone, touching her eyelashes and her cheeks. She would look across at me as she did this, like she was waiting for me to confirm something, but I never knew what she wanted me to say, so I didn't say anything at all.

They slipped her in through the back door, in a puffy black jacket with a furred hood. When we unwrapped her from the jacket in her dressing room, she was laughing. Her eyes were panicked. I sat her down on a chair and Charlie hovered nearby, sending an assistant to get some water.

'You can do this,' I said, kneeling beside her.

She nodded and nodded, but it didn't seem as if the words were going in. I knew that she was replaying the voice of the man from the park in her mind, because I was too. She took the bottled water from the assistant, drank a third. I stayed kneeling on the carpet, letting the pattern of it print on to my bare knees as she jiggled her legs and took deep, shuddery breaths. The door opened, and I tapped her on the leg. She rearranged her face into Callie's. It was the host for the event, a bubbly woman in a black pantsuit, coming to say hello. Inese stood to greet her, keeping one hand on the back of the chair. They chatted for a few minutes about traffic and the weather. When the woman disappeared, Inese fell back into the chair with a gasp.

'She thinks I'm a fake.'

Charlie and I rushed to reassure her that of course she didn't. How could she? She (Inese, Callie, it didn't matter) was completely authentic in everything she did. People were crazy to think otherwise. It was such a strange little scene we were acting out, each feigning innocence for each other, or maybe for her. We were like three people staring at the earth from space and swearing to each other that it was flat as a pancake. The truth was, as well, that Inese wasn't playing her part perfectly just then. There had been several moments with the host that had made my stomach clench. Outside the dressing room, we heard the host, just as bubbly in public as in private, start to warm up the assembled crowd.

'Knock, knock,' came a voice. It was Gene, putting her head around the door, grey hair severely coiffured. 'How are we feeling?'

'A little nervous,' said Inese, as brightly as she could manage.

'Well, put those nerves to bed. You're going to be fabulous. Just let the art do the talking.' She looked at Inese over the top of her glasses. 'Yes?'

Inese swallowed, smiling, and nodded.

'Let's hear that gorgeous voice.'

'Yes,' she said, a little squeaky.

My face must have betrayed how I felt about this interaction, because Gene's gaze landed on me. 'Oh, hello,' she said. 'Here again, are we?'

'Always,' I said.

'Well, it takes a village. I'll be out there. Let's give them some of that Calista magic. No need to look so frightened.'

She smiled, over the top, and Inese imitated her. As soon as Gene stepped away, her face dropped. We all sat in silence for a minute.

'How many people are out there?' asked Inese in a very small voice.

'Just fifty or so,' said Charlie.

'Fifty's a lot.'

'And you've seduced crowds of thousands. Stay calm.'

She nodded, skittishly. He was handling her all wrong. 'Don't focus on them,' I said, taking her hand. 'Don't focus on anyone else.' I pushed a lock of hair behind her ear. 'Remember when you played for me in the music room? Remember what it did to me?'

'Yes,' she whispered.

'Do that to them.'

'I feel like I'm going to be sick.'

'You can't be sick. Your throat will be raw.'

She nodded, like I made a good point, and like me making it had done away with her nausea altogether.

They started with a discussion about the album. Charlie and I stood near the back of the room, watching her onstage over rows of heads. She looked nervous, but no more than anyone might have been presenting something they loved to all the people that mattered for the very first time. She and the host had a little preliminary chatter about the album before playing a few tracks over the speakers. Charlie had prepped her well for this and she had something insightful to say about each one: an anecdote from the studio, a personal story, a detail in the production the room might otherwise have missed. As she spoke, she became more confident. Callie's tinkly laugh circled the walls, leaving a trail of stars as it went. She was hypnotising. No one could have said that this wasn't her record.

When it came time for her to perform – 'Now, I hear you've got a little treat for us,' grinned the host – she seemed delighted to be asked. She rose gracefully from her chair like there was nothing else she would rather do. But as she watched them bring the standing mic onstage, it was like thumbing through that flick-book again – Callie, Inese, Callie, Inese – her face in one moment calm and professional, in another terrified to her core.

'Hi,' she said when she stepped up to the mic, with a winning little wave. The audience laughed. Charlie looked pleased. Unbeknown to him, we'd rehearsed that wave, me and her. 'So, one thing that I've been conscious of is that I know a lot of people are going to see this record as performance art, because it is so self-referential. And while I have often approached music from a place of concept, I've also always approached it from a place of emotion. I wanted to strip this one back for you and just sing it, and hopefully you can see what I mean.'

She held the mic and took a breath. Her eyes found mine. Neither of us acknowledged the other – it was enough just to see and be seen. Someone handed her a guitar. She hooked the strap around herself and began to play.

One thing that I had begun to fear might give her away was that while Inese could do a pitch-perfect imitation of Callie's voice, she actually played guitar and piano much better. Callie had always treated her instruments as secondary to her voice and songwriting, but for Inese they were passions in their own right. They also became part of her imitations – she would play guitar as Joni Mitchell or Bob Dylan, piano as Elton John or Norah Jones. When she was nervous, as she was now, and focused on getting Callie's voice and mannerisms correct, the muscle memory in her fingers took over and she played guitar more expertly and with more feeling than Callie ever had. Perhaps that clue would fly under the radar – Callie could always have improved, after all. But my mind was wired to high alert, searching for anything that the truther accounts might use to unravel her.

The production for this song on the album was inventive and interesting, but I preferred it played like this. Inese's guitar, and Callie's voice, and the echo of a very quiet room.

In every crowded basement

In all their ugly faces

In the most unlikely places

My thoughts go back to you

She was Callie on her very best days. Callie at her most magical. Watching her under those lights, on that unassuming stage, no one could have doubted her. Every social media conspiracy theorist would have deleted their pages immediately. The mental flick-book stopped. She settled into herself, whoever herself was, now. After this, she would never be just Inese again. Her outline had melted, like we had held her up to a flame.

Charlie looked at me, as if to confirm this. 'I'll miss her,' I blurted, before I could stop myself, and then closed my eyes, mortified. He raised his eyebrows, but he let the words lie where they did, with no comment.

When she finished playing, the room did not erupt into applause. Rooms full of industry people rarely did, Charlie told us later. But as they clapped for her, Inese looked out into the crowd and glowed. She was seeing what we couldn't from where we stood, on every face. *Conviction.*

She wasn't expected to come out and shake hands afterwards, because that kind of thing was never expected of stars as bright as Calista. But she chose to, walking through the small audience to thank them all for coming and for being so supportive of the album. Now that she was sure they believed in her, it seemed that all she wanted to do was parade herself in front of them. Occasionally, mid-conversation with some man in a suit or woman in a sensibly floral dress, she would catch my eye across the room and grin. It was like getting away with a crime in plain sight. Her anxiety was gone – she was drunk on it.

When everyone cleared out and we were stowed safely back in the dressing room, she held me for a very long time. I wondered if she was tearing up, but when she pulled back her face was dry and almost wild.

'Let's go out,' she said.

'You know we can't do that.'

'I'll wear a wig.'

'Where on earth are we getting a wig?'

'Callie's closet. She has loads of them.'

It knocked me sideways for a second, the same way it always did when I learnt a new secret about Callie. 'What does she have wigs for?'

'Stevie,' said Inese, like she was talking to a particularly slow child, 'I would guess, for exactly this purpose.'

We let ourselves be driven home, giggling like we shared a naughty secret. Back at the Hampstead house, I sat on the bed and watched her bring out wig after wig, about eight of them in total. She laid them out across the long footstool like scalps won. 'Which?' she asked.

I pointed to a long black one, pin straight. Callie had caps and wig glue in a box above her shoes – we had quite a time getting everything on and convincingly secured. Even then it looked a little like a Halloween costume, as Inese paraded in front of a mirror, throwing long black hair over her shoulder. 'Sunglasses,' she said. 'Both of us – they recognise you too, now.'

'Should I wear a wig as well?'

She took the ends of my brown waves between her fingers. 'No. Yours is too lovely.'

I was still standing there with the feeling of her fingers tugging gently on my hair when I realised she was across the room, taking off her top and disappearing into Callie's enormous closet. She emerged in only her shimmery dancer's tights, two small breasts exposed. She was the same build as Callie but her nipples were different – they were larger and darker, one pointing straight forward, the other slightly off to the side. She held a leather jacket on a hanger. Ignoring me entirely, she shrugged it on around her shoulders, leaving the sleeves dangling. She disappeared again and reappeared in a pair of tall red boots. She danced a quickstep around the room, long black hair falling over her shoulders and her bare chest, stumbling a little on her thin heels. The leather jacket fell off and she gasped and dove for it, like it had been protecting her modesty. She was so many different girls. Right now, she was aloof, carefree and cool. I noticed that her belly button was pierced. She caught me looking, painting her lips red in the mirror, and grinned.

'Did you get yours done at the same time as her?'

'The very next day,' she said. 'Two years ago. The next time I saw her, she apologised to me. Said she hadn't realised what it would mean. This—' She rolled her tights down a little and pointed to the star on her hip. 'She already had it when I was brought on board.'

'I know. I—' I needed to tell her suddenly. 'I have one too.'

'You do? Where?' I pulled my sock down so that she could see it on my heel. She covered her mouth with her hands. 'You got matching tattoos? Does anyone know?'

'No, not even Mel. I was embarrassed. It was only a few months before we broke up. She knows Callie has one, of course, but she's never seen mine.'

'Now we match too,' said Inese. 'Funny. She told me it was her lucky star, keeping her safe and healthy.'

It was strange to remember that Inese was the way she was because Callie had been sick. Callie had been sick and I hadn't known. Callie had been suffering and I hadn't felt it.

'What's wrong?' she asked, coming over to lift the corners of my mouth up. It was hard not to look at her chest and also not to look like I was deliberately avoiding looking at it. 'You look sad. You shouldn't be sad.'

'I'm not. I'm happy.'

'I'll get us shots,' she said, and she led me downstairs, still in her leather jacket and red boots and virtually nothing else.

We sat at the kitchen table and drank two shots each of gin and one of vermouth, because Inese had never tried it. She asked me to close my eyes and think of her and then tell her the first colour that came to mind. 'Gold,' I said, so we went back up two flights of stairs to Callie's closet and found a glossy gold top with lace along the hem.

'Oh!' said Inese, and opened a drawer to reveal underwear in every colour imaginable. She pulled out a gold sparkly thong and turned back towards me. 'Do you mind?' she asked. So that was where her boundaries lay. I turned to face the wall as she peeled the tights from her legs and slipped it on.

'You wear her underwear?' I said to the wall.

'Of course,' she said. 'You should too. It's all lovely quality.' She found a red slip dress for me and red underwear to match and closed the closet doors on me without switching on the light. In the dark, I dressed, discarding my clothes on the floor. When Inese pulled the doors open on me without warning, she was, just for a second, blindingly bright.

'Look at you,' she said, turning me towards the mirror. Her thumbs brushed over my shoulders. 'Such a pretty girl.'

'Are you drunk?'

'No,' she said unconvincingly.

'You're supposed to be able to drink. You're Eastern European.'

'That's an offensive stereotype,' she said. 'Anyway,' she said in Callie's voice, 'I'm not Eastern European. I grew up in Brighton.'

'Stop it.'

'Stop what?' She blinked innocently at me in the mirror. Even under all the long black hair, I still saw Callie's face. 'I'm just being me.'

'You're being Callie.'

'I am Callie.'

'No,' I said, 'you're Inese. You're Inese.'

'I'm both,' she said. She kissed me on the cheek. Her lipstick left a bright red mark. 'I need trousers,' she said in her own voice. 'Or a skirt. Something.' I left her rummaging through racks of clothes and went into the bathroom to touch up my make-up and breathe. The drawers were packed with Callie's expensive products. I ran my hand over them – smooth plastic, soft bristles, cold and gentle – and picked out a few to try. Moments like these had a little triumph in them. She had forced me out of her life, and here I was, inside her home, with everything she owned at my disposal.

I opened an expensive foundation and tipped a little into my hand, then a little more, letting it run over my fingers and splash on to the ceramic. Then I upturned it and tipped the entire thing down the sink, watching it collect over the plughole, glossy pink-ish yellow, like melted skin.

'Nearly ready?' asked Inese, now properly dressed in a black miniskirt. She didn't seem shocked at the waste. 'Careful,' she said lightly. 'You'll block the drains.'

We didn't call a car. We did another shot, and then we walked to the Tube. Inese moved like someone was after us, her neck twisting with every pace we took, her steps irregular. 'I wouldn't put it beyond Charlie to have me microchipped,' she said. I laughed. She linked her arm through mine. 'I feel like I'm floating above myself,' she said.

'That's not good.'

'No, it is good. I like to feel like that. I feel my best when I hardly feel in my body at all, like I'm just watching it and wondering who's inside it today.'

'You can't just say things like that.'

'Why not?'

'They're scary. They make me worry about you.'

She laughed. 'You shouldn't worry. I like being all the people that I am.'

We both wore sunglasses on the Tube. Inese's were large and round, and she was almost unrecognisable, not just because of the glasses and the wig, but because her body language was entirely different – she stood in this slouchy way I didn't recognise, moved differently, coughed differently.

'Who were you being?' I asked her, when we got off.

'This girl from back home,' she said. 'She was an absolute bitch, but she knew how to party. She was the first person I ever let inside my body. We were in the toilets in a club and I was obsessed with the way she spoke to me – so filthy.'

'That did it for you?' I asked, feeling a wave of inadequacy come over me.

'No, it didn't turn me on, Stevie. I just found it fascinating. I started imitating her after that. She knew I was doing it but she could never prove it. It sounded crazy, her shouting about how I was standing like her. It drove her mad.' I stopped walking and she looked up at the red neon sign over our heads. 'Where have you brought me?'

'It's a karaoke bar.'

'Did the two of you used to come here?' I didn't reply. 'It's okay, Stevie,' she said. 'I don't mind you bringing me to the same places.'

'No?'

She kissed me gently, her teeth softly dragging along my bottom lip, and pulled me inside.

It was busy but not full, plenty of space for us to slip through pockets of people towards the stage. Inese took off her leather jacket and held it over her shoulder. People looked at us, but more in curiosity than recognition. A man around my age was singing an awful version of 'My Way', so sincere and out of tune that not even his friends were cheering him on.

I turned back to Inese. She looked uncertain again – the bravado of the last couple of hours had slipped off her and now she was vulnerable like she had been earlier in the dressing room, looking for reassurance. My hands ached to touch her. 'What if someone sees us?' she asked.

'It's okay. You look so different.'

'We didn't think this through properly.'

'Inese, you can be nothing like her, when you try.'

'I know,' she said. 'I'm being reckless, though. I've worked so hard to build this all and I'm being reckless.' She shook her head at me. 'You weren't supposed to make me reckless, Stevie. You were supposed to make me better at my job.'

'I do,' I said, a little plaintively.

'You do,' she agreed.

I dropped my gaze. I felt her hand on my shoulder. She turned my face towards hers. I was afraid she was drawing attention to us. She examined me.

'What?' I asked, a little breathless.

'I remember sometimes that you didn't have a mother,' she said, 'and it makes me want to take care of you.'

'Did your mother take care of you?'

'Yes,' she said, 'where it mattered.' Then she reconsidered. 'Not in the way I mean. But I think I need that less than you.'

'I don't need to be taken care of.' I've always been the one who wanted to take care of the people I loved.

'Oh, Stevie,' she said, her head on one side, like she didn't believe me.

We went to the bar and ordered vodka. Inese had hers with tonic water, and I had mine with Diet Coke. Onstage, the man singing 'My Way' had been replaced by a woman singing Britney Spears, with a lot more stage presence and semblance of tuning. There were whoops from the audience.

'I'd like to hear you sing,' I said to Inese.

'You heard me sing already today. I think I sang very well, actually.'

'I'd like to hear you sing as yourself.'

She let out a nervous laugh. 'Here?'

'Why not? No one will know.'

'What if someone realises?'

'They won't. Just sing as you. None of Callie. Something you like.'

'I've been drinking. My voice will be bad.'

'You want to,' I said, and she put the straw between her teeth and grinned, like a child caught in a lie.

She went to the DJ to queue her song. He didn't give her a second glance, just nodded, eyes on his screen, and put both thumbs up. She didn't move back towards me, but stayed beside the stage, slowly dancing, moving her body in this strange, torturously slow way, individually stretching and retracting each arm. It was gruesome. I couldn't stop watching her. I was afraid that she was drawing too much attention to herself, but then again, it hardly mattered when right now she was as far from being Calista as she could have been. She rolled her neck in blue light, put both hands in her long black hair. I hoped she wouldn't dislodge the wig.

She'd chosen 'At Last' by Etta James. When the song came on, she ascended the steps to the stage in a trance. The wig had become tangled at the ends. She pushed them back over her shoulders. The DJ handed her the mic. The crowd looked unimpressed – no one had told Inese that you weren't supposed to pick downbeat songs at a karaoke bar. She didn't care. They might as well have not existed. She stared over their heads towards the black door we'd entered through, covered in band stickers. Her make-up was messy and smudged.

When she sung, she was better than Callie had ever been. I knew it instantly, from the first note. It was something about the tone of it, the placement, the way it cut through the air, the way her face scrunched up and then relaxed, the trembling emotion she shot through it, aiming the pistol with a steady hand.

An intense feeling of gratitude came over me, electrifying, so huge an emotion I wanted to jump up from my chair and sprint down the street just to burn the edge off it. Not too long ago, I had been stuck in this soul-sucking routine in my boring flat, in my boring job, with my boring boyfriend. Now, I had my life with Callie back, and even more. I had all of it, and on top of everything,

I had Inese. This wild, intense, crazy-talented thing that I could sneak out into the city with in dark hair and dark sunglasses, to sing for me in dusty bars, to love me through clouds of smoke, to tell me that I was her saviour. Everyone around me had spent years instructing me to move on and leave Callie behind. But I hadn't wasted years over her – I had invested time, and my investment was returning tenfold. This was the wicked, wonderful, ridiculous life that I had always known I was supposed to be a part of.

Tonight, I would take Inese home. Tomorrow, when Charlie came over, I would sit with Callie on the sofa, and we would talk about her career. I would watch Calista sing onstage and drive home with Inese in the back of the limo. It was all too extraordinary. I was the luckiest girl in the world.

◆ ◆ ◆

At home in her bed, with our make-up staining pillowcases, wigs thrown over the back of the chair and real hair tangled in hairbands, she touched my cheek and said, 'Sometimes I wish you knew me only as myself.'

'Why?'

'Because I want to know if you would love me anyway.'

'I've never said that I love you.'

'You do,' she said. 'You just do.'

I closed my eyes. Her fingers wiped mascara from under the sockets.

'But there's not just me in here,' she said. 'It's not so clear who it is you love. Maybe both of us at once.'

'Maybe.'

'That's okay,' she said. 'That's enough.'

She twisted her body towards me, so that her chest was facing me, her hips still flat on the bed. The black miniskirt was hiked up around her waist, the gold glimmering between her legs. She ran her finger over the strap of my red dress, pushed it down over my shoulder.

'Inese . . .'

'You don't have to call me that,' she said, 'if you don't want.'

I closed my eyes, tried to swallow. 'What?' I said, my throat dry.

'You know what,' she said. Her finger pushed my strap down further. My arm pressed the dress against my side, holding it up. She moved her hips, and her skirt rode up higher. She took my hand, walked my fingers down towards the glinting. 'You can say it,' she said. 'It's okay.' She let go of my hand and began to trace other places, other parts of me. I gasped. 'Stevie,' she said. 'Stevie . . .'

I closed my eyes again, tighter this time. I felt her voice in my ear. Her fingers made me see red behind my eyes. 'Callie,' I whispered. Her body reacted to it.

'It's okay,' she said, when I fell silent. Her hands kept moving.

'Are you okay with this?'

'I am. Are you?'

I nodded into her hair. 'Callie,' I said, a little louder.

'I love you,' she said.

'I love you too. I—' I wanted to find a way to say I loved both of her, all of her. Whoever this creature was in bed beside me, I loved her. The words for that didn't exist, or if they did, they couldn't be easily gasped out among the rest of it. So, I said it again. 'I love you.'

If to love someone is to know them entirely, and if to love someone is to love the parts they keep hidden, I loved her both ways. Nothing had ever felt as euphoric as that.

Loser (2017)

This is the first year that people start to call her 'prolific'. It's a word that will become heavily associated with her over the years, and people will stop being astonished at how quickly she is able to turn around an album, and always to such great success. When Loser *is announced, though, just a year after* Calista, *people are astonished. 'She's one of the hardest-working women in pop,' one of her producers claims. 'No one should worry about any part of this work being rushed. Calista spends more time in the studio than anyone else I know. Including me!'*

The lead single is a break-up song. She's never written a break-up song before. It isn't very specific, but it's very emotional. She describes not being able to get out of bed, all her food tasting the same, how empty her hand feels on public transport. It's called 'Only'. I listen to it again and again, until Mel, who I've temporarily moved in with while I get my living situation in order, tells me that if this song is about me then so is the album title. The album cover shows her staring through someone's window into a cosy house party, tears running down her cheeks. It's exactly how I've been feeling for the last year. The image elates me. She's been feeling it too.

I buy standing tickets for her O2 Arena show without telling Mel. On the day of the performance, I queue for seven hours with a group of seventeen-year-old girls who are skipping school for the day and who proudly show me their homemade I'm A Loser *t-shirts. The line slowly forms behind us – teenagers with their mothers, students my age holding signs written in felt pen. Everyone around me has brought something to hold up and show her, or something they are hoping to pass her onstage. All I want is to catch her eye. I'm half fearful and half hoping that one of the friendly seventeen-year-old girls might recognise me, but none of them seem to know who I am. It is baking hot, and I have to ask them to hold my spot in line while I go and buy myself a bottle of water. When I return, a large woman a few spots behind me tries to argue that there isn't any space-holding, as if this is an official system and not a collective madness that we are all participating in. I ignore her, and eventually she calms down. During our fifth hour of waiting, one of the seventeen-year-olds gives me a chocolate teacake and it is the best thing I have ever tasted.*

Eventually they start to funnel us in, with a stern 'No running'. We head towards the barriers at the front of the empty stage. The seventeen-year-olds are walking as fast as their skinny legs will let them, batting each other like they're trying to squash mosquitoes on each other's arms. One of them grabs my hand and drags me forward. We are right at the front, in the centre, the four seventeen-year-olds and me. This is closer to her than I bargained on being. I want her to see me, but I don't want to look this keen. I panic and take a step backwards, but the girl beside me grabs my shoulder. 'Don't let them take your spot!' she says. 'You waited for this!' I did, I think, oh god. What's wrong with me?

It's another two hours before the warm-up act comes onstage, another hour after that before the lights dim. I expect the girls to start flagging – I certainly do – but they only seem to gain energy as we get closer. They're drunk without drinking. They're caffeinated without coffee. When a stagehand comes onstage to check the mic, they scream so loudly that I think they can't possibly be any louder for Callie herself.

But they manage it, of course. When she steps out, I feel the sound deep in my skull, and I think I will probably be hearing like I'm underwater for several days. She's in a pleated skirt and a baggy t-shirt that reads LOSER *in capital letters. The girls puff their chests out, point to their own t-shirts. She notices and smiles at them. I turn my head and slip backwards into the crowd while she is distracted. There's a scuffle for my spot that alarms her for a second. I can't tell if she sees that I've caused it. She's singing 'Don't Save Me', the lead single from* Calista *that she accused me of not liking.*

From my spot in the crowd, I stand and watch her, light-headed just from being in the same room as her, like she's taking in all the air. She sings 'Only', and then a song from Put This On My Headstone *that holds me by the throat. I want to cry. She's luminescent. I mourn the months she has spent hurting, the heartbreak that she poured into 'Only'. It didn't have to be like that. She didn't have to feel those things. I would have loved her forever. I can make her know it.*

'London,' she says then, with her hand on her hip. 'Would you like to hear something new?'

The crowd screams. I want to jump up and down and yell, 'Yes! Yes! Tell me anything, anything at all!'

'I went through quite an intense heartbreak this year,' she says. 'It wasn't like anything I've felt before, and it really made me understand that all those heartbreak clichés are true.'

Callie, I can make it better. I can fix it all. I promise.

She fiddles with the mic, slotting it back into the stand.

'It was quite a brief relationship—'

It wasn't brief by my standards, but I suppose it was, in the grand scheme of things. In the context of forever. One day we'll look back and consider this time apart brief too.

'—and I fell super quickly, which isn't something I'd experienced before. My first relationship gave me quite a clear idea of what feeling in love was, and then this one really just turned it all on its head, and I realised that love really doesn't have a timeline.'

There is a coldness gnawing at my stomach. Something is wrong here.

'And even though he and I parted—'

He?

'—and even though it was the worst heartbreak I've ever experienced—'

The worst?

'—it really gave me an important perspective on love and relationships, and I'm grateful for the experience. And, as a songwriter, the inspiration.' She laughs. The crowd laughs too. It feels mocking. Their heads jump on their shoulders like ventriloquist dummies. 'That's what this album's about; how feeling like a loser, feeling all these uncomfortable, negative emotions, can actually help you to grow.'

The crowd are cheering. I feel like dying.

'I really hope you love the album when it's out, and I really hope you love this song. It's about that realisation, and it's called, "Stomach It".'

I listen half in hope, but even by the end of the first verse, it's clear. This song is not about me. I take a step backwards, and then another. Someone swears at me. I push through the packed crowd into the aisle. Even outside the doors, I can hear her. The O2 is massive. I can't remember which way round I need to go in order to get out. The nausea is coming back over me, a fresh wave, and I find myself retching into a bin. Thankfully, no one is there to see.

She's loved and lost again, since we broke up. Not only that, but this loss hit her harder. It made her grow. She's processed it. She's turned it into art.

I am the far, far bigger loser out of the two of us. I will stop loving her, I decide. I will let it go. When this album comes out, I won't listen to it. I will let myself move on.

But of course, I listen to it, at the kitchen table when Mel is working late, with a glass of wine, like a total fucking cliché. And even though the songs aren't about me, and even though the feelings she describes have nothing to do with me, listening to it makes me feel less alone.

Chapter Seven

The final text Rich sent me was three weeks after he'd turned up at the Hampstead house. *I hope you know that youv massively masivley fucked me over but have a nice life I guess x.* I assumed it was a drunk text from the single kiss and the fact that 'massively' was spelt two different ways. I checked for a while after that, expecting to see his name pop up again, but nothing. Not too long after that message he posted a picture of his hand at a pub table, with another, smaller hand resting on top of it. I hadn't fucked him over all that massively in the end then – either that, or one of his mates had very feminine hands.

Mel never stopped texting me. Almost three months since we'd last seen each other, I would still get a message from her almost every other day. The longest stretch of silence was four days – I wondered if she had forgotten, or finally given up. But then, on the fifth day, a text came through.

> *Got a candle shaped like a butt today. I'll buy you one, if you like.*

She was either very lonely or very deluded, or she loved me very much. I didn't like to think about which it was, and I didn't like to think about why I couldn't text her back. If I did, I had to admit that what I had here didn't feel like winning three lotteries at once; it felt fragile, and easy to disrupt. And it felt like making some deal with the devil, whereby to have what I'd wanted for so long I had to leave my old life behind.

'You could just block her number,' said Inese one day, when she saw me scrolling through the unanswered texts. She never asked me why I didn't reply, and when I continued to let the texts come through, she didn't ask me about that either. We weren't interested in finding any kind of normal or thinking about how to make all of it sustainable. We were happy to live in this weird, not-quite-reality for as long as we could.

I couldn't block Mel's number. We'd agreed without really agreeing, Inese and I, that I wasn't leaving the Hampstead house anytime soon. I'd been feeling for a while that I should initiate a proper conversation about it. I knew that I wanted to stay – this world, Calista's world, felt more like home to me than anything had in the years since I'd been ousted from it. Then, one day, unprompted, Inese asked me if there was anything I thought we should do to the house.

'What?' I asked.

'I just wanted to get your opinion,' she said. The implication was clear – this was my home too.

I daydreamed about redecorating Callie's bedroom, pulling her strange wall décor down, making the room something that was reflective of Inese and I, rather than a refuge for Callie's ghost. There was no job for me to go home to, no boyfriend. There was no reason for me to want to be anywhere else. But, still, there was Mel. Mel, whose name kept coming up on my phone, no matter how many times I swiped the messages away.

The text that upset me the most came through at the album release party.

It's really hard not having you to talk to, Stevie-girl.

Inese found me crying in the bathroom.

'Stevie,' she said as Callie, kneeling in front of me, wiping the tears from under my eyes with her thumbs. She'd been Callie from the minute we'd sat down in the car, even when it was just the two of us. There were far too many people around and she was far too much the centre of attention to risk anything. 'You can't let her get to you like this.'

'I feel like I've abandoned her.'

'You haven't,' she said. 'You're just growing apart from her. You've got this whole other life now.'

I slowly unwound toilet paper. There were black smudges on Inese's thumbs. 'I am going to tell her everything, when it all calms down.'

'Stevie,' she said lightly, but I could tell that it was a warning to watch my words. She kissed my forehead. 'You're missing the party,' she said.

'So are you. You should get back out there.'

'I don't go anywhere without you,' she said, holding her hand out to me. 'You know that by now.' She'd bought herself the same silver tennis bracelet that Callie had owned and now we both wore them every day. Some fans had started wearing their own versions too, particularly lesbian couples. Calista's queer fanbase had grown exponentially since we'd gone public. I took her hand and let her pull me to my feet and lead me over to the mirror, where she fussed over me, fixing my make-up. 'Do you need some water?'

'I'm okay.' I lowered her hands. 'Go. I don't want to keep you from your party. This is your night.'

'It's both our nights,' she said.

She'd hardly let go of me the entire party, keeping her arm linked through mine the whole time. This was as much strategic as it was affectionate – I was a fantastic decoy. It was hard for people to get too familiar with her while also being polite to me. I allowed her to keep everyone at arm's length. Back in the old days, I had often felt pushed to the side at industry events, as she shook the hands she needed to shake and talked on and on about herself. I loved being so essential to her.

When it hit midnight and *Haunt Me Haunt Me* officially dropped – an industry word I loved, like something heavy was being released from Inese's clenched fist, hitting the ground with a clang – a mic was pressed into her hand. She sang along to the lead single. The track was a blend of her and Callie – it had been thought prudent to replace Callie's vocals, just so the songs would sound as close as possible when Inese sang them live. Still, I heard Callie in the mix, in the backing vocals, like she was cheering Inese on from beyond the grave. I held on to Inese's other hand and sang with them both, and when she missed the song's final line to kiss me, there was a cheer from all the people in the room that we hardly knew. It was a new beginning for both of us.

I was by her side in every meeting now. Gene Parrison didn't like it – she never said so, but women like Gene were able to be openly rude to you with a lot of plausible deniability. Charlie accepted it quietly. Inese swore that Charlie liked me – she could tell, she said, and I chose to take her word for it. They all liked me, by Inese's estimation. They were all so pleased that I was there; they saw how important I was to her. She would repeat it to me after every meeting, clasping my hand in hers, her expression reverent. I was crucial to all of this. It was all my victory just as much as hers. She said it often enough that I started to believe it.

Sometimes she was different with me. Sometimes the help I tried to give wasn't accepted. My words were harsh, or I was too distant, and then she would pout and shut herself in a separate room for hours at a time. I knew that she was being childish because of the overwhelming pressure she was feeling, that she had to be allowed to have these moods, but it aggravated me how suddenly she could switch up. Then she would emerge, apologetic, regretful, and put her arms around my neck, and I would love her again. If I noticed her being Callie in these reconciliations, copying Callie's mannerisms, doing her smile, I never said anything about it.

When news of the show had first been delivered to Inese by Charlie, along with a bottle of champagne and box of Fortnum & Mason chocolates, she had received it calmly. She'd sat with the champagne and chocolates on the coffee table in front of her, nodding along, as Charlie gently talked her through the plans that had been made and I drew hearts on her knee with my finger. Callie had been planning a tour anyway, of course, to go along with the album. It had all been pushed back to allow her more time to recover, but Gene proposed that one of the London dates stay in the diary. A one-night-only comeback show before Calista toured internationally next year, something to show the world that she was the same performer she had always been. Something – although this was never said out loud – to shut everyone up once and for all.

'Exciting, huh?' said Charlie, wiping dry hands on his jeans. 'Wembley.'

She barely reacted to the word. After a second she reached forward and took the pink lid off the box of chocolates. I watched her search for an almond truffle, her fingers hovering, pinching air, until she found what she wanted. She turned my hand over and placed a heart-shaped caramel in the centre of it.

'Thoughts?' asked Charlie, as she chewed.

She didn't have any thoughts, not just then. She couldn't. The album was about to come out, and Wembley was too large an idea for her to process. Charlie left in a good mood, as if the meeting had been a successful one. He didn't see how, in the coming days, the thoughts found her – slowly at first, showing themselves in jittering legs and nails bitten down to the quick, and then so fast and relentless that they threatened to overwhelm her.

They pulled her into rehearsals the very next week. Every day we would go to the studio and I would sit and watch her sing and play. She would belt out her entire setlist while jogging on the spot – the first time they made her do this, she threw up, and rehearsals ended early. She had to learn choreography as well, which was when I realised that there was something she was noticeably worse at than Callie. The steps weren't anything complicated, but they panicked her when she couldn't get them right straight away. She never broke in the room, or in the car on the way home, or even for several hours afterwards. But when it got dark, when we were sat on the sofa watching something, or curled up in bed, I would look over and see that there were tears falling down her cheeks. Sometimes, when I held her at night, she would tremble for hours.

One night, kept awake by her sobs, I said into the dark, 'If you can't do this, you need to tell them.'

Silence. Eventually, after a few sniffs, she said, 'You don't think I can do it?'

'That's not what I said.'

'You come to these rehearsals,' she said, 'and you sit there, and you watch me, and you don't smile.'

'What are you talking about?'

'You don't smile. You don't say anything on the ride home. You know they're going badly. You know, but you don't say anything.'

I was quiet. Beside me, sullen and hungry, lay the weight of her expectation. She rolled over and the mass of it shifted, jutting into my side.

'You feel as if I'm ruining her,' she said. 'I know. I feel it too.'

It became harder and harder to sit in the rehearsal room and watch her. She would forget choreography she'd spent four days mastering. She was tense and nervous as she moved. She started to mess up the stuff she'd always been able to do, stumbling over lyrics, backing off from high notes. Her fingers on the piano keys were a jumbled mess. Every time she made a mistake, she would look over at me, her eyes enormous and frightened, and I wouldn't know what to do with my face. At home, she would cry with her head in my lap, my fingers in her hair. I tried to stay soft, safe, something for her to sink into when she could no longer hold herself up. I would search for wonderful reviews of the album – of which there were many – and read them to her. She would be quiet, listening, but when I was done the sobbing would start again. It was Callie's work, Callie's genius, and she couldn't sustain it. She was going to fail. She knew she was going to fail.

The horrible truth was that I was becoming weary of all of it. In her most panicked moments, she would turn her blotchy face to me, and the only thing in the world she would need was for me to tell her that when I looked at her, I saw Callie. But this was becoming harder to do. The more I watched her struggle through rehearsals, the more I saw her stooped and made smaller by failure, the more I saw Inese. Just a girl from Riga, who had spent her life pretending to be other people and now couldn't outrun herself.

Eventually, there came a morning where she turned to me at the door in her rehearsal clothes, with the car engine running outside, and said, 'Ready?' And I couldn't go with her.

'I think I might hang back for today,' I said.

She didn't say anything. She looked at me for a second, and then she left, closing the door quietly behind her. The car pulled away. I walked down to the end of the garden and sat in the grass, eyes shut, feeling the wind on my face. I spent the day doing very little.

When she came home, she said, 'You didn't make dinner?'

'No,' I said. She started taking ingredients from the fridge without another word about it. 'I'll order something,' I said. She slammed a tin of chopped tomatoes down on the counter and started rifling through drawers for a can opener. 'How was it?' I asked, sat at the table, on edge.

'Fine,' she said. I watched her put two slices of bread in the toaster. She ate in the living room alone. If she cried that night, I didn't know about it. The next day, she didn't ask if I was coming with her. That became the new normal – me at home, Inese at rehearsals, evenings when we pretended nothing was wrong. She stopped telling me how it was all going, and I stopped asking.

I thought about trying to get my job back, or trying to find a new one. Maybe this was settling into things – maybe this was life now, and I had to find a version of it that didn't feel like a holiday from reality. I brought it up to her one night as we sat at the kitchen table eating takeout pizza that definitely wasn't in Inese's food plan. 'Do you think I should look for work?'

'Work?' she said, around a mouthful of pizza, like she'd never heard the word.

'Since I'm less . . . involved. Since you're just . . . doing your thing now. Maybe I should find my thing.'

'You don't need to work,' she said, dismissive.

'I might want to.'

'Why would you want to? We're rich. You could do anything you like.' I wasn't sure what to say to that. 'Unless you're planning to leave,' she said. She said it calmly, but her eyes wouldn't let go of mine.

'I can't be fully dependent on you,' I said.

She looked down at her pizza, and then smiled bitterly.

'What? Do you want me to be?'

'I just don't get it,' she said. 'She said that's all you wanted.'

'Who said?'

She smiled again, picking cheese from the top of her slice.

'She told you that?'

'No, Stevie,' she said. 'We never talked about you.' The words hurt, like she'd known they would. 'It was in her diaries,' she said. 'She said it in her diaries.'

The cheese stuck in the back of my throat. 'You're missing the full context,' I said.

She lifted an eyebrow at me.

◆ ◆ ◆

Later, I sat in bed and tried not to look at the final volume beside me. I'd been telling myself for a while now to get it over with. There couldn't have been anything too surprising in the last diary – if there was, Inese would have said something by now. Perhaps what I was afraid of was any hint of disapproval, a slight indication that this cause I'd turned my life upside down for wasn't what Callie had wanted after all. Perhaps I was just scared that reading it would make her feel dead again. She was so alive, all around me. I didn't want to go back to grieving her.

But had she really written that I wanted to be fully dependent on her? That I didn't want a life of my own?

Inese climbed in under the covers and peeled her t-shirt off. I could smell her sweat. The blue photo album that I'd made for Callie was on her bedside table. I ignored the diary – I couldn't have read it just then with Inese beside me, anyway – and nodded towards the album. 'Were you the one who wrote in that?' She nodded. 'You wrote like you were her,' I said. 'Why did you do that?'

'I was imagining what it would have been like,' she said. 'To be her. To be loved by you.'

I laid my head on my knees. She took my hand, brought it up to her lips. She liked to do this, in moments where she wanted me to know that she cared, honestly and deeply. I knew that for her it was the tenderest way she had to show me that she loved me.

‘I never would have thrown it away,’ she said. ‘You know that.’

Her lips brushed the skin on the back of my hand like something had briefly tickled it – a cat’s whisker, a butterfly’s wing. ‘I know,’ I said.

◆ ◆ ◆

Inese’s body was getting stronger – I could see the evidence of it in her shoulders and upper arms. In the garden she chased a wasp away from our table and her legs were lean and toned. Her body looked less like Callie’s now but was more equipped to do what Callie’s body had done. She didn’t seem to mind so much that I had stopped coming to rehearsals. I felt less needed, something that embarrassed me, especially since Inese’s comment about me craving some unhealthy dependency. It wasn’t something I’d thought I felt. It made me retroactively self-conscious of the way that I had behaved in my relationship with Callie. I’d always seen myself as the thing keeping her grounded, not hanging belligerently on to her ankle.

When Inese was out at rehearsals, I went back to that first volume and opened it to May 2016, to the entry that I hadn’t been able to bring myself to read.

> *We finally broke up a few days ago. I haven’t been able to write about it. It was horrible, but not because I wasn’t ready to do it. The worst part was that I had left it far too long and was so, so ready, and I almost felt like I hardly had any sympathy for her, which made me feel like a monster. She asked me why so many times, and I just had to keep giving her the same answer. We’ve grown apart. Which sounds like nothing, so I couldn’t convince her it was a real reason.*

'I don't understand what changed,' she said.

I pointed out that lots had changed.

'So, we can't be together anymore because you're famous now?'

I tried not to get angry when she said that. I know that's what she thinks it is. She thinks I'm moving forward and leaving her behind. She's always been afraid of that, I think, right from the start. She was devastated. I had to sit and listen to her cry for hours. I sound awful, writing that. I suppose I've just listened to her cry so much that I've sort of disconnected from it. I should have done this far sooner. I should have done it when I first felt myself falling out of love. That's what first relationships are though, I suppose – you learn from your mistakes and you carry the lessons forward.

The thing that's hard to say to her is that you can't really stay in love with someone just because of how much they love you. Because what do they do when you leave the room? Whenever I leave a room, I just picture Stevie sat there patiently, waiting for me to come back. I would never sit in a room and wait for someone like that. I want to be with someone who chooses to be in that room with me because it's the thing they like best, not because it's the only thing they have.

I really do hope she'll be happy. I really did love her, for a while.

I wanted to throw the book across the room again. This mousy little lapdog wasn't who I was. She wasn't who I'd ever been. I'd seen Callie entirely, I'd known her, but clearly she had never really known me. She had never really tried. She had loved how much I'd loved her and then she'd started to grow tired of it. Isn't that how every star feels about their fans after a while?

I was ready to lay her to rest.

◆ ◆ ◆

Callie's final diary began strangely.

> *A new diary means a fresh start, which is something I desperately need. I'm proud of myself for how well I've stuck to doing this over the years – long may it continue. I haven't felt myself in a while, but I'm coming back to who I was now, little by little.*

Not too different from how she'd written before, but as she continued there was something a tad robotic in it.

> *Went to meet a fan today who lost her mother to cancer. Adorable little girl. I gave her some presents and we played some music together for a while . . .*

I skipped ahead a little, to a different entry. None of them in this volume were dated.

> *Have finalised the concept for the new album. This resurrection theme is something I'm incredibly excited about. I've started collecting visuals and will go in for my first sessions very soon . . .*

I was disappointed to find that the final volume I had of her seemed, after that first paragraph, to be much drier and more factual. It was largely about the conceptualisation and creation of *Haunt Me Haunt Me* – not the insight into her creative process that I had come to expect and still craved, but more the admin of it. When she had taken certain meetings, how she had pitched it to the execs. She said over and over again that she was 'so excited' but never quite seemed to convince herself. Her words sounded tired. It was a damp squib of an end to her explosive life; a short, infrequent, matter-of-fact record of her final days. Perhaps if she'd known, she would have tried to make it more exciting. I suppose what I was really looking for was some kind of retraction. *I was completely wrong about Stevie. She was the love of my life and no one else has really compared to her since.* Nothing of the sort. Not even a mention of my name. In fact, I hadn't been mentioned since volume three, when she met an actor who'd grown up in my hometown.

She wrote a bit about Inese. *I'm so grateful to her for continuing it all for the fans, even when I'm not able to. If anything ever did happen to me (touch wood) then it's nice to know that Calista is safe at least.* There were a few more mentions of that sort, dotted throughout. Her conflicting feelings about Inese's involvement seemed to have vanished entirely by the end – which was good, I thought. At least Inese could trust that she was doing exactly as Callie had wanted.

Inese's car pulled in and she came upstairs to the green bedroom, which is where I always went to read Callie's diaries, ritualistically.

'You must be done by now,' she said from the doorway. Her hair was in two braids, which meant she'd got up early enough to do it. She'd had more energy lately, getting up earlier in the mornings to work out and warm up her voice, or to make herself breakfast, or just to make herself look pretty.

'Just finished.' I'd actually finished half an hour ago, and had been contemplating the diary's back cover. The final entry read as follows:

> *Rio is next week, and after that it all starts up again. I've been doing this so long now and it's still my favourite thing in the world. The show is going to be a real celebration of everything I've accomplished, all the people in my past who made it possible, no matter how small a role they played. I can't wait.*

That was it. It read like a press release. The final words she would ever say to me – well, not the final words, I reflected. Not actually.

So, Stevie. This one's for you.

I was meant to be one of many surprise dedications, by the sounds of it. Probably most of her exes would have heard their names that night. She was acknowledging her past with simpering gratitude, but she was moving ever forward. She had never been looking backwards, not really. I had been crazy to imagine she ever could have been stuck like me.

'What are you thinking?' said Inese, sitting down opposite me.

'I'm glad I've read them.'

'I'm glad you have as well.' She was waiting for something that I wasn't giving her, so in true Inese fashion, she pushed for it. 'What do you think of her?'

'What do you mean?'

'You've seen inside her mind now,' she said, moving hair out of her mouth. 'All those years you were apart. What do you think?'

'She seems like she was very happy, for a while,' I said, 'and then she wasn't.'

She nodded thoughtfully, like this was an astute observation.

'She talks about Calista almost like she's a separate person,' I said. 'She acts like Calista is more important than she is. More important than anything, I guess. What did you think of her, when you read them?'

'I was full of admiration,' she said.

'Really?'

'More than anything else. She's going to be remembered, I thought. I was proud to be a small part of it.'

'You're hardly a small part.'

She nudged me with her toe. 'Will you come to rehearsals tomorrow?'

'Do you want me there?'

'They've been going really well,' she said. 'I want you to see what we've been doing.'

She smiled at me from behind the sleeve of her hoodie. I wanted to kiss her, which was an urge I hadn't had in a few days.

'You're good, then?' I asked.

'You know I'm good,' she said as Callie. 'I'm the best there ever was.'

She could have been. I wasn't in a place to be objective, in that rehearsal room. She was in leggings and a t-shirt, performing to a handful of crew members in a studio with tape on the floor, but it didn't matter. She wasn't even the same girl she'd been just a few months ago. It didn't matter, just then, whether she was doing a good enough impression of Callie. She was a new Calista. She was the next stage of evolution. She was furthering the legacy. No one could have found fault with it.

Charlie was there, of course. He'd been there every day. We sat in folding chairs beside each other as she sang with her guitar around her shoulders, easy and light, like nothing had ever come more naturally. He acknowledged me as little as possible, as always. At one point I looked across at him and asked, 'Are you proud of her?' I couldn't help it. I had to know. He exhaled through his nose, with a hint of a smile, and raised his eyebrows at the stage.

'Harma says the ticketing sites might crash, when this goes on sale tomorrow,' he said, after a while.

'I suppose everyone wants to see her up close at this point, even if they weren't fans before.'

'She'll sell it out,' he said, as if he hadn't heard me. 'You know, I've been afraid she wouldn't be able to do it.' Almost as if he heard me holding my breath, he glanced over at me and added, 'She's been a long time out of the game.'

'Not that long,' I said. 'Rio was only a few months ago.'

He looked across at me with something like amusement, but he didn't say anything else.

When Inese was finished, she came towards me, all elation, and said, 'Did you see? Did you see?' As if I hadn't been sat right there the entire time. I kissed her without caring who was looking. 'Charlie's very pleased,' she said, with my arms around her shoulders. Inese could always make Charlie break a smile, if she tried.

At the kitchen table, eating toast with scrambled egg and smoked salmon, I said, 'You know he's in love with you.'

'Who?' she asked, astonished.

'Charlie. Obviously.'

'He's engaged to Harma,' she said. A bit of scrambled egg fell off her toast. 'Honestly, Stevie,' she said, pushing it back on with her finger. 'I'm not convinced you ever know how anyone's really feeling.'

'Maybe not,' I said.

'Why have you brought that down?' she asked, nodding at Callie's final diary, which sat in front of me.

'I wanted to check a few things.'

'Alright,' she said, perplexed. She took her plate to the sink. There were several days' worth of plates piled up – Charlie had signed off on a cleaning staff coming to the house once a week and we'd both become a lot laxer about chores as a result. 'It's late,' she said. 'When did it get so late?' She was forever surprised by the time. I would have loved to know how time moved for her – it seemed different to how it moved for me. 'I should sleep before tomorrow,' she said.

'Yeah, you should.'

'Are you coming?'

'I will. Just let me—' I tapped the diary.

'What are you looking for?' she asked. 'Mentions of you?'

'No. I know there aren't any. There's just a part I wanted to reread.'

She kissed me on the cheek and slipped away. For the first time, I wondered if Inese was ever jealous of Callie.

I flicked through the pages, trying to remember what it was that had sat weirdly, but increasingly I realised there was hardly a page that didn't give me a twisting sensation in my stomach. There had been a sadness in finishing the diaries, of course, and another minor humiliation in realising how little she'd really thought of me by the end. But neither of those things was causing the feeling that came over me as I sat staring down at the page in front of me. I thought of the story Mel had told me once, about a man who sits for days staring at a lamp, knowing there's something wrong with it, only to come to the conclusion that the lamp isn't real and his whole life is a dream. The diary was perfectly rectangular, perfectly bound, perfectly filled with her neat handwriting – but there was something wrong with it. There was something that made it feel not quite real.

I'm so grateful to her for continuing it all for the fans.

Callie might have changed her mind on that word, 'fans'. She might have come round to it, at the level of fame she'd reached by the end. And if these books had proved anything, it was that I didn't really know her. Even when we were together, I hadn't known her half as well as I'd thought.

But somewhere in me, I knew with an itching certainty that Callie had never written that sentence.

I missed her voice. Rather, I missed the sense of her voice that rose from the scribbles of her biro on the page. I felt cheated – I had been saving the last of it, and there was nothing there, nothing to hold on to. I wanted more. I wanted something new, impossible newness, newness that maybe existed somewhere in this house still. Scribbled lyrics in back pages, jotted thoughts in a margin. A grocery list, even. Something, something more than this damp squib of an ending to her narrative.

I went into the office, which was never used, to the cupboard where the stacks of blue spiral notebooks were kept. They were all piled on top of each other – I pulled the whole lot out on to the carpet and flipped through each one, but they were empty. So much space for words she would never write. I went through the bookshelf in the living room, but there were no notebooks pressed between her romance novels and clothbound classics. None of the books I picked up had inscriptions in them. I slid out what she had always said was her favourite novel – *Brideshead Revisited,* Evelyn Waugh – absolute crap when I reflected back because that was no eighteen-year-old's favourite novel – but the pages were undecorated. There weren't even any corners folded over. I felt foolish, but not foolish enough to stop.

I climbed the stairs. In our bedroom, Inese had one leg thrown over the duvet, the rest of her body tucked beneath it. She always slept very still, her breathing very quiet, in the same strange positions all night. Trying to be quiet, I stood up on my side of the bed. The mattress dipped beneath me. I ran my finger over the volumes on the shelf, then turned my phone torch on and counted them. I had read them all. I knew that I had read them all, but there was some ridiculous part of me that hoped they might have divided or multiplied, or that some other slim volume had been hiding between them.

I went to the drawers, rifled through charging cables and adapter plugs and loose hair ties. A lot of the drawers in the unit were empty. Had they always been empty, or had someone cleared them out? Her wardrobe was a mess – between us, we had turned it upside down searching for things to wear, and the place hadn't been cleaned in a while. I pushed my hand to the back of one of the wardrobes and rifled.

'Stevie?' came Inese's voice from the bedroom.

I came back into the room, my phone torch still on. She shielded her eyes.

'What's wrong?'

'I was just looking for something.'

'For what?'

'There's no . . . more? Of her writing?'

She was too sleepy to understand the question. I watched her eyes start to close again.

'Come get into bed,' she said.

'Are you sure she wrote all of them? The diaries?'

'Yes, Stevie.'

'Are you sure? Who told you? Are you sure she wrote any of them?'

'Charlie told me.' She rubbed her eyes. 'She's had them for years. You recognised the first one – you said that. You remember her writing in it. You know she wrote them.'

'This last one isn't right. There's something wrong about the last one.'

'Come here,' she said, pushing herself upright a little on the pillows. I walked over to her bedside, but I didn't climb in with her under the covers. She reached out with a tired arm to touch my cheek. 'Stevie, not everything is a conspiracy.'

'That's rich, coming from you.'

'It's a big morning tomorrow,' she said. 'I have to sleep. So do you. We'll talk about it tomorrow.'

'If you believed me we'd talk about it right now.'

'That's probably true,' she said. 'Go to sleep, Stevie.'

So, this was what it had come to. Even Inese thought I was crazy.

I let her sleep. I went back to searching the wardrobe, more quietly this time, and then I padded in bare feet down the stairs and out into the garden. The stone path was cold and littered with leaves – I pointed my phone torch down in time to see my toe touch a slug, and I squeaked. At the bottom of the garden, in the music room, I went through everything, but it was all Inese and Charlie – pages of their notes, annotations on sheet music and lyrics. Some of it was in my writing too. How could there be more of me in this room than her?

I was supposed to have laid her to rest. But of course, that had been a delusion. I needed more of her. I always would.

I climbed the stairs once more, but I still didn't go to bed. I stood up on the mattress again, ignoring Inese's mumbled protest, and I took Callie's first diary off the shelf. I went back down to the kitchen with it under my arm. I read the scenes of us in our flat, the gorgeous domesticity of us, two people making beds and eating cereal, Callie describing it like it all had some larger meaning, like two people making beds and eating cereal was the point. Her dreams of Wembley and Red Rocks and Copacabana Beach had been so far away. When dreams are that far in the distance, it's so much easier to be happier with what's in front of you. It was only when her dreams got closer that it all stopped being enough for her – pasta from Carla's, bowls of dusty granola, a new shoe rack in the hallway, supermarket flowers just because. New guitar strings for her birthday, a Twister left for her in the freezer. Collecting her hair off the shower walls because it was her least favourite chore. All the things that you're adored for, while someone loves you, until they stop noticing them altogether.

The sun was starting to come up. In the pantry, up on the top shelf, there it was – the box of orange and cranberry granola, the awful, sawdusty stuff that Callie had liked and that I had pretended to like too. Suddenly I craved the tasteless mush of it, the way it disintegrated in milk, the toughness of the dried fruit. The taste of a life perfectly dull, a quiet prelude to a glossy enormity; the only life that had ever felt real to me. The shelves were stacked with Inese's ridiculous supermarket orders. She'd taken to searching online for all the things she fancied she'd like to try, and her shopping lists for Charlie's assistant had got longer and longer. I pushed aside boxes of fancy pasta and pastries we were never going to get around to eating and reached for the granola.

The box was strangely heavy as I lifted it down. I gave it a shake.

It didn't sound like granola.

It was a book. A blue spiral notebook, only this one wasn't empty.

12/1/25

Here we are: another new book. I used to be proud of myself for keeping up with these and now the larger the pile gets, the more ominous it feels. For one, they now all go to Inese if the worst should happen. How morbid. But I discussed it with Gene, and we've decided it's the right thing to do. If the poor girl is ever put in that position, she'll need all the help she can get.

There had been a diary missing. But the one I'd read upstairs had picked up where the previous volume had left off and carried right through to Rio, so when had she written this one? At the bottom of the box, rattling around amid a few stale pieces of granola, were two black pens. I sat on the floor of the pantry, landing more heavily than I intended, dazed. It felt as if I had willed this book into being. It was some kind of mirage, a desperate hallucination. I could hear her voice again.

1/2/25

The Haunt Me Haunt Me sessions are some of the most fun I've had in a long time. I was worried the whole thing would feel trite and like I'm out of new ideas, but I think the work is great. Only played it to Shane from the label so far but he loved what we had.

There was a noise upstairs – it was morning, and Inese's alarm had gone off. Charlie and the rest of the team would be arriving soon. She was calling my name – I ignored her. I skipped ahead.

14/2/25

Saw Inese today, and she had new teeth. It's ridiculous, to feel like you're torturing someone by giving them expensive veneers, but it's how I feel. Every time I see her, she's a little more me. It's like I'm eating her. Sometimes I can't sleep, thinking about everything she's giving up. She's so young. She doesn't understand that one day she might want herself back. I told Gene I felt conflicted about it, and she reminded me that we're all making sacrifices for Calista. I didn't ask her what sacrifices she's making, because I already know she paid someone to stop the leaks coming out. I don't know who, and I don't know how many tracks they had, but I overheard Charlie and Harma discussing it the other day. They both speak so differently, when they think I'm not listening. I wanted to confront them and tell them that this kind of stuff should always be brought directly to me, but it won't make any difference. You'd think after all this time I'd be the head of the operation, but as time goes on, more and more I feel like they don't even need me there half the time, especially since Inese.

'Isn't it good to know,' Gene said the other day, 'that if it's ever too much for you, we've got someone who can step in?'

The deeper into this album I get, the more I remember that Calista is just an idea. Inese is a person.

I sat down on the pantry floor against a shelf of baking ingredients and turned a few more pages. Every noise from outside made me skittish. I read as fast as I could.

27/2/25

So tired today. Went in for some blood tests. There might be something seriously wrong with me, and what then? Can't get Inese out of my mind. Too tired to say anything else, and I've said it all before anyway. Gene floated that she thinks Inese's jawline is a 'problem'.

'Her jawline is fine,' I said.

She showed me two photos of us side by side.

'We've come this far,' she said.

This is Gene's way of reminding me that if anything comes out, it'll probably be much worse for me than any of them. Still, I told her that I don't want Inese to have any more surgeries.

'Well, it's ultimately up to the girl, of course,' she said. Like Inese doesn't ask how high every time they tell her to jump.

3/4/25

Told the whole team today that I'd like to change the name of the album and call it Postmortem. *They're not happy – they like the self-parody thing better, but the art is the part I still have control over. The art is where I can change my mind wherever I like. They can whisper about me behind my back all they want, but if I say that's what the album's called, that's what it's called. It wasn't always like that. Maybe I have gained some ground in all these years.*

I'm supposed to start rehearsals for Rio in a couple of weeks and I don't know how I'm supposed to get through them, let alone the actual performance. Hoping my body starts feeling more like my body soon.

10/4/25

Never seen Gene so furious. She doesn't get furious outwardly, but she goes cold and hard like no one I've ever known. She asked me if I've really thought this through, and I said yes.

I wanted to say, Gene, when have I ever been reckless with Calista? It made me just as angry with her as she was with me. To suggest I would ever take Calista lightly, when she is the heaviest thing on my heart, and everything I am revolves around the gravitational pull of her. The fact is, she can't exist anymore, not with me being the way I am, and I can't give her Inese. I just can't. Every time I look at that girl's face, I'm so guilty I feel sick.

So, I'll put Calista to sleep, like an old loyal dog laying her head down for the last time. I won't let them make her into some reanimated corpse. Postmortem will bury her, beautifully. I'll tell them all at Rio. I'll give them one last glorious night of her, with everything I have, all the energy left in my body. I'll tell the whole story, or at least the parts I can tell and still protect Inese. And then I'll say goodbye.

Maybe, if it stops here, I still have a chance at a good legacy. And Inese still has a chance at a life.

The doorbell rang. I could hear Inese's voice – Callie's now – calling to me as she ran down the stairs, but I didn't come.

20/4/25

Have an appointment made with my solicitor for after the announcement to take Inese out of my will. It feels shitty on some level to blindside her like this, when she's sacrificed so much, but I hope one day she'll understand why I'm doing it. She's so talented, that girl. If people want someone to fill the gap when I go, then they can take Inese instead, exactly as she is.

My biggest regret is telling Gene as early as I did. She barely looks at me anymore. Every time I'm in a room with her or Charlie, my skin is crawling. Charlie doesn't work with that woman, Bo, anymore. I don't know where she went. Maybe she started to feel exactly how I'm starting to feel about the whole thing.

25/4/25

Gene came over today to talk through the dissolution of my contract and when I went to make tea I lost track of her. I found her in my room, taking my diaries from the shelf. 'Wanted to ask,' she said. 'Inese might have to step in and do a few things in the transition, and she might need these now rather than later.' I asked her what transition. 'Press after Rio,' she said.

'There won't be any press after Rio,' I said. 'I'm done after Rio.'

'I know,' she said. 'You're done. But people will want an explanation, and if you aren't willing to give it—' I think I just stared at her. 'I wouldn't have taken them without your permission,' she said. I told her to put them back. 'Do you still write in them?' she asked.

'No,' I said. 'I'm too tired now.'

I've started keeping this one in a granola box, which is ridiculous and paranoid, but I'm not going to stop. Writing these diaries has always been an outlet, but it's starting to feel like a necessity. One day, maybe I'll tell everyone everything. Maybe I'll do exactly what they're all afraid I'm going to do.

I've thought about calling Mum to tell her that I'm retiring, but what would be the point? I haven't even told her about my diagnosis. I don't want to hear that it's all in god's plan for me to be sick and giving up everything. I want it to be my plan, or none of it was ever even worth it.

The final entry was two weeks before Rio.

12/5/25

Feeling much more myself, thank god, and rehearsals are going well. Everyone is very chipper and I think they're hoping that I'll forget wanting to stop. But I won't. I wrote another song for Postmortem *today, a true goodbye. I wrote it alone, with just my guitar, the way I used to. I've been thinking a lot lately about what life will be like after Calista, about what life was like before her. About those first songs, the ones I wrote mostly for Stevie, and how I didn't write them for an album or a live show, how I didn't write them thinking anyone would hear them but her.*

I'm ready to be Callie again. I'm tired of putting Calista first. I want to write songs just because I want to write them, not because I think they'll be a hit or they'll have some kind of cultural impact, not because I can hear people singing along to them in my head but because they're fun to sing just by myself. I thought I'd feel more conflicted about this as the end approaches, but I don't. I'll announce my retirement, and then Postmortem will come out, Calista's posthumous project, because she'll be as good as dead. And then I might just sleep for years.

I'm at peace with it, but I'm still afraid. I'm not even sure what of. I'll just get through Rio, and then I'll feel calmer. Then nobody can try to talk me out of my decisions anymore.

That was it.

I put the book back in the box of granola, almost knocking the rest over.

The Rio show hadn't been just an anniversary celebration. It had been a farewell tour. That's why she'd said my name. Calista was saying goodbye to everyone who'd mattered.

Callie had never wanted any of this. Her team had known that.

And right before she could tell the world that Calista was retiring, she had fallen to her death.

A loud cheer went up in the living room. I made my way out of the pantry and through the now empty kitchen, feeling like I might throw up. About fifteen people were crowded around Gene's laptop, which sat on the coffee table, showing a floorplan of Wembley Stadium with all the sections coloured in grey. A couple of them had their arms around each other's backs, raising themselves up to see. Someone was pouring glasses of champagne at the buffet table.

Inese, crouched on the floor right in front of the screen, turned and saw me. She wore a small blue t-shirt with a butterfly on the front and a pair of leather trousers, too big around the waist, like most of Callie's things were on her. She was a strange mix of mannerisms, impersonating Callie, her own excitement bleeding through. When her face lit up, it was her face.

'There you are!' she said. 'We're going to sell out.'

She turned back to the screen without waiting for my response, which was lucky, because I wouldn't have been able to muster one if I'd tried. Reflected in the screen was the faint outline of her, blueish and strange, and slightly inhuman.

Dry Ice (2020)

A month before the UK goes into lockdown, it is a chilly February and I am on a date, trying to figure out how to answer when he asks me what I do for a living. I have been out of university for well over three years now and have found myself in and out of jobs, taking temporary copywriting contracts, doing as much freelance as I can on the side, hunting for something permanent with a nice, reliable pay cheque and dental benefits. The thing I find myself thinking about more often than anything else is how I'm going to come up with my half of the rent that month. 'You could always move back in with your dad?' suggested an almost-friend from university that I had coffee with the other day. I walked home considering the casual use of the word 'always'. The money troubles are about to get worse, although I don't know it yet. No one does.

'I'm a writer,' I tell my date. Nice and vague.

'Novels?'

'Marketing text.'

'Oh,' he says. His tone conveys that this is less sexy.

Callie is about to release her fifth album, and every shop and café is playing the title single. It's extravagant, glittery, a little funny, both widely loved and widely derided for being such unapologetic chart fodder. When it comes on, the barista bobbing her head along to it behind the counter, I have the pleasant feeling of enjoying it without pain, without regret, without shame. My relationship with Callie's music has changed for the better as I've felt further estranged from her. Now she's just someone I used to love and no longer do, and her fifth album will be something I can enjoy purely for what it is.

'God,' says my date, 'I don't know about you, but I'm getting so sick of this song.'

'Ha,' I say. 'Yeah.' I've made a pact with myself not to let Calista impact my relationships going forward, but I can still feel that this comment has ruined the date.

We're in a café near Tottenham Court Road. Mel is meeting me to go window shopping afterwards, so that we can debrief about my first date since Jeremy, or as she put it, with startling foresight, so that I can complain. He's spent twenty minutes talking about his job – I'm still not clear on what it is – and the remaining ten interrupting me. It's a relief when my phone buzzes. 'Ah,' he says, 'so you're the kind of person who checks their phone mid-conversation.' I physically can't help the look I give him. 'Take your time,' he says. Whatever the notification is, I'm going to say that my grandmother has just been rushed to hospital and leave him with the bill.

Tags. Quite a few of them flooding in. I went through a period where it hurt me, when her fans tagged me in things, but I'm starting to love it again. They're paparazzi photos of Callie in dark sunglasses and a fluffy black hat, swarmed by fans. Then a video. She looks a little overwhelmed. Cameras shutter loudly. My heart squeezes. Maybe she should be used to this by now, but I hate how lost she looks in it all.

Then I recognise the shop behind her.

'Is that—' I squint at my phone, then show it to the guy across the table from me. 'That's Carnaby Street.'

'I guess,' he says.

'No, it is. *Isn't it?'*

'Yeah. So? Who is that?'

I don't answer. I'm already on my feet. How recent are the posts? *I ask in the comments and am redirected to a livestream. There she is, with a forced smile, trying to sign everything being thrust in front of her. Callie is two minutes from me.*

I sprint out of the café. The guy, whose name I've already forgotten, doesn't even call after me. I'm glued to the livestream, bumping into people as I run. She's completely lost in the crowd. They pack the entire width of the street. I turn the corner, and there's the whole mass of them. There doesn't seem to be a way through them, but her breathing on the livestream is gaspy and panicked and I know I have to try.

'Calista! Calista!'

The crowd is still growing. A group of teenage girls further down the road scream and drop their shopping bags. People flood out of shops. One man runs past me with his name badge still on. It's all happened so fast that I barely have time to process it. I begin to move through the crowd, slipping into gaps at first, and then pushing – hard. I elbow people out of my way. I can see her blonde hair now, and I call her name, but she can't hear me. Two or three men are trying to hug her. She's fending them off gently, quietly making a call, preserving a smile. I push closer, cup my hands around my mouth, and yell as loud as I can over the noise. 'It's Stevie!' It takes me two tries. 'Callie, it's Stevie!' Eventually her head turns towards me.

It's really her. Even under the hat and sunglasses, the familiarity of her face takes the breath out of me for a second. The paparazzi press closer, a camera hitting my shoulder, and I come back to myself. I gesture for her hand. She thrusts it towards me, desperate. I pull her through the mass of people, more aggressive than I've ever been, ignoring shouts for photos and autographs, ignoring the way they cry and shout abuse. 'Keep your head down,' I say. She nods. 'Do you have anyone with you? Security? Anyone?'

'They're on the next road over,' she says quietly, pointing me in the right direction. 'They're pulling up.'

'What were you doing here?'

'Shopping,' she says. 'Is it really you, Stevie?'

'It's really me.'

She nods. There's no curiosity about how I found her, no questions about how I've been. She seems hardly to be in the real world. The crowd follows us along the street, growing all the time. Someone tries to snatch her bag and I stamp hard on their foot and keep walking. Someone calls me a bitch. Someone else yells that I'm kidnapping her. The two of us just keep moving forward. 'That's my car,' she says finally, panting a little, and points.

A final push through the crowds of people. Opening the car door is hard – security gets out to help us, holding the mob back, but a couple of people still try to climb inside. She doesn't say anything to me, but just before the car door slams closed behind her, she takes off her sunglasses. Her face is thinner. I try to remember the last time she looked me straight in the eyes like that. Another second, and she's driving away, and the whole thing has happened so quickly it already feels like a dream.

Every time I listen to Dry Ice *that summer, cooped up in the flat, only venturing out for a walk around the empty neighbourhood or a trip to the supermarket, I think of her eyes in the back of that car, before the door closed. The way she looked at me like I'd saved her.*

Chapter Eight

The night after the Wembley show sold out was the hardest I'd ever seen Inese cry. I'd thought I was used to it, but that night she cried like she was trying to expel her own stomach, gripping the skin on her arms and around her hips, scratching at her scalp. I tried to help at first, but she shook me off. After a while, watching her, I felt that there was something ritualistic about it, something cleansing. I was concerned for her voice, but she didn't seem to be. She slowed after about forty minutes, and after about an hour her cheeks were dry and the thickness in her voice was gone. She looked across at me and gave me a small nod, as if to thank me for waiting.

'You're a very strange person,' I said.

'Only a very strange person could have done what I have done,' she said, which was likely true.

I watched her pull her hair back from her face, wipe her sleeve over her eyes one last time. 'So?' I asked eventually.

She scratched her cheek, prised mascara from the corner of her eye. I waited.

'I'm okay,' she said.

Callie's real final diary, the one I'd found in the granola box, sat between us, in the centre of the bed. There was a faint smear of Inese's mascara on the back cover – she licked her finger and rubbed at it.

'I always thought she was proud of me,' she said.

'She was proud of you.'

'But also afraid for me.' She left the book alone. 'I thought this was what she wanted. I thought— I thought this was my purpose. Who I was meant to be.'

'Maybe you were just meant to be you,' I said.

She looked down. 'I was always afraid of that.' She studied her arms, her fingers, spread out in front of her, like she was just now realising they belonged to her. 'It's so much harder,' she said. 'Being myself. Being her – that's easier, really. Strangely.'

'Maybe. But I think you should try.' She turned her arms over to look at her wrists. 'Inese,' I said. 'You have so much talent. Maybe this is a chance to create something new. Write something that's wholly yours. Own it yourself. Callie wanted that for you.'

'Maybe,' she said. 'Yes. Maybe so.'

She touched the diary lightly with one finger, like touching the nose of a pet.

'She wrote it for us,' she said. 'So we would know.'

'Not for us. For you.'

'She left it in the granola for you to find.'

'That was just a place she put it,' I said. 'She didn't think about me. You were the one that mattered. You always were.'

Inese looked over her knee at me, dry-eyed but wrung out. 'What will happen?' she asked. 'If I stop?'

'I don't know.'

'It would have to be public,' she said. 'I would have to do it in a way where they couldn't shut me up.' She paused, and looked at me, and I knew we were thinking the same thing. 'That scares me,' she said. 'Stopping.'

'I know.'

'People will hate me.'

'I don't think so. Not if you explain. And we have this.' I tapped the book. 'It's yours now. You could make it public. If everyone heard it from Callie herself—'

'They might think it's a fake,' she said.

'How could they? You're all the evidence they need, surely.'

'Gene will say I'm lying.'

'Inese, all you have to do is get a DNA test to prove you aren't Callie. Then they're screwed. You have the power here. You always did.'

She took the book, turned it over in her hands.

'She wanted you to have a career as yourself,' I said. 'You could do that. You could introduce the world to Inese.'

'That scares me too.'

'It shouldn't,' I said. I took one of her hands. She was still staring at the notebook. 'You're brilliant, Inese. With your voice, and this story – you'd have the world at your feet. Let them fall in love with you, just as the person you are.'

'Do you think they will?'

'Of course they will,' I said. 'I did.'

She smiled gently, but she looked as if she didn't believe me.

'It's your choice to make,' I said.

'It's not my choice to make,' she said. 'It's Callie's. And she made it a long time ago.'

The only thing, I think, that can really prepare you for walking out on to the stage at Wembley is having done it before – which meant that Inese couldn't react like it was her first time, but I could. The crew had been building the stage for two days, adding a long extension out into the audience. I sat in the middle of it and stared up at the empty arena, the rows and rows and rows of seats, feeling a funny urge to count them. Inese hung back, pacing the top of the stage, but after a while she came and sat beside me.

'It's dizzying,' she said as Callie.

'A little.' She shuffled closer to me and put her head on my shoulder. 'Excited?' I asked.

'Maybe. Something like it.' Down by her side where no one could see, I squeezed her hand. 'It feels too big to take in,' she said, and I knew she wasn't just talking about the stadium.

'Frightened?' I said, quieter now. She nodded into my shoulder, very slightly. 'I'll be here,' I said.

'I know,' she whispered. 'I'm still afraid.'

Calista was famous for inviting fans to her soundcheck, and the general feeling – not expressed, but widely understood – was that it would be suspicious not to do it this time too. Keeping with tradition, Inese, in a t-shirt and jeans, sang pared-down versions of some of Calista's biggest songs, as well as a couple of acoustic covers requested by the small crowd of superfans, most below the age of twenty-five and close to passing out. I watched her for a few minutes before whatever I was feeling – nerves, grief, some mixture of the two – took over, and I had to walk away. My pass – access all areas – bounced on my chest. I had never had one before and felt, amid the cocktail of feelings that the day brought up, strangely proud of it, as if I had done something to earn it.

I wandered the stadium for a while, never venturing too far towards the other side because the place was enormous and I didn't want to get stuck walking thirty minutes back the other way. I occupied myself going where it felt like I shouldn't – behind the counter of food stands and bars not yet set up, through every staff door I came across. Most led me into uninteresting corridors and storerooms but through one I found a huge stock of merch – the face on the t-shirt so airbrushed that I couldn't tell if it was Inese's or Callie's – and through another, a staffroom. This was occupied by about thirty people in orange vests receiving the tail end of an onboarding speech. I went to close the door, but at that moment the meeting broke up, and thirty faces turned towards me.

One was familiar.

She seemed more relieved than taken aback to see me, because of course, what reason would she have for taking temp work at a stadium other than trying to track me down and corner me into a conversation?

'Hey, Stevie-girl,' she said.

Most of the orange vests moved past me into the stadium, but a few looked back. I caught some whispers. I gestured for Mel to follow me, which she did, ignoring her colleagues, intently focused on my face. I led us back towards the merch stockroom. Staff members and temps were starting to appear along the concourse, some of them watching us as we went. I pulled her in and closed the door behind us.

'What are you doing here?'

'It's decent money,' she said. She looked ridiculously good in fluorescent orange.

'Please.'

'It is. A friend brought it up with me, and I thought, why not? Decent money, I might get to see the show, and yeah, I thought maybe there's a chance I'd get to see you too.' She looked me up and down. 'You look great. You look stressed, though.'

'How many times do I have to say that I'm fine?'

'A few,' she said, 'I guess.' It was hard to stand there in front of her and not feel like a sulky child. She sighed. 'Look, I get that you're an adult. I get that you don't owe anyone an explanation for your actions. But fuck it, I *want* one. Alright? You've been in my life longer than basically anyone and you're acting like none of it means anything to you anymore now that you're back with your girlfriend. Being uncommunicative with your dad I get – not like that's too different from normal. Breaking up with Rich I wholeheartedly support, even if the way you went about it was a little messy.' She took a breath and folded her arms. 'But cutting me off? Maybe I'm big-headed, but that I don't get, Stevie.'

'I didn't cut you off,' I said. 'I just— I needed time.'

'How much time?'

'Some.'

'You don't need this much time when you get back together with an ex. You don't need over three months with no job and no friends. It makes me feel like there's something fucked-up going on.' She held up both hands. 'And you can tell me to leave, and you can say you're fine and you're happy and you just don't really want us to be friends anymore. It'll break my fucking heart, Stevie, but I'll leave you alone if that's really what you want.' A pair of footsteps came right up to the door and then went past. 'I just had to ask you in person,' she said. 'If this is actually it. If you're happy.'

'I'm happy,' I said, hating how small my voice sounded.

'You don't really look it.'

'It's complicated.'

'What is? What's so complicated that you can't tell me?'

'I did tell you,' I said. 'I told you and I told Rich. Neither of you believed me. Neither of you took me seriously. No one ever does, when it comes to her.'

She frowned. 'Told us what?'

'That—'

I listened, but everything was quiet outside the door.

'That Callie wasn't Callie. That— That she was dead.'

Mel stared at me. For a moment, she looked truly horrified. It was an expression I had never seen on her.

'She isn't dead,' she said. 'You're dating her.'

'I'm not. I'm— I'm, well, I'm not really dating anyone. I don't know what it is.'

'Stevie, what you do you mean she's *dead?*'

'She died at Copacabana Beach. Everyone saw it. We all just chose not to believe it.'

'No, crazy people chose not to believe it.'

'She died, Mel,' I said. 'She's dead. The person I've been with . . . she isn't her.'

She looked at me for a second longer, still horrified. I thought she might laugh. Instead she said, a reedy dread in her voice, 'You actually believe that, don't you?'

'This is why I couldn't tell you,' I said. 'She'll be done with soundcheck soon. I have to—'

She grabbed my arm. 'Stevie, look me in the eyes and swear that you haven't lost your fucking mind.'

I looked her in the eyes. She wanted to believe me. 'I swear. Just stay until the end of the show. Right until the end. Watch what she does. I swear you'll believe me then.'

Mel held on to my arm for a second longer, staring at me. Finally, she said, 'Okay.'

'Okay?'

'Okay. I love you. If I have to trust you on this one, if that's what it takes, then that's what I'll do.'

I wasn't even aware that I was crying until she reached up to wipe my tears away. 'Mel,' I said, 'it's been—'

'I know, Stevie.'

'Wonderful.' She blinked. 'And a lot of other things,' I said. 'It's been— It's been a lot.'

'I can see that,' she said, still wary.

'I still can't believe you brought Rich to the house.'

'Yeah, I regretted that. He was properly annoying on the Tube. Had to put him on an iPhone game like a fucking three-year-old.' I laughed through my tears. She hugged me to her, and I held her for so long that I started to feel the warmth coming back into me, like she was recharging me, like I hadn't even realised how depleted I'd become.

◆ ◆ ◆

When I made it back to the dressing room, Inese was already in there, doing her own make-up. She hadn't wanted anyone else. 'Where's Charlie?' I asked.

'I said I didn't want him to come in,' she said, applying her lip-gloss. 'He's not happy, but he's not pushing it.'

'Did you say anything to him?'

'Of course not,' she said tersely. She didn't like lying to Charlie. She handed me a green bottle. 'Can you set my face? Just spray it.' She closed her eyes and turned her face towards me. I coated it with a fine mist that covered the tops of my fingers as it settled. She blinked rapidly a few times, then put her hands under her chin and smiled at me like a pageant kid.

'You look beautiful,' I said honestly.

She turned to the mirror and ran her fingers through the ends of her curls. 'The last time,' she said.

'Do you have the diary?'

'It's at home. I hid it back inside the granola.'

'Maybe you should have brought it,' I said.

'They never found it there before.' She was distracted, watching herself in the glass. She shook her head. 'I've had weeks to think about who I'll be, after this, and I still don't know.'

'You don't have to know right away. You've got time.'

Still watching herself in the mirror, she reached behind her and took my hand, bringing it forward to rest on her shoulder. 'Do I?' she asked.

'Why wouldn't you?'

'I'm scared,' she said.

'Don't be,' I said. 'What can they do?' But we both knew that question had an answer. The idea that Callie's death might not have been an accident hadn't left my mind since I'd read her final diary. I hadn't voiced this to Inese. I guessed I didn't have to.

'These are powerful people,' she said. 'And the world won't forget. People don't like to be tricked.'

'It wasn't a trick,' I said. 'You can tell them that tonight. It was a second chance at life.'

She smiled at me in the mirror. 'A second chance at life,' she repeated. 'That's good. I like that. I'll say that tonight.'

There was a knock on the door. I left her in her chair playing with the ends of her hair and went to open it. Charlie stood there, looking out of place in Calista merch – a white t-shirt with a cheerfully spooky blonde cartoon zombie. 'Is she there?' he asked me.

Inese leant back in her chair and nodded, her frown telling me to be normal. Charlie eyed me as I stepped aside, like he suspected me of keeping her from him.

'How are you feeling?' he asked.

'Good,' she said. 'Ready.' She smiled at him in her usual manner. He shifted his gait.

'Good. They've just opened the doors.' There was a vacant chair against the wall – I saw him notice it, but he didn't sit down. 'They can bring a guitar in for you,' he said, 'if you want to warm up.'

'I warmed up at soundcheck,' said Inese, turning back to the mirror.

'If you want to stay warm, then.'

He looked over at me, a little helplessly. I'd never seen Charlie at such a loss. He jerked his head at the doorway and I stepped outside with him, Inese catching my eye as I went. She frowned harder.

In the corridor, he pulled me to one side and said, 'Is she alright?'

'She just told you she was.'

'Do you think she seems quite . . .' He looked for another word, but could find no better one. 'Herself?' he finished reluctantly.

I couldn't resist. 'Which self?'

I wanted to see him taken aback. Instead, he looked at me with exasperation and a little pity. 'I hope neither of you is going to be stupid,' he said.

'Of course not. She's been rehearsing for months.'

'And she'll do everything as rehearsed?'

'Ask her yourself.'

'I'm trusting you, Stevie.' We both knew that he'd never even liked me, let alone trusted me. 'We're all here for Calista. Or we should be.'

'We are. She and I are, at least.'

He regarded me. 'Can I tell you something?' I shrugged. 'Sometimes I worry you're more in it for yourself than anything else,' he said.

'That's rich.'

I knew the words were a mistake, but it was hard to regret saying them, not when he raised his eyebrows at me like that, so smug.

'Don't say anything thoughtless,' he said. 'Not here.'

'I wouldn't. Because I'm here for her, no matter what you might think of me.' That same smug expression on his face, unmoving. 'You still don't understand that what you think of me doesn't matter. It only matters what *she* thinks of me. You've all fooled yourselves into thinking you have power over Calista, but you don't. Without her, there wouldn't be any Calista. It's all about her.'

'That would be an awful thing,' he said. 'A world with no Calista.'

It was an unnecessary risk. But I'd come so far, and learnt so much, and I'd earned the right to look into his face and see just a little bit of fear. I leant in. Still amused, he did the same.

'I know what you did,' I said quietly.

He wasn't looking back at me. He was looking over my shoulder.

'Really?' came a voice from behind me. 'What on earth has he done now?'

It was Gene Parrison, walking towards us with all the urgency of a woman for whom the rest of the world would wait. To look at her, you wouldn't have known that tonight was special – she was in her usual business casual, her hair set like a Lego piece. She smiled at me, to let me know how small she thought I was.

'Something you want to tell me?' she asked.

I took a step away from Charlie. Gene checked her watch.

'I'm going to go see if she needs anything,' I said.

When I got in the room she was lying down on the sofa with her feet crossed on the armrest, wearing a white robe. The evening's outfits were hanging on a rail behind her head.

'What did he want?' she asked.

'To tell me he doesn't trust me.'

She swung her legs down and pushed herself upright. 'Do you think he knows?'

'It doesn't matter either way. There's not much he can do at this point.' I didn't tell her what I'd said to him, or that Gene had overheard. I didn't want to make her more frightened. She was chewing on her bottom lip, getting lipstick all over her top two teeth. 'Don't,' I said, touching her leg.

'I don't like lying to Charlie,' she said.

'Why do you care?'

'He's always been honest with me.'

'Really? You think he didn't know that diary was a fake? You think he didn't oversee the writing of it?' She shook her head. 'Come on, you're not stupid.'

'That was Gene.'

'You're Charlie's whole job. You know that. Gene, or whoever hired him, brought him in to be in charge of all things you.'

She was on the edge of arguing with me, but she sat up and sighed. 'You're right. You're the only one who never lied to me.' She reached for my hand, pulled me over to her. I let her wrap her arms around me. 'My saviour,' she said into my hair. 'I knew it from the moment I met you.'

'That I'd save you?'

'You did save me. Remember Carnaby Street?'

My chest lurched. I pulled back to look in her face, and pictured it behind dark glasses, underneath a dark, fluffy hat.

'That was you?'

I felt the motion of her nod. 'That was me.'

Her hand in mine, moving through the crowd. Her wide, grateful eyes, the second between the raising of her sunglasses and the car door slamming shut. Not my Callie needing me, but Inese trusting me. Trusting me when I'd appeared from nowhere and pulled her from that throng of people all those years ago, trusting me when I'd brought her the diary and showed her what Callie had really thought. Trusting me now, when I promised her that I would save her.

The people who had made this happen had hidden or disposed of a body. They had paid off plastic surgeons and curious minds to keep quiet and practically scrubbed Inese from the record. Somehow, under their guidance, a death had gone unrecorded. A girl who had been on TV in her home country had vanished with hardly any fuss. That was power and resource that we couldn't match. Those were quite some lengths to go to, only to have it all brought suddenly to light.

But Calista wasn't ours. It was Callie's wish that she be laid to rest, not be rewound and pushed back out there again and again, for album after album and tour after tour. To keep her alive for Callie and the public was one thing. To keep her alive for Gene Parrison was quite another.

So, one more night. The world's final few hours with Calista. Let them enjoy her one last time. And then let her go quietly into the dark, to die a good death.

That evening in the dressing room, she was the calmest I'd seen her in quite some time. It felt like the hours before her execution, with her confession made and all her demons laid to rest. I leant back against her, listening to her heartbeat, remembering Carnaby Street, the way I'd almost felt her pulse through her hand, and wondered if maybe I'd got it all wrong. Maybe it had never been Callie. Maybe Inese had always been the one that I was meant to love.

They dressed her all in black. Harma put her head round the door to invite me to come and watch from backstage, as if that were her right, as if I shouldn't have been the one inviting her. 'Our star!' she said with a smile at Inese. She didn't wish her luck. She looked tense. I wondered what Charlie had told her.

They came to take Inese away. She didn't say anything before she went – she couldn't with all the other people in the room, but she took both my hands in hers and pressed them, and the expression on her face was rapturous.

Harma led me on a winding march through the stadium's insides, until we emerged at the side of the enormous stage, standing well back so that we couldn't be seen. A thin white curtain hid the thousands of people from us. It wouldn't be the best view of her, but when the curtain went up I would be able to see so many of them. Right now, they would be waiting with their phones out. They would be finishing off their drinks, taking photos of each other with arms in the air, eyes closed, open-mouthed smiles, in the middle of a silent laugh. So many of them would cry tonight. It would be a beautiful thing, all of us crying together.

To give my hands something to do, I took out my phone. Someone way up at the back had already started livestreaming. The stage waited, empty, as people scuttled like ants down the walkways and into the main pit. You could see the whole stadium from this vantage point, all the many rows of people. The white curtain rippled. I took a ginger sweet for nausea, offering the tin to Harma.

'No, thanks,' she said, but then, a second after, she paused and said, 'Oh, go on,' as if I'd offered her a shot at the end of a long night out. She put it in her mouth like she was doing something naughty.

The music quietened. Screams, from my phone and the thousands of real-life people just ahead of us. She was under the stage at this very moment. Momentarily, I was rapt – Calista was about to rise through that floor, metres from me. Then I pictured Inese, playing with her mic, inspecting her nails, putting on the right face, and I felt sick again despite the ginger.

The intro to 'Eat Me' began. I wanted to climb the walls. My stomach was throbbing. The floor opened. The top of her head crowned the floor of the stage. On the livestream, she was a shadow, looming far larger than herself, slowly emerging, like she was forming from the ground up. The *sound* of it. I wondered how she heard it. It terrified me. Had Callie been terrified like this, when the crowds grew and grew, when they roared their love at her with all this fury? Or had she been made for it in a way I could never understand? Maybe Inese was made of the same stuff. Maybe I would never quite get it, no matter how near to them I was, no matter how close I edged from the wings to the stage, almost in her light.

She was standing on the stage now. She looked at me, and she winked, and I didn't know where I was. Slowly, she turned to face the curtain, her face hidden from both me and the audience. Her expression all her own. Was she Callie yet, or still Inese? Or perhaps she was some secret third thing, some part of herself that she had never shown even to me.

Through the phone, through the speakers, from just across the stage, from all directions, her voice came.

'Shall we?'

The screams were deafening. The curtain rippled upwards, too fast, the moment gone. On the livestream, there she was: a single figure onstage, holding a white microphone above her head. The dancers ran past in two diagonal lines, out into the centre of the stage. One of them rushed right past me – I felt the lace edge of a skirt brush my thigh, and I shivered. It was so strange to see her like this, so close and from such a distance all at once. What was happening on my phone felt somehow far more real than what was happening in front of me.

She sang 'Eat Me' like she had written it. She sang it like it had meaning only she could comprehend, like there were secrets hidden in it she would never tell. When she finished, her back to us, and the music transitioned into the lead single from *Haunt Me Haunt Me,* she took just a few seconds' pause, her chin turned up towards the top rows. On the livestream, I could see how wide she was smiling.

The comments had started.

SHE'S BACK

all the internet weirdos screaming crying rn

omg still looks nothing like her

Harma was looking at me, I realised, clearly confused as to why I was staring at my phone and not watching Inese. 'Everything alright?' she whispered.

A little way off, Charlie stood with Gene Parrison. They shared the comfortable silence of two people who had recently had a lengthy conversation about something important. It rattled me.

'Fine,' I said, but I didn't put my phone away. Onstage, Inese and two female dancers performed a part of the choreography it had taken her weeks to perfect. She did it now as if it were the easiest thing in the world. I felt blinding pride for her, and somewhere underneath, intense fear that I couldn't place.

Once there was one dissenting comment, more followed, and then the chat was flooded with people loudly disagreeing with the conspiracy theorists until it dominated the entire conversation.

Can't believe people are still trying to claim this isn't her!

can anyone who is here to spread misinformation please just LEAVE, Calista is alive and well

Shit. I opened all of the apps and started to move between them. I watched the conversation on each one become muddied. People were talking more about the conspiracy than they were about the actual performance. They theorised where it might have come from, what her management might have done to squash it earlier. Every little thing Inese did onstage, even if it was completely true to Callie, needed to be run through seven layers of internet discourse. Over the top of my phone, Inese danced on. Over the top of the comments, a smaller version did the same, her face animated, her movements sharp. *How does she do it?* wondered someone in the comments, and even though I had watched her rehearse for so many weeks, even though I had seen all the frustration and fear of failure, all the effort that had gone into making it look effortless, I wondered the same thing.

But increasingly, so many of them were starting to doubt. I couldn't understand it. She moved on to a song from *Dry Ice,* dancing through clouds of sparkly smoke, and they wondered if all the special effects were there to hide her face. She twirled to an upbeat, hyperpop offering from *Pointelle,* and they suggested that the conspiracy theorists might say her vocals were slightly pitchy, her movements a little too frantic. And they weren't. This was exactly how Callie would have done it. Every beat of it was perfect. But the conversation had run away from us. It wasn't even about Inese anymore. It was about the joy of speculation.

They were ruining it. I wanted to run out onstage and yell at them all just to stop, to tell them that there would be months for this afterwards, there would be years, so much time in which to analyse every detail of it, to look for all the clues. This was the last time they would ever be able to enjoy Calista, purely, the last time they would ever stand there and gaze up at her like she was something beyond human. The last time they would listen to these songs and not remember everything that had come after. The last time they would ever live in her world.

I couldn't run out onstage. But I could post.

Angling my phone away from Harma, my blood hot, I typed.

Can we all just end the speculation and enjoy tonight for what it is.

The comments started immediately.

For what it is???

nah there's something so weird about this relationship

Stevie knows something for sure

I read my post again and couldn't see what it was that would have set them off. Maybe I could have said anything and they would have found a way to twist it into something suspicious. Freshly nauseous, I deleted it. But it was too late – a screenshot of the post was already being shared on fan accounts. I turned back to the livestream, but they were talking about it there too. I tried to ignore the comment section, to just focus on Inese. She was waiting for the applause to die down so that she could speak. Eventually, she had to lift the mic and, laughing, talk through it.

'Wembley!' she said. 'You guys are too much!'

Another round of cheers. She gave them a few seconds this time before she spoke again, just as she'd rehearsed.

'We're going to be playing a lot of old favourites tonight, but I wonder – would you guys be okay if I played you something from my new album?' The noise was so deafening it rattled the floor we stood on. Charlie's drink, placed down beside his shoe, spilt. 'Would that be okay?' came her voice, laughing, through it.

So curious about how she handles this, someone wrote.

It was the song she'd played at the label event, with its full arrangement this time. But even amid all the noise, I heard her voice, sweet and clear, as if we were lying in bed and she were singing right into my ear.

In every crowded basement

In all their ugly faces

In the most unlikely places

Something strange was happening in the chat. Slowly, the naysayers were being buried by a new outpouring of love for Calista. This was new material – there was no point of comparison, no other renditions to compare to, just the joy of hearing her sing something live for the first time. On my phone screen, she danced through a stream of hearts, her face and voice bright. She walked away from us down the thrust of the stage, kissing her hands to the audience, and she was far from me now, she was out among them – she was caught between us, me and them, suspended at a distance from all of us, floating in muddied waters, something so impossibly crystalline and pure, something that none of them deserved.

When she turned and ran back down the length of the thrust, lightly, just like Callie would have, I saw her face in person for the first time since she'd begun, and there was none of Inese in it at all.

I followed the dressers as they hurried ahead to the dressing room, leaving Harma on the side of the stage. When Inese burst through the door, an explosion of glitter and blonde curls, I padded the sweat from her forehead with a cloth and she grinned up at me in uncontrolled pleasure. Her new dress was short and trailed behind her like smoke. She pulled her heels off to quickly rub her toes.

'Did you post something?' she asked me.

'What?' I stalled. The dressers look shifty.

'Gene mentioned something, when I ran past her. She was telling Charlie that you'd posted something.'

'I deleted it.' She gave me a quizzical look. 'People were . . . It doesn't matter now.'

'Tell me.'

'They were saying things. I was tired of seeing it.'

'Stevie,' she said, with a glance at the dressers.

'How do you feel? Out there?'

She slipped her shoes back on. 'I feel like the very brightest star,' she said.

She was perfect, curls falling down over her shoulders, her eyelids silver, her lips red. The smoky trails of her dress gently touched her thighs. Her jaw was healed now, no more yellow and green bruising along it, and her skin was peachy and sweet, her lips curved, her eyes that hypnotising kind of crazy. The dressers stood back to examine her, and I heard a soft gasp from one of them. She didn't look quite in the real world anymore. She didn't even really look like she lived and breathed. Inese wasn't in her, just then, but neither was Callie.

'You are,' I said. 'The very brightest.'

She looked back at her entourage. 'Give us thirty seconds.' No one moved. 'The audience can wait thirty seconds,' she said. 'I need this.'

The dressing room emptied. She turned back towards me, and I felt her disappointment, hot and forceful, my skin withering under it.

'I knew you'd done something,' she said. 'Gene was weird with me just now. Did you speak to her at all?'

'No,' I said. 'Not really.'

'Not really?'

'She overheard something I said to Charlie.'

'Well, what did you say to Charlie?'

'You shouldn't worry about this now.'

'Don't tell me what I should and shouldn't worry about.'

'I can't stand him acting like he cares when I know what he did. That's all.'

'Oh, for *fuck's* sake, Stevie,' she said, suddenly loud. 'Charlie *does* care, okay? Whatever nastiness happened, whatever they did, whatever the real story is, he is a *good man.* He has a job to do. If I can understand that then you should be able to as well.'

'You're so blind when it comes to him.'

'Raise your voice if you're going to speak to me,' she spat.

'Fine! You're fucking stupid about Charlie. Charlie doesn't protect you.' I was very close to her, up in her face, and she stepped away from me. 'I protect you! All I have ever wanted, *ever,* was to be the one that protects you. *No one* understands like I do. *No one* will be here for you like I am here for you. How do you *still* not get that?'

There was a tentative knock on the door.

'I have to go back onstage,' said Inese.

There was the sickening feeling coming over me that I'd ruined something. 'I'm sorry,' I said. 'You'll be wonderful. You can do this. Don't trust them, okay?'

We stared at each other, chests rising and falling.

'I'll come with you,' I said.

'Maybe it would be better if you didn't,' she said. 'Maybe you should stay here.'

In her anger, she was even more glorious. Even more blindingly Calista. When she let the door close hard behind her, I knew that no matter what happened from here, I would never see that girl again. No one would.

I rushed to my phone and scrolled for a few minutes. What I saw calmed me. Social media had changed their minds. My post no longer mattered. The conspiracists were quiet. The naysayers stayed away. Those of us who loved her gathered in every corner of the web to praise her. We held hands and swayed together and sang songs about her beauty, about the art she gave us, about the way she looked – luminous, legendary – weaving her tales in this largest of fairy circles. We promised to pass down the stories. We promised to love her forever. Everything was as it should have been. This was my home, in her house of worship. I might have raised my voice, but only because I was so passionate about her, like I was about nothing else. She would understand that, when this was all over.

Still, I felt displaced, out of my body. I wanted to look into her eyes and be restored. Her voice over the speaker called to me. The siren song of her ran with light steps up the corridor and curled around the sides of the door, sliding in past the hinges, leading me forward. I had to see. I left the room and followed it towards the stage – not the wings, where Gene and Charlie and all the other heretics waited, but through a door into the main stadium.

The stage was bleeding white light, ropes of it slithering across my vision, reaching strange fingers out into the stands. From down here, the rows of people continued, impossibly high. The people right at the top could hardly have been able to see her, and still I knew, somehow, that they were so happy. That maybe she was making them the happiest they'd been all year. Those on the floor worshipped below, faces turned towards the shining, and no matter their age every single one of them looked young – far younger than her – needing her, waiting for her to tell them who to be. I slipped in at the edge of the crowd.

'Are you Stevie Stone?' someone asked me, under the music.

'Just watch,' I said. 'Just watch her.' Uncertain, they turned back to the stage. She was playing a song from *Want Me Want Me*, pure pop, unabashed joy, a song they played in supermarkets, a song that little girls around the world made dance routines to in their bedrooms, a song that would never be cool, a song that some had claimed was only designed to worm its way into your brain and never leave. But that was magic, wasn't it? For something to bury itself so deeply in your head that you couldn't hook it out. For a song to stick to you like a burr you couldn't untangle from your clothes, like last words from a lover, like childhood memories, like honey, like glue. No one understood the art in it better than she did. No one loved her for it more than me.

The love slowed time. The love vanished the world. I stood there and watched her for however long I did, and I knew, finally, that this was goodbye. Calista and me. This was where it ended.

'Wembley,' she said, 'you guys have been so magical. And I trust you enough to share something really big with you right now.'

This had been Gene's idea. Something to show the world that we could let go of what had happened in Rio, a moment that wouldn't define her legacy. On its wires, the white bench descended from the ceiling. Gasps from the crowd, and then an enormous swell of sound. She walked over and strapped herself in – I watched her closely – and held on to the wire as the bench began to rise.

'I've had some scary moments in my life, London,' she said. 'What happened in Rio is one of them. But to live a life like I've lived, with you, I'd take the scary moments. I'd do them all again, again, again.'

High in the air, she hung like mist, like a wisp of cloud. The music came in, a swell of it, a thick soup of strings in the arrangement, unlike I'd ever known this song to sound – and I'd heard it so many times, in so many different ways. She raised the microphone to her lips and sang to me. I don't know how she found me in the crowd, but she did. Calista, singing our song to me.

So, Stevie. This one's for you.

A chill worked slowly through my chest. I thought of Charlie's face in the corridor, the way he almost seemed like he wanted me to say it, out loud, my finger pointing in his face, listing all the things I knew. She was on a harness. It was different this time, but still—

No one in the stadium completely relaxed until the bench was back on the ground again and she had unbuckled herself and stepped on to the stage, but when she did, there was a swell of relief so great that the building shook. The people lining the walls were stamping their feet hard and fast, too much love to contain in just a sound – it had to come out in action as well. *We love you,* said the rumble, *we love you. We'll make earthquakes for you to show it. We'll bring buildings down. We love you, and we know you love us too.*

She stood for a moment, her eyes closed.

'Wembley,' she said. She took a breath. In that moment, she became Inese once more. 'Wembley,' she said again, in Inese's voice now. The crowd sensed the shift, although most of them didn't know what to make of it. A low chatter started around me. Inese swallowed, smiled, blinked away tears. 'There's something very important that I have to tell you—'

The power went out.

The confusion was immediate. Phone torches turned on, but not enough of them – the stadium was dark and the sound was gone, and that was enough to panic people. A scream to my left, another behind me. I looked around in the darkness and thought, *Inese. Inese.* I needed to get backstage. I tried to push through the crowd, but people were pushing back in all directions. Someone bumped into my chest, hard; I staggered backwards, and someone's elbow hit my side so hard that I was winded. They started to push in earnest then, a screaming, panicked mass of them surging for the doors. I tried to move with them, but they weren't taking me where I needed to go. Then, like a wave, I felt the weight of bodies pressing forward, forward, even though there was nowhere to go, and I was knocked to the ground. Under their feet, I searched blindly for a hold, something to help me push myself up, but the shoes around me were coming down heavily and I didn't want to risk my fingers. Someone reached to help me up and was carried off in the crush before I could find their hand. I curled up, heart hammering, feeling feet on my back, on my legs, and prayed that no one would kick me in the head, that it would soon be over.

A break in the movement let me struggle to my feet, a stranger's hands under my armpits, a few murmurs of 'Stevie? Is that Stevie?' – and then the lights came on again, and someone shouted over a mic, 'EVERYONE STOP MOVING. STOP MOVING.' The stadium staff had started to regain control, people in orange vests separating us out with barriers, creating walkways, telling people that there was no need to panic, it was just a power failure, they were going to lead us out slowly now and everyone would be fine if we just didn't push—

I searched for Mel but couldn't see her. I moved with the crowd towards the exit, but when I got there and tried to head back towards the stage, a man in orange put his arm out to stop me. 'Please,' I said, 'I need to go back there.'

'That's not possible, I'm afraid.'

'I have a pass—' Only, I didn't. When I reached for it around my neck, it was gone, lost in the crush.

'You'll need to evacuate with everyone else,' he said.

'You don't understand,' I said desperately, 'I'm her girlfriend, she's expecting me—'

'Sorry, miss,' he said, his arm still in my way. 'You'll have to contact her yourself.'

I got out on to the concourse and tried to call her, but there was no signal. People around me were crying.

'Is it terrorists?' one girl asked her friend, both of them holding tightly to each other's arms. They looked and sounded so young. *Was* it? Was it all some strange coincidence, and some outside force had struck just as she'd tried to speak? I was frantic. I ran back along the concourse in the direction of the stage, trying to find a door, a friendly face, some way back there, someone who I could convince to let me through. Nothing. I tried to go back down the stairs into the standing area again, but the staff weren't having anything. Without my pass, I wasn't anybody. No one even seemed to recognise me. Even the fans were ignoring me, too focused on whatever emergency we'd found ourselves in.

'Inese!' I started shouting in the direction of the stage. 'INESE!' Surely someone would have to come out to shut me up at least. 'INESE!'

They let me yell. I stood there, bleating her name, my fists scrunched up, as thousands of people flooded past me. The stadium emptied. The staff began to turn to each other, arms out in bewilderment.

'Stevie?'

Someone put a hand on my arm. Mel, still in her orange vest.

'Who are you calling for?' she asked.

'I can't find her. They won't let me back there. I promised her I'd be backstage. What's going on?'

'I don't know,' she said. 'I was wondering if you would.'

'She was going to tell them, Mel. They cut her off before she could. They knew what she was going to say.'

'I think it was just a power failure, Stevie,' she said, but she didn't sound sure.

I must have got a bar of signal just then, because a message came through. Inese's phone, but I still had her saved as Callie from that first meeting.

I'm sorry, I think we need some time apart

Mel peered down at it. 'What happened?' she asked. 'Did you fight?'

'It's not from her.'

'It says it's from her.'

'It's not, Mel. I promise you.'

But I could hear the crazy in my voice. I could feel that my eyes were wide and intense and that I was trembling. She stared at me for a second, looking so lost for words that I wanted to cry, and then she put her arms around me. ‘Oh, Stevie,’ she said.

‘It all happened,’ I said. ‘I’m not crazy. I’ll explain it all to you. You’ll believe me. It was all real.’

‘I know it was, Stevie-girl,’ she said. ‘Let’s get you home.’

Put This On My Headstone (2014)

Callie doesn't often get stage fright, but when she does, it starts in the mornings. She'll wake up knowing that it's one of those days, and then for hours and hours she'll sit with this gnawing sickness in her stomach, unable to eat or drink, knowing that it's all going to go wrong. She'll tell me that she can't do it. I'll tell her she can, she can, and she'll repeat, 'I can, I can,' dully, like she's trying to cement the words in her brain. These are the days when she needs me the most.

I don't tell her that I saw her parents outside the venue. I bring her a black coffee (no milk, not for six hours before she sings) and I sit beside her in the dressing room, and I say, 'Baby.' I only ever call her this when she's very stressed and her walls are all the way down. It's the only time she won't laugh. 'You're incredible.'

'You have to say that.'

'I don't. I could easily say you were shit, if it was true, but it isn't.'

She smiles a little at that. She adjusts herself on the sofa, laying her legs across my lap, curling her body into me. Nothing feels quite like this.

'It's Brixton,' she says.

'I know.'

'That's huge.'

'I know it is. You're going to be so much bigger than Brixton, one day, baby. You'll look back on this as a cute little local gig that you absolutely killed.'

She doesn't say anything. After a minute she gets up and starts pacing, takes a sip of her coffee. I had offered to bring her something stronger, but she didn't want it, just a jolt, she said. Something to wake her up. She doesn't want any of her senses dulled.

There's a cheer outside. Five minutes. Her team are by the door, ready to get her into the wings, but I've asked them to give us space. 'Do you want me to walk with you?' I ask.

'Yes,' she says. 'Just you. No one else.'

So we walk, the two of us, to the side of the stage. Her palm is sweaty in mine. Her mascara has left marks below her eyebrows. With my index finger, I wipe them away. She shakes out her arms, breathes in little puffs. A day of feeling this sickness. I wish I could have felt it for her. But it'll be worth it. I know it, even if she doesn't.

'Do you know why you're my favourite artist in the world?' I say.

'Because none of the others will have sex with you.'

'Not just that. Because you're so honest. The things you say are so beautiful and true. You go out there and you share a piece of yourself.'

'Other artists do that,' she says.

'Not like you. None of them.'

She smiles at me, calm for a second.

'What?' I ask.

'Sometimes I wonder what it would be like,' she says, 'to see myself as you see me.'

'Just look out into that crowd tonight. They'll all look at you like I do.'

'Not like you,' she says. 'None of them.'

She holds on to me for a second, her fingers in mine, not letting go until the last possible second. She takes a few steps backwards. The crowd cheers suddenly, which makes her jump. I can't help laughing. The music starts.

'Will you be here?' she asks.

'No, I want to go watch with everyone else.'

'You'll have a better view from here.'

'I don't care. I'd rather be out there.'

'You'll boil, Stevie.'

'I won't.' She rolls her eyes at me tenderly. 'I have to be among them all,' I said. 'I have to really feel it.'

'Silly Stevie,' she says. She's supposed to be walking onstage but instead she comes forward again, to kiss me on the cheek. I'm holding her hand again now, until it slips out of mine and I'm left reaching for her. She mouths an 'I love you'. I mouth it too. I let her go. She turns, shakes out her shoulders. They rise and fall as she breathes. I watch her walk forward, into the light. The noise is like nothing I've ever heard. She doesn't look back.

I make my way out of the backstage area, to stand at the edge of the crowd. Someone next to me is crying. I've never seen anyone cry for her before. I watch the crying stranger for a few seconds, fascinated by the gulping breath she takes, the tears splashing on to her t-shirt. She doesn't seem happy. She seems like her love is too much. At the front of the stage, hands reach for Callie. She squats down to hold them as she sings, and each one hangs on as long as it can. She stands up, pushing her hair back from her face, laughing a little. She looks disbelieving. I watch her search the crowd for me, to share the feeling with her. This is crazy, *she wants to tell me with her eyes.* Isn't this crazy?

I wave. I call to her. I want to let her know that I'm here, that I'm witnessing it too, that I can't believe it either, except I can, because I always knew she'd get here. I knew it through every empty venue and every gig that fell through, every late night of frustrated songwriting, every no, every doubt. My faith in her has rivalled any great faith in history. When she wasn't sure, I was. When no one else believed, I did. I'm here, *I think,* I'm here, we did it, I'm so proud of you, *and I put my arms in the air, and I yell her name.*

She doesn't see me.

Chapter Nine

Some evenings Mel would find me in the park behind her building, sitting on the bench that faced the block of flats perpendicular to hers. The building was two storeys tall and, at the right time of day, cast a long rectangular shadow over the grass, rows of perfect yellow picture frames rising up from the join. Those who lived alone and kept their blinds open were beautifully unselfconscious, dancing with headphones on while they cleaned, napping on sofas, studying or reading with heads bent over desks and lamps half lighting them. Sometimes I would see them in various states of undress, men pulling clothes from their racks in their underwear, or girls tiptoeing through the living room looking for a phone charger, one hand over their bare chests, aware that they might be observed but only half-heartedly covering themselves, no concept of who the observer might be and as such unconcerned. The flat shares were less interesting – some of them seemed to actually be friends, and it was nice to see them crowding together on sofas in front of the TV or uncorking wine together, but mostly they all lived around each other in a disappointingly self-aware way, never showing much of who they really were. They meal-prepped and ate and sent emails with no personality. They didn't give me what I needed.

The couples were my favourite. The mornings spent rushing around getting ready for work, putting toast in for each other, sometimes kissing goodbye, sometimes forgetting. The evenings curled up sleepily together in front of whatever they were watching, cooking for each other, starting to have sex before they disappeared off into the bedroom and closed the blinds. I loved the fights. Some of them fought wildly and passionately, with gesticulating hands. Some cried, holding each other all the way through until the conflict was over. Once I saw someone throw something and made the mistake of telling Mel when she came outside to sit with me on my bench.

'You should call the police,' she said.

Mel didn't understand. These people weren't real. I just needed something to watch.

The first week it had felt as if something was coming – they put a statement out immediately, supposedly from her, saying there had been a safety issue at the stadium which meant they'd had to pull the plug quite abruptly, and she was sorry for any distress caused. Some theorised that it was a marketing stunt. Some theorised that it was something more sinister. She then released a new photo, not seen before, convincingly recent, but I knew it was an old one that Charlie had taken of Inese in the music room.

Thank you all for giving me some time to recover, said the caption. *The truth is, there is something I've been keeping from you all. My health hasn't been the best for a while now, which is as much detail as I'm ever willing to go into about such a personal matter, and I've been doing my best to push through for you all, but I think I need to put myself first for a bit and take a break. I'm going to be taking some time off, and when you see me again, I hope I'll be able to bring you something wonderful. Until then, I love you all, and I'm so beyond grateful.*

C x

We all waited. I was tagged in the picture over and over, reposted by a thousand different accounts. People asked me to speak out, to say something. I couldn't. Eventually Mel told me that she thought I should delete my social media.

'What if she posts?' I asked. 'What if she tries to message me?'

'She's got your number. And I'll tell you if anything important happens – I promise.' I stared down at the folder on my phone. 'You can't move forward like this,' she said.

One by one, I held them down and, as they squirmed, ended them.

Mel didn't quite know how to speak to me. It was the first time in our friendship that we'd been that way. I'd explained everything to her and I knew that she wanted to believe me, that she did, mostly. But I could see she had moments of doubt. It all sounded too insane. She watched me send text after text to two different numbers, one saved under *Callie*, one under *Inese*, neither of which answered. I cried that they had done something terrible to her, and she hugged me and said, 'Stevie, things like that don't happen in real life.' Which wasn't much consolation, because I was becoming more and more convinced that they did.

The day after the Wembley concert, I made her get in an Uber with me and drive straight to the Hampstead house, where she hung back and watched me rap on the door, calling Inese's name. When the door finally did open, it was Charlie.

'Where is she?' I asked.

He looked awful. I could see that he hadn't slept. He was still clean-shaven, no wrinkles in his shirt, but he carried himself with an uncertainty that hadn't been there before and there was a hollowness in his eyes that reminded me of Inese on the cover of *Haunt Me Haunt Me.* He stood in the doorway, blocking me from entry, and said, 'Stevie, she doesn't want to see you.'

'I don't believe you.'

'She thinks you were bad for her,' he said. 'A bad influence. You tried to push her to do things that wouldn't have been right for her to do.'

I stood on my toes and called her name over his shoulder. 'Inese! Inese!'

'Stevie,' he said, putting a hand up to quiet me. 'Come on. We both know there's no one here with that name.' He sounded tired.

'What have you done with her?'

'No one's doing anything with her, Stevie,' he said. 'It's just over.'

His voice gave out just a little as he said this.

I stared at him. He held my gaze for a minute, not unsure what to say so much as entirely depleted.

'Do you have it?' I asked.

I couldn't read his face. He turned away from me. 'Go home,' he said, closing the door. 'Your friend will take care of you.'

As if he'd given her a cue, Mel came forward and took my arm. 'Let's go, Stevie-girl.'

'He's lying,' I told her, as she led me towards the car.

'Maybe,' she said. 'Maybe it is just over.'

I went back to the Hampstead house a few times, but Charlie was always there, insisting that she didn't want to see me. Over time, he seemed to become restored to himself, turning me away with more confidence. The colour came back into his face. His eyes lost their dark rings. Maybe he was learning to live with whatever had happened, or maybe I was just reading into it. Once, I went in the middle of the night and stood in the driveway calling her name. The next week, Mel showed me a headline: *Calista Sells £6 Million Hampstead Home, Sources Say Stalkers Drove Her Out.*

'They don't mean me,' I said.

I tried to sneak into the garden, to gain access to the kitchen and find the final diary, but it was impossible. Maybe it was already gone anyway.

Mel encouraged me to find another job, to look for a more permanent place to stay than on her sofa. And I did try a few times – I sent off applications, called estate agents. I just couldn't ever seem to see anything all the way through. Every time I took a step, my body caved under the effort of it, and I needed to retreat back to Mel's sofa and recover for a week. She was gentle with me, but insistent. Once I said, tentatively, that maybe I should get out of her space and see if I could move back in with my dad for a bit, while I figured some things out.

'Stevie,' she said, 'do you think I'm that bad a friend?'

She kept all my stuff for me, after Rich moved out of our flat and our contract ended. Her entire living room was taken up by boxes of my clothes and kitchenware. I think walking in and seeing those boxes was the moment that I realised just how much she loved me, that I was family to her, and it was hard to realise that and understand how much I must have hurt her by cutting her off. I wanted to get better, for her. For myself, I only wanted quiet and darkness, and windows into other people's worlds.

There was a couple I was particularly obsessed with in that block of flats. Two girls, and one of them played guitar, of course. They were stupidly in love. I never saw them fight. They rubbed each other's feet in the evenings and wore all of each other's clothes. One night, the one who played guitar sat and serenaded the one who didn't. I could never see the faces of any of the people in the windows that well from where I sat, but on that night every detail was piercingly sharp, and I had to leave before the song was over.

Mel was already home, frowning down at her phone screen.

'What is it?' I asked, slipping my shoes off. She had her knees tucked up on the sofa, still in her work clothes.

'She's released something.'

'What?' I rushed over to her side. 'A statement?'

'No, a song. At least, I don't think she released it, but it's been leaked.'

'What song? From when?'

'They're saying from the most recent album, just never made the cut.' There was something weird in her expression. I peered over her shoulder. She wasn't on a news page – she was reading the lyrics.

They said my name.

I pulled my phone out of my pocket and searched for the leak. Mel might have been talking to me, but I couldn't hear her. The song started to play – it was hardly produced, just her at the piano, playing simple chords.

I'll lose my mind in waiting for

The day that I can't fake it

Remembering how Stevie said

She always knew I'd make it

So if I go by sickness

Or by poison or by pill

Remember me, remember me,

I know you always will

'Morbid,' whispered Mel.

'She said my name,' I said.

'Yeah,' she said. 'How about that.'

'It's a goodbye.' Her voice swelled over the piano. It didn't sound quite like Inese. It didn't sound quite like Callie either. Mel glanced at me, wanting an answer that she could see I didn't have. When the song ended, I played it again, and I knew that it was

Inese, right up until the end, when Callie's tremor convinced me otherwise. Again, and Callie's sniff in the background warred with Inese's throaty low notes. Again. Again. Callie. Inese. Inese. Callie.

'Stop it,' said Mel, when I went to tap the screen and take us back to the start one more time.

'I need to know which one of them made this.'

'You'll drive yourself crazy.' We both knew that I was crazy already. Mel was still trying to figure out to what degree. After a while, she went to bed, and I kept playing it. Callie. Inese. Inese. Callie.

Remember me, remember me,

I know you always will.

I went to my empty social media folder and redownloaded the first app that came to mind. I found *@whathappenedtocalista* and unblocked the account.

@steviestone5: Have you listened?

@whathappenedtocalista: Hi, Stevie. Yes, I have. There's definitely some hidden messages.

@steviestone5: I'm going to send you something. I need an email address.

They replied with one immediately. It betrayed no name, no date of birth. Nothing to indicate who I was talking to. I preferred it that way. I sat down at the table, and I started to write. Everything that had happened since Callie fell in Rio, every conversation between Inese and I, the years she'd spent becoming Callie, the night I'd brought her that diary and it had all come crashing down. I told whoever was behind the account what I believed to be true – that Inese had been going to tell the world the real story at Wembley, before the power had gone out, and that they'd had to do something drastic to keep her quiet.

Then, my heart aching, I edited myself out of it. I kept it as factual as I could. I told them what I knew, but not how I knew it. I asked them not to reveal their sources. I had no reason to trust them – but somehow I believed that I could.

@whathappenedtocalista: Do you think she was planning on disappearing?

@steviestone5: No, I don't.

I can't believe that. But not believing it always sends my mind to worse places.

@whathappenedtocalista: Do you think something bad happened to her?

@whathappenedtocalista: ??

My piece was released in several screenshots on @*whathappenedtocalista*'s page the next morning. It told of two girls, both talented in different ways, both combining those talents to keep Calista perfect. It outlined how those talents had been exploited. It lamented that Callie's voice was gone, and that Inese's – unusual, insightful, wildly moving – had never been truly heard. It said they were both missed. It didn't say who by.

I deleted the app as soon as I saw it had gone up and swore to Mel that it hadn't come from me, even though she knew it had.

By midday, it had been picked up by a couple of news sites, but not as news.

This is the wildest celebrity conspiracy you've heard yet, read one clickbait piece. The irony of it was that they'd used a picture of Inese as the header image. I couldn't resist a peek at the comments.

> *This just HAS to be real. The coincidences are too crazy otherwise.*
>
> *I LITERALLY KNEW SOMETHING WEIRD WAS HAPPENING*
>
> *okay we can all agree that this 'source' is Stevie right? like?? girl you're not slick*

The next day, this headline appeared:

> *Fans Suspect Calista's Girlfriend, Stevie Stone, Might Be the One Behind Wild Body-Double Claims*

That one was from a major news site. Mel was worried about me when it came out, but it made me want to kick my feet. A major news site had published the story, even if they thought it was crazy. It was out there, just like Callie and Inese had wanted, and some people would believe it. It would never be enough. But it was something.

> *Calista's Girlfriend, Stevie Stone.*

I didn't mind that they had named me. I wanted the plausible deniability, just in case. But I didn't want to fall out of her story.

I'll never want that.

One night, when it was very late and I couldn't sleep, I logged into my account on Mel's laptop. I had hundreds of DM requests – I trawled through them. Theories pouring in, most of them crazy, or at least what I would have called crazy a year ago. The word had lost all meaning. Secret pregnancies, aliens, lizard people, cults, devil worship – I read it all and I pictured it all, and even though some of it made me laugh, most of it just washed over me.

I thought, *I get it.*

In among it all—

@remembermerememberme000: I know it was you.

@remembermerememberme000: Thank you.

@steviestone5: Inese?

My message wasn't delivered. The account had been deactivated.

I lived with Mel for a year. Slowly, I stopped staring up at other people's windows, and I started going on job interviews. Eventually I got a job subediting copy for a pet food brand. The first week was horrendously depressing, but I've been there two years now and it isn't so bad. The people are dull, and the conversation is inane, but there's a sort of comfort in the inane. There's a sort of safety in knowing that you have a life that can never surprise you. I don't miss being surprised – or at least I try not to.

I live in a house share with two university students and a twenty-four-year-old who podcasts. The podcaster stays in his room most of the time, unless he's drunk, and then he wants to chat. The university students are very sweet. They massage each other's shoulders in the living room. They try making blusher out of strawberry juice. Sometimes they fall asleep on each other watching *Sex and the City*, and I think they might be in love, but I don't think they would ever admit it.

One day I asked them if they liked Calista. Um, they said, they did, but she hadn't done anything in a while, and her last album was sort of weird. They like other music that I don't get, music that makes me wonder if this is what people like Rich think Calista sounds like.

I wonder what I'd think of her music, if I hadn't loved her first.

They say she releases a single next month. Nothing's been confirmed, but I've been around the block enough now to know that whispers in the industry – at least whispers of that kind – are usually quite deliberately planted. Three years away, and she's finally preparing to show her face to the world again. Whoever that face might belong to. Perhaps it's Inese, whisked away from me when they decided I was getting too comfortable, reconditioned, reconvinced of her responsibilities. Perhaps it's someone else entirely. If Callie herself rose from a shallow grave, at this point I'd hardly even be surprised.

I don't listen to her music anymore, but I do listen to 'Remember'. I like that I don't know who sings it, because it means that I get to choose. Sometimes it's Callie, ready to retire, ready to lay Calista to rest, remembering that I believed she'd make it to these heights even when no one else did. Sometimes it's Inese, so frightened, but with so much faith in me to protect her. Sometimes it's neither of them. Sometimes it's just Calista, that strange, possessing force. A voice without a body. Asking not to be forgotten.

Remember me, she asks. *Remember me.* Then, with a small, smug smile – *I know you always will.*

ACKNOWLEDGEMENTS

Every book is fun to write, but this was a blast. Thank you to Maisie Lawrence and Celine Kelly for a super-smooth editorial process and feedback that turned a draft I liked into a book I loved. Thank you to my agent, Silvia Molteni – with each new book I feel freshly lucky to be your client. Thank you to Melissa Hyder for straightening out the timeline and to everyone else on the Amazon Publishing team who had a hand in editing, proofreading, formatting, designing and marketing this book. Thank you also to Rebecca Hills for being the best, most generous cheerleader an author could ever ask for and the whole lovely team at Tandem Collective, who are always wonderful.

Thank you to my amazing parents – I couldn't let another book come out without putting you in that dedication line. To my siblings, always. I love you both the most in the world. Thank you to Paul, who is brave enough to look at unfinished manuscripts and give honest feedback, and who is always ready to tell strangers I'm an author. To the many, many wonderful friends and family members in my world who make life so joyful and massively overhype me. And thank you to everyone who has read one of my books, posted a kind review, followed along on social media, or been a part of this journey in any way. I'm having the time of my life, all because of you.

If you were utterly captivated in this novel by Stevie's search for the truth, and the woman she once knew, then you'll adore *The Real Deal* by Caitlin Devlin.

Belle Simon was just twelve when she was one of six girls plucked from obscurity to star in reality TV sensation *The Real Deal* to become a world-famous star. Now twenty-six, Belle is trying to live anonymously until a producer offers her a big pay cheque to join a reunion special. Everyone watching thinks they know what happened, but only Belle knows. Is she ready to go back and confront her past? And will anyone believe her if she reveals the truth?

Available now or keep reading for an exclusive extract!

Most people don't know that Donna was the one who taught me to smoke. It was Howie that first put a spliff to my lips and told me to inhale, but he didn't teach me how. He laughed when I coughed, which I did, every time, and when I complained about the burning feeling he said, 'I'm not baking you brownies, Belle. Sorry.' And took another drag, smoke drifting easily over his knuckles.

Once, in LA, I had an audition for some indie film. I don't remember what it was called – *Knife's Point* or something similar – but they wanted an edgy girl, someone with a bit of grit. Actually, the casting call said 'damaged', which Donna and I interpreted as heavy eyeliner and tights with a ladder in them. The damaged girl was called Velma, like in *Scooby Doo*, and she had a twelve-line monologue about jacking off her teacher. And she was a smoker.

'Have you ever smoked?' asked Donna, lighting the cigarette on her deck and handing it out to me.

'No,' I lied. 'Never.'

At around eight every evening on Donna's deck it became vibrantly orange, the light hovering low and close to us, so that the orange was hazy and a little dusty. A perfect tangerine of a sun rippled in the centre of the pool. There wasn't much of a view of anything from her back garden, tall trees blocking our line of sight at every angle. I liked this because it meant that nobody had much of a view of us. At that moment, it really did feel like nobody. I knew this wouldn't make the edit.

'Hold it between two of your fingers,' said Donna. She moved them for me, one over, one under. Red eyes winked at us from the patio table and the roof of the pool house. 'That's good.' Her voice, crackling like an old radio, took on a note of laughter. 'You don't need to look scared of it.'

I made myself laugh with her. 'Do I look scared?'

'Like cancer's going to jump up out of it and bite you. It's just for the part.'

'They won't make me smoke in an audition, will they?'

'No,' she said, 'but when you get it, and you will, you don't want to have a coughing fit on set. Besides,' she added, 'you can always tell by looking at a young girl whether or not she knows how to smoke.'

The house was a little way out from the centre of LA but it wasn't far from a main road, so that beeps and honks and the shouts of taxi drivers became as much a part of my waking and sleeping hours as they had in London. They buzzed like cicadas in the background as Donna gently cupped my small hand in her slender one and raised the cigarette, still held between my two fingers, to my bottom lip.

'Gently inhale,' she said. 'Hold it for a second. Exhale.' I inhaled as gently as I could. 'No,' she said, 'not enough. Try again. Slowly, but be sure of yourself.'

It burned, but not necessarily in a bad way. I coughed, but only a little.

'Not bad!' said Donna. She gave me a little round of applause, nodding her head so that her earrings jangled. 'Not bad at all. We'll make damaged goods of you yet.'

Through the burnt-orange dusk, the red eyes sparkled.

Reunion special

Everyone always wants to know what I'm doing now. The nicer voices say it like that – 'What is Belle from *The Real Deal* doing now?' in loopy font, sometimes over an out-of-date photo of me shyly waving. The other voices ask it differently. 'What happened to Belle from *The Real Deal*?' There's always a photo of me on these ones. I am always crying.

Whoever asks it, however it is phrased, the answer is always the same. Nothing. I am doing nothing now. Nothing happened to me. They conclude it sadly, or gleefully, and then they ask you to subscribe.

'You don't understand the appetite for it,' Rupert says on the phone. 'I mean, Belle, you do this, and who knows? All the world needs is a little reminder of you.'

'Is that what you told Donna the first time around?'

He laughs. Rupert has always been remarkably good at laughing through his discomfort. 'Yes, more or less.'

'Well then.'

'Well, it was true, wasn't it? We put her back on the map.' A pause. 'It's hardly our fault she sort of . . . dropped off it again.'

I want to ask if this is the kind of sensitivity I can expect throughout the experience, but I already know the answer. Besides, Jane is already watching me closely from the kitchen table, Biology homework forgotten and a cheese sandwich held halfway to her mouth. I stick my tongue out at her and she reciprocates, but she still looks concerned. A small piece of grated cheese falls onto the front of her PE top.

'I just don't really want to drag it all up,' I say into the phone, gesturing to Jane to brush off the front of her top. She looks down, surprised. Her messiness definitely comes from Cameron's side. Mum and I were always neat to a fault.

'That's understandable,' says Rupert, and his voice dips lower, into the register he uses to show faux concern. It's so familiar that if Jane hadn't been watching, I might have shivered. 'But we can proceed gently.'

'So we don't have to talk about it.'

Another pause. 'Belle, I'm going to be straight with you,' says Rupert. 'We can't do this special and not talk about it. But we *can* be delicate.'

'Do *I* have to talk about it?'

'We can negotiate on that. *We* have to cover it, certainly, but that could be done with witnesses and news stories. No one has to ask you about it directly, if that's what it takes.' He waits. 'Belle? How does that sound?'

'What's the money like?'

He laughs. 'That's what I always liked about you. You're all business.'

'Well?' I know the number I'm expecting him to say. It's double.

'That's what the other girls are getting, at least,' he says. 'But I won't bullshit you. We'd pay what we needed to. You're our most valuable player. And like I said, this is going to be huge.' He quietens. 'Belle, I was so sorry to hear about Sofie.'

'Thanks.' It's not as if he could say anything different, of course, but it's still strange to hear. He never liked her.

'I keep thinking about that little baby she went home to have. It'd be what, ten now? Your little brother or sister?'

'Eleven. She just started Year Seven.' Jane is surprised to hear herself referenced. She drops another bit of cheese.

'And what does Sofie's partner do?'

'He runs a bookshop.'

'In London?'

'Bethnal Green.'

'Lovely,' said Rupert. 'Sounds idyllic. You'll think about it, won't you? Like I said, we'd pay what you want. And all the other girls are going to be involved.'

'Even Paget?'

'Well, the other four. I know they'd love to see you again.' He knows no such thing. He adds, because he's probably aware I don't believe him: 'Faye said as much when we spoke.'

I still don't say anything. There is a commotion behind me as Jane's pen rolls off the table and under the fridge. She scrambles for it. I hear the sandwich hit the floor. '*Belle*,' she hisses. I am very still, frozen in the half-light of the kitchen.

'Please think about it,' says Rupert. 'The world deserves to have Belle back on their screens. Have your people call my people and they can negotiate to your heart's content.' He hangs up before I have a chance to tell him that I don't have any people, any more. It's just me.

I tell Cameron that the money isn't what sways me.

'Then why?' Cameron asks me as the three of us sit outside on our camping chairs, Jane eating the chocolate off a Magnum.

'Closure,' I say. 'I suppose.'

This isn't a lie, not entirely. Closure sounds nice. And Faye wants to see me. That sounds nice too.

But it is the money, really. Mum's life insurance and Cameron's savings from his years in law have so far been enough to sustain a bookshop that struggles month on month to keep afloat, but they won't be enough forever. I don't want Cameron to give up the bookshop. And I don't want Jane to notice.

Jane is very small and slight, like I was at her age. She has Cameron's tanned skin and Mum's sharp nose and big eyes. She's a very pretty child. My throat seizes every time someone's head turns to look at her in the street. She thinks that this is because I am scared of paedophiles, which is the kind of thing that is hilarious when you're eleven and feel invincible.

She plays netball and hockey and shows no interest in acting or singing, but she loves to dance. I try to be happy for her when I watch her, sat in the audience with my hands curled in a claw shape under the chair and Cameron periodically whispering, 'You okay, Belle?' into my ear. I can't always manage it. She doesn't like me to come to her shows any more because sometimes I cry and it unsettles and embarrasses her.

Jane hates her name. 'Yours is so pretty. Mine's so flat and nothing.' I tell her again how carefully Mum chose her name, but it's hard to make her understand why.

She's never watched the show, even though she's asked me many times if I'll show her an episode. I'm not stupid – I know that any day now she could look it up online and watch it all in secret under her duvet. I'm just waiting for her to figure it out. I hope it takes her a while.

Before Mum died, she made us promise to be there for each other. I am there for Jane by being hypervigilant, conscious of any and all possible threats to her person, to her mind, to her innocence. Jane is there for me by letting me hold her hand through her wonderfully normal eleven-year-old life. I'm not always sure which of us is raising the other.

Rupert tells me that the special is going to be called *The Real Deal: Ten Years On*, to mark the anniversary of the final episode. I ask Rupert if we'll all be meeting up before filming starts, but of course he says no.

'And obviously I can't stop you, but I'd rather you didn't reach out ahead of time. We want to see all the electricity of that first reunion!'

I sit on my bed for half an hour after receiving this email and stare at the wall, until Jane knocks on my door and offers me a pouch of chocolate raisins. We eat them together in silence. After a while she says, 'Do you want me to come with you next week?'

'You've got school.'

'You seem scared,' she says.

'You seem like you're trying to get out of school.'

She grins. 'Belle, more than one thing can be true at the same time.'

She's much funnier than I was at eleven. She's sharply observational and very quick with her words, and she has far more confidence. In some ways she reminds me of Kendra, or at least, the parts of Kendra that I always secretly admired. But sometimes I imagine her being observed like that, the weight of all those eyes on her, trying to stay one step ahead of the adults around her, ducking and weaving to avoid their disappointment, and the image leaves me shaken. I can't see how her small frame could stand it.

The week before, Roni is on an American talk show. She wears a floor-length purple dress with a long slit and her hair is in lots of small braids with purple flowers scattered amongst them. She looks like a princess. She and the host talk about the second season of her show, and the film she's just finished making where she and an ex-pro-wrestler rob an art gallery, and then he tells her, 'Now, you actually started in the world of reality TV!' as if she doesn't know.

'I did!' she laughs. If there's any weariness in it, I'm probably imagining it. The host pulls out a picture of her in her black leotard, her arm around Kendra's waist. An *aw* from the audience.

'So that's you and Kendra Hale,' says the host, 'who was also on the show.'

'Yes, there we are. We were babies.'

'How old are you there?'

'Twelve,' she says, with another white smile.

'Just twelve. And now it's almost been ten years since the show ended. How do you feel about that?'

'I feel old,' she laughs, her hand on his arm.

'Oh, stop it,' he says.

'I do!' She laughs again. She has a perfect laugh: controlled, cheerful, a little throaty. You can tell she's worked on it. 'But, no, it was a complicated time. It was a baptism of fire, really, but it gave me a platform, and it gave me the girls . . .'

'You're all still friends?'

'Yes,' she lies, smiling.

'So,' says the host, 'I guess what we're all wondering is, hypothetically, if there were to be a reunion—' Whistles from the crowd. Roni smiles demurely. The host holds his hand up. '*If.* If. I'm not trying to get sued.' The studio laughs. 'Would that be something you'd be up for?'

'I mean,' she says, 'never say never.' More whistles. 'It's a complex one,' she says. 'Anyone who's seen the show, you know that's true. We all had a hard time at points. Some of us more than others.' She's not even looking into the camera but it's like I can feel her eyes on me, suddenly. The host rearranges his features, appropriately sombre. 'It's a complex one,' she repeats. 'But no matter what else there was on that set, there was so much love. We had so much love for each other.'

It's almost like I can see Rupert standing just off camera, mouthing the words.

She's been asked about it before. They both have, her and Kendra. Kendra especially, because her PR team is worse – Roni's seem to mostly axe the questions ahead of time. *What really happened in that final episode?* Whenever Roni is asked a variation of this question, she'll say, 'I mean, I think we all saw what happened. My heart really goes out to Belle. I really just wish healing for her.'

'I don't know,' Kendra will say. 'I wasn't there. You'd have to ask Belle.'

They have asked me. In the weeks after the final episode aired, press would call my home phone number and wait outside my door sometimes, asking me. *What happened? How are you doing now? Do the two of you still speak?* My social media comments became so repetitive that I eventually shut down all of my accounts. Into my silence, they spoke. I'm sure some of them spoke with nuance, but the voices I saw screamed with deafening certainty. *ABUSE ON THE SET OF THE REAL DEAL* read the tabloids. It wasn't phrased like a question. A Twitter account popped up – @therealdealtruth – supposedly to share 'evidence', but all they posted were compilations of clips from the show set to sad music, my micro-expressions slowed to a fifth of their original speed. There was much debate in the comment sections of these compilations as to whether this was proof of anything or not. Nonetheless, they inspired copycats.

Then the think pieces rolled in. First online blogs run by individual freelancers, and then *Variety, Cosmopolitan, The Washington Post.* Our phone rang so much that Mum redid our answering machine message with an additional warning: 'Journalists will be hung up on or sworn at, depending on what kind of day I'm having.' The few times I did pick up and heard an unfamiliar voice say, 'Hi, is that Belle Simon?' I would stay silent on the phone until they gave up. 'Hello?' they would say. 'I'd just love to talk, if you had a moment.' One man persisted for so long that I sat the phone down on the sofa beside me and painted my nails, listening as his polite frustration become steadily less polite.

When I wouldn't talk, they talked without me. The conversation closed with me on the outside of it. Like the rest of the world, I was a spectator. 'What *The Real Deal* can teach us about the warning signs of abuse,' they wrote. 'Why Belle Simon from *The Real Deal* has never been a villain,' they wrote. 'How Belle Simon's story on *The Real Deal* is helping Gen Z learn about power dynamics,' they wrote. It was scary, to let go of the reins and let them all run with it, but it was better than trying to explain it all myself. The details didn't matter so much to me. Not whilst everyone was speaking about me with so much warmth.

Within a year, it was no longer a matter of speculation. Nothing was up for debate. Which suited me fine because no one felt the need to ask me anything, any more.

We're shooting at a studio in Soho, which I'm grateful for. I know we'll be heading back to the Southbank at some point but perhaps even Rupert and Fred recognise that we all need that chance to acclimatise. To slowly lower ourselves into the water.

Jane helps me lay out my outfit the night before. We've been told to keep it casual but I can't help thinking that maybe this is a trick, a way to make me look like I'm doing worse than the others when they show up in cocktail dresses. With Jane's help I find the perfect compromise – a slightly slouchy but still tailored jumpsuit and low heels which Jane, with all the authority of an eleven-year-old social media addict, calls 'day to night'.

We stand at the foot of my bed and stare down at the jumpsuit like we're examining a body.

'I think it's good,' says Jane.

I don't say anything. I feel her skinny arms go around my waist, head pressed into the crook of my elbow. She doesn't know why I'm scared but I can feel that she doesn't like it. It must be hard for her, not knowing and feeling like she can't ask.

'Hey,' I say, squeezing my fingers into her side. She wriggles. 'Come here.' We sit beside each other on the bed, careful to avoid the jumpsuit. 'What do you know about what's happening tomorrow?' I ask.

She tilts her head at me. 'Um,' she says, with emphasis, to let me know that she thinks I'm being weird, 'I know you're going to film a TV show.'

'Do you know what the show is?'

'The one you used to be on.'

'Do you know what it's called?'

'*The Real Deal*,' she says, biting the skin around her thumbnail.

I've never actually heard her say the name of the show before, but of course she knows it. Even if she's never looked it up, friends will have told her. Maybe they've even shown her a clip or two – although the show is not as easy to access as it used to be. A journalist who I've never met started a conversation online a while ago about the ethics of having *The Real Deal* available on streaming services.

Anyone who knows anything about what went on behind the scenes on this show recognises that this is not entertainment, she wrote. *This is people's childhood trauma you are consuming whilst you make your lunch or brush your teeth. Imagine being one of these girls and having these clips come up on your social media feed day after day.*

She'd avoided naming any of us, but I was the one that got tagged, over and over, as the post circulated on social media. The result of it was that the official YouTube page for the show was taken down (*We hear you and we're sorry,* wrote some PR rep) and most channels stopped airing reruns. But it isn't as if the show is gone. A quick search can turn up any scene you want, and in many ways the censorship has only made *The Real Deal* more salacious viewing. It's more than possible that Jane has come across it, especially now that she has her own laptop and phone.

But when I ask her if she's ever seen it, she shakes her head. 'Do you know what it's about?' I ask.

'It's like, a dancing school, right? And you're taught by that woman—'

'Donna.'

'—and she wanted to make you all famous.'

She looks at me, like it's a question. I pull up the Wikipedia page on my phone. 'Here.'

She takes the phone cautiously, but I can see the eagerness in her face as she starts to read.

> The Real Deal *is a British docuseries that aired from 2009 to 2014. It follows six children placed in an elite performing arts programme under the mentorship and tutelage of actress, singer and dancer Donna Mayfair. Set first in London, England and later in Los Angeles, USA, the show follows the girls as they attend their first auditions, book their first jobs, and build their careers. The show is often credited with reviving Mayfair's career as well as breaking out performers such as Veronica Owayale and Kendra Hale. Due to backlash online, particularly surrounding the fifth and final season, reruns of the show now air post-watershed only.*

I see Jane's fingers lingering over the 'Controversy' link in the menu and I take my phone back from her, gently but firmly. 'There you go.'

'So all six of you are . . . what? Going back to school?'

'Five of us. We're just talking. Remembering stuff.'

'Can I watch it?'

'I don't think it'll be very interesting for you.'

'Are you nervous?'

'Probably a bit,' I say. 'I haven't seen most of these girls in for ever.' I'd run into Hannah in King's Cross a few years ago. We'd had a brief, awkward hug and a promise to stay in touch before she ran to catch a train. She still had trouble meeting my eyes. She'd been doing her masters at UCL and she was heading north again for the holidays, to see her sister, she said.

How is your sister? I asked.

Oh, she said, *she's making pottery now. You know Faye.* I looked it up online later, half disbelieving, but she'd been telling the truth – she had an online storefront full of dishes and ceramics. I almost bought a glazed turquoise mug, before I thought better of it. It wouldn't have gone with anything else in the house.

Cameron makes me pancakes in the morning and sits with me whilst Jane gets ready for school. Before she leaves, she runs into the kitchen, hockey stick slung over her shoulder, and kisses me on the same cheek three times in short, sharp pecks. I squeeze her ribs on the third time and she wriggles away, brandishing the hockey stick at me.

'Good luck,' she says.

'I could have sworn I sent her to a state school,' says Cameron, as Jane rushes off to get her rucksack.

'You did.'

'That hockey stick makes her look like she's off to Malory Towers.'

'They play hockey at state schools too,' I say.

'I wish they'd stop.'

She turns back again at the door, to wave at me. Through the open doorway, I see a dark shadow pull up behind her.

'Car's here,' says Cameron, who is watching too.

He waits for me to gather my things, to collect myself, and then he hugs me tightly, a bone-splintering, tear-stinging kind of hug, and I know he's hugging for two.

Drivers sometimes tell me that they recognise me from TV. They mostly aren't in the show's target demographic, but occasionally one will take me by surprise. Then I'll have to keep the conversation on track for the length of the drive, distracting them with the celebrities I've met and the TV shows I've been on, so that no one asks what they all really want to ask.

This one looks at me in the mirror and opens his mouth.

'Do you want the radio on?' he asks instead. I tell him no, thank you, and then regret it. 'Soho?' he asks. 'Doing anything fun?'

'No,' I say.

He leaves me be after that. Silently, I watch the familiar silhouettes of buildings grow and gather over the river. It's rush hour and movement on the roads is steady but ominously slow. I said I'd never complain about London traffic again after LA. Now I find myself wishing I'd just taken the tube.

My finger moves over the hills and dips of my knuckles, back and forth, like waves coming and going. I make myself remember what I did on each of my birthdays from five to twenty-five, and then on Jane's from one to eleven. I count up all the countries I have visited. I recite the entirety of *The Sound of Music* in my head (safe, because I never got cast in that one).

'Here we are then,' says the driver.

The Soho studio is a large, square building, much squatter than the place on the Southbank with all its many stairs. No part of it is familiar to me. This is comforting. An assistant with a clipboard is hovering on the pavement. I don't know her either. She smiles at me. I smile back, my hand on the handle, taking a deep breath in through my nose.

We drive past, the assistant following us with her eyes. Alarmed, I look up at the driver in the mirror. He's glancing down at his phone.

'Sorry,' he says. 'We're just going to do another couple of loops.'

'Is something wrong?'

'It's all good,' he says. 'They're finishing up another shot.'

Someone else is arriving first. I turn back, staring through the back window. A black car, much larger than this one, with tinted windows, has pulled up on the pavement. A security guard exits from the front seat to open the door. We turn the corner before I get a chance to see who steps out.

'Was that Roni?' I ask the driver. 'Veronica, I mean?'

'I'm not sure,' he says. 'Sorry. I only know what I've told you.'

'Am I supposed to be the last one in there?'

'I don't know the order. I just know that you're next.'

He's probably lying. They've probably told him not to tell me. Shakily, I settle myself in my seat and start on Act Two of *The Sound of Music.*

We do another two laps before we finally pull up on the pavement outside the studio, now empty again save for the unfamiliar assistant in her black headset.

'Hi, Belle,' she says, shaking my hand. She looks younger than me by at least a couple of years. This is briefly disorientating. 'Sorry about all the faff. We're so pleased to have you.'

'Pleased to be here.'

'Just give me one minute.' She turns away from me. 'She's here,' she says, into the headset.

No name. I'm last.

There's Rupert, suddenly appearing from seemingly nowhere. I'm disassociating. *Focus.*

'Belle!' He gives me an unasked-for hug. I'm stiff in his arms. 'Goodness,' he says, grasping my hand and stepping back to take a good look at me. 'Aren't you grown up? Fred won't believe his eyes.'

'Hi, Rupe. You look well.' He looks old.

'We're ready for you in there,' he says. 'Everyone's so excited.'

To see each other, I think, sure. Then I force myself to remember what Rupert said on the phone: Faye's looking forward to it. Faye wants to see me.

I've never been brave enough to call her. I suppose I was always waiting for some external force to place us in a room together. And this is it.

'You okay?' asks Rupert, hand on my arm. 'You want some water?'

'So I just . . . walk in? That's it?'

'Just walk in and say hello. We've got a nice set up, there's some drinks . . .' He waves a hand. 'Just catch up! It's a chill one today.'

'Okay.' I brush him off and flex my fingers. He leads me to a small red door at the side of the building, his hand firm in the small of my back as he opens it and pushes me forward. 'Go on!'

And there it is.

It's a shoulder-operated Canon held by a grip in black who I don't recognise. The sound guy beside him looks vaguely familiar, holding his boom aloft. My eyes dart over them both for only a second before the muscle memory kicks in and I carry myself as if I'm alone, as if I'm not being watched, looking anywhere except at that dark shape just in the corner of my eye.

We move down a short corridor, turning the corner. Two double doors stand open at the end of it. The space inside is big and bright. I can see the edge of a pot plant, fairy lights. A velvet sofa comes into view, a glass of prosecco on a small wooden table beside it. A hand reaches out to pick it up. A thin hand, pale and small, with silver jewellery tinkling against the glass. It rings like a doorbell.

In my head, I am still singing *The Sound of Music.* I'm midway through 'The Lonely Goatherd', which is funny, although I can't show it. The camera can't see my lips turn up. The camera can't see my eyes crinkle.

I don't think I can do this.

Kendra notices me first. She's settled in an armchair, legs crossed, drink in hand. She looks at home. She doesn't change position when her eyes land on me, but she stiffens just for a second, cold like stone. It takes her a second to take me in – the shorter, darker hair, the wider face. Then she smiles, slowly, and her other hand comes to the base of her champagne glass.

'Belle,' she says.

'Hi, everyone.'

The sisters, their backs to me, turn to stare. I can't look at them. Roni is sat on Kendra's right, impossibly beautiful in a lavender suit. She's openly frowning.

They didn't know I was coming. That's why I was last. Not Roni, arguably the show's biggest success, but me.

I'm the twist.

'Oh my god,' says Kendra. She laughs.

I don't want to be the twist. I can't do this.

But there are two cameras in the room with me now, one very still, one circling, moving round to capture the sisters' faces with the boom stalking just behind. Somewhere else in this building, down the corridor or on the floor below, there is a room of people watching us on monitors or sketching plans for upcoming scenes based on an energy, a hint of tension, an interesting look at the wrong moment. In the doorway at the far end of the room, two dark shapes in suits stand side by side and watch us with a cool, passive interest.

I force myself to look at the sisters. Hannah is still wide-eyed in her disbelief, hair tucked behind her ears and an expression of surprise so genuine I can suddenly see the nine-year-old in her again. Faye is calm. Gentle, silvery, unflappable Faye. Very slightly, she nods at the empty armchair.

My eyes on her, I take my seat.

ABOUT THE AUTHOR

Photo © 2023 Caitlin Devlin

Caitlin Devlin studied English and Creative Writing at Warwick University before graduating to work in music and theatre journalism. As a teenager, she started writing novels as Christmas presents for her younger sister and brother. Her work has been recognised by competitions such as the IGGY & Litro Young Writers' Prize, the Flash 500 Short Stories competition and the Exeter Writers Short Story Competition. She is also a performed playwright. Her debut adult novel, *The Real Deal*, was published by Lake Union in 2024.

Follow Caitlin on TikTok at @catmdevlin.

Follow the Author on Amazon

If you enjoyed this book, follow Caitlin Devlin on Amazon to be notified when the author releases a new book!
To do this, please follow these instructions:

Desktop:

1) Search for the author's name on Amazon or in the Amazon App.
2) Click on the author's name to arrive on their Amazon page.
3) Click the 'Follow' button.

Mobile and Tablet:

1) Search for the author's name on Amazon or in the Amazon App.
2) Click on one of the author's books.
3) Click on the author's name to arrive on their Amazon page.
4) Click the 'Follow' button.

Kindle eReader and Kindle App:

If you enjoyed this book on a Kindle eReader or in the Kindle App, you will find the author 'Follow' button after the last page.